The Coniston Curse

Hugo Miller Mysteries 5

Joseph Allen

Published by Rogue Phoenix Press, LLP
Copyright © 2021

ISBN: 978-1-62420-608-5

Credits
Cover Artist: Designs by Ms G
Editor: Kitty Carlisle

Dedication

For Angus, Isabelle, Xixi, John, Nancee, Toni and the Fellowship of the White Boar

Chapter One

I seldom stay up to watch the late news unless there is something going on that I am super-curious about – or sometimes if I come home right at eleven from a movie or dinner or whatever. It's because when I feel sleepy, I go to bed. If I try to go to bed when I'm not sleepy, I'll toss and turn for what seems like hours.

That night, though, I walked into my apartment a few minutes before eleven from a movie. My mind was racing in all kinds of directions about the film, which took place in northern Italy during the summertime. Like a gauzy dream of sunshine and wonderful food to look at, kinda, but it was a coming-of-age movie full of teenage angst and dirty talk. I knew I would have to calm down if I wanted to go to sleep, so I turned on the television, which had news on almost all the channels, and poured myself a martini-glass of vodka, which I keep in the freezer instead of on the liquor cabinet, because vodka is only drinkable if it's chilled.

The first story on the news was a breaking item about two kids disappearing. I live in New York and although homicides and most major crimes are at a near all-time low, it's not unusual for the late news to feature a shooting or somebody getting hit by a speeding car or whatever. But this was no ordinary crime story. Apparently, two kids whose wealthy father died recently were missing – never came home from school – and the cops had no clues to go on. Plus, the two boys were both from the Coniston family, social-register and inherited money all the way, but usually with a low profile in the papers or gossip columns.

The Coniston home on upper 5th Avenue was one of the last gigantic nineteenth-century townhomes left on the avenue that was still a family residence. Most of the townhomes that lined the avenue one hundred years earlier had been torn down to make room for high-rise buildings, and the few that survived were mostly museums, like The Frick Collection, the Cooper Hewitt (Andrew Carnegie's home) and the Ukrainian Institute of America (Fletcher-Sinclair Mansion at 79th Street).

Eddie Coniston, the father of the boys who disappeared, died several months before the kids disappeared, but his passing wasn't really a news story because there was no foul play. Coniston had been the head of a family conglomerate that had interests in real estate, construction, property management and a bunch of other things as well. It was private and totally owned by the family. There had never been any financial filings that would give the media an idea of the size of the Coniston empire. The news coverage of his death said there was no information on why he died or from what (he was in his late forties), but speculation was a coronary or respiratory failure. Eddie had been a football player in college, but, over the years, had gotten grossly fat. He had to be helped in and out of cars. He was a big contributor to charities, but stopped going to events. In fact, he stopped appearing in public at all a couple of years back.

He left all his estate to his elder son, also named Edward, who was twelve. Eddie's brother Ricky Coniston was appointed CEO of all the Coniston companies. Now young Ed Coniston and his younger brother, Richie, had gone missing. To make things more confusing, Ricky Coniston had a son named Edward, called Ned, as well, and so did the third brother, George, who had died some years back. George's Edward was called Ted.

I signed onto the computer in my office, actually a guest bedroom, but serving two or three purposes, and sent a quick email to my friend, Mike di Saronno, a bigwig detective in the NYPD, asking him if he saw the coverage. I am Hugo Miller, a civilian criminalist for the NYPD – basically a *pro bono* consultant, and more or less deputized back-up for the department's investigative arm. I copied my friends, Ruth Jensen and Gabriele Cortese, who have helped me help the NYPD. Mike knew Ruth and Gabriele well from having worked with them over the years. In addition, Ruth is a well-known socialite and philanthropist. Gabriele is the co-owner of one of the chicest restaurants in SoHo, Ora di Pranzo. It's one of those places where people make reservations months in advance of special occasions – and even then, they have a hard time getting a table. Think of a hit Broadway musical that is sold out until two years from now.

Ora di Pranzo is kinda like that. Me, I am semi-retired from a sports PR company I founded in the 1980s, and I still own a big chunk of it. Fortunately, it has done well, so I have been able to sock away some savings, and am ahead of my expenses, sometimes way ahead. My work for the NYPD is a freebie, no pay, although sometimes my expenses are reimbursed.

I live in Long Island City, which is the part of Queens that is directly opposite the United Nations across the East River. From my subway station at Vernon-Jackson, it is one stop to Grand Central Station, about a four-minute ride. Gabriele lives in Brooklyn Heights, one of the swankiest places in New York City. Ruth has a big apartment on Park Avenue at the corner of 61st Street, her home with her husband, Murray, who died about three years back.

After finishing my vodka, I knew I would be able to go to sleep, and as I drifted off, I tried to go over anything I might already know about the Conistons, which, if it was sugar, would not have been enough for a single spoonful to stir into a cup of coffee. I made a note on the notepad next to the bed to look into the Coniston family first thing in the morning.

It was late summer, but the sun was still coming up early and going down late. There was a pervasive humidity that seldom lifted in the hot weather. For icing on that cake, about three out of five days, we'd have a thunderstorm in the afternoon, so there would be steam rising off the streets, as if it wasn't already hot enough to feel like you might melt like ice cream that had been dropped on the sidewalk.

Although I hate the heat and humidity, I can't sleep without a sheet on top of me. So, I turned on the air conditioning in my bedroom. The white noise of the AC unit blanks out a lot of what might be going on outside, including the sounds of rain and traffic. Even so, when the sun came up at about five thirty, I woke up just like it was an alarm clock.

I've been having a bit of a tremor in my hands sometimes. My doctor says it's nothing to worry about, called a 'familial tremor'. Almost everybody on my father's side of the family has it. It's not a degenerative condition – it can get worse if I don't take care of myself, but it's not possible for it to get worse enough to ruin my health or kill me, like multiple sclerosis or amyotrophic lateral sclerosis, 'Lou Gehrig's Disease'. Caffeine seems to bring it on unless I'm eating a meal while I consume the caffeine. So, I was struggling to eliminate my cuppa joe first thing in the morning.

My pattern is that I usually have a beverage in the morning – always had been coffee, but now it was usually orange juice with or without any vodka in it. The advantage of a jigger of vodka for me is that it stops the tremor before it starts. Any alcohol does that.

I did without the vodka that morning, and dived into the seemingly limitless world of the Internet, to see what I could find out about the Coniston family. Just as I was getting started, Mike called me.

"Hey, Hugo," he said. "Yeah, I did see the coverage of the Coniston kids last night. More than that, I've been assigned to the investigative team. I hope you'll have time to help us out."

Music to my ears. "Already on it, boss," I said. "Trying to get up to date on the family. I guess they go way back to before the Revolution. I was just going to check on Amazon to see if there is a family biography by chance. Are you interested in where the family name comes from?"

"Sure, why not?"

"It's probably from northern England. There is a town called Coniston in the Lake District in northwest England. There is also a Coniston Lake and a land formation called The Old Man of Coniston, which is a pointed hill with barren sides like moors."

I hiked up it, years earlier. It had some geological significance that I couldn't recall, but I remember the town, very picturesque, as most of the Lake District is. Coniston was called Coningeston in the Middle Ages, a name derived from the Old Norse word for king, combined with the Anglo-Saxon suffix -*ton*, indicating a village. A lot of history in that area. England then was a little like California or Korea now, with the north quite different in most ways from the south.

"I'm guessing the family has been in America for a long time, probably since the early 1800s, so it probably doesn't matter," I said. "There was a great migration out of much of Scotland and the northwest of England in the late eighteenth century, and I suspect that may have been when the Coniston family arrived."

"I bet Ruth knows somebody in the family."

"That occurred to me, but I didn't want to call her so early."

There was a pause as I visualized Mike looking at his watch. "Oh," he said, "it is early. Sorry. Do you want to talk later instead?"

"No, I'm okay. So, what happened to the kids? The news didn't have any details last night. I haven't turned on the tube this morning yet."

He explained the boys, who were students at The Trinity School on West 91st Street, left school at their regular time, and never showed up at home. The NYPD was trying to search out any video that might have caught the boys as they walked to the bus stop, or as they walked across Central Park, where their home was only a couple of blocks north of 'uptown' East 91st Street. So far, not much help.

"Any ransom demand?"

"Negative. No calls, no letter, no email. Their mother, Lizzie Coniston, was distraught, of course. She had recently lost her husband, and now her children disappeared. Ed and Richie were the only boys, but there were two girls. There are two guys around the clock with Mrs Coniston, one from the FBI and one from here. No decision that I know of about whether to pay any ransom that's demanded, but we think the family will do almost anything to get those two boys home safe."

I told Mike I would call him back after I had a chance to check in with Ruth and Gabriele. He agreed, and suggested when I talked to them, it might be good for the four of us to caucus before long.

"As you might guess," he said, "the mayor is all over this like white on rice. So, I have no idea what will happen an hour from now. If we can do it, let's try to get Halal food from the food truck downstairs and meet at my office."

I went back to my computer and turned on the television to CNN, although I doubted there would be much coverage of a crime story in New York on a global news service like CNN.

The phone rang. It was Ruth.

Ruth and I have known each other for decades. We were introduced by a financial analyst with a penchant for matchmaking back in the early 1990s, after my second divorce and after Ruth's breakup with a longtime boyfriend who finally decided he was not going to divorce his wife. I never remarried, but Ruth met and married Murray Jensen, and was now widowed after ten years of marital bliss.

I told her I had a bet with Mike that she knew somebody from the Coniston family.

"He bet against me?"

"Negative. I bet against you."

"Well, now you owe me a drink, because I don't know one of them, I know several of them. One is even a member of the Opera League," she said, mentioning a social club she and Murray belonged to at the Metropolitan Opera.

"You gotta tell me all about everybody, and Mike suggested that you and Gabriele and I go over to his office and we can grab some lunch from the Halal truck that parks outside the precinct."

She said that was good, and I told her I would text her a time to meet. I also suggested that if she felt like doing some background work on the family, it would be appreciated.

"I'm doing what I can online, but I suspect you will have better places to look. Why would anybody take their kids?"

"Money, my dear. Money."

I texted Gabriele about my conversation with Mike, and asked if he could meet me at a restaurant called Thalia so we could walk over to the precinct together.

OK when

11:30

CU

Chapter Two

Gabriele was already waiting at Thalia when I walked in. He is an unusually handsome Italian fellow. He and his cousin, Dante, own a super-popular restaurant in SoHo called Ora di Pranzo. Dante is from Naples. Gabriele is from the famous Isle of Capri, setting the theme at Ora di Pranzo, where the menu is heavily weighted toward seafood.

He was standing, resting his back on the bar so he could see the front door of the restaurant, and I did a quick scan of the room, where virtually every female with a line of sight was staring at him, and some of the men.

I knew a tennis player, from my years in sports PR, who was a famous beauty, and I remember waiting at a bar on the east side for her to join me for dinner. When she walked in, every head turned as she walked down the bar to where I was standing, calmly put her hand on the nape of my neck and kissed me on the cheek. I could see all the men at the bar thinking, *she's with that old guy?* Similar sort of thing happens when Gabriele walks into a room.

It doesn't hurt that wherever he goes, the food and drinks are comped because he is so well known for his restaurant.

He held his hand out and I shook it, then we did the European kiss-kiss thing, one on each cheek.

The bartender put a dirty vodka down on the bar for me – I used to live a block away from Thalia before I moved to Long Island City. It was only a few minutes after noon, but I didn't turn it down. Gabriele sipped on a glass of red wine. Although I am fond of dirty vodka, vodka with olive 'juice' – the liquid in the bottle, very salty, I decided to stop after a couple of sips. We were going to the police precinct, after all.

Gabriele told me he watched coverage of the Coniston kidnapping on television. Like Ruth, he knew some of the family from times they had been at the restaurant, including the recently deceased Eddie, his wife, Lizzie, and his younger brother, Ricky. He had never met any of the children.

I reluctantly left a lot of the vodka in the martini glass, and left a big tip for the bartender, something you do when the food or drink is comped. Then we walked over to the PD precinct. The Halal truck was in front of the precinct. I had my taste buds primed for some falafel, which looks like meatballs, but is made with ground dried beans, olive oil, scallions, lemon juice and parsley mostly – no meat of any kind, and usually green or yellowish when you bite into them, depending on what kind of beans were used. It sticks to your ribs like meat does. I don't eat red meat, haven't for years.

We ordered two falafel lunches, falafel on top of yellow rice and what the truck guys call 'salad', which is lettuce and tomato with a couple of French fries and pickle slices on top. Then we ordered a chicken lunch and a gyro lunch, pronounced like "year-oh" in Greek and a combo of beef and lamb. If you've never had Halal food from a truck, you have no idea what six bucks can buy, or how wonderful it tastes. We took the four lunches upstairs to Mike's office.

Ruth and Mike were camped out in one of the interrogation rooms and had left the door open so we could find them. I claimed one of the falafel lunches. I could eat the chicken lunch, but I prefer the falafel. Surprisingly, Gabriele chose the gyro lunch, Ruth took the other falafel, and Mike took the remaining lunch, chicken. I got some containers of white sauce, mayo and yogurt, maybe something else in it, and red sauce, fiery peppery liquid that's hotter than Tabasco sauce, and offered them to everyone. Gabriele and I dumped both sauces on our lunches, Ruth chose white only, and Mike chose red only. Glad I'm not a betting man, because I would have lost every bet, I could shake hands on.

Together, Ruth and Gabriele are like a society data base. I listened closely to what they had to tell us. Mike taped the whole meeting and took notes, too.

Ruth said Eddie and Ricky's mother, Cecily Coniston, started a minor scandal some years back, when Eddie decided to marry Elizabeth

Westbrook Harrison, a girl Cecily didn't approve of. They had an argument in the Grill Room at the Four Seasons that was overheard by enough people it was reported on most of the television channels that night. Eddie maintained it was his right to pick his own wife. Cecily said, loudly, she found a suitable young lady whose family was distantly related to Cecily's own branch of the Neval family. She then instructed him unequivocally that he was to marry this young woman who was Cecily's second cousin once removed, which made her Eddie's third cousin, no impediment to marriage.

Eddie wasn't having any of it, because he had fallen in love with Lizzie, 'no family at all' was Cecily's comment, and fully intended to marry her at Saint Bart's on Park Avenue in short order.

The two of them kept ordering drinks and arguing, although they were never loud enough to be asked to leave.

"She is already married, and has a bunch of children," Cecily said, loudly enough to be heard across the room.

The maître d' started to walk over, and she waved him away, lowering her voice.

"She is divorced," he said, "no impediment to marriage there either."

"She's a nobody."

"She's gonna be my wife. Tell your cousin thanks but no thanks."

The next morning, the gist of this hour-long discussion was reported in a daily tabloid that was read widely in New York, following the late-news coverage on television. Naturally, a reporter called Eddie, who hung up with no comment, then called Cecily, who did. What Cecily said threw everyone in the family in a cocked hat.

"Eddie is not Richard Coniston's son," she said bluntly, referring to her deceased husband, "and should never have inherited the Coniston fortune."

According to what she told the reporter, Richard had gone on an extended business trip to Australia, and while he was gone, Cecily had an affair. "I loved Richard, and I don't know why I did it, but it was a long time ago, and I never told him. But I guarantee you that if someone does a DNA test on Eddie – or on Eddie's children – they will find no matches to Richard, or to Ricky (her youngest child), who is the only legitimate heir. Look in your files for a picture of my husband and see if you think he could have been Eddie's father!"

The question in the gossip columns was simple: why would Cecily Coniston tell the world that she had an affair and an illegitimate son if it wasn't true? It would ruin her own reputation, of course. She was many years a widow and clearly had no intention of re-marrying, but her friends would shun her, of course, and she would become a nobody herself.

A couple of days later, Cecily was found dead in her bedroom at the Coniston Mansion on 5th Avenue. The coroner labeled her death a suicide, based on the high level of opioids in her blood and digestive tract.

Eddie married Lizzie, and faced the world with pride and defiance. After a while, the kerfuffle died down and was largely forgotten.

"Then, to cap it all off, George Coniston, who, like Ricky, was Eddie's brother, and the next-eldest in the family, sued Eddie to reclaim the family businesses for the true heir – himself," Ruth harrumphed. "Cecily wasn't in the ground yet, and George wanted everything for himself."

"George was the one who drowned, right?" Mike asked.

"Yes," Ruth answered. "He took his yacht to California and one evening that summer, he drank too much and fell overboard in Avalon harbor and drowned. No evidence of foul play is what they said."

"There are some rich families it's a blessing not to be related to," I said.

Mike nodded his head and added that Richard Coniston, Cecily's husband and Eddie's putative father, was murdered years earlier by a cousin who had accused him of trying to steal the land the cousin's home was built on. It had been such a bitter relationship that when Richard was killed, the cousin cut off his head and put it on a pole in his front yard. He spent the rest of his life in a private psychiatric hospital in northern Westchester County.

"It's like the family in the House of Seven Gables," I said. "A curse that runs from generation to generation."

Gabriele looked like a spectator in a tennis match, watching intently as Ruth, Mike and I talked about Cecily's bombshell and death.

When we all took a breath, he said, "I not know about this, but Ricky and Eddie Coniston both come often to Ora di Pranzo. Eddie big tall man with blue eyes and leave big tip for waiter. Ricky small man with black hair, very how-you-say *magro*."

"Skinny," I translated.

Gabriele held up three photographs, clearly printed out from an online source. One was a tall, wide-smiling, beefy man with very symmetrical features and blondish hair. "Is Eddie," he said.

The second was a beetle-browed young man with very shaggy eyebrows, but quite good looking in a puppyish kind of way. "Is Ricky."

The third was a middle-aged man, very thin, with dark hair and the same shaggy eyebrows, dressed in a suit with a very wide 50s-type tie. "Is Richard, father of Eddie and Ricky."

"Yes, and I gather that Richard and Ricky were six or eight inches shorter than Eddie too," Mike added. "But that doesn't mean much. I'm taller than my father, but I don't look like either of my parents. I've been told I look like one of my grandfathers, but I've never seen any photos of them that look like me."

"Well, Cecily Coniston is dead, so we can't ask her what she was thinking when she had that shouting match with her son. Too bad it wasn't at home or in Central Park or someplace where people wouldn't have heard every word."

"What do you know about Ricky Coniston other than this picture?" Mike asked. "Have you ever seen Eddie's children?"

"Not know *bambini*," Gabriele offered. "Signor Ricky is good man, have wife very beautiful, remember name of waiter, and even bottle of Barolo for me at Christmas."

"So, it's easy for him to get a reservation?" I asked.

Shrug. Nod.

Mike changed the subject to the kidnapping. There had been no contact from the kidnappers, no communication from anybody about ransom. There were an FBI agent and a cop in Coniston Mansion twenty-four/seven, and the phone lines were monitored. "So, we have to ask ourselves why anyone would want to kidnap these kids. Seems like it might be a very bad time to get a ransom paid."

"Maybe not," Ruth volunteered. "Maybe they think the mother might be more inclined to pay than the father would have been?"

"Except, as far as we know, there hasn't been a ransom demand. So at least for now, it doesn't matter who would be more inclined to pay."

Mike said the K9 unit tried to pick up the boys' scent inside and around Trinity School and on what they surmised might have been the route they would have taken if they walked home. "Too much going on. The dogs were no help. No telling how many thousands of people walk those streets and walk across the park every day. One thing we know for sure is they never made it home.

"We're searching for outdoor video on any route they might have taken, but so far, nothing except right around Trinity School."

"I think the older son, Ed, is twelve or thirteen, not yet in high school, so he would be old enough in a few years to make decisions for himself. I wonder if that has anything to do with why they were snatched when they were," Ruth mused, staring at the floor.

I hadn't thought of that. But what difference would it make?

Mike looked frustrated. I wondered if he was thinking the same thing I was.

"Turning eighteen is important. When he gets there, it gives him the right to vote, and have an adult driver's license, but that's about it," he said. "If he was coming into a fortune at eighteen, that might account for why somebody would want to hold onto him, but snatching him when he's in seventh grade would just mean he couldn't access anything he would inherit five years later."

"Unless they wanted to keep him from inheriting anything," Ruth said. "His younger brother would be an insurance policy in that case."

"Why he want boy, not want *riscatto*?" Gabriele cocked his head to the side.

Ruth shrugged. "You mean ransom? No idea."

Mike tapped out a note on his phone. I must have looked puzzled, because he said, "Interesting idea, that someone would kidnap the boys to keep them from inheriting. Not sure what that would mean, but it's worth remembering."

Chapter Three

Meanwhile, the NYPD was searching high and low for the boys. They found literally hundreds of video cameras that would have been operating the day the boys appeared – on about seven different routes the boys might have taken to go home after school. Trinity School is on 91st Street between Amsterdam and Columbus Avenues. There was plenty of video as they left. Although they were in different grades, they always walked or rode home together, and the school itself provided video of them until they turned uptown on Columbus Avenue. For some reason, they disappeared as they rounded the corner, maybe intending to walk up to 96th Street, where they could walk across the Park just to the north of the Reservoir.

"Maybe they went into a bodega or a deli to buy something," Mike said when I saw him at his office the next day. "Kids are always hungry, maybe a snack. Did you watch to see if they came out any of those doors?"

The CSIs were certain that the boys were no longer on camera shortly after they turned the corner onto Columbus Avenue going uptown. They viewed the videos for an hour after they disappeared, and no one looking even vaguely like two Trinity boys showed up.

"Go back and look at all the cars driving down Columbus in the half-hour after the boys turned onto Columbus Avenue," Mike said, "and see if they had any kids in the back seat. Get the license plates if you can. Maybe if we can get in touch with them, they would have seen the boys, especially if there was something unusual going on."

There were several cars where the view of the driver and passenger area was obstructed by other cars, or by something on the lens that obscured the picture. You had to combine what was seen by one camera with what was seen by another camera, and try to fit them together as seamlessly as possible.

"It's easier to concentrate with less people in the room," he said to me. "Not that they don't contribute to the conversation, but I think better when there is some quiet, not so many people talking."

It's like working on a room-size jigsaw puzzle. Trying to find pieces that fit is frustrating and more laborious than a tortoise climbing up a slippery rock.

Mike said he preferred to leave it to the CSIs. They would find everything there was to find. "They really know what they're doing, and they're very methodical. If we try to interfere with their procedures, the potential for a mess increases."

"The one who comes out smelling like a rose is Eddie's brother. He takes control of the family businesses, even though theoretically the boys own them."

"What's theoretical about that?"

"We don't know for sure whether the boys are even alive. As days pass with no word, we have to begin to consider the worst, don't we?"

Mike stood up and paced around the room. "The first forty-eight hours are critical in a kidnapping. If it's a kidnapping."

"What else could it be?"

"Well, as you were intimating, it could be a double homicide. It's also possible the boys could have run away from home on their own steam, or could be hiding out with a friend. We know they weren't hit by a car or whatever, because they probably would have showed up at a hospital or the morgue."

He pulled a manila file folder off his desk and opened it up. "Ricky Coniston," he said.

"Why him?"

"I didn't mean I thought he grabbed the boys, but he is a family member, and did stand to gain in some way if the boys were gone."

"What do we know about him?"

Mike glanced down at the papers in the folder. Ricky was forty-seven, bachelor's degree in European history from Harvard, MBA from the NYU Stern School of Business. Married, one child, a boy, died young. He worked for a large pharmaceutical company for ten years or so after getting his MBA, and moved to the Coniston family business portfolio after his brother, George, drowned. George had been litigating with Eddie to take over the family's assets following Cecily's claim that Eddie was illegitimate.

"From all that we could find, Ricky had always been the good brother, loyal to Eddie and Lizzie, and an indulgent uncle to the boys, who spent part of the summer at Ricky's place near Katonah. Unlike the middle brother, George, who turned against Eddie, Ricky tried to fill in the best he could, and never was a cloud on Eddie's horizon. He worked in a variety of different capacities for companies in the Coniston portfolio, and Eddie appointed him to the Board of Directors after he had been there for about four years.

"He seems to have stayed in the background, didn't live at the Coniston Mansion on 5th Avenue, bought an old house in northern Westchester, became a historic preservation activist." Mike paused. "He worked on renovating falling-down houses with a claim to history, raised money, donated his own money, and was invited onto the boards of two charitable groups trying to save old Broadway theaters from being torn down to make room for more skyscrapers. He also plays several musical instruments, and was in the vestry of his local church."

He flipped through the pages. "Nothing negative. No enemies. Treated like royalty in the area where he lived between Briarcliff Manor and Chappaqua. Showed up to serve Thanksgiving and Christmas dinners to veterans' groups for several years. Married Annette Neval, a distant cousin of his mother, and had a child, a boy they named Edward after his uncle Eddie. The son, who was called Ned, went to a few private schools, none of them in New York City, and although they were respectable, none of them was a 'social register' school.

"Ricky and Ann were stars. Almost every year at the Metropolitan Museum's Costume Gala, rubbing shoulders with the great and the good. According to Page Six, the perfect couple. Then a couple of years back, Ned died suddenly from pneumonia when he was thirteen, may have started as influenza that Ned tried to ignore.

"After the boy died, there's not much more about Ricky. He

commutes on MetroNorth trains to the Coniston office on East 56th Street, and parks a Mercedes C Class sedan at the Pleasantville station most days. Does his own driving. Gave a eulogy at Eddie's funeral." He shrugged. "That's what we know."

I asked if anybody interviewed Ricky.

"Not yet. I think I'll set something up now." He thought for a couple of seconds. "If I can get him to come in here, I'd like you and your friends to be in the observation room."

"How do you get his phone number?"

"I already have it. The CSI team compiled a cast of characters with contacts. I'll send him an email." He pulled out another file folder and scanned down the list of people, then opened his Outlook and tapped out a note on his keyboard. He is a two-finger typist, but fast. "There," he said. "Let's eat some lunch and give him a chance to respond."

We walked down 9th Avenue to 50th Street and were lucky to find a table at Chez Napoleon, a tiny eatery that featured traditional French food cooked by an elderly woman called Grand-mère, who hailed from Brittany. The food was always superb, and the prices were more than reasonable, especially at lunch. The waitress, also a family member, was very friendly with Mike, and I got the impression that he ate there often. So maybe it wasn't luck that got us in.

I sent texts to Ruth and Gabriele explaining what Mike wanted us to do, and telling them I would let them know when a time was set up with Ricky Coniston. Gabriele said he could do it as long as he was at his restaurant by about five o'clock, because his cousin and co-owner of the restaurant, Dante di Benedetto, was out of town for the day. Ruth responded with a text: *okay*.

There's something about duck *confit* that makes it pop right off the menu when I look at it. Actually, I very seldom eat it; only when I find myself in a place like Chez Napoleon where I know it will have been roasted very slowly so the meat is falling-apart while the skin is crispy. Usually, they serve a leg and thigh together, and some starch and vegetables with it. I caved as soon as I read it on the blackboard on the wall by the door to the kitchen.

Mike gave me a knowing smile when I ordered it, but he voted for a dozen Belon oysters with fresh horseradish, and an order of fries. I like oysters but the Belon oyster – which French people prefer over all other types – tastes, or maybe smells, like it was raised in a sewer to me. Not that I think they are likely to make me sick, but there is a smell to them that makes me want to spit them out. I smiled back at Mike and said something about liking oysters, but loving duck confit.

"Both Ruth and Gabriele have met Ricky Coniston," I said. "They move in the right circles, I guess."

"I haven't actually met him, but I have seen him when I have been at events," Mike said. "I used to be assigned every year to the Met Gala, for instance. Put on a tux and make sure there's no hanky-panky or pick-pockets. I would see Ricky and his wife – I think her name is Ann – often, or it seems like often. He's very ordinary-looking. Kinda short for a guy. Dark hair, not bad looking but not good looking either. Athletic, I guess, or slim anyway. Big smile. Makes you wonder when you see a couple where she's gorgeous and sexy, and he looks like Joe Six-Pack."

"Money helps."

"I'm fairly sure she was okay in the money department – not wealthy, but not down-and-out either – before they were married," he said. "As a matter of fact, I think she is the reason they moved up to the country, because she grew up in someplace like Mount Kisco. Rich family. I think Ricky and Ann may be distant cousins."

"What do they say? The apple doesn't fall far from the tree."

"That usually means something more along the lines of the son acting like the father."

"That's what I meant. Weren't Ricky's parents also cousins? And isn't Ann a cousin of Ricky's mom?"

"Ann and Cecily are definitely cousins, and had the same maiden name. Don't know offhand about Ricky's parents. The father died when Ricky was a toddler, I think."

I ordered a glass of *Cahors*, a red wine from the southwest part of France, on the west side of the Rhone, mostly Malbec grapes. It complemented the duck and had an astringent quality that cleaned any residual grease out of my mouth. At least it felt that way. When the waitress asked Mike, he declined.

"On duty."

"I guess I am, too," I said slowly.

"Nah, you're a volunteer." He slurped the last oyster down and quickly finished off the last few fries. His phone beeped. It was a text message and he responded with a few taps. "We ought to be getting back though, looks like Ricky Coniston will be at the precinct in a half-hour or so." He stood up and waved at the waitress, who handed him the check. I pulled out my wallet, and he said, "Nah, Hugo, this was a police discussion. On me."

I love it when somebody else pays.

Chapter Four

Ricky Coniston was way shorter than I expected. When you think about captains of industry, for some reason they're usually tall and well-dressed. He was about five foot seven and slim, wearing old jeans, cowboy boots and a well-worn cotton flannel shirt in a faded checked pattern. His hair was long enough to make him look like a rock musician gone to seed. But flashing blue eyes and an ingratiating smile.

Ruth, Gabriele and I were sitting with Mike in his office when Mr Coniston was announced by the sergeant downstairs at the door. Mike told us to go to the observation room next to Interrogation Room 2. We were safely ensconced when Mike opened the door and showed Mr Coniston in. He brought two cups of vending-machine coffee with plastic lids, and put those on the table with some sugar packets and a couple of creamers with wooden stirring sticks. Gabriele groaned.

Everything about Ricky Coniston said he was comfortable, not threatened, but he had the attitude of an animal that constantly sweeps its environment to make sure that no danger is lurking nearby. He handed Mike a business card.

"Coniston Industries," Mike read. "What kinds of products or services, if you don't mind my asking?" He was looking at the card, not at Coniston.

Ricky leaned back in his chair and gazed at the mirror that was keeping him from seeing us. "Well, the card is for the family office, not a particular company. We own several industrial companies one hundred percent, but we have partial ownership of more companies than the ones that we own all of. Each company has its own management and executive leadership, and a good piece of the profits that we earn are allocated to the Coniston Foundation, which was established by my brother, Eddie. I guess I'm more of a portfolio manager than an industrialist. I keep thinking I should change the business cards, and maybe the name of the company. We're really a family office, just one family – although we have a lot of different households in the family who benefit from the assets that are in the company."

"Do you own the company?"

"Me?" he looked taken aback. "No. I get a salary and benefits from the company, but the actual ownership is with my two nephews, the ones who were kidnapped."

Ruth made a disapproving noise when Ricky said that.

"Not to disagree," Mike said, "but we're not certain that your nephews were kidnapped."

"I hope they were kidnapped, because that might mean they're still alive."

"So why do other people in the family get pay-outs instead of having it all go into the estate of the boys?

"Because that's how my brother set it up." He looked up at the ceiling and then back at Mike. "The family is fairly close-knit, and although it was Eddie who put the company together, he always intended to share it with virtually everyone in the family. Some of that goes through the foundation, but most of it is sent to payees as a dividend, more or less. They pay taxes on it. And yes, I get a pay-out in addition to my compensation. I have made my income taxes available to the police if they want to look at them."

"Mr Coniston," Mike said, "I want you to know that I'm not asking these questions for any reason other than to understand better what's going on."

"He seems like somebody you'd meet in a bowling alley," Ruth whispered to me.

"Very rich man," Gabriele said to Ruth. "Come in Ora di Pranzo many times. Wear expensive clothes, have car with driver wait outside while he eat."

He certainly isn't coming across that way today.

"One of the friends of the department is a young man who owns a restaurant called Ora di Pranzo," Mike said, looking down at the table.

21

Then he raised his eyes to look at Ricky. "He says you have been in his restaurant, and that everybody there likes you."

"Dante?" Coniston asked.

"No, Gabriele Cortese. He and Dante are cousins. Gabriele is the man at the front of the restaurant most of the time."

"Small world." He looked at the ceiling again and then back down. "We haven't been going out as much since our son died, about a year ago. My wife doesn't want to go anywhere. I worry about her. But she would be willing to go to your friend's restaurant, very friendly place."

"Very expensive, too," Mike said.

Gabriele made a disapproving noise. "Not expensive. Good food."

"C'mon Gabriele," I said. "When two people eat dinner at Ora di Pranzo and have a bottle of wine, I bet the average tab is over two hundred dollars. That's expensive, even in Manhattan."

He put his arm over my shoulder, around my neck and squeezed with a grin. "*Bel uomo.*"

I know I blushed because I could feel it, but the room was darkened, and I hoped it didn't show.

"I don't have any idea how expensive or not it is," Ruth said with a big smile, "because I have never paid." She paused, then said, "Thank you, Gabriele. You're a very generous friend."

He kissed her hand like he was Marcello Mastroianni. She cooed.

Mike was going over the details of what Ricky was doing the day the boys vanished, and when he found out what had happened.

"I had an appointment with my dermatologist, who removed a couple of small skin cancers from my face, so I was bandaged up pretty much. Lizzie called me on my cellphone when the boys weren't home at the regular time," he said. "She was worried that something had happened. She knew that not everybody loved Eddie the way she did. There were many people who didn't like him at all."

"Would that be the same for you now?"

"Beg pardon?"

"Are there people who don't like you?"

He nodded. "Partly because I'm Eddie's brother, and partly

because I'm the CEO of the company."

"The king in his castle?"

A sour look from Mr Coniston.

"What would happen if the boys weren't found?"

"To what? What would happen to what?"

"To the company you work for."

"I suppose the Board would continue to oversee everything. We're following protocols that Eddie set up decades ago."

"Who would own the company?"

"The boys."

"Even if they never showed up again?"

Coniston grimaced. "I'm not a lawyer, but I suppose at some point they would be presumed dead by a court. That would take years. But we're hoping they come home, and that would make it irrelevant."

"And if they didn't come home – what then?"

Coniston looked directly at Mike and said, with an iron tone, "And then probably the Board would convene the family and decide what to do." He stood up and stretched, with his hands above his head. "Sorry, I've been very stressed, and I feel it when I sit still for a long time."

Mike looked at his watch. "We've only been talking for twenty minutes."

"I just have problems with anxiety," he said. "It's better when I'm working, because I feel like I'm getting something done. Sitting here with you, all I can think about is what happened to the boys, and what would happen to Lizzie if they didn't come home." He looked at his hands. "I know what it's like to lose a son, and I've seen the damage it did to my wife."

Mike said he would try to speed things up and gestured to Coniston to sit back down. "I don't want to have to trouble you again because there were some other questions. Can you tell me if there have ever been any threats against the boys?"

"If there ever were, I never knew about it."

"That's a no?"

He nodded.

"Any threats against Eddie that would have been bitter enough that they might take it out on the boys?"

"Not that I know of. Eddie wasn't the best-liked man in Manhattan, but nobody thought he was a bad guy."

"There were a lot of civil lawsuits against Edward Coniston, alleging all kinds of unfair competition, and some accusations of not being totally truthful in testimony."

"Whatever you say."

"Did you grow up in the house on 5th Avenue?"

He nodded.

"Big place."

"Huge. Unnecessary. It was built when families were bigger, and there were servants around every corner."

"Does your sister-in-law feel comfortable there?"

He shrugged. "She wouldn't be comfortable anywhere with her sons gone."

"Sorry, I meant did she enjoy living there before this happened?"

"I suppose. It's a nice house. She hasn't entertained since Eddie died. At least not that I know of."

"I can't imagine what it would be like wondering where the boys are and whether they are okay," Mike said.

"You're right. You can't imagine unless you've been through it. Do you have children?"

Mike said he had never married, had no kids. "And I live in an apartment a few blocks from here, not big enough to feel lonely in."

He added, "Sorry, one other thing, and I apologize for bringing it up. There were some statements made by your mother about your brother, Eddie, to the effect that his father may not have been your father."

"Yes."

"What can you tell me about that?"

"She was a dementia patient. She had a ruptured aneurysm that scrambled her brain, but she managed not to die when most people who have that don't survive. Sadly, she didn't always know what she was saying."

"Would it be correct to say that you don't believe what she said?"

"It would be correct to say that whatever she said, it didn't matter." He stood up again, and was clearly ready to leave.

"Thank you for coming by, Mr Coniston. I'm sorry that some of my questions were unpleasant and probably seemed hostile. I do my job, just as you do your job. Thank you again." Mike stood up and they shook hands before Mr Coniston left.

Mike looked at the mirror and said to us, "Meet you in my office."

We got to his office before Mike did. When he got there, he was balancing four coffees.

All three of us said virtually the same thing about Coniston: he was credible, didn't seem hostile or afraid of questions.

"I knew him a bit from the Opera Club," Ruth said. "His brother, Eddie, was a member for decades, and sometimes Ricky and Ann used Eddie's tickets. Nice fellow, but they didn't seem to want to socialize with the other members. And after Murray passed, I didn't always go to all the performances. I remember Eddie and Lizzie very fondly."

"He have big memory, know all names in Ora di Pranzo. All people like him." Gabriele looked somber. "Is *terribile* what happen to him."

Mike said that he had a hard time believing that Ricky, who had lost his own son, could have anything to do with what happened to Eddie and Lizzie's boys. "Having to bury a child is unnatural and gut-wrenching," he said. "Somebody's going to have to talk to other family members."

"Just let us know when and where," I said.

"I think the CSI's can take it from here. If they dig something interesting up, we can decide what to do then. I can't keep an open mind in a situation like this."

Chapter Five

Ruth, Gabriele and I walked the four blocks over to Thalia, an eatery on 8th Avenue with a good bar and a good menu. The bartender knows me, and he lifted a bottle of Tito's vodka with a questioning look when we walked in. I nodded.

"Me, too," Ruth said.

I waved two fingers at the bartender, and pointed at Ruth.

It was mid-afternoon and there were plenty of places at the bar.

He nodded and took out two martini glasses from the freezer. They frosted up immediately. He shook the vodka over his head – entertainment for the others at the bar. When he brought the glasses over and poured the dirty vodka into them from the shaker, he said to Gabriele, "Signor Cortese, an honor to have you at our bar. What can I get for you?"

"You have chianti?"

He nodded and reached under the bar to retrieve a bottle of Ser Niccolo, a modestly priced but famous vineyard that is said to be on Machiavelli's farm in the countryside east of Florence. Old vines. Gabriele gave him a thumbs-up.

"I didn't know they had Ser Niccolo by the glass," I said to Gabriele.

"Always have good wine for good customers. He no charge us for drinks."

"Everything's better when it's free," Ruth said with a simpering smile. She pecked Gabriele on the cheek.

I asked them what they thought about Ricky Coniston.

Ruth said he seemed unexpectedly normal for someone who was so wealthy and socially prominent. "Very sexy eyes," she said, "and good features, but a little short for my taste, and skinny. I like men with some meat on their bones."

"I wasn't asking if you want to date him," I said, then thought better of it. "I meant, did you think he was being straight with us? Truthful?"

"I don't remember him being asked much that wasn't already public. The family has been in the papers ever since I can remember. Yeah, I think he seems like a straight-shooter. I don't know if I would buy a used car from him, if that's what you're asking."

"He wearing *maschera*," Gabriele said, using an Italian word for a stage costume. "Not look like cowboy when he come Ora di Pranzo. Look like business, *ricchezza e bellezza,*" he said, quoting a common description of the upper class, meaning "wealthy and beautiful." He stroked his chin with his right hand. "Maybe he want police think he different from real."

"You mean you think he was acting different from the way he usually acts?" Ruth cocked her head to the side.

Gabriele nodded. "Maybe you see him different at opera, too."

"Or maybe the man we saw is the real Ricky Coniston, and the businessman or the opera-goer is the masquerade," I offered.

I wondered why he would go to the trouble of inventing a new persona for his meeting at the precinct. *Maybe we saw the "real" Ricky Coniston, and the public persona is the fake one.* "Are you sure he wasn't putting on airs when he was at Ora di Pranzo? Acting the way, he thought a rich man ought to act?"

Gabriele shrugged. "I know Signor Coniston only at Ora di Pranzo. And he wear very fine clothes."

"Honestly, I don't remember him very distinctly from the Monday-night operas. I mean I recognized him when he walked into the interrogation room, but not a lot of memories came back. No idea which opera or operas he saw, for instance. Or even when the last time I saw him was. I think he and his wife only showed up when Eddie and Lizzie couldn't go. And frankly, he isn't physically a stand-out in any way; not ugly, not a gargoyle or anything like that, just ordinary-looking except his eyes are remarkable. I don't think Murray and I ever exchanged anything other than a wave across the room with them. I don't recall ever talking to him or his wife. A lot of people put on a haughty front at the opera. We always dress up, only time I wear a floor-length dress. Is that the real me? Probably not. In my case, it's kinda fun to dress up. But a lot of people go to the opera just to show off. I happen to love opera."

"I found him credible, and laid-back. He didn't seem nervous the way some people might if they were in an interrogation room at a police precinct," I said. "He looked straight at Mike a good deal of the time, and I didn't see anything about his behavior that was at odds with what he was saying."

He didn't look familiar when he walked in, so I probably wasn't at any of the operas he saw.

"He seemed like he still is in lot of pain from the death of his son," Ruth said, "and it doesn't seem likely to me that he would have anything to do with kidnapping his nephews. I doubt he would put the boys' mom through a living hell of worry and anxiety, so soon after her husband's death. Poor thing, she must feel like the world is ending."

Although Gabriele may not have been completely on board, we agreed that we found Ricky Coniston a credible man in the interview we witnessed. Not that it mattered, because we wouldn't be asked for our opinions. We also decided that Mike should try to persuade Lizzie to agree to an interview. If there was anybody in the family who would have a reason to suspect Ricky based on long acquaintance, it would be her. And if she didn't suspect him, it might be enough to almost clear him of anything we might suspect him of, which at present was nothing at all.

I sent a text to Mike: *Recommend interview Eliz C*
Why
Best view of family, incl Ricky
OK will try to set up, U3 can be here?
Probably LMK

"He wants us to be there if he can get Lizzie to agree to an interview."

"She's not going to want to leave her home if they're still hoping for some kind of communication from the kidnapper," Ruth said.

I sent a new text to Mike: *What if she wants to stay home bec*

kidnap
> *Then u go w me and I'll figure out the rest*
> *Just me or all 3*
> *3 if u can*
> *OK LMK*

We decided to walk up Central Park West to 91st Street. A long walk, about two miles, but we knew that once we got to Columbus Circle, we wouldn't have to deal with cross-streets if we walked on the park side of the street. We wanted to see the way the boys would normally have walked to get home from school.

It was a sunny late afternoon, and muggy. The sky looked like we might have a pop-up thunderstorm, a not-unusual phenomenon along the lower Hudson River. The air gets so heavy with humidity that it makes rain seem like an almost daily event – sometimes with spectacular lightning shows and ear-splitting thunder. Fortunately, although the storms can be fierce, they usually only last a short time, and then move on to scare children and dogs somewhere else.

"If it starts to rain, we can duck in someplace and grab a nibble," Ruth said as she changed her heels for a pair of track shoes she carried in her bag.

"Or a glass of something," I added.

"*Caffé*," Gabriele chirped with a slightly disapproving look.

I sweat easily – or maybe I should say I sweat quickly, and sometimes profusely. There were a gaggle of vendors at Columbus Circle, and I bought three bottles of water for us to stay hydrated on our way uptown.

Since I didn't grow up in New York or the northeastern part of the United States, I have always been amazed by how overwhelmingly green the landscapes are in the summer. I lived most of my life in southern California, where the landscapes are largely brown in the summer, speckled with eucalyptus trees and other non-native trees like flowering pears or jacarandas that turn streets into lavender fairylands. Central Park was designed to look like the English countryside by Frederick Law Olmsted, the man who invented landscape architecture. Central Park was created on paper when the street grid above Houston Street was laid out in 1811 in a grand plan that has given Manhattan much of its character to this day.

Mr Olmsted disliked flower gardens, and there are almost no flower gardens in the wonderful park that some people call "New York's back yard." When he started, much of the land that was to be parkland was in actuality a pig farm – flat, smelly and uninteresting. The landscapes there are amazing flights of Olmsted's imagination. He wanted it to look like the Cotswolds, which he had visited in his youth, rambling through the rolling hills and the then-unspoiled areas of the Midlands. It looks for all the world like a wild forest with some areas tamed into meadows or baseball diamonds, but much of it with hilly walking paths. Completely worth several hours on any spring or summer day.

In reality, the trees are not native – everything was planted, because the land had been totally cleared for farming, and many of the trees originated in other parts of the world, like the ginkgo trees, which are only native to China, and are ideal for city landscaping because they are not susceptible to any of the normal pests that kill trees in American forests. Unfortunately, some ginkgo trees bear a fruit that looks for all the world like a large yellow cherry, but smells like sewage. It is the pit of that horrible fruit that is converted into ginkgo biloba that is sold as a miracle-working food supplement in natural food stores. Olmsted also designed bridges, fountains, ponds, streams and a variety of recreational areas.

That's a long way of saying that the walk up the side of the park was calming and seemed to go by very quickly. I drank my bottle of water by the time we were halfway to 91st Street, and began to feel the call of nature around 72nd Street. We detoured into the park, heading for the restrooms at the Loeb Boathouse, a very chic eatery and watering hole on the romantic artificial lake-let where you can rent a rowboat and row your lady-love or your kids around and there are clean public restrooms.

We walked the rest of the way to 91st Street inside the park. It's easy to find your way and the only danger is usually from bicyclists who sometimes ride faster than speeding bullets. In fact, most of Central Park at 91st Street is water – the Jacqueline Onassis reservoir – so we opted to walk on the Bridle Path that follows the edge of the reservoir, which looks like a big fenced lake. That way we could exit the park on 5th Avenue a few blocks from the Coniston Mansion.

If the boys had dropped bread crumbs like Hansel and Gretel, the birds had long since eaten them, and there weren't many places where somebody could pop out from a hidden perch and grab two young boys on their way home from school. Then we turned around and walked across the downtown side of the reservoir, which took us to just north of the Metropolitan Museum of Art, with just a short uptown walk on 5th Avenue to the Coniston boys' home.

"If I don't miss my guess, they would have taken the 86th Street crossing," Ruth said. "Easier, shorter, and more people to keep it safe."

Gabriele disagreed. "If I school boy, I take uptown crossing. Is cooler, more shade, and not take longer time." He stepped over to a tree behind the Museum garage and urinated onto the tree trunk, glancing around to make sure he was not being ogled. "*E posso fare pipì.*" I certainly sympathized with that. Ruth was studiously looking in another direction.

"Finished?" she asked.

I gave an uh-huh grunt and she turned around to face me. "Boys will be boys," she said. "I guess."

"I may be all wet, but I haven't seen any place that two boys could be kidnapped without being seen," Ruth mused.

"No, you're not all wet," I said. "I was thinking along the same lines. How about you, Gabriele?"

"When I was little and we go to Napoli, many children was *rapimenti*, like you say kidnap. Taken on sidewalk in fast car. No possible have fast car in Manhattan, and too many people in park for take boys there. Maybe we walk west part of park and look at walk from school to park."

I reminded them that the video cameras in the area never saw them after they turned uptown on Columbus Avenue. "Maybe we should look on Columbus and see if there is a bodega they could have gone into."

It was a frustrating afternoon for anyone looking for clues. That block going north from 91st Street on Columbus didn't have a neighborhood-ish bodega. There was a supermarket and a little outdoor restaurant on the west side of the avenue, and a little pocket park with no apparent rear exit – and plenty of video cameras everywhere we looked. The east side of the avenue was entirely taken up by a medical office building with guards inside ready to check IDs for anyone who wanted to go upstairs.

"The video on 91st Street saw them turn north on Columbus, and then no video saw them on Columbus," I said out loud, but I was really talking to myself.

"So, they must have gone into the supermarket," Ruth said, taking some pictures of the neighborhood. "Hard to believe the supermarket wouldn't have video, if for no other reason, to catch shoplifters. Children are the best shoplifters, I think. When I was a child, I swiped candy fairly often. Never got caught."

We walked around inside the supermarket. It looked like any other supermarket, but with very narrow aisles and product shelving that would take a ladder to reach for most people. Manhattan square footage is expensive, so merchants get the maximum use out of it.

Ruth asked a young man who was stocking tomato sauces if they had a restroom. He pointed to a large doorway with plastic sheeting instead of a door in the back of the store. She told us to wait and she would be right back.

When she came back, she said the restroom was cleaner than she expected, and there were several ways to leave the store in the back. Almost all of the openings she saw were on the loading docks, where two Trinity boys in uniforms would have looked really out of place. "So, I guess it's unlikely that they ducked in here, stole a Hershey bar or a bag of chips and then ran out the back door." She paused and then added, "but even if they did, they would probably have re-appeared on 91st Street, so we would see them on video."

"Well, we should ask Mike if the CSIs reviewed any video from inside the supermarket," I said.

Gabriele stared at me. "Maybe they call Uber."

"Maybe I'll call Mike," I said, intending it to be good-humored.

He answered after the first ring. I put the phone on speaker so we could all hear, but there was too much background noise where we were, so I turned off the speaker. I explained to him what we had been up to, and what we thought might have happened, based on the evidence we knew of.

It wasn't impossible the boys that vanished had Uber on their smartphones, but it seemed likely that if they did summon an Uber car, their mother would have been notified, since most likely she would be paying the bills. It made me wonder if they could have met someone in a car who offered them a ride – like somebody they knew. As it happened, there was no video that showed the boys getting into a car.

"That doesn't mean it didn't happen," Mike said. "It just means that with what we have now, we can't prove it."

"Do you think it's likely what happened?" Ruth asked.

"It's one scenario that could explain the gaps in what we know," Mike said, "providing we're willing to say that the boys were abducted by someone they knew."

But it's the only solution to how the boys disappeared, I thought. I couldn't bring myself to think that the boys were taken prisoner in the supermarket or the outdoor café, and then spirited away in disguise, or the back of a truck or whatever.

The CSIs had gone back over all the video they had gathered, concentrating on the corner of Columbus Avenue and 91st Street, which was only a couple of blocks from Trinity School, where they were students. They found that three cars drove by a camera mid-block on Columbus, twice or more times within a few minutes. That excluded trying to spot repeats by taxis, because taxis are too much alike.

"That by itself could be a bit unusual," Mike said, "but all of us have circled blocks looking for parking spaces – sometimes a bunch of times around the same block – and that may be what was going on. But I asked them to see if they can find anything about those three cars that would help us identify them. One was a silver current model Mercedes Benz sedan. One was a dark-color, maybe black, two-year-old Lincoln four-door with what looked like a livery sticker on the windshield on the passenger side. The third was a light blue Honda sedan that was a current design, but there was no way to say what year it was."

"The black Lincoln could be an Uber," Ruth said.

Gabriele nodded agreement.

"We thought about that," Mike said, "so we checked the congestion pricing entry points where there are cameras, and we didn't see it crossing 61st Street going downtown, where it would incur a surcharge if it was a livery car."

"That doesn't mean it wasn't an Uber," I said. "Ubers may try to stay south of 61st Street to avoid getting passengers hit with the surcharge more than once in a day. All they'd have to do is decline rides that were going outside the congestion area."

"But the congestion fee is paid by the passenger," Mike said. "Not by the driver. And in the case of Uber, it's a couple of bucks automatically charged on the passenger's Uber account credit card. Maybe not a concern about having enough passengers; no drag on a driver's income. And there have to be Uber drivers who live inside the boundaries of the congestion zone. So, they could drive all day or all night inside, and not crossing back and forth."

Gabriele asked if the CSIs had been able to identify any of the cars.

"Not so far."

We decided to table it and wait a day or so to see if the CSIs could come up with something on at least one of the three cars – and hopefully all three.

It was starting to get toward rush hour, and Gabriele was antsy about not being at his restaurant, so I told him to peel off and take the subway. Ruth didn't want to go home, so we walked back over to 5th Avenue and caught a yellow taxi to take us to the Peninsula Hotel, where I know the bartender who would be on duty in the Lobby Bar. He wouldn't comp us, but he would pour with a heavy hand.

Chapter Six

Sure enough, Juan was behind the bar. I hadn't been there in a while, so we spent a couple of minutes catching up, and then he seated us at a table for four where we would be comfortable, then brought me a dirty vodka with olives. I pushed it over to Ruth, and asked him for one more like that. He brought a bowl of roasted nuts with some kind of flavored salt on them. Nice.

When the runner brought my drink to the table, I was telling Ruth that I had seen numerous celebrities in that same bar, including a very famous French actress who was virtually a legend of elegance and beauty…

"Wow," Ruth said, "this must be where the elite meet. Ricky Coniston just walked in." She waved and he walked over to our table.

He was wearing a navy-blue suit, white shirt and a tie with blue and yellow stripes. Quite a different persona from the guy we had observed at the police precinct.

Ruth introduced me, and then said, as if explaining, "Ricky comes to the opera on Mondays sometimes."

He said he didn't want to intrude, which prompted Ruth to ask him if would join us for a drink. "We won't be here very long, just thirsty after a long walk in the park."

Ricky ordered a single malt scotch with a longish name neat (no ice, no water). When it arrived, we welcomed him and clinked. He seemed more relaxed than he had when he was talking to Mike, and I could hear the trace of a Massachusetts or Rhode Island accent ("pahk the cah in Hahvahd yahd").

He smiled when I asked if he was a Red Sox fan. "Not a Red Sox fan," he said, "but guilty as charged about Harvard."

Ruth said, "Hugo's a fan of A.B.B. in baseball."

He looked puzzled.

"Anybody But Boston. A.B.B."

"We were sorry to read about the boys being missing. Any progress on that?" Ruth asked.

He looked uncomfortable and sat up straighter. "That's a twenty-four/seven worry for all of us. I just wish we'd get a ransom letter or call."

"Is your home swarming with cops all the time?" I asked.

"Not mine, no. I live in Westchester. But Eddie and Lizzie's house, yes. They try to be unobtrusive, and stay out of her way, but I know every time Lizzie sees one of them, she feels her heart break all over again."

"I can't even imagine how horrible it must be for the whole family," Ruth said. "I don't have any children, but I come from a large family, and I know how close we've always been. My brothers have kids, and I know I would be destroyed if something happened to one of them."

"I think I'll have another drink," Ricky said, and waved at Juan, drew a circle in the air over the table, telling him to bring another round for all of us.

I could tell that Ruth almost said no, but then thought better of it.

When the drinks came, he said, "I lost my son last summer. Everybody said it's unnatural for a parent to have to bury a child. I still wake up in the mornings expecting to see him at breakfast. And of course, my brother Eddie died a few months ago. It's been a bad period for the family. My other brother, George, died eight or nine years back, drowned after he had been drinking in Catalina harbor in California. But it's worse when something happens to a kid."

He was sipping the whisky instead of drinking it. That was reassuring, but there was something odd about what he said. Like he had rehearsed it.

He looked at me looking at him. "Everybody offers sympathy, so there's no time when the family tragedies aren't front and center."

"I'm sorry," I said. "How 'bout dem Yankees?"

He smiled and looked relieved. "That house is a museum. Hard to live there."

36

"Westchester is better?"

"It's not a new-built house, but it's new to Annie and me, lets us relax."

"I bet the house on 5th Avenue is beautiful," Ruth said. "And I bet when you were a child you felt more like it was home, instead of a museum."

"My father died when I was young, but Mom was always there, always had a smile for everybody. And Annabelle, who was in charge of our kitchen, adopted me and showed me how to cook. She said everybody needs to learn how to cook, because no matter how much money you have, there are times when you need to make your own dinner. So yeah, it was home then. It was when Annie and I got married and my son was born, that I didn't want to live there anymore."

I said my family had lived in northern Westchester when I was in college, town called Briarcliff Manor. "I was at school in California, but I visited, and stayed with them for a year once, when I needed to get a job and sock away some money, because I was paying my own way through college. So, I learned a fair amount about Westchester, just wandering around."

"We live near Pleasantville, if you know where that is," he said. "A lot of people know it because *Reader's Digest* was founded and published there."

"Close to Chappaqua?"

He nodded.

"Pretty over there. I've been to Horace Greeley's home. It may be in Pleasantville, or may be in Chappaqua, don't remember. Difficult to get there without a car."

Greeley was famous in his day as a journalist, founder of the newspaper that became the *New York Herald Tribune*. These days he is mostly remembered for something he said: "Go west, young man, go west and grow up with the country."

"It is confusing about Horace Greeley," Ricky said. "The thing is, he lived in Chappaqua and his home is a museum there now. But he died at Choate House in Pleasantville, which was a sanitarium in the nineteenth century, and Greeley was being treated there. I think a lot of people call Choate House by Greeley's name. Today it's part of a college."

"There is a train between Pleasantville and Grand Central," he said. "I usually commute on the train and leave my car at the station. I could just as easily commute from Chappaqua, but I don't. When I need to get home fast, I take the train to North White Plains, which has way more trains arriving and departing than Pleasantville does. Then I can take a taxi home from there."

"My dad never wanted to leave his car at the station in Briarcliff. He was afraid it would get scraped and dented, so my mom or I would drive him there and then pick him up in the evening."

Ricky said he had never had a problem with the car. "But I work at home on Mondays and Fridays sometimes."

"How's your beautiful wife?" Ruth asked. "Those seats at the opera have been empty the last few times I was there."

"I hadn't thought about the opera. We've had several bad things happen in the family. My brother died, then my son died. Now Eddie's boys disappeared, probably kidnapped. And my wife has been sick, too, off and on since our boy died. I think that's why I have been having a few drinks before I go home."

"Well, I sympathize. My husband died a couple of years back, and I thought I wouldn't be able to go on by myself. But the opera is dark for the summer anyway," she said. "I hope things improve for you by the time the fall season opens. Like they say, time heals all wounds. Some new productions that are probably going to be spectacular this year."

"I never thought I would like going to the opera," Ricky said. "But Eddie was a real fan, and he convinced me to give it a try. Annie loved it, and I admit I enjoyed it every time I went."

"I've always loved the opera," I said. "I don't have much of a voice, but when I was in college, I sang in opera choruses when the Music Department was staging something. At least I learned to read music well enough to more or less figure out what the notes were without somebody playing them on a piano, which a lot of people needed."

He asked where I went to school, and I told him I went to UCLA.

It was obvious looking at him that he was anxious about something. He kept looking at his smartphone and his watch.

"Are you expecting someone to meet you here?" I asked. "Because we don't want to get in the way."

He shook his head. "No, I'm not. I've been wondering whether I should go to Grand Central to get the train, or whether I'm okay to drive."

"You have your car here?"

He nodded. "The doorman is holding it for me."

"If you want to take the train, I'll park your car in the garage in the middle of the block here, and give you the ticket before you leave for Grand Central," I said. "How much should I tip the doorman?"

"Twenty," he said. "Thanks, but I think I'll drive. I need to drink some water, but I don't feel like I'm impaired."

"You sure? Let me walk down to the front of the hotel and make sure your car is there."

"I'll get the check," Ruth said.

"No need," Ricky said. "I have a tab. My treat." He stood up.

I got up, too, and we walked down the two short flights of stairs to the revolving front door. The Peninsula Hotel is new, but the building is old. When I was a kid, it was called the Gotham Hotel. It's the same period as the St Regis Hotel across 5th Avenue facing it, and both buildings are steel reinforced but solid stone. When the UN General Assembly convenes in September every year, the two hotels are commandeered by the NYPD, and held for heads of state from the Middle East or other hot spots, because the St Regis and the Peninsula are the most bomb-proof hotels in Manhattan. The last thing the NYPD wants is to have a head of state assassinated in his sleep in some modern, glass-fronted hotel.

Sure enough, the doorman, whom I also knew, had Ricky's silver Mercedes waiting in what was surely a no-parking zone. "It pays to have friends," I said to him as he got into the car. "Good meeting you, Ricky."

He smiled and said "Same here. Thanks."

"Thank you for the drinks."

I started to walk back up to the bar, but Ruth was standing just inside the revolving door waiting for me.

She said she hadn't intended to have two drinks, and really wanted to eat something before she went home. We walked a block and a half over to Bice on 54th Street between 5th and Madison. Giancarlo, the maître d', is an old friend, and seated us as soon as we walked up to him, though we didn't have a reservation, and there were other people waiting for tables. The name looks like it would rhyme with "dice," but it's Italian, and pronounced BEE-chay. Excellent food, pretty mainstream in terms of using old recipes, but with a remarkable wine list – the kind that has five pages of Barolo wines in the best vintages. Pricey, too. I thought *this would be a good time to have Gabriele here, so we could get comped.*

I think in past lives I was a peasant, maybe in Italy. Even in the fanciest restaurants, I head straight for the pasta section in the menu, and almost always end up with something common, like spaghetti *cacio e pepe* or *penne arrabiata*. For my taste, there is nothing more rewarding than *cacio e pepe*, which is one of the simplest of all Italian dishes. You dump the hot pasta with some of the pasta water it was boiled in, into a concave dent in the top of a wheel of *cacio*, which is a cheese that is usually a sheep cheese, frequently Pecorino Romano because it's from Rome and therefore is the best. Douse it with freshly grated black pepper. The water softens and slightly melts the cheese, and the starch in the pasta and the pasta water causes it to adhere together, so that every bite has cheese and pepper sticking to the pasta. A little grated parmesan cheese on top – heaven. And sheep cheese is very low in cholesterol.

Ruth wanted *coda alla vaccinara*, a stew made with vegetables, tomatoes and oxtails, cooked for a very long time together so the tough fatty meat of the oxtail is tender and the veggies are coated with the drippings from the oxtail. It smelled good to me, one of those times when I wished I still ate red meat, but I haven't for the last thirty-five years.

"Ricky was driving a silver Mercedes sedan," I said to her when the waiter put some bread on the table with a saucer of olive oil that had black pepper stirred into it.

I decided I would have a glass of *barbaresco,* an everyday wine with a nice tang to it. Ruth just wanted water.

"From the way you said that, I know I am supposed to connect it to something," Ruth said, "but I'm drawing a blank."

"Unless I'm remembering wrong, a silver Mercedes sedan was one of the three cars that drove by three or more times where the boys were when they disappeared. The CSI's got that from the video they scavenged from the neighborhood the boys were walking through. "

"I think you're right, now that you say that. I wonder how many silver Mercedes sedans there are in the Tri-State area."

"Probably hundreds, maybe thousands," I said. "But this one belongs to the boys' uncle."

Chapter Seven

Mike told me, on the phone, later that he would check the toll bridges to see if Mr Coniston's Mercedes showed up at any of the crossings. He said if someone was driving from Westchester, there would be a lot of routes that would take them into Manhattan without hitting a toll. If you drove down the Major Deegan Expressway and then across the Willis Avenue Bridge or any of several other bridges that cross the Harlem River, there wouldn't have been a toll. Or if he went across the Whitestone Bridge to Queens and then across the Queensboro Bridge, he'd be in Manhattan midtown without ever paying a toll except going into Queens. All the East River bridges are exempt from the congestion toll. And, he reminded us, they had already checked the 61st Street congestion cameras and no silver Mercedes sedan showed up on those.

"But I thought we were looking for a silver Mercedes that might have crossed into the congestion area around the time the boys were getting out of school. What if it drove in during rush hour? Maybe seven or eight hours before Trinity School students would be on their way home?"

"Could be. Coniston told us that he had some skin cancers removed that morning; could have already been in Manhattan."

We agreed we should talk again later, and disconnected.

Manhattan has an exceptionally large population of world-class hospitals, physicians and specialists, but Westchester is no slouch in healthcare, so it was not a slam-dunk that his morning appointment would have been in the City.

I made it home by a little after ten pm, and decided to have a snack while I watched the eleven o'clock news. I'm a sucker for avocado toast, just some toasted bread with mashed-up avocado spread over it (and it's healthy food, too). Also been a news junkie most of my life, frequently devouring the online versions of several newspapers every day, and keeping either CNN or CNBC on the television during the day – mostly as background noise, but I listen when an interesting story comes up. I'm not a big fan of news programs that default to opinion all the time. Seems to me the news ought to be the news, not a long editorial rant. Would Walter Cronkite have engaged in the sort of meandering supposition that dominates CNN for much of the day? Jim Lehrer? No.

But that evening when I turned on the ABC news, the lead story was about the Coniston kidnapping. There was some video footage of the boys at a backyard party someplace that looked like it was captured on a smartphone, and news coverage of the Met Costume Gala a few years earlier, featuring Ricky and Ann Coniston, the boys' uncle and aunt. No footage of Eddie, but a brief clip showing Lizzie smiling in a restaurant-type setting in happier times. The news hook was that it was three weeks since the boys went missing, and so far, there had been no communication from the kidnappers. There was a brief interview with a noted criminologist from the John Jay College of Criminal Justice on the west side near Lincoln Center. He said that the first forty-eight hours after a kidnapping is key to figuring out how to get the victims released. When nothing developed to support the assumption that it was a kidnapping, hope that the boys were still alive would inevitably wane.

I had been thinking the same thing, but any time I brought it up, somebody – Mike or Ruth – would pooh-pooh the idea. The words 'homicide" or 'murder' never came up. Instead, the conversation would turn to the idea the boys probably ran off on their own, maybe hiding out with a friend. That's the old 'boys will be boys' idea. Whatever the direction of our speculation, each day must have been beyond painful for Lizzie Coniston, who stayed at home, probably staring at the telephone, waiting for it to ring.

I thought about our conversation with Ricky Coniston, who more or less refused to consider the idea that the boys might no longer be alive. He wouldn't speculate on what would happen to the Coniston companies if the boys couldn't inherit. He was in a particularly painful position, too, because he had lost his own son.

It was especially difficult to figure out who could benefit from the boys' disappearance. Clearly Ricky Coniston was already fixed for life, whether the boys were around or not. He was, for all intents and purposes, the head of the family, even though it was by default, with his elder brothers both deceased. The thought that he might have snatched the boys and then maybe even killed them goes against everything he seemed to be – and the reality of his own son's death a few months prior made it seem well-nigh unthinkable.

So, who else might benefit from the boys disappearing? I asked myself.

There was Edward, the son of Eddie and Ricky's brother George, who drowned several years back. He might stand to inherit if Eddie's sons weren't able to. Eddie and Lizzie had two daughters as well, but for some reason they did not seem to be in the running to inherit the Coniston Companies.

The Edward who was George's son was a college kid, and lived with his mother outside Boston. It took a vivid imagination to visualize a very young man arranging the kidnapping and eventual disappearance of two boys who were his cousins. There might be disaffected employees or other stakeholders of the Coniston Companies, but you'd think Ricky would be aware of people like that, if there were any. If Lizzie Coniston had any close relatives, maybe they could benefit if the boys were gone, because they might move closer to inheriting part of the estate, even though there might be no blood relationship to the Coniston family. And the extended family included lots of people who were receiving dividends from the company, even though it was, strictly speaking, not public. So, there could be third cousins twice removed with dreams of riches – but there had been no demand for ransom, so how could they profit? Ricky was solidly in control of the estate, and also seemed close with Lizzie, the widow and mother of the supposedly kidnapped boys.

That sounds like a parallel universe, not the one we live in. Not anything like reality.

I needed to talk to Ruth and Gabriele for a reality check, and to try to figure out what we hadn't seen that could open up new possibilities. I texted them to see when they might be able to meet up. We decided to meet at ten am for breakfast at the Pershing Square Café that faces Grand Central on 42nd Street just under the Park Avenue ramp. It's always mobbed at breakfast, but if you go to the bar, which is usually deserted at breakfast, you can order breakfast there. One of the best 'power breakfasts' in Manhattan – and convenient, because I can take the subway one stop to Grand Central and walk upstairs. For Ruth, it's easy because she can either walk or take a subway to Grand Central and do the same. Gabriele can take a subway from Brooklyn Heights to Bryant Park and then transfer to the crosstown subway and hit Grand Central without ever having to go outdoors.

I got there first and ordered a black coffee and a screwdriver. Before the bartender got it to me, Gabriele showed up. Cheek kisses and he ordered the same. I started to explain things to Gabriele, but then Ruth arrived and made the coffee and screwdriver three.

I suggested that we order food first, because I had refrained from eating other than coffee and toast and felt like I was starving. I'm very conservative at breakfast – scrambled eggs, rye toast with butter and jelly, and maybe some potatoes. I don't eat red meat, so no bacon or sausage. At home I eat vegetarian sausages or turkey sausages occasionally, but restaurants seldom have those things.

Gabriele wanted Belgian waffles with strawberries, and Ruth had a bagel with a shmear and some lox. Whatever. I think most people want to have the breakfast they grew up with. In my case it was always bacon and eggs, but I abandoned meat about thirty-five years ago, so the potatoes stand in for bacon. Ruth grew up in Brooklyn, thus the bagel with lox and cream cheese. I doubt seriously that Gabriele grew up with waffles, whipped cream and strawberries, since in Italy breakfast is usually coffee, cold cuts, cheese, fruit (maybe fruit juice) and maybe some pastries for breakfast. But he's very adventurous when it comes to food, probably because he virtually lives in his restaurant, and is delighted to see a menu that has different things on it. He seldom orders Italian food when we go out.

"I feel like we've hit a dead-end about the Coniston boys," I said.

"No ransom demand, no clues about where they went or with whom. Seems to me like we ought to be rattling whatever skeletons there are in the family closets – there's no way the boys disappeared into thin air, so we have to go back over that, too."

Ruth said she thought it was likely that, since the boys were set to inherit the family business, the whole thing was done to get the wealth redistributed.

I asked whether they thought there was a chance the boys were still alive. They both shook their heads.

"I hate to say it," Ruth offered, "but it seems to me that either they had an accident of some kind or met with foul play. Since there was no ransom, the only obvious conclusion is that the boys were nabbed and disposed of somehow."

"The problem is," I said, "that it's hard to figure out who would benefit from the boys vanishing without a trace. So there doesn't seem to be an obvious suspect. There was no sign that the boys were into drugs or had a history of running off, and nobody has ever thought they high-tailed it out of town on their own hook."

Gabriele asked what Mike thought. I told him that Mike might be running into a brick wall, too, as far as I could tell.

"The most obvious suspect would be a family member, but there are so few of them other than Ricky and Ann, Lizzie of course, and a bunch of cousins," Ruth said. "I tried to construct a family tree from what I could find in the papers, but never got very far."

"What about using Ancestry or one of the other genealogical companies?" I asked.

"If boys dead, what happen to bodies?" Gabriele asked. "Bury? Drop in ocean? Impossible to burn body up. Smell bad and leave bones."

"It seems from reading the news that when somebody disappears, the most likely is that they get buried in a shallow grave," Ruth said with a frown. "I never met the boys, but it's horrible to think they might be dead and moldering in somebody's back yard."

"Gone are the days when bodies could be buried in the cellar. Cellars these days are all concrete floors, so you'd need a jack-hammer to get through to dirt." It gave me a chill to say that. Vision of some kind of serial killer. "I wonder if there have been any similar disappearances."

"Rich kids disappearing without a trace?"

"Maybe not rich, maybe just kids."

"There certainly are lots of runaways," Ruth said. "There are those public-service commercials on television about kids that have gone missing, sometimes for years. So, it's not unheard of that kids head for the hills on their own."

"Wouldn't there be warning signs if kids were ready to run off from one of the wealthiest families in New York?" I mused. "Mental health warnings maybe? Abuse? Maybe we should talk to the family doctor. That would have to be Mike, not us. No way a doctor is going to talk to us about patients."

"And boy mother?" Gabriele asked. "Mother know if boys unhappy."

I called Mike with the phone on speaker. He answered quickly and I told him Ruth and Gabriele were with me. "Has anybody interviewed the boys' mother?" I asked.

"Yes, of course. About what?"

"I don't know. Were the boys complaining about being bullied, like at school? Any chance they were being abused in some way? Did it seem like they might want to leave home? If they did leave home, where might they have gone?"

He said he would have to go back over the interviews, because there had been a few. "I wasn't there for all of them. Mostly, I think they were asking her about the disappearance, or about who in the family might have a bone to pick with her or the boys. I'll check and get back to you."

"Are there still cops at the Coniston home?"

"No, we pulled them, but they check in there a couple of times a day to see if there has been any word from someone who might be holding the boys. And we're still monitoring their phones."

"So, Mrs Coniston is there all by herself?"

"She's not alone, Hugo. She has family, relatives staying there also. It's a big house. There are maids and a cook and other staff to help out, even a nurse the time I was over there. This is a rich family, you know. The boys are missing, but the money isn't. I don't recall seeing any kind of mental profile on the boys, but I'm gonna check. The older one, Eddie Junior, had been being briefed almost every week at the Coniston offices, I know that. Could be disorienting, I guess. Kinda doubt there was any problem at Trinity School. Mrs Coniston doesn't seem like a shrinking violet to me. More kinda in-your-face, to tell the truth."

"Not for nothing," I said, "but it turns out that the three of us all think the boys aren't alive anymore."

Silence.

"You don't agree?"

I could hear him clear his throat. "It's not time for that yet."

"Why?"

"Because if we thought the boys were dead, this would be a homicide investigation, not missing-persons."

"Is that what it is? Missing persons? Why did we think all along it was kidnapping?"

"Rich kids disappear, the first thing you do is you start looking for a ransom demand. It looked like a kidnapping from the get-go. But even though it started out as a kidnapping, I don't think the NYPD ever used that word. You're right, it may have morphed into homicide. If we decide to act on that, it will come down like a ton of bricks on the family – and the media, the newspapers in particular, will go hog-wild. Readers like scandals in rich families. For now, though, we should swallow what we individually think, and keep on slogging ahead the way we're going. I'll talk to the higher-ups and let you know if they want to change course."

Sounds like there's politics in everything.

"I wonder why the cops are worried about the media," Ruth said. "Seems like something they would try to ignore."

"When children killed, people very angry," Gabriele said. "Is why *ndrangheta* not kill children. Even *cosa nostra* afraid of media sometimes. Make *gente arrabbiata.*" He used two Italian names for mobs we would call Mafia in New York, and an Italian phrase for 'angry people'.

The restaurant was starting to empty out as breakfast ended and lunch hadn't yet begun. I wondered if we could move from the bar to a table. Gabriele walked over to the maître d', who moved us to a booth on the east side of the restaurant. You could see the cars above us on the ramp reflected in the windows of the building just outside. Strange.

I ordered some more toast and a refill of my coffee. The others didn't want anything more. My phone buzzed and Mike's name appeared on the screen.

"Hugo, I think we may be headed in the direction you were talking about, but I think it would be good for you and your guys to come over here if you can." He paused, then said, "Because Mrs Coniston is coming in to talk. Although she didn't say so, I believe she thinks the boys are dead."

Chapter Eight

Needless to say, we hot-footed it over to Mike's office at the Midtown North precinct on 54th Street. Mike was waiting for us, and put us in the observation room behind a two-way mirror. One of Mike's detectives joined us.

"We'll be able to hear Mike and Mrs Coniston, but they won't be able to hear us," he said. "No need to take notes because the entire conversation will be on video, and there will be a transcript within a few hours. Mike wants your thoughts after the interrogation is over."

I was anticipating that Mrs Coniston would arrive with a lawyer, but she didn't. She was wearing a pair of what looked like camel-hair slacks with pleats from the thin blue belt that emphasized her small waist. She was taller than most women, probably five foot ten. She was wearing heels that almost made her taller than Mike. Topped off with a Peter Pan blouse and a light blue cardigan sweater that looked like cashmere. No jewelry except a pair of gold hoop earrings and a silver-colored wedding band, probably platinum. She was probably in her late forties, but she could have been a runway model if you didn't already know who she was.

"It's easy to see why Eddie fell in love with her," Ruth said. "She is a physical match for him, and they were always hand-in-hand every time I saw them, which would have been mostly at the Met. A powerful woman, but charming. Eddie was about six foot four and bubbling over with charisma. She kept up with him all the time."

Mike was formal but gracious with Mrs Coniston, who nevertheless opened the conversation by saying "Call me Lizzie. Everybody does."

"We anticipated that you might have a lawyer with you, Mrs Coniston."

"Lizzie."

"Okay, Lizzie."

"No need for a lawyer. I just wanted to talk to you about what's happened, and where you think you can look to find out who did it." She had a slight accent, a flavor of the South.

She told Mike that she had been at home without going outside the house for the three weeks and more since the boys vanished. She had, like everybody else, been expecting a ransom demand that never came.

"So, I started wondering if it was possible that they ran off to stay with friends or with somebody in the family. I called around to every name I could come up with, and nobody knew where they were, or had even heard from them."

"If I may be so bold, Lizzie, if someone was involved in the boys disappearing, they might not come clean when you called them."

"I wasn't born yesterday, officer. But I've known everyone in the family for a long time, and I think I could tell if they were acting like they had something to hide."

Mike nodded but didn't respond.

She had been married before and had three daughters from that marriage who were half-siblings with the boys who disappeared.

"I have my girls still," she said, looking at Mike from the corner of her eye. "But I also have plenty of assets to take care of them, make sure they have everything they want. Eddie saw to it that I have my own assets, not just what the estate would allot to me."

She knows it might look like her daughters would benefit from the boys' disappearance.

"Hmmm," Ruth muttered.

"She not hurt boys," Gabriele said clearly and in a normal voice.

"Your daughters use their father's family name, don't they?" Mike asked.

"Yes, they are Harrisons, not Conistons. And they stand to inherit from my family, if you were going there."

Mike shook his head. "Just curious why Mr Edward Coniston didn't adopt them."

"We talked about it. He always took care of them, but he felt that the Coniston family might be upset if it looked like my girls might inherit shares in the Coniston Companies that they might not be entitled to by birth."

"May I ask you – and I apologize in advance – what your reaction is to the statements by Mr Edward Coniston's mother about who his biological father was."

She smiled briefly, as though she had expected this question, and answered, "Mrs Coniston was a dementia patient at the time, and no stranger to delusions and odd ideas. She and I always got along well, even when she was getting close to the end. She adored my girls, and of course she adored the boys. I remember a time when she said the house was a cruise ship and she was afraid it might sink. Her statement that she had an affair when she was young and how that might relate to Eddie, was about the same as saying the house might hit an iceberg and go down like the Titanic."

"So, you weren't angry about her comments?"

"No. I just hope I would be able to hold myself together like she did if I were slowly losing my wits. She never lost her dignity, and never stopped loving all her family."

That sounded like she wrote it down before she said it.

Mike asked her how she felt about Ricky Coniston. She looked puzzled and cocked her head, maybe not understanding the question.

"I mean, do you think Ricky Coniston – since he lost his own son recently – is handling the whole thing well?"

"I guess so," she said, glancing around the room and at the two-way mirror. "He's been a hero at the Coniston Companies; don't know what we would do without him."

"Is it possible that he could end up better off if the boys don't come home?"

"How?"

"I don't know, just more control of the business?"

"He's got total control of the business now. Well, the Board does, but he's the Chairman as well as the CEO." She looked very puzzled.

"Not trying to suggest anything or be offensive, Mrs Coniston. My job now is to learn how everybody in the family is being affected by this situation. I'm not pointing any fingers, just trying to learn more so we can decide what direction we need to go so that we can find out what happened."

She smiled and looked at her hands. "I've just gotten jumpy and scared, that's all."

"My apologies."

"No worries. I'm just not quite myself these days. I never stop wondering what happened to Eddie and Rich. I never let myself think they might not still be alive, but it's been so long." She paused. "Maybe they're not."

I could see her eyes looking watery.

"It leaves a hole in my heart," she said.

"No point assuming the worst until we know more," he said. "That's why I'm asking these questions. I'd like to talk to the rest of the family, too. Would you like some coffee?"

"Last thing I need. I feel like I could jump right out of my skin most of the time. What I need is a glass of wine."

Mike smiled. "Afraid we don't have any of that here, but if you'd like to walk down the street with me, there are some nice places where we could have a bite to eat and you could have some wine."

She shook her head. "I really need to get back home. I know they would have called me if someone had called, but I feel antsy if I'm not there. Somebody might find them, you know. It could happen."

"Of course." He offered to have a squad car take her home.

She shook her head, but smiled. "I have a car downstairs."

Mike stood up and motioned toward the door. "If you need to get home, I don't want to be keeping you here."

She smiled and held her hand out. They shook and she walked out. Mike opened the door to the Observation Room after a couple of minutes and suggested that we go over to his office.

"Waddya think?" he asked.

"She seems like a woman with a lot of grief bottled up inside," Ruth said. "But man, does she go on the defensive fast when you push her buttons."

Mike looked puzzled.

"When you get the transcript, check out how she responded to your question about Mrs Coniston, Eddie's mother. She memorized that one, because people have asked her the same question before, more than once." She paused and then continued, "And how fast she delivered an oration about how well-off her daughters from the first husband are."

Mike nodded.

"I'm the only one of us with any children, and I've never been very close to them, to say the least. But if I thought somebody might have killed them, it would rip me up. I was there when they were born, and I'll never forget how happy I was then. I felt like I might start to cry as soon as I saw her walk into the room," I said. "Very obviously working hard at maintaining control of herself."

"She not say everything she know," Gabriele said harshly, then softened. "Is good mama. *É molto triste.*" I am always surprised at how quickly he makes judgments about people, and how often he goes to the heart of things. I knew why he said what he said. I had been thinking she was holding back, too, although I didn't realize it until he said that.

Mike nodded again. "I don't think she's keeping any secrets on purpose. She just doesn't want to talk about everything that's going on and causing her a lot of pain. But we need to find out if there's anything eating at her other than worrying about her kids."

"As though that wasn't enough," Ruth said with a harumph that exploded out of her mouth as a humorless laugh.

"It's a heavy burden to have to carry," Mike said, looking at Ruth, "but, unfortunately, that doesn't mean it's the only problem she's got to deal with. Even rich people have problems."

Chapter Nine

Ruth, Gabriele and I decided to walk over to Thalia for a bite and a drink. I was feeling very much at sixes and sevens on this case. There was no path to follow, not even a direction to look.

Although we usually sit at the bar when we go to Thalia, I suggested we get a table and eat lunch like regular people. The restaurant is large and there were empty tables, so I asked for a table in the back, on a small balcony-like area that was higher than the rest of the space. It seemed like we might be able to talk more freely there.

I told them I just was looking for a ray of light someplace. "I suppose if I had been to the Police Academy or taken a degree in Criminology, I might have a framework for something like this. But right now, I feel like I'm treading water."

"I think you should leave the police-work to the police," Ruth said. "I think our value to Mike and the department in general is that we *aren't* cops. So, we can think outside the box, or at least that's what I always assumed."

Gabriele said he thought somebody was going to try to find out if Ricky Coniston's car was one of the cars that was seen passing by where the boys were when they disappeared, apparently on Columbus Avenue between 91st and 92nd Streets. "Is working on?" he wanted to know.

"You think Ricky Coniston could be involved in the boys going missing?" I asked.

He shrugged and made an 'I don't know' face.

"I thought you liked him," Ruth said.

"I like him, *é vero*. That not mean he always good guy, also not mean he my friend. He is good guy at Ora di Pranzo. Make good tip for *cameriere*," he said, using an Italian word for a waiter. "He drink good wine, smile and friendly. In Napoli and Capri, many people like Coniston

55

have much money, good for business, *ma forse* not good people."

I knew he was thinking about the Camorra, which is the Naples version of the Sicilian Mafia or Cosa Nostra.

"Well, anyway, you're right about Mike," I said. "He did say there would be somebody checking out that car. I think he asked the CSIs to try to get a clearer picture so we can distinguish one silver Mercedes from all the other silver Mercedes in the area. Maybe if we get lucky, they'll be able to read a license plate. I'll ask him and let you know."

I told them I thought it would be good to try to assemble a family tree of sorts, so we could know who else in the family might be somebody we should interview.

"I have a membership in a website that can help me construct a family tree," Ruth said. "How far back do you want to go?"

"Not any farther back than necessary to find who the cousins are who might be closely related. What I think would help most is if we could figure out the cousins and other family members who might be getting dividends from the Coniston Companies," I said. "That might give us a list of people who might have a gripe with the management, or maybe an old gripe with Eddie Coniston that might have morphed into problems for Lizzie or the boys."

She said that if I wanted to get a current family tree that showed a lot of branches of the family, she might have to go back several generations to know what all the non-Coniston names were. That made sense.

"If we want a list of who gets dividends, why not just subpoena the list from the Coniston Companies themselves?"

"No idea about that, way above my pay grade, but I'll tell Mike you suggested it."

"So, I'm hearing you may not want a family tree, but just a snapshot of the current family."

"No need to make it artistic either. I just need some idea of which people out there in the world might turn out to be receiving dividends from Coniston. Could also be helpful if I could just get a list of family names other than Coniston. Like I think Ricky's wife and his mother both had maiden names of Neval. Distant cousins, I think they said. Maybe like Neville Chamberlain? Spellings change over time or because of politics. My family name used to be Mueller, but now it's Miller – because my German ancestors, who were from Prussia but emigrated to the United States, didn't want to be German during the First World War. The royal family of the United Kingdom did the same thing, but they changed their name to Windsor from Saxe-Coburg. When Prince Charles becomes king, the name will change again, this time to Mountbatten, which itself was changed from Battenberg during World War I."

"Is there going to be a quiz on that?" Ruth asked with a look of boredom all over her face.

"Not this time, sweetie," I said. Gabriele snorted.

"I got this started on my phone, but I need a computer so I can see more information than the screen on my phone is capable of displaying," she said.

I told her I could give her my laptop if we went over to my apartment. Gabriele was getting bored and signaled the waiter, whispered something to him when he came over to the table, and the waiter took off, returning quickly with a platter that had a mountain of boiled shrimp and what looked like two or three dozen oysters.

"Just what the doctor ordered," Ruth said. "*Traife*."

Gabriele looked puzzled. Ruth took one of the shrimp, bit it in half and dipped the part that had the tail on it in the red sauce on the platter. "*Traife*," she said. "It's Yiddish for something I love but shouldn't be eating."

He still looked puzzled.

"It's not Kosher, but I love it," she cooed with a smile.

The waiter brought three glasses of a nearly colorless white wine that had a terrific, astringent quality to it, Perfect for seafood from the raw bar. I looked at Gabriele and motioned to the wine with a questioning look.

"*Spagna verde,*" he said.

"Green Spain?"

He touched his right index finger to the tip of his nose in an old gesture meaning 'yes'.

"What does that mean, *spagne verde*?"

"Mean north part of Spain, wine green color. *Chocoli* is name." He held the glass up to look at it with a light behind it.

He was right, it had a greenish cast to it. I had learned a long time back not to question Gabriele's wine knowledge, which ran to encyclopedic. But I did wish I had a photo of him looking at that wine with the light behind it.

My cellphone buzzed. It was Mike, who told me that it looked like the boys had been found.

"Are they okay?" I asked.

"No, they're dead. At least the two who were found are dead. They were in the woods near Pocantico Hills, near the Rockefeller estate. And some animals had found them before the local police did. So, they're difficult to identify."

"Cause of death?"

"The M.E. is working on it. Looks like they might have been stabbed according to the cops who were on site, but it's had to tell from the photos. They might have been attacked by an animal, maybe a bear. And then apparently other varmints found them later. I haven't seen any photos, only talked to the local police, who found the bodies and thought they might be the Coniston kids."

"You gonna call Mrs Coniston?"

I was starting to feel faint, like if I stood up, I might pass out. I started clenching and unclenching my toes, in order to get the blood flowing. Lightheadedness is sometimes, I am given to believe, the result of blood surging to the lower limbs, leaving the brain starved for oxygen temporarily. The idea of those young boys being killed and left for animals to eat was more than I could deal with. I found myself thinking if Mike tried to show me any photographs of that scene, I would refuse to look at them.

"Already did, leaving to go over there now," he said. "Can you meet me back at my office in about an hour? Maybe an hour and a half?'

Ruth said she could, but Gabriele said he needed to get to the restaurant unless it was important that he be there. Mike said if Ruth and I could come, that would help him.

We agreed.

Ruth and Gabriele finished demolishing the mound of seafood and had another glass of the delicious greenish wine, and talked about what Mike had just told me, which I summarized for them. I marveled that they could chow into the raw seafood with such gusto after hearing such disgusting news.

"How the heck did the boys get from Columbus Avenue and 91st Street to northern Westchester?" Ruth asked rhetorically.

Now it's even more important to identify any cars that the boys could have got into. Obviously, they didn't walk all the way to Pocantico Hills, which had to be more than twenty miles, and most of it not pedestrian-friendly either – crowded roads and parkways with cars sprinting way over the speed limit.

I realized I was still hungry, which is something that plagues me in times of stress. I'm not the only person who ever wanted French fries and ice cream as 'comfort food', but I tried to ward off an obvious pizza-and-cookies binge. The oysters I had been munching on may be a nearly perfect food nutritionally, but they aren't filling, and I really only like them with fresh horseradish, which is tangy but not burning hot like it is when it's been aged. I seldom eat shrimp or mussels because I have friends who have gout. I have been told many times shellfish tend to aggravate the gout, but that oysters seldom seem to do that. I waved to the waiter and asked him to bring an order of fries, no truffle oil, with some mayonnaise on the side. And a glass of montepulciano, which Ruth subscribed to as well. Gabriele stood up and took his leave, saying he didn't want to stick Dante with the whole place, and he didn't want Dante to be annoyed either.

I don't know whether the alcohol finally kicked in, or whether I gave up on the anxiety that had suddenly taken over in my mind when I heard of the Coniston boys being found in a wooded area, where some animals had been feeding on them. But when it was time for Ruth and me to go back over to the Precinct, I was feeling calmer, though I still felt like I might be nauseated almost any moment (I never did feel that way, fortunately – I think the fries soaked up any acid that had been in my stomach).

Mike arrived just about the same time we did, and we took over an interrogation room that wasn't being used.

Sure enough, Mike said he had some photos of the crime scene, which he could show us if we wanted to see them. We both demurred. When that was decided, I felt the wave of almost-nausea subside.

He said Mrs Coniston had taken the news like a woman in a trance, showing little or no emotion, but with a face as pale as a corpse.

"Was it near Ricky and Ann's place?" she asked.

He told her it was not anywhere near where her brother-in-law and his wife lived, although it was closer to Chappaqua than it was to Central Park.

She asked if the boys appeared to have been buried and then dug up by the animals. Mike told her that he couldn't answer that, because he hadn't been there, but the forensic team and the Medical Examiner would have reports ready quickly.

"I felt so sorry for Ricky and Ann when their boy died last year," she said. "I was glad I couldn't imagine what it would be like. Now I know what it is like." She stared at the ceiling, not making eye contact with anyone in the room. But no tears.

Mike said that although the CSIs hadn't finished their work at the scene where the bodies were found, they had told Mike that it appeared that the boys were dead before they were deposited in the woods. There was virtually no evidence of bleeding from the predation of the animals. The M.E. would have a report right away, Mike said, indicating that it might be as soon as that same evening.

Ruth said that it looked to her like somebody must have picked the boys up on Columbus Avenue.

Mike agreed. "There's no way for us to tell yet if the boys died there, or if their bodies were dumped there. If they died someplace else, it could have been someplace close to Trinity School."

I asked Mike if I could have a bottle of water. I felt like my mouth was full of cotton. I couldn't help thinking about my own children. Although I was a piss-poor dad for them, I was like Lizzie Coniston, in that I couldn't imagine the pain that a parent would go through. My kids are all in their thirties and forties, so the only ones in my family who would be school-age kids are my grandchildren, most of whom I have never seen face-to-face, although I keep photos of them in my apartment. I had two wives, five children, and both marriages ended badly. That's why I have been living alone ever since.

The water helped. It came from a vending machine and was cooler than tap water would have been.

"You look a little green around the gills," Mike said.

I told him I would be okay, but I had been feeling bad since I heard what happened to the two boys.

"Truth is, we don't know what happened to them yet," Mike said. "We don't know when or where they died, or from what. Although both bodies showed signs of animals biting into them, there was no evidence that they were alive when that happened. They'll be using luminol and hydrogen peroxide all around where they were found, to see if there is any evidence they died there. But right now, all we know is they were in all likelihood dead – even long dead – before the animals found them. You should concentrate on taking deep breaths and exhaling completely."

"Any progress on the video front about seeing the boys get into a car?" Ruth asked.

Mike said there was a 'maybe'. It was a silver Mercedes that seemed to stop next to the curb, but there were so many people on the sidewalk that the CSIs weren't able to see into the car, to see if someone got into it, or what the license plate was. "No distinguishing marks. No dents, for instance."

"You know Ricky Coniston drives a silver Mercedes and he was in town that morning for a dermatologist appointment in the east 60s, near Hunter College," I said.

"Correction. The Conistons do own a silver Mercedes like the one in the photo, but it is usually driven by Mrs Coniston. Mr Coniston traveled to Manhattan on MetroNorth that fateful day. No car at all."

"You sure about that?"

"That's what they told us. Mr Coniston told us he took the train as usual and then a taxi to the doctor's office. Said he didn't want to drive after having an anesthetic."

"But nobody outside the family?"

Mike shook his head. "But the manager of the closest gas station told us that the car we were asking about belonged to Mrs Coniston."

"When you were married, how many days would there have been when people outside the family would know what car you drove to work last Tuesday?" Ruth asked.

"I wish I could…" I didn't know how to finish the question I was trying to formulate.

"Shimmy like my sister Kate?" Ruth completed my unfinished sentence and put a question mark at the end.

"You're showing your age, my dear," I said, but smiled, remembering the old song. "I meant that I wish I could figure out who could have picked them up, and why, and what could have happened before whoever it was left the kids dead in the woods in Pocantico Hills. We don't have any clues about any of it."

"We are, but that's because the boys disappeared in Manhattan. That doesn't mean we can interfere in Westchester County when they find dead people in a public place like a forest."

"So did the Westchester M.E. decide how the boys died?"

"Not yet."

"Is the NYC Medical Examiner assisting in any way?"

"Not yet."

"What has to happen for the NYPD to get involved in Westchester?"

"The Department is negotiating with Westchester on how we can work together."

He's avoiding my questions.

"What is it you're not telling me?"

There was a long pause. "I told you there was no bear saliva, so they decided no bears were involved in spite of the claw marks. There aren't any other animals anywhere around here that could or would kill humans. There were some traces of saliva that contains DNA that's possibly compatible with a primate, but so far there's been no firm identification of what kind of ape it could be. Humans are apes, I guess, so maybe it could be human."

"King Kong? Some kind of monkey that might be a pet?"

"Apes aren't supposed to be kept as pets. They are very dangerous. There was a woman who was mauled by a chimpanzee in Connecticut some years back, but that one was a pet, and the owner had a license. Even so, that chimpanzee was seized by the state, euthanized and autopsied to make sure it didn't have a disease like rabies. It's strictly illegal to own any ape in New York State – or in most other states, including Connecticut now. Chimpanzees are apes, but they're much smaller than, say, gorillas. Even so, they are completely capable of killing an adult human, much less a child. I gather there is a possibility that the saliva is human, but it's degraded, difficult to tell exactly. That's what they tell me anyway. And I understand why the Department doesn't want to say that an ape was involved in the boys' deaths. It could cause a huge panic. Did you ever read 'Murders in the Rue Morgue'?"

"Yes, I've read most of Edgar Allan Poe's stories, and I know that particular murder was attributed to an ape. I think I remember that the story was based loosely on a real murder and a real ape. But that is not only fiction, it's from nineteenth century Paris. Science and zoology have come a long way since then, haven't they?"

"There are still people who believe there is a creature like Bigfoot. The last thing we need is a headline that Bigfoot killed two children in Westchester County."

"But if there is an ape out there that could have done this, isn't it important to find it?"

"I suppose, but there's no firm evidence of an ape, just that trace of saliva that could be from either a human or another primate. By the way, they tell me that chimpanzee DNA is ninety-nine percent the same as human DNA."

"How could human saliva have got on the boys?"

"Lots of ways. A sneeze, maybe. A bite. A kiss. Spit. Drool." I sensed he was smiling, and didn't appreciate it.

I told him I needed some time to absorb this, maybe have lunch with Gabriele and Ruth and get their reactions. He said his desk was covered with new files he had to study, but he would let me know if there was new information.

I texted Ruth and Gabriele, asked if they were free for lunch. They were. I asked them if they'd be okay if I ordered some Thai food when they got to my place, and they said that would be good. I felt like I could eat some vegetarian Thai food, but it was risky to try to eat meat of any kind. I remembered reading about a child a few years back who was killed by a mountain lion somewhere in the southwest, and I felt sick when I read that, too – something about the lion grabbing the little girl in its mouth and dragging her away. My imagination can run riot when I read something like that.

Gabriele and Ruth arrived within five minutes of each other. Gabriele was wearing jeans with a thick belt and a tight t-shirt, a distinct James Dean or young Marlon Brando look. Ruth was Ruth, always astonishingly put together, but with a theme color of pink. I called Tuk-

Tuk, a Thai restaurant a couple of blocks away, named after a motorized rickshaw type of vehicle that is used in Thailand. It's supposed to mean 'fast', because the food is delivered by bicycle and is surprisingly fast. It is a huge neighborhood success, because not only is the food tasty and reasonably priced, but it arrives within about fifteen minutes of the time an order is placed.

Gabriele brought a bottle of Il Falcone, a hearty red wine from Puglia, on the southeast coast of Italy. I set the table and he opened the wine while Ruth opened the containers of food. I chewed up another Dramamine pill.

"There's a fake-duck salad that I ordered for myself," I said to her. "The other dishes are house specialties, and they're for you and Gabriele. The pad thai is a specialty, has shrimp in it. And green papaya salad is always good."

"Fake-duck?"

"It's probably made from soy beans, but it's good, and vegetarian, even though it seems like meat."

"I didn't know you like to eat vegetarian."

"I never eat red meat, at least not for the last thirty years or so. But I'm not vegetarian. I've been talking to Mike about the Coniston boys, and how their bodies were found in the woods up north. Animals had been dining on them. So, vegetarian seems best, at least for now."

They had both read about it in the newspaper.

We ate the food while it was hot. It's quite remarkable how tasty the food from Tuk-Tuk is, and so fresh always. And the wine Gabriele brought was mellow enough that it didn't overwhelm the food at all. I don't know whether it was the food or the wine or just being with my friends, but I felt more normal, and the feeling that I might be sick was gone.

After we ate, I summarized for them what Mike had told me. The most gruesome parts had been withheld from the media.

"Who can do this thing?" Gabriele asked with his head back, looking at the ceiling.

Mike said more than once that the boys were already dead when the bodies were dumped in the woods. "It's not the animals' fault that they did what they did," I said. "It takes a human being to do something evil. Animals act like animals, and wild carnivores will eat just about any kind of meat. One of the puzzles is how they died, and another one is how they could look like they were mauled by a bear and still have no bear saliva on them."

"*È impossibile.*"

"But it happened, so it's not impossible," Ruth said.

"How boys die?"

I explained that there was no finalized cause of death. "Mike said it looked like they died from a fall. Could have been accidental or could be murder. Given that they were moved to the woods after they died, it looks like it might be homicide."

"Do we know how the family is taking this?" Ruth asked.

"You mean the mother? I don't know."

Chapter Eleven

Elizabeth 'Lizzie' Coniston withdrew from view when the bodies of her sons were found, and was not seen, even at a window, for quite a while. Because she was very wealthy, two very high-end lawyers met the media and asked everyone to pray for the souls of her sons and for the rest of the family, all of whom were mourning the loss of two innocents. The funeral was closed, family and invited friends only, and there were no photos of it released to the media. The interment took place at St Joseph's Cemetery on the Canadian side of Niagara Falls in a family plot where generations of Conistons had been buried for well over a century. An Anglican bishop presided, the family having been Anglican or Episcopalian from very far back. Those details were released to the press several days after the burial.

A group of reporters mobbed Ricky Coniston outside his office in Manhattan. He stopped, turned to face them, held his hands out to them and said, "No comment. If there is news, it will be given to you by our attorneys. This is a time of grief, and we hope you will respect our privacy." Then he turned, walked back to his office, and left them on the street.

I saw Ricky's statement on television. It was breaking news, according to the channel I had turned on in the background while I was writing a news release for a client. It was one that usually only covers the stock market, but when one of the richest men in the nation has a murder in his family, they stopped the action at the Exchange and went to the front of the building in midtown where Coniston Companies had offices. He didn't look angry, he didn't look like he wanted to hit one of them. But he was extremely serious and spoke loudly and with conviction. I admired the way he was handling the situation.

You have time to bring me up to date? It was Mike.

Sure, you want me to come over there?
That would be good, thanks
Ruth and Gabriele?
Maybe not this time, thanks
C U in an hour

It felt like a dress-shirt-and-tie occasion, so I did the businessman thing, polished up a pair of cordovan penny loafers and did my best to impersonate a successful investment banker.

Whenever I saw him, Mike was always wearing a nondescript business suit, a white shirt and striped tie, with broken-in dark brown, wingtip Oxfords. He joked that he dressed like an IBM salesman from the 1960s, which was probably about right. He would have been in grammar school in the 1960s, though.

He had an undertaker look. The suit was charcoal, the tie was solid black or midnight blue. And he had a somber expression that made him look like he was getting ready to preach a sermon.

"Reverend Doctor di Saronno, I presume?" I said with a grin. "You look like you should be wearing a Roman collar."

"Not exactly, no. More like Mike the Midtown West gumshoe."

"I can't imagine what the Coniston family is going through. Not only are the boys dead, but their bodies were mangled and unrecognizable. Have you spoken with any of them?"

"No, not even once since the bodies were found. They have a wall of lawyers protecting them. If I were as rich as they are, I'd be doing the same thing. Leave me alone in my grief."

"This is a new experience for me, Mike. Dead children, I mean. I have kids, and although I haven't been in touch with them regularly, now that they're grown, I can only imagine what it would have been like to bury one of them – much less two – when they were in school."

"Being rich is not a bed of roses, I guess."

"Wealth has its advantages, but nothing makes life a cakewalk. Murder in a family like this is heart-rending. Maybe it's always heart-rending, but the Conistons are so careful to be out of the spotlight, and when they need their privacy most, they get it the least.

"Are you seeing any cracks in the family from this?" I went ahead and just asked him what I was wondering.

"You mean like are they spitting at each other?"

"Or are they cutting each other off?"

"No way to tell that. The only people I speak with are the lawyers. And, of course, the crew in forensics."

"Any idea where the boys were when they died?"

"The real answer is no, not yet. We're looking at a variety of places to see if we can find blood splatters with luminol, which reacts with the hemoglobin in blood, even after it's been washed away, or even bleached. No way to clean up blood when we're using luminol."

"And does your nose tell you where to look?"

"I suppose. We've been all over the loading docks behind the supermarket at 91st and Columbus, and along the paths in Central Park. So far, nothing. The M.E. is certain they fell and were killed on impact, so that would indicate a building window maybe? Or a cliff? Kids sometimes take huge risks when they're playing, so it could be someplace like the Belvedere Castle in Central Park, so we looked there. Nothing."

"So, what's left?"

"Well, it's fairly clear that they were dead before they were left in the woods. And they weren't bludgeoned with a baseball bat. It was like they climbed a tree and fell onto a driveway or something."

"And have you checked family homes? Like the mansion on 5th Avenue? Or Ricky Coniston's place up in Westchester?

"Fifth Avenue yes. Westchester, not yet. And we don't have an answer to the old question of whether they fell or somebody pushed them."

"How were they dressed?"

"They apparently were still wearing Trinity uniforms."

"So, they were grabbed on their way home from school, like we thought originally?"

"Probably, yes."

"So, it has to have been on that block of Columbus between 91st and 92nd, right?"

"I don't think I'm as sure of that as you are, but I guess that's probable."

"Any progress on the silver Mercedes?"

He said there just wasn't enough video to identify it, but it looked to be the same model as the one that Ann Coniston usually drove.

"Any idea what the lay of the land is like where Ricky Coniston lives?"

"Like a lot of Westchester, some rock outcrops, forest, lots of trees, but more flat than hilly. It would be unusual to find a cliff in that area, as I recall. The parts of Westchester that are hillier would be close to the Hudson River, like in Pocantico Hills where they were found, or what they call the River Towns from Tarrytown south to the Bronx. If they fell off a cliff, it would more likely be someplace like Yonkers, which is super-hilly, lots of huge rocks sticking out of the soil."

"What's next, boss?"

"I kinda hate to say it, but I think we need a subpoena to inspect the cars at Ricky and Ann Coniston's place. With luminol."

"And others in the family?"

"There are a couple of others in the family who might have been jealous of the boys, or who could possibly think they might gain from their deaths, but it would be hard to convince a judge about Lizzie or her one surviving nephew."

"What about the Boston nephew's parents?"

"Father's dead – drowned in a boating accident a few years back. The mother moved to Boston after her husband died, and put the son in a classy boarding school in Connecticut, neither the mother nor the son would've been anywhere near New York when the boys went missing."

"And the nephew? what age would he be?"

"Late teens, maybe twenty or so. Not sure."

"Ruth has been researching the Coniston family so that she can construct a family tree," I said. "Any interest?"

He said they were working on something similar, but he'd love to see what Ruth was coming up with. "I think we probably know who the main players are already, but there's a lot of money and power at the

Coniston Companies, so somebody could come out of the woodwork."

"How can I help best?" I asked. "Obviously I can't go with your team to the Coniston home to search the cars there."

"Get together with your team and do some brainstorming. I need to know what I'm forgetting or overlooking."

He looked at his watch and shook his head. "Damn. I have a command performance with the Commissioner downtown and I'm gonna be late."

That's why he's dressed like that. Nobody in the NYPD wants to be called on the carpet by the Police Commissioner.

I walked down the stairs with him. He broke into a trot outside, waved to me, and disappeared around the corner. I called Ruth, and said it would be good if we could have a conference call with Gabriele. As I thought, she told me she could hook the three of us up on her phone.

"When is good for you?" she asked.

"Well, I'm standing on the sidewalk outside Mike's office. So, I need to get someplace where there's a good signal, and where I can talk privately."

"Why not just come over to my place and we can call Gabriele together?"

I told her I would walk to her place, but I decided to take the subway from 49th and 7th Avenue to Times Square, to Grand Central, and then to Lexington and 59th Street. Then I walked the three blocks to Ruth's building at Park and 61st Street.

"You must have speed-walked all the way over here," she said.

I explained that I had taken a 1, then a 7, then a 6. "I had a good talk with Mike. It'd be good to tell you and Gabriele what he told me."

We went into one of the bedrooms that was outfitted as an office. She put the phone on speaker and dialed Gabriele's cellphone number. He answered after one ring. He was at home, so nobody would hear our conversation.

I told them about my conversation with Mike, and that Mike wanted the three of us to try to figure out what we thought should be a next step.

"You know, I did some research on the family, and maybe there's something you forgot," Ruth said. "Elizabeth Coniston was married before she met Eddie, and she had children – two girls – both of them adults now. So, she still has some family, in addition to the Conistons. Her first husband was older, and eventually died, but she was divorced when she married Eddie."

"Where are daughters?" Gabriele asked.

She opened one of the drawers in her desk and retrieved a sheaf of paper. "Sorry, but I don't remember everything. Here it is. Margaret and Isabelle are the girls' names. Late twenties. Last name is Harrison. Mrs Coniston's maiden name was Westbrook. I'll have to try to find out where they are. I'd guess Easthampton or someplace near there, since that is where the Westbrook family hail from. No idea whether they are married or have kids."

I suggested that if she could check on the girls, it would be good. Not that there would be any reason for the girls to be involved. "And if you could check on others in the Westbrook family, that could be helpful, too. Did Mrs Coniston have any brothers and sisters?"

She flipped through some of the sheets of paper she had taken out of the desk. "Several siblings. Looks like three boys and two girls. No names, sorry. I can probably fill in the blanks. Should I send it to you and Gabriele when I get done?"

"Just attach it to an email. Gabriele, you seem to know a lot of people. Does the name Westbrook ring any bells with you?"

"Sound familiar, but maybe is common name?"

I told him I didn't think it was a common name. "There is a town in New Jersey, not far from Newark, named Westbrook. Maybe that's why it sounds familiar. There was a well-known political writer named Westbrook Pegler, but he's way before your time."

"I talk to Dante, *forse lui sa.*"

"If you think maybe Dante might know, then you think Westbrook might be a name from Ora di Pranzo?"

"*Sì forse.*"

"Let me know if you figure it out. Like I said, Lizzie Coniston's

Joseph Allen

children from her first marriage are Westbrooks. So, she still has some grown children – Ruth says there are two Coniston girls and two girls from her previous marriage – even after losing her two Coniston boys."

"Do we know who will inherit the boys' shares in the Coniston Companies?" Ruth asked.

"Sorry, I don't. Mike asked Ricky Coniston that question, and as I recall what he said was the stock would probably go to others in the Coniston family, maybe split between several. Whatever the Board decided."

Ruth said she would get to work on the Westbrooks and see what she could come up with. Gabriele said he would call Dante and let us know if he found out anything.

I headed home.

Chapter Twelve

I found myself wondering where the boys had been and how they got wherever they were when they died. I kept thinking about the silver Mercedes. When I got back to my apartment, I signed onto my computer and started looking for any pictures I could find of the house where Ricky and Ann Coniston lived. It wasn't particularly close to Pocantico Hills, but closer than 91st and Columbus Avenue. And we knew that Ricky Coniston had been in Manhattan that day for a doctor's appointment.

When I woke up the next morning, I texted Mike for Ricky Coniston's address which, surprisingly, he sent without asking why I wanted it. It was 7 Long and Winding Road. Easy to remember, just like the song. I looked it up on the computer. It was in an area between Chappaqua and Millwood, so, since I couldn't figure out which town I should enter, I figured I would have to fiddle with the GPS to make it work.

Not wanting to go up there by myself, I texted Gabriele to see if he would keep me company for the drive. He was up for it, said he would be over as soon as he could get a subway from Brooklyn Heights. I fished out an old basket that some fruit had arrived in one Christmas, then I lined it with wax paper because it was blackberry season, and I thought we might be able to find a patch of them. I found a couple of pairs of work gloves to protect our hands from thorns, and threw them into the basket. There's nothing better than a bowl of fresh-picked blackberries with milk. I figured Gabriele would be game for berry hunting, and I know he likes getting out into the countryside where it smells like nature, not like a city.

He showed up faster than I thought he would, and we were off. I have an old Jaguar XK8, from the years when Ford owned Jaguar. Never had a problem with it, and now it's fifteen years old, but in good condition. It's a convertible, and I never get tired of driving with the top down when the weather permits.

I told him I just wanted to see where Ricky Coniston lived, maybe poke around a little if we could.

"Ricky Coniston not kill boys," he said.

"I didn't say he did, and that's not what I meant either."

There was very little traffic going over the Triboro Bridge, and even the Major Deegan was moving along at a good pace. We were in Westchester about twenty minutes after we left the garage. New York State is beautiful, and a vibrant green that a Californian like me never really gets used to.

I wear boots when I go for a walk in the woods. It's a good way to avoid thorns and insects, especially ticks, which can carry a lot of yucky illnesses, including Lyme disease. It also protects against snake bites. I'm a bit of a germophobe. Gabriele is the opposite, would go barefoot if he could, but when he got to my place, he was wearing high-top athletic shoes and jeans. *Perfetto.*

The GPS talks to me with a British accent and a woman's voice, which I have always found either amusing or annoying depending on my mood, but it always gets me where I want to go. When I was a kid, the only way to find a place was to locate it on a map, and then there was the hassle of trying to read it while you were driving, or getting a passenger to read it.

I pointed out to him where Pocantico Hills was when we passed it on the Saw Mill Parkway. That was where the boys were found. It's also where the Rockefeller estates are, as well as a small but famous church with stained glass windows by Matisse and Chagall. The Rockefellers never had to worry about money, and neither did the church. The name of the town is a Native American phrase that refers to a lazy little rivulet or creek that runs through the town. Lots of movies have been shot there because the whole little town looks like a postcard. Probably a thousand acres of forest and a lot of hiking trails.

The British lady told us to change to the Taconic Parkway, which we did, and there was a sign for the Hardscrabble Wilderness Area, so I pulled off the parkway for a little jaunt to show Gabriele what the geography was like in the area. It really is true that the west part of Westchester, close to the Hudson River, is very hilly and rocky, and the rest of the county is either flat or rolling hills. There were several hiking trails in Hardscrabble, and we walked a way into the forest. There were a lot of people on the trail, some with dogs and some on bicycles.

The forests of New York are mostly deciduous trees, so the soil can be very rich from centuries of falling leaves. Lots of wildflowers wherever there is sun, and tangled, jungle-like undergrowth everywhere. Very unlike the forests in California, which tend to be mostly evergreens and a fairly open forest floor, unlike the machete-hacking tangles of New York. The two places – California and New York – are very different in important ways, particularly rainfall. New York has rainy days in every month, and probably double or triple or more the amount of rain or snow that California gets on average. As a result, it would be easy for a child to hide in a New York forest, and just as easy to get lost. The ground is also soft in a New York forest, so digging is easy, which means burying would be easy.

After about forty minutes at Hardscrabble, we got back on the Parkway.

Gabriele was hungry. So was I. So, we got off again at the exit for Briarcliff Manor and Millwood. There was an English-looking restaurant with a parking lot, and we pulled in. Like a lot of suburban eateries, it looked a lot like a tavern when we walked in, people lined up at the bar, and a baseball game on big-screen televisions. The dining area was off to the side, in a high-ceiling room with shiny wood walls and comfortable chairs. Gabriele had a hamburger and fries with a Pilsener beer. I had a turkey and Swiss sandwich with potato chips and a bottle of mineral water (I was driving).

The GPS Brit lady guided us to Long and Winding Road within about ten minutes after we left the restaurant. It looked no different from other country roads. There was forest on one side and what looked like pasture on the other. The pasture was fenced with a white board fence with metal poles every ten feet or so, and what appeared to be two one by six-inch wooden slats painted white. It looked like pasturage for horses, not for cattle, who could easily destroy a fence like that. The first home we came to was number 7. It was an elegant, white, three-story building with the severe lines of federal style, but faced with white brick, and with what looked like fairly recent improvements, such as a portico that led to the left of the house. There were three dormer windows poking out of the roof line at equal intervals. They broke up the otherwise boxy shape, as did two thick, tall, brick chimneys on each side of the house, set about halfway between the center of the building and the sides, so there would have been fireplaces on both sides of the house and on each floor. Set back about a football field from the road, there was a tall, brick-faced gatehouse near the road and a cattle-guard starting a long driveway with mature oak trees on either side. There was no gate, just the cattle-guard to keep livestock from crossing to the street. It looked like a horse farm.

"Is flat," Gabriele said. "No cliff. No rocks."

"That's what I was expecting," I said. "The rocky cliffs are west of here, close to the river. Beautiful house. I think I remember Ricky saying it was old. Looks like early nineteenth century, but I'm not good at architecture. I bet they kept the old flooring as much as possible. That oak-plank flooring is super-expensive these days."

There was a grassy setback that formed a small shoulder between the street and the fence, but it was large enough that I could pull the car onto the grass and be clear of the pavement.

"Maybe boys fall from roof?"

"I doubt it. Even if Ricky Coniston was involved, he's far too rich and far too smart to do something like that at his own home."

"*E fantasmi.*"

"Do you believe in ghosts?"

He smiled, shook his head, but also made the hand sign that wards off the evil eye.

I opened my door and said I was going to have a look at the forest. "It doesn't seem to be posted. I haven't seen any No Trespassing signs."

He hopped over the door on his side and jogged around the car to join me. The forest was atwitter with birds until we got to that side of the road, and then there was some fluttering and the birdsongs stopped.

"What make birds quiet?"

"Bigfoot."

"Non capisco."

"Come un mostro o satiro, ma molto più grande."

Again, the evil eye gesture, which I interpreted as being similar to the middle finger raised solo.

"Just wait and keep your eyes and ears open," I said, and stepped into the woods. "I want to see if there are rock outcrops in the woods. That land across the street was cleared of anything and everything a long time ago. That's why it is so smooth and even. If there are schist formations here, they could easily be high enough to kill you if you fell off."

Making progress was slow, but finally we got through the thicket of vines that grow where the sun can get to the ground. Once inside the forest canopy, it was easier to walk. It was flat-ish, but there were in fact some schist outcrops, as there are very commonly in lower New York. It's schist that makes Central Park so beautiful. Before it was a park it was farmland, and all the rocks had been covered with soil. Nothing impressive on Long and Winding Road, though. There were lots of blackberry vines, but no ripe fruit.

We got back to the car, and I made a U turn in the street and headed back the way we had come from. It was the middle of the afternoon, bright sun and not super-hot or super-muggy. I wanted to look for blackberries, which I had not seen in our hike into the forest. I also hadn't seen any on the side of the road, where they commonly grow.

"Let's go back to Sleepy Hollow. I think I know where there may be a blackberry patch. I used to have relatives up there when I was young."

He smiled his magazine-cover smile. I felt bad there was no camera to preserve the picture. He opened the glove box and looked through the CDs. Soon we were listening to selections from "La Boheme," and Gabriele was singing duets with the tenor. It's unfair that in addition to everything else, he has a good singing voice. He tells me everybody sings in Italy.

As it turned out, the semi-swampy area that I recalled from my twenties had been developed into a neighborhood of McMansions. But all was not lost, because as we drove along Old Sleepy Hollow Road, we ran across a meadow-like area that was covered with the brambles of blackberry bushes. I grabbed the basket and tossed a pair of work gloves to Gabriele. After we picked what looked like a couple of quarts of berries, we got back in the car, and headed south on Route 9, which is a long extension of Broadway in Manhattan. It goes all the way to Albany.

When we got into the north part of Yonkers, I pulled into the parking area for Untermyer Gardens, an enormous public park that had been part of an old estate that was willed to the city. Gabriele and I walked around and looked at the many rock formations, some of which looked like they could be very dangerous to climb around on.

"*Non ha senso*," Gabriele said, indicating that it made no sense, "kill boys here and take them to forest."

"I didn't say the boys were killed here, although I've read that the infamous satanic killer called Son of Sam killed people here a few decades back – but he shot them, they didn't break their necks falling on the rocks. This is just a place like a lot of others, where there are natural or artificial rock outcrops. There are many places like this on the west side of Westchester County close to the Hudson River. Many hills, many rocks. This place is a park, not a good place to murder boys." I pointed to the Palisade on the other side of the river. "You see, we are as high here as the top of the cliff on the other side of the river. There is a cool breeze that blows up from the river here, too, even in the summer."

"Maybe boys fall from tree? Or fall off roof of house?"

"Okay, maybe they did. But then how did they get to Pocantico Hills?"

Chapter Thirteen

Ruth had been trying to locate relatives of Eddie and Ricky Coniston, basically using online information from a genealogy site. She had also been exploring what little was available on the Internet about the Coniston Companies family office. I texted her when I got home from the Westchester jaunt, and told her about the day. She asked if I had plans for dinner. I told her I didn't and she offered to come over so we could have a good talk.

I suggested that we have a drink at my place and then go to my favorite fish joint a couple of blocks away.

When she arrived, I made a couple of dirty vodkas. We clinked our glasses and sat down on the couch.

"You have a hard time working on the Conistons? I bet it must be like searching for hen's teeth. They seem to be allergic to the media. There's basically nothing online except coverage of the supposed kidnapping."

She said that the genealogy sites were easy to navigate, and given their gargantuan data bases, it was just a matter of being persistent.

"The Westbrooks are a fairly large related family that is attached to the Conistons by marriage only," she said. "It is easy to see them as a close-knit family that hangs together tightly, and happens to be close to the Conistons. But from another viewpoint, they look almost like parasites. They've become wealthy and proud of it since Lizzie and Eddie's marriage. Whether that's because they sucked up to the Conistons and got some moolah for it, or for some other reason, no way to tell. They're certainly upwardly mobile, and they became tastefully rich by some fortunate land transactions in the Hamptons. Their ancestors are mostly solid working-class. Very few of them seem to have stayed in school beyond twelfth grade until some of the current Westbrooks. I'm getting the impression from little hints in the newspapers that more than one of the Westbrook women or girls has virtually taken up residence in the Coniston Mansion on 5th Avenue. Maybe they could be her daughters, who would be grown up now. I guess they'd say they were there to keep Lizzie company and help her out. It must be a terrible time for her, with her husband and her Coniston sons gone."

"Would they stand to gain from the boys' deaths?"

"That's a legal question. No idea."

"I just meant that maybe Lizzie would now own whatever her husband left to the boys. So maybe her relatives would see that as an opportunity."

"Well, apparently Lizzie is in favor of keeping Ricky as CEO of the family office, so it seems to me that the biggest asset is already assigned. Of course, Ricky's son died recently, too, so Ricky is the last of his line."

"Maybe she feels like the Coniston fortune should stay with the Conistons."

"Did you find out anything about the Coniston Companies?"

"Not much. If you search for them, you don't get anything. They don't have a website that I can find. They don't file anything with the SEC or on EDGAR. Bloomberg publishes a list of the largest family offices, but Coniston apparently has only one family to invest for – themselves. Long story short, they're not included on the Bloomberg list at all. Maybe they're not a family office by the strict definition. Maybe Mike could subpoena their records, but aside from that, I don't think we're going to find out anything useful."

The doorbell rang. I wasn't expecting anyone and when I opened the door there was an old teddy bear that fell forward into my apartment. But nobody else.

"Ruth, come look at this please," I called out.

She was there in a trice, and bent over to pick up the stuffed animal. It looked like a child's bedtime friend, but one of its arms had been augmented with something like wire to create four claws.

"That's a little creepy," she said. "Nobody was there to explain?"

"Not that I could see."

"If it was a joke, it looks like it fell flat. Maybe whoever did it will get in touch again."

"I wonder if the claws are supposed to be a reference to a real bear. There was some reason to believe the Coniston boys had been mauled by a bear or bears, but the M.E. decided there was no bear. I checked and as far as I can tell, there haven't been any bear sightings in Westchester County except in some towns considerably farther north. No problems, not nearly the menace that coyotes are. Bears are unpopular on the other side of the Hudson. I guess they can be dangerous, and they tear garbage cans apart. New Jersey has a hunting season for bears, to help reduce the population."

I grabbed a plastic bag from the kitchen cabinet and put the bear in it. "Weird, but nothing I can do about it now." I threw it on the floor of the coat closet. "Where were we?"

"Talking about the Westbrooks, I think."

"Why not finish off our drinks and toddle over to the fish restaurant?"

She smiled and nodded. There wasn't very much to finish off, so we were on our way to the Crab Shack a few minutes later. It is an old place in an old building, and they have had more than one fire, but they seem to come back each time. The food is good and the prices are very reasonable. There's sawdust on the floor and red-checked tablecloths. They also have surprisingly good wines by the carafe for a low price. Needless to say, I go there often.

"I can't get that teddy bear out of my mind," Ruth said when we sat down. "Bizarre."

My phone rang. It was Gabriele. He wanted to know if I got the teddy bear, he sent over.

"That was from you? What the hell is it supposed to mean?"

He said that was what he wanted to ask me. It had been delivered to Ora di Pranzo in a bag with my name on it. Gabriele opened it and threw away the bag, and asked one of the restaurant runners to drop it at my door.

"I bet you thought it had something to do with our little trip to Westchester. Why would anyone send it to me at your address?"

"*Forse chiunque abbia mandato l'orso non sapeva il tuo indirizzo.*"

I translated for Ruth: "Maybe whoever sent it didn't know your address." Then I told him, "Ruth is here. We're at the fish place."

"*Ciao ciao, bella signorina.*"

"Same to ya, buddy," she said.

I thought I heard him chuckle.

"Ugly little thing, isn't it?" Ruth said.

"*Spaventosa,*" he said, then added, "Scary. Is toy for dead child."

"Okay," I said. "Who do we know that would send something – anything – to me at Ora di Pranzo?" It was a rhetorical question, and I supplied at least the beginning of an answer. "Mike di Saronno if it was a joke. Ricky Coniston, who only has met me there and at the Peninsula Hotel bar. After that I draw a blank."

"Or somebody that one of them talked to," Ruth added. "We need to take it to Mike. He can send it to a lab to see if there are any clues about what it is or where it came from. No fingerprints on a stuffed animal, but maybe a hair or some DNA. I don't know. If it was a child's toy, there might be some DNA on it."

"I wonder if it is possible that someone saw us tramping around in front of the Coniston home and across the street in the forest."

"If they did, why would they send you a teddy bear with claws on it?"

"Got me."

"Do you suppose it's possible that someone is trying to help us?" I said.

"Help us?" Ruth echoed.

"I wonder if it could be a clue of some kind."

"If it is, it would have to be somebody with a morbid sense of humor."

I suggested that if he had time, Gabriele should go with me to Mike's office, so that he could explain how the teddy bear was sent to me at his restaurant. He agreed and said he would meet me at my apartment at nine o'clock, and we could take the subway over together.

I had ordered fried shrimp with french fries. Ruth had ordered oyster stew. The oversized portions kept us busy for a while. We dropped the subject of the teddy bear and enjoyed the food.

"There used to be places like this in every neighborhood when I was a kid," she said. "Family, neighborhood kinds of places, where you might run into the man from next door, or the kid who bags groceries at the market."

"Actually, I seldom eat shrimp, because they tend to bring on a flare of gout sometimes. But I grew up loving shrimp back in the days when Fridays were for fish – and I didn't like fish when I was a child. But I can't remember anyplace that made them better than the Crab Shack."

"And I seldom eat oyster stew, but this is heaven. It's also *traife*," she said. "I love it, makes me feel warm, all the milk and onions. Lotsa garlic. Peppery. Perfect."

My cellphone buzzed, indicating a text message. It was from Gabriele.

Look at your Facebook

I showed Ruth, who quickly dialed up my Facebook page on her cellphone. She showed me a photo of the teddy bear with claws over a caption of "What the hell?"

It had been posted by a screen name XYZXYZXYZ – obviously somebody who didn't want to be identified. We agreed that Gabriele would show up at my place bright and early the next morning.

"Well, that's a pisser," I said softly to Ruth.

She nodded.

"I'll let Mike know, and I'm going to take the stuffed animal to him tomorrow anyway. My guess is it's someone just wanting to harass me. Probably will go away on its own. Seems harmless unless there's something about it I haven't noticed."

"Hey listen," she said, "dinner's on me. You always pay for everything."

"No way, no how. You're the one who gets all the first-class plane tickets."

"Pish-tush." She already had her credit card in her hand and waved to the waitress. "This place is a find, Hugo. It's going on my list of favorites."

"Thanks for dinner, then. You should try the cracked crabs sometime."

"Never got into that," she said, "They look like monsters from a million years ago, especially the big ones, like King Crab. Not food."

"Lobster?"

"Better. Not anywhere near the top of my wish list though."

It was getting on for midnight, so we left. I walked her to the subway, stayed there behind the turnstiles until I saw her get on a train, then headed home.

Chapter Fourteen

I knew I was going to have a hard time going to sleep, so I turned on my desktop computer and poured myself a vodka. It occurred to me that the teddy bear had four claws, not five. I went to a search engine and asked it how many claws were on a bear's paw. The answer was 'five'. A bear's claws are not retractable like cat's claw are, so the claws are easy to see in a footprint and they're long. A bear's back legs are bigger than the front legs, and so are the back feet. But the scratching would be done with the front paws.

Then I found that I could look at tattoos of bear scratches. I don't have any tattoos, grew up thinking tattoos were for people with weak minds or something. Today a lot of people have them – male and female – and a surprisingly large number have many tattoos. I had seen tattoos of bear claw scratches, some of which are fairly gruesome-looking. Sure enough, there were images of all kinds of tattoos of bear scratches, all of which were, as far as I could tell, on males.

What surprised me was that some had the marks of five claws, some had four and a few even had three. Artistic license? Or do bear scratches vary? I looked up pictures of bear scratches, which fortunately were all on trees (not people), and the most common number of claws doing the scratching was four. Bears sharpen their claws by scratching trees, like cats scratch furniture or upholstery.

Then I started looking for information on the Coniston Companies. I found a few references in articles about philanthropy, and one where Coniston Companies had sponsored a 10K race. There was an article on a small company that had gone public a couple of decades past, and had been partially funded previously by Coniston Companies. I noted that it was in Tarrytown, which borders on Pocantico Hills. It had a name that turned out to be Basque: Euskal Corp. I checked for current trading or value, but there was no quote and no ticker symbol. There was nothing for that name in the SEC's website, www.sec.gov. I figured either the IPO never happened, the company ceased to exist, or maybe it was acquired.

But aside from scattered references, Ruth had been right about the scarcity of information. I doubted the NYPD would be able to get the D.A. to subpoena anything from Coniston Companies, and wondered if some more aggressive sleuthing would turn anything up. I went to the website of the New York Public Library, and quickly realized that if I wanted to find anything in their enormous data bases, I would have to go there in person to get help.

I was feeling more relaxed, so I refreshed my vodka and put a history of early Christianity on my bedside table. An academic book accomplishes two things, because I learn something and then I fall asleep. I wanted to be awake and alert when Gabriele got to my place the next morning.

When I woke up, it was brightly sunny, about seven o'clock. I knew I needed nourishment if I wanted to be at my best, so I put some turkey sausages in the skillet with some butter and scrambled two eggs in the skillet when the sausages were done, so the eggs could pick up some of the flavor. Rye toast with butter. Breakfast of champions.

What I really needed was coffee. Hard to start the day without coffee.

Gabriele was right on time at nine o'clock. Of course, he looked like he had just come from having a makeover at a salon, where I look like I was dragged behind a horse a lot of the time. How he had managed not to be on the cover of Gentleman's Quarterly, I do not know. As we walked to the subway, I opened the plastic bag I was carrying and showed him the teddy bear.

He gave it a sour look and said, "*Maloik,*" which is Neapolitan slang for *malocchio*, or the evil eye.

"There's really nothing to connect the stuffed animal to the Coniston boys, but it's creepy anyway," I said.

"Is not from boys, is from killer."

"How would anyone know that I was helping the police on this case?"

He shrugged. We took the 7 train to Times Square, and then took the 1 train to 50th Street, then walked the five or so blocks to Mike's office.

"Did you touch the teddy bear?" Mike asked me as he looked at it in the plastic bag.

"Yes, I picked it up when I opened the door, but pretty quickly put it into that bag."

"I don't think I ever told you that the boys' bodies had been scratched by something that was intended to look like bears had mauled them. That's why the local police thought bears had been there. Of course, there was no saliva, as you know."

"Well, I said it was creepy, but why me?"

"I gather you drove up to Mr Coniston's place in Chappaqua."

"Gabriele and I both went up there. We didn't trespass on their property, just wanted to see the lay of the land in a forest area across the street."

"And did you go to Pocantico Hills?"

"We did but we only walked along a public hiking trail, didn't try to find where the bodies were. We also went to Untermyer Gardens to look at some of the rock formations there. Not because I thought Untermyer Gardens was somehow involved, but just so Gabriele could see what kinds of rock formations there are close to the Hudson River."

"Signor Cortese?"

Gabriele smiled and pointed to the plastic bag. "Is from killer, no?"

Mike shrugged.

"If Gabriele is right, still why send it to me?"

"Because it might scare you, and you might throw it in the trash, not give it to me to send to the lab."

"How would anybody know that I was working with you on this?"

"You watched me interview Ricky Coniston when he was here, so maybe he was able to find out you were here. Or it's possible that Ruth Jensen told someone from the Opera League, I guess. The Conistons were members, don't know if Ricky picked up that membership or whether maybe Elizabeth still has it."

Mike added that it made sense that the home in Chappaqua had surveillance cameras, so they might know that the two of us were poking around there.

"Have you been there?" I asked.

Negative.

"I was guessing that the boys were climbing rocks or trees and were either pushed or fell accidentally. But when we were there, we saw a tall gatehouse, maybe thirty feet tall. If you fell off the roof of that, it might be just as deadly as falling from a tree or falling off a rock ledge."

He listened carefully, but didn't respond directly. "What makes you think the boys were killed at the home in Chappaqua?"

"I didn't say I thought that."

"But clearly you do."

I shrugged. "Actually, whoever left that stuffed animal for me at Ora di Pranzo, it could have been a warning – I get that. But maybe it was somebody handing us a clue."

"What kind of clue?"

Gabriele perked up.

"Maybe the reason it looked like they were killed by a bear is that there were claw marks inflicted on them with an artificial set of bear claws. Like the claws were added to the teddy bear."

"Congrats," Mike said. "As it happens, the M.E. measured the claw marks on the bodies, and they were all exactly identical. She said it had to be something artificial because no bear paw could be so precisely the same all the time. And of course, there was no bear DNA either. "

Gabriele's eyes widened. *"Ugo genio."*

"Hardly a genius, *amico mio*, but thank you. I just couldn't believe *quell'orsetto* was sent to me to scare me. It looked more stupid than scary. So I had to figure out another reason for someone to have left it. Not that it helps much, I guess. But I still have to figure out why it was left for me, instead of somebody else."

"Not to mention that we already knew what you guessed from the stuffed animal," Mike said. "So maybe it wasn't there for exactly that reason."

That was a little chilling, even on a warm humid day.

Mike said he would get the teddy bear to the forensic lab right away, to find out what we couldn't see by just looking at it. I could tell by looking at Gabriele that he wanted to leave. When we were walking to the subway, he grabbed my hand and held it while we were walking. It's not unusual to see men holding hands in New York City, but I felt like everybody on the avenue was staring at us.

He dropped my hand after a couple of blocks, so I put my arm around his shoulder. He grinned, but kept looking straight ahead.

Who's your daddy?

"So," I moved my arm and put my hand in my pants pocket. "What do you think the teddy bear was for?"

"Is from killer, laugh at you." He had a very stern look on his face.

I suggested we should stop and have a drink at Thalia. He agreed.

My phone rang. It was Ruth. I told her Gabriele and I had left the precinct and were going to Thalia for a drink.

"It's a little early, no?"

"Well, you know it's always five o'clock somewhere. Both Mike and Gabriele seem to think the stuffed animal was a threat to me. Frankly, that calls for a drink, since two kids have already been killed. "

"You've been in worse pickles than this. Keep calm and carry on, as the Brits say."

"I'm not crazed, it's just strange and scary to think some anonymous guy may be threatening me."

"Or anonymous gal." She said she would join us, and I told her we would be at the bar. "But remember there was a time when somebody fired bullets into your apartment in the Theater District a few years ago, so this is fairly non-threatening compared to that."

The bartender took one look at us and whipped up two dirty vodkas. "On the house, Mr Miller. Relax and take some deep breaths."

I realized I must have looked as tense as I felt. Tried to give him a relaxed smile, "Thanks, Brian."

"I take care of you," Gabriele said softly. "I protect you."

I touched his face with my hand and nodded. I couldn't help wondering what other people at the bar would think was going on.

They probably think I'm his father. I'm certainly old enough to be.

Ruth crept up and whispered in my ear, "Boo!"

I flinched or jumped or whatever, and she laughed. "Lighten up, Hugo. How you guys doing?"

Gabriele beamed at her. "Signorina, good to see you always time."

Brian brought her a dirty vodka. She blew him an air kiss.

"I wanted a drink because we just came from Mike's. The consensus seems to be that somebody wants me to get the hell out of Dodge, not to put too fine a point on it."

"And who might that be?"

"Man what kill boys," Gabriele said matter-of-factly.

"We don't know who," I said. "Whoever sent the stuffed bear with the claws to Gabriele's restaurant with my name on it, I guess. We took it to Mike. He sent it to the lab, so we'll see if there are any clues about who that might be. If somebody killed the boys, that doesn't mean that same somebody did this."

"I saw it, remember?" Ruth said. "It didn't look like a joke, but it also didn't look like a threat of some kind. It did look like somebody wanted you to know that they have an eye on you – and probably on Gabriele and me, too."

"Look, let's just assume for now that somebody wanted to kill the boys. That means making them disappear, taking them someplace where nobody would know they were there, and then killing them. And then, of course, taking their bodies to Pocantico Hills – without being seen – and leaving them there for animals to eat.

"Number one, no single person could do all that, so if it happened, there has to be a group of people who were in on it. Number two, we still don't know if the boys fell or were pushed, and we don't know where. But the teddy bear with the claws is a child's toy with a stupid – maybe gruesome, but still stupid – addition. Anybody but the three of us would have just thrown it away. It has to have been sent to Ora di Pranzo by someone who maybe didn't know where I live."

"Is like Cosa Nostra in Napoli: somebody kiss you and you know you gonna be dead."

"Has there been any follow-up to the teddy bear?"

"Not that I know of."

"So whoever left it doesn't care if you understand or not. Maybe it was a prank," Ruth said. "Right?"

I finished my drink and waved to Brian to bring another one.

"Ugo, vodka not make everything good."

"There's nothing magic about vodka, except it helps me cope with things that scare me. Liquid courage, they used to call it." I took a big slurp of the new drink, and picked the olives out of the old one, popped them in my mouth.

"Hugo's a big boy," Ruth said directly to me. "He knows vodka isn't an answer. But sometimes it helps you find the answer. You know, *in vino veritas*."

"That's not what that means. That means you tell the truth if you're drunk because it's hard to lie when you're soused."

She put her hand on my shoulder and smiled. "So not only are you a big boy. You're a smart boy, too."

I understood what they were saying, and suggested that I should get some lunch. When I stood up to talk to the woman at the front desk about getting a table, Gabriele hugged me and patted me on the back.

I asked Brian if I could order a turkey burger at the bar. Yup. "And fries. No ketchup. Mayo."

Chapter Fifteen

When I got home, I sent Mike an email to see if he knew of any surveillance cameras outside Ora di Pranzo that could have caught whoever left the teddy bear there with my name on the package. A few minutes later my cellphone buzzed.

"Hugo, I got some results from the lab on the stuffed animal. There were a lot of almost microscopic dust mites all over it, indicating that possibly it had been in an attic or a garage or maybe a second-hand store – someplace where there might have been dust in the air – could be a library; books are notoriously attractive to dust mites because they gather dust. I knew a lawyer who had to wear work gloves when he consulted law books because he was allergic to the mites. The claws that were added to the bear were made from coat hangers that had been clipped with a wire cutter and then bent to look like claws. They are sharp enough to cut fairly deep. Some DNA on the bear, by the way, probably from flakes of skin."

"So nothing useful to tell us where the teddy bear came from?"

"They said the dust mites could be a clue."

"Yeah, you said a garage or a second-hand store."

"I believe if we had a specific garage in mind, they could compare the dust mites to see if they were a match."

"I doubt the Conistons store old toys in their garage, so I don't know how that could help."

"There's nothing that says it has to be a garage. It could be an attic or a closet, maybe the trunk of a car."

"Did they ever check the Coniston cars with luminol?"

"Not all of them, no. They checked the Mercedes. Negative."

"The trunk of the Mercedes?"

"Also negative."

"Did they take any samples from the car and the trunk? Could there be dust mites?"

"I see where you're going. There was no mention of dust mites, but it wasn't something they were looking for. I can ask."

"You said not all the cars were checked, just the Mercedes. How many cars do they have?"

"Several. Not sure. They don't collect them or anything like that. I think there was a pickup truck, some kind of ATV, a horse trailer. There are a couple of limos at the 5th Avenue home. I agree, we should look at all of them."

"A horse trailer might be exactly the right thing if you needed to move a body, especially a trailer with stalls for two horses – that way you could put the body in one stall, and a horse in the other one, in case you needed someone to see that you were transporting a horse."

"I suppose any vehicle that has good horsepower could tow a horse trailer, and a Cadillac pulling a horse trailer wouldn't look out of place in most of Westchester County."

"Is it difficult to get a warrant to search the garage in Chappaqua because it's a different county?"

"They can make it difficult if they don't want it to happen."

"They? Who are they?"

"The Westchester officials. No reason to think they would be difficult, though."

"But the Conistons couldn't get in the way?"

"You really think Ricky Coniston had something to do with this, don't you?"

"No, I don't. I just don't know anything that would eliminate him from the lineup, that's all."

"And who else would be in the lineup?"

"No idea, to tell the truth. I'd say any other Conistons or relatives who could make a play for the Coniston Companies."

"I don't think there are any other Conistons who could stand up to Ricky," he said. "There's the Westbrooks and the cousin whose father drowned about five or so years back. He may be twenty-one or so, but it's hard to imagine someone that age taking on Ricky Coniston. His name is Edward, like a lot of the others. Lives in Boston with his mom."

"If he's twenty, he might be a rock star for the younger cousins. I bet they may have been close. When I was a kid, I hero-worshipped some of my cousins who were older than me," I said. "For sure there are too many Edwards and Richards. You wonder why they recycle the same two names in each generation. You can't tell the players without a scorecard. That's what my father would've said."

"I wonder where he was when the boys went missing," Mike said. "And I wonder if he has a silver Mercedes. Probably doesn't have any money problems. His father tried to throw Eddie out, but couldn't make it happen. He was a drunk, so the kid may have had a bumpy childhood."

The doorbell rang, so I told Mike I would call him back. I looked through the peep-hole in the door and didn't see anyone. I opened the door cautiously and looked out.

Nobody. There was a piece of paper on the floor of the hallway. It was printed in lower case letters and read "meet me at the bar downstairs Ted."

I don't know anybody named Ted. Theodore, I guess, but I don't know anybody named Theodore either. Maybe whoever it is left his message at the wrong apartment. Whatever.

It was getting on for five o'clock. There isn't a bar downstairs in my building, but there's a restaurant that has a bar, so I put on a fresh shirt and brushed my hair and went downstairs.

The entrance to the restaurant was around the corner from the front door of the building, which gave the place a nice view of the East River, the United Nations and the Chrysler Building. Even so, it was not a place I went often because the food was mediocre and overpriced. I was surprised at how many people were there. It wasn't crowded, but there were a lot of people at the bar. I didn't recognize any of them.

A young man stood up from the bar and walked toward me. He was dark-haired with good symmetrical features, about average height, wearing jeans and a rayon shirt with some palm trees on it. He held out his hand without smiling.

"Ted," he said. "Thanks for coming."

"I don't think we've met."

"That's right, we haven't met."

I should turn around and walk out, but I wonder what he wants.

"I guess you already know who I am, but my name is Hugo Miller."

"I'm Ted Coniston."

"Ted?" I didn't recall a Theodore or Ted on Ruth's charts.

"Actually, my name is Edward Coniston, but there are so many Edwards in the family that I've always been called Ted, like Ted Kennedy – his name was Edward, too." A slight upturn on his face, not quite a smile though.

"Also like teddy bear?"

He nodded, but looked puzzled and said, "I guess."

"Do you live in Boston?"

He nodded.

"And you didn't send a teddy bear to me at a restaurant in Manhattan a couple of days ago?"

"No."

"What can I do for you?"

"I believe you are connected with the police?"

"I am a civilian criminalist, not a police officer, but I work with the NYPD when they ask me to, yes." I handed him a card.

"And I believe you have been helping with the investigation about my cousins?"

"The boys who were found in the woods in Pocantico Hills, yes."

"Their father and my father were brothers, but they never got along. My dad actually tried to have Eddie Coniston removed from the Coniston Companies, but he didn't succeed. There were some in the family who thought that Uncle Eddie wasn't actually a Coniston. That his real father was somebody else. I guess everybody's forgotten about that now."

"Yes, I've read about that."

"But Ed and Dick – my cousins – we were very close when Mom

and I were still living in Westchester and I'm hoping I can help in some way."

"How did you get my name?"

"My Uncle Ricky told me he met you after my cousins disappeared. He said he thought maybe you would be easier to talk to than a cop."

"I almost didn't come down because I thought your note was a joke. If you want to help, you should get in touch with Michael di Saronno, who is in charge of the investigation." I asked the bartender for a pen, and wrote Mike's name and phone number on a napkin, and added my cellphone number, too. "He works at a precinct just off 8th Avenue on 54th Street." I handed it to him.

"Can you just tell me what you think happened?"

"Like I said, I'm not a police officer. Anything I knew would be confidential, so I couldn't talk about it."

He looked downcast. Nice looking kid, obviously related to Ricky Coniston. Strong family resemblance, but put together better.

"Are you old enough to drink legally?"

He nodded, pulled out his wallet and showed me his driver's license. Twenty-three.

I waved at the bartender, who sidled over. "So, I'm gonna have a dirty vodka with olives, straight up."

"That's a little strong for me. I'm gonna have a Corona, please."

"You mind if I ask you a personal question?"

He shrugged an okay.

"Since your cousins are both dead, is there a chance you'll inherit their ownership stakes in the Coniston Companies?"

He looked bewildered. "Why do you want to know?"

"Like I said, I work with Mike di Saronno. Plus, I'm just curious."

"Well, the answer is I don't freakin' know. And I don't freakin' care. When my dad died, he left Mom and me plenty for us to be comfortable and do whatever we wanted. And if you're thinking I had something to do with what happened, you ought to see a psychiatrist." He was kinda steamed. He drank a big gulp of his beer and let out an explosive "ahhhh" after he swallowed.

"I wasn't implying that you had anything to do with it. I just asked if there is a chance you might inherit, that's all. Otherwise, it seems from what I've been told that your Uncle Ricky will basically be head of the Coniston Companies for life."

"Ricky is doing a great job. Payouts have almost doubled since he took over. Hard to argue with that. Uncle Eddie never did that."

So, I changed the subject. "Did you drive down from Boston?"

He nodded. "My mom's old car. Don't have one myself."

"An old folks car?"

He smiled a little. "Yup. Mercedes sedan, four doors, but it's in good shape."

"Hard to be upset about that."

"What do you drive?"

"Jaguar XK8, old in years but low mileage. Convertible. Zero to sixty in about five seconds, if you want to get a ticket. Easy to park though."

"James Bond car."

"Well, same frame, but Bond drives an Aston-Martin."

"So, call me a liar over a label."

"Mine's British racing green with a champagne top and champagne-colored leather interior."

"Of course, that's what it ought to be. One of the most beautiful cars on the road, even today."

"I bought it out of the showroom and it's about fifteen years old, but only has a little more than thirty-five thousand miles. All the maintenance done by the dealer. Somebody's going to get a real good deal whenever I can bring myself to give it up. They say that Jaguars start to appreciate after twenty years though, so maybe I'll just wait."

"Mine's my mom's, and it's kinda platinum colored, I guess. Not real shiny though. White leather inside, some of it kinda cracking. But everything works."

"Saddle soap helps the leather."

"Seriously? Soap?"

"Yeah, saddle soap, not like hand soap. It comes in a container like shoe polish, probably can find it in a drug store or an auto parts store or a carwash. It takes all the grime off and leaves the leather soft. I use it on my car. It's easy."

I was going to have to decide whether to order another drink or leave. I signaled for the check.

"This is on me," he said.

"I'm old enough to be your grandfather, and I'm used to paying." I had my wallet out. The bartender signaled to me that it was already paid for.

"I gave the bartender my card before you got here. Thanks for meeting me. And remember, if I can help, call me. I want to find out who fucking did that to Ed and Dick. I can afford to buy drinks, too."

I thanked him and we shook hands. "Call Mike. He's a good guy. You'll like him. He cares about his job. And he cares about people."

When I got back upstairs, I sent an email to Mike with copies to Ruth and Gabriele, telling them about my meeting with Ted.

Met with Ted Coniston this evening, son of George Coniston (the one who drowned). He lives in Boston with his mother. He drives his mother's silver Mercedes and he told me he wants to help with the investigation. I gave him your cellphone number. Didn't tell him anything. Nice kid. Looks like Ricky Coniston, maybe a couple inches taller. His driving license says he's twenty-three.

Then I made a grilled cheese sandwich and wolfed that down with another dirty vodka. I made it through the eleven o'clock news and went to bed when I started seeing lightning bolts in the sky. The forecast was for heavy rain and thunderstorms. Where I grew up in southern California, it never rains in summertime. Fog maybe, but no rain. Rain is only between about November and April.

Chapter Sixteen

When I woke up, the sky was blue and the sun was shining. It was about six o'clock, so I thought I should turn over and close my eyes, since I'd only had about six hours of sleep. I can do that occasionally, but I really need something closer to eight hours. But instead, I got up, got dressed, made the coffee, and drank a full mug. I couldn't stop thinking about Ted Coniston.

My cellphone beeped, indicating a text message had arrived.

Hey, sorry if I was rude last night. Ted

No apology needed. U weren't rude. Did U call Mike? Hugo

Not yet. If you have time, would like to talk to you again

I told U I can't discuss police business

Understood. I want to tell you some things

What's Ur schedule?

I'm open. This morning okay?

Obviously, you know where I live. You want to come over here?

OK

Where are you now? What time works?

I was driving back up to Boston, but I turned around and I'm outside the entrance to your building

Come on up.

CU in a few.

I shook the coffee pot; it sloshed a little. I poured what was left in the sink and put on a new pot so it would be fresh. I put a bowl of mandarin oranges on the coffee table and put the mug I had been using in the dishwasher. Set out two coffee cups with saucers on the pass-through from the kitchen. For me, breakfast at home is usually fruit, toast and coffee.

When the doorbell rang, my cellphone beeped again. It was Mike.

Call me when you're free. Want to talk about Ted Coniston.
Ted's here, call you later.

Ted was smiling when I opened the door. He stuck his hand out. I shook it and said I had put some coffee on, invited him into the living room. He walked around the room looking at the paintings, and nodding his head.

"Beautiful pictures. You collect them?"

"Nah. I just have bought things over the years when I fell in love with them. Have a seat on the couch, and I'll pour some coffee. What do you take in yours?"

"Anything you got. Sugar, milk?"

I pointed to the mandarins and said, "Help yourself."

He picked one up and followed me into the kitchen. He started to peel the mandarin, and asked, "Trash?"

I pointed to the pantry door, and took the two coffees into the living room. It was easy to tell which was which, because I drink mine black. I put a sugar bowl on the table with a spoon. The milk was already in his coffee. In New York City, a 'regular' coffee is one with milk. If you don't want milk in your coffee, you have to order it black.

"Tangerine was good," he said when he sat down. "Look, I don't want to bother you, or take you away from whatever you should be doing, but thanks for letting me come over." He paused, then said, "I know I was rude last night, no point pretending I wasn't. I've been on edge ever since Ed and Dick were murdered."

I looked at the floor and nodded. "Understandable. I can't imagine what your family must be going through."

"I used to babysit for them when we still lived in Westchester."

"Where in Westchester?"

"Dobbs Ferry."

"Nice town, some good restaurants, too. I have a bunch of relatives in Westchester, scattered around. Valhalla. Ossining. Some other small towns in the northern part of the county. Pocantico Hills?"

He shook his head. "I haven't been to where the bodies were either."

"Why wouldn't you stay with Ricky if you were going to be around there?"

"Auntie Ann isn't in good health, and it makes Ricky jumpy."

"Sorry to hear that. I hope it's not something serious."

"It's called Pick's Disease. Kinda like Alzheimer's, but different, I guess. She doesn't recognize people she knows really well, like Ricky, but she doesn't act crazy, doesn't see ghosts or anything. She eats too much and she's getting fat."

"I wonder if that's related to losing her son and then her nephews."

"She didn't know me. I don't think she would have known Ed and Dick." He stared at his knees.

"Does she have nursing help?"

"Oh, for sure. Around the clock. She might wander off or something."

"What causes it? I've never heard of Pick's Disease."

"I don't know, and the doctors don't either. Ricky told me it's always fatal though."

"It's like the family in 'The House of Seven Gables.' No end to the bad things that happen."

"Aunt Lizzie thinks there's a curse on them."

"What does your mother think?"

"My mom didn't want to stay around after Dad died. She stayed until I finished high school, and then we moved to Boston. She thought Eddie probably had something to do with Dad drowning."

"Did you go to college up there?"

"I went to BC, studied finance."

"Good for you. When I went to school it was still hippies at UCLA. Didn't want to get involved with filthy lucre. I studied Latin and EngLit."

"Did you get a teaching credential?"

"No. Had no intention of teaching."

"Why Latin then?"

"I was raised Catholic and back then a lot of things at church were still in Latin, so I was curious, and I was always curious about Ancient

Rome anyway. Rome's a beautiful city, although I never went there until after I was in college. I think it was kinda like a secret language."

"Grad school?"

"No. Hated school. Did you really come here just to say you were sorry?"

"No. I feel like you might be unbiased about my family. I just want to find out what happened to Ed and Dick. Everybody in my family suspects other people in the family when anything goes wrong. Especially the Westbrooks."

"Westbrooks?"

"Aunt Lizzie's family."

"So, you wanted to help the NYPD figure out what happened. Do you have a theory about it?"

"No. I hope they died in an accident, and then somebody tried to get rid of the bodies in the forest. I hope they died fast."

"I shouldn't talk about the case, but I'll tell you that we have not been able to figure out how they disappeared. It was like they vanished into thin air while they were walking. We have video of them walking from school to the corner of Broadway and 91st Street, and then nothing."

He was tearing up and breathing fast. "I met them there. We had set it up, they just jumped into the car and we were off."

"You drove all the way from Boston to pick them up after school?"

"Not exactly. They wanted to go up to visit Uncle Ricky and Auntie Ann, and they didn't know how to get there. Their mom kinda turned into a hermit after Uncle Eddie died, and there were always Westbrooks hanging around. I didn't have anything special going on, and I was finished with college, so I told them I would take them."

"You were their big brother?"

"Kinda, I guess. They had a hard time at home. Uncle Eddie had made sure the Westbrooks were wealthy, which they weren't before Eddie and Lizzie got married. He bought houses for them, changed the Coniston Companies dividends around so that the Westbrooks started getting a check every month, too. Conistons basically don't have much use for Westbrooks. "

"Like a feud?"

"No. We're always polite, and everybody loves Lizzie."

"If you call Mike, I know he will appreciate hearing what you have to say. You still have the phone number?"

He reached into his jacket pocket and pulled out the paper napkin with the number on it.

"Do you want me to call Mike? I can introduce you on the phone."

He smiled and nodded vigorously. I got up and motioned to him to follow me. I walked into the little bedroom down the hall that I use as an office. The desk telephone there has a good speaker. I picked up the handset and dialed Mike's number. He answered right away.

"Mike, it's Hugo. I have Ted Coniston here with me, and I'd like to put the phone on speaker and introduce the two of you. Does that work for you?"

"Sure, but I need to speak with you, too."

"Maybe later?"

"Okay."

I pressed the speaker button and introduced them.

"Hugo tells me I should tell you what I know about what happened. I picked them up the day they went missing, because they wanted to go and visit Uncle Ricky and Auntie Ann."

"Can you come over to my office in Manhattan? I'd like to talk here so we can record the conversation if that's okay."

"Okay."

"Can you come over now?"

"Sure."

"Hugo, pick up please."

I picked up the handset, which disconnected the speaker.

"Hugo, thanks for all of this. If you can, come over with him. I think if you're here, it will help him not be nervous. I'll get Ruth and Gabriele to come over if they can, and they can watch from the observation room. Congratulations, Hugo, this may be the big break we need."

"I'm going to take a quick shower and we'll take the subway. Ted can leave his car wherever he parked it when he came here. Trying to park near the precinct is impossible."

Ted needed to find a bathroom. I pointed him down the hall to the second bathroom next to the office room.

I turned on the shower, but didn't get undressed. Just wanted to take some time so that Ruth and Gabriele could get to Mike's office before Ted and I got there. I changed my shirt to a Hawaiian style rayon shirt and read a few pages in my book, then went in and turned off the shower, threw some water on my hair and brushed it.

"Nice shirt," Ted said.

We walked to the subway station and hopped on the next train which pulled into the station about a minute after we got there.

Chapter Seventeen

It was about eleven thirty when we got to Mike's office. He told Ted the best place to have a conversation was an interrogation room because there were audio and video recording that would be made automatically.

"Should I call a lawyer?"

"If you want, but you're not a suspect in any way."

"Okay. If I feel like I should call a lawyer, I'll tell you."

I saw Ruth and Gabriele walk out of Mike's office while we walked over to Interrogation Room 1.

Mike showed Ted where the video camera was and where the mic was for the audio recording. "Can you just tell me in your own words what happened the day the boys left school and never got home?"

He repeated pretty much in the same words what he had told me, and that he had picked them up on Broadway to take them to Ricky and Ann Coniston's home for a visit.

"Were Mr and Mrs Coniston expecting you? Did you tell them you would be bringing the boys?"

"No, I hadn't told them. We wanted it to be a surprise."

"And how did they react?"

"Well, Uncle Ricky wasn't there. Auntie Ann's nurse told me that Ricky had some minor surgery in the City that morning, and they didn't expect him home until later."

"That must have been a disappointment."

"It was, but we wanted to see Auntie Ann. We knew she had been sick, and that the nurse was there to make sure everything was okay, that Ann wasn't at home alone."

"And was she happy to see you?"

"No, she had no idea who we were." He explained about the

disease that robbed his aunt of the ability to recognize people, even people she knew very well, like Ricky himself.

"Did she have any trouble talking, or did she seem okay other than not knowing who you were?"

"She was kinda hesitant when she talked, like the words wouldn't come out. I told her who we were and she seemed to understand, but she didn't – or couldn't – call us by our names. The nurse offered us an iced tea and some cookies, and suggested that we go into the kitchen. An aide stayed with Ann when we went to the kitchen. While we were there, the nurse told us about Pick's Disease, and I realized that was why she hadn't been out with Uncle Ricky for a long while. It seemed to have come on when her son, Edward, died. Nobody in the family knew, not even Lizzie. She can't even recognize herself in a mirror."

"Good grief," Mike said. "What a horrible situation for Ricky, and how horrible for you and the boys to find out the way you found out."

"Well, we decided we didn't want to stay, so we left – the three of us. Ed and Dick said they wanted to go home, but they were worried that Aunt Lizzie would be worried and angry that they didn't go home after school, so they wanted me to drop them off at the Botanical Garden in the Bronx. That way they could text Lizzie, tell her where they were, and take the subway home."

"And that was the last time you saw them?"

He nodded. Even I could tell that he probably couldn't see much or say anything because tears were dripping down his cheeks.

"And they didn't call their mother."

"There must be video of them at the Botanical Garden," I said. "I think there are a lot of surveillance cameras. I'm a member and go there often."

Mike nodded. He looked at Ted. "I won't ask you to stay in New York City, but please try to be available to answer some questions if we need something you didn't already tell us. But if I heard you right, there were people who saw you at the Coniston home in Chappaqua, which would support what you told us. If we can get video of the boys at the Botanical Garden, that will fill in some of what's missing. But now we know how they got from Broadway and 91st Street to the Botanical Garden."

Ted nodded again and made some choking sounds.

"A word of advice," Mike said to him. "Splash some cold water in your face in the Men's Room, and find a way to tell your Aunt Lizzie what you just told us."

He looked into his lap and nodded, looked back up with a smile plastered on his face, still wet from crying.

"I got a text message after I dropped the boys off from Uncle Ricky, and I told him what happened."

"I'll go with you back to Long Island City so you can get your car," I said. "Give me a minute with Mike. I'll meet you downstairs."

"Unfortunately, not the kind of break we would have liked, but it's better than not knowing anything," I told Mike, feeling a little thunderstruck myself.

"You did good, Hugo. You can only find what's actually there, not what you thought was there. Everything we learn gets us closer to knowing what happened. Now we know that Ted told Ricky where the boys were. He may still have been in Manhattan when he found out, after whatever minor surgical procedure he had."

"Pick's Disease sounds like a perfect horror. I looked it up on the internet. Nobody knows what causes it, but it hits much earlier than Alzheimer's."

Mike said he knew something about the disease because of a case he had worked on a few years back. "An individual who was wandering around but couldn't identify himself. He had a wallet, and the officer who intercepted him looked at the driver's license. The man said he wasn't that person, and when the officer showed him the license, the man said he had never seen that person before. But it was him. He later got back to where he knew his name, could recognize himself in a mirror, but he didn't know who anybody else was. We were able to notify the family, and they found a nursing home that would care for him. I remember thinking he looked and acted close to normal, but he was an overeater, like Ted said about Ann Coniston. They called it something else, something I don't remember."

"Frontotemporal dementia?"

He nodded.

"Same thing, different name."

Ted was waiting in the downstairs lobby when I got there. "I don't get why things like this happen," he said. "Seems like God would have saved them."

"You mean your aunt or the boys?"

"Both, I guess. It was like when my dad died. He was too young to die."

"But it was an accident, wasn't it?"

"They never decided. He drowned, but nobody saw him go overboard from his boat. He hadn't been drinking, or if he had, it wasn't much because there wasn't much in his blood. He could have slipped and fallen, but then he wouldn't have gone into the water, would've just been on the deck. The coroner ruled it an accident, so yeah, I guess it was. My mom never said, but I could tell she thought he was murdered. Who knows?"

"Life isn't fair. Lots of things happen at random."

We walked to the subway at 50th Street and 8th Avenue. Before we went downstairs, I texted Gabriele and asked him if he could come over to my place to meet Ted Coniston. By the time we were at my stop, Gabriele had sent a reply: *On way CU soon*

I told Ted there was someone I wanted him to meet, and asked if he could hang out with me for a little longer. He was agreeable, and we went up to my apartment. I poured each of us some Montepulciano D'Abruzzo, an Italian red. We toasted and I got some crackers and cheddar cheese.

True to his word, Gabriele arrived quickly. I introduced the two of them and poured some wine for Gabriele. It occurred to me that we were like an illustration of three ages – Ted in his twenties, Gabriele forties, me sixties. Two, four, six.

"Ted was telling me about how he picked the boys up on Columbus Avenue and took them up to see Ricky and Ann Coniston, whom they wanted to visit. Ricky wasn't home ..."

"We call them Uncle Ricky and Auntie Ann," Ted said, picking up the conversation. He told Gabriele about Pick's Disease, and said he dropped the boys at the Botanical Garden. Theoretically, they could get home from there by taking the MetroNorth train from the Botanical Garden station and changing to the Green Line at 125th Street, where they could get off at 96th Street and walk home.

"So they not ride bicycle," he said. "But they go where we look at house *e la foresta*."

"But the boys were obviously still alive when Ted dropped them off," I added.

"Who you told where boys are?"

Ted looked puzzled. I reworded Gabriele's question. "Did you tell anyone where the boys were?"

"Umm, well I sent a text to Uncle Ricky and told him we had gone to visit, sorry we missed him, but the boys were either at the Botanical Garden or on their way home."

"Izzy is my mom. Her name is Isabelle. She's cousins with Auntie Ann."

"So, you probably spent a lot of time together when you were still living in Westchester," I said.

He nodded and sadness returned to his face. "I should take off if I want to get home for dinner," he said. "Nice to meet you, and I really want to help find out who did this, so keep me in mind."

He stood up and we shook hands. Gabriele started to kiss him on the cheek, but Ted clearly didn't know what was going on.

"He's from Italy," I said. "People kiss each other on the cheeks there, same as we shake hands."

"Gotcha," he said, and spread his arms out to hug Gabriele, but Gabriele just shook his head slightly.

"Glad I meet you. Hope see you again sometime. I have *ristorante* in Manhattan with Dante, *il mio cugino*. Maybe you come and we cook something for you. *Signor Ugo* maybe he bring you. *Simpatizzo*."

After Ted left, Gabriele asked if there was any wine left. I refilled

Joseph Allen

his glass and poured a couple of swallows in mine.

"What do you think about Ted?"

"Is good man." He paused for a moment, then added, "But you my man." He hugged me, then stepped back with a look that said he was giving me my space. "You come Ora di Pranzo tonight?"

I told him I would be there for dinner, and realized he was getting ready to leave, so I hugged him. Then he was gone.

Chapter Eighteen

I never turn down an invitation to Ora di Pranzo. It's the best Italian food in Manhattan, and that's saying a lot, because Manhattan is the foodiest place on Earth. But on this particular day, I considered calling in sick. There was something going on with Gabriele that I didn't understand. I felt a negative vibe from him and wondered if it was related to Ted being there. There was something of the rich kid in Ted, but I didn't think he was dislikable. I usually consider Gabriele to be a formidable judge of character, but this time there was something going on that I could almost smell, but couldn't put my finger on.

I kept thinking about Pick's Disease, and what that would do to Ann and to Ricky. I had a relative who eventually died from dementia, maybe Alzheimer's, and it was very upsetting to visit her, because she didn't know me from Adam. I couldn't imagine what that would be like for Ricky coming home from some kind of surgery. She wouldn't know him, any more than she knew Ted or Ed or Dick.

What could have happened to the boys after Ted dropped them off at the Botanical Garden? It's in the Bronx, almost next door to the Bronx Zoo. It has its own train station ("Botanical Garden"); it would have been a piece of cake to get home from there. A short train ride and then a short subway ride. The Botanical Garden has a semi-wilderness area that is intended to look like what the area must have looked like before Europeans took over. Plenty of places to climb up on a rock and fall off. But then how would they have been moved to Pocantico Hills?

What if they decided to go back to Ricky Coniston's home in Chappaqua? Uber? No, there were no Uber charges that could have been the boys. What if they took a Citi Bike from one of the hundreds of public racks? We knew they could have ridden bicycles on various old trails to get to northern Westchester. How they could have gotten to the Coniston home was another conundrum. They had probably been there more than once since they spent summers there, but people who haven't driven a route seldom know all the turns to take.

Ted said that he sent a text to Ricky telling him that the boys were at the Botanical Garden. Ricky hadn't told the police that he had received a text like that. As though I knew what the CSIs had found, of course. Maybe they knew about it, and nobody had told me.

When it got close to five o'clock, I spruced myself up, put on a fresh shirt and took the subway to Ora di Pranzo.

Gabriele was smiling broadly when I got there. We did the European double cheek kiss thing and he winked at me as he pointed to the last seat at the bar, next to the wall. They had kept it reserved for me. He waved at the bartender, who put a martini glass at the place. Dirty vodka with olives.

After I sat down, he stood next to me and mouthed *te amo*. I couldn't remember why I had thought he was acting strangely.

"Did you have a bad impression of Ted?" I asked him.

"Ted not tell you what he know."

"About what?"

"About boys. About anything."

"What do you think happened?"

"*Non lo so*, but he not tell you all things he know."

Gabriele was a sex worker earlier in life, and developed a knack for spotting lies or incomplete truths – or people who shouldn't be trusted. I get the impression it was a survival skill from the little he says about it. He still radiates sex appeal without seeming to try. It always amuses me to watch a room that he walks into. Men and women follow him with their eyes. He's taller than average, but not tall, Italian looking – dark hair, tanned skin, green eyes, v-shaped torso and small waist. No tattoos or facial hair. He sometimes looks like he might be a reincarnation of Elvis – but Italian.

He and I have a platonic relationship, but more than a regular friendship. To be truthful, I think it is father-and-son on my side. He is older than my two sons, but not a lot. His father died when he was a small child. I've been married twice – unsuccessfully – ending in two divorces. He had a lot of sex with clients and without emotion, and says he doesn't yearn for it. It's a balancing act that I intend to continue. If I were attracted to men, he would be the only one on my list – but I'm not. And I'm old enough to hide behind my age. I keep thinking he will fall in love with someone, and I would be happy to dance at his wedding, but it hasn't happened so far.

As for me, I'm a two-time loser. Third strike and you're out, right? So I think it's a stalemate, but I have to admit, I am never more happy than when I am with him. Well, there's Ruth, who gets my male juices flowing easily, but there's for sure no future for me there. Her husband died a couple of years back (cancer), and it's obvious that she's not dating, although she is closer to Gabriele in age than to me. Besides, I considered her husband, Murray, a friend of mine, too, and it would be strange at best if I asked her out on a romantic date.

I changed the subject. "I was thinking about driving up to Boston. I want to go to the Oyster House, maybe even drive up into Maine."

"You want talk to Ted?"

"I could, I suppose, but I'm really thinking about seafood. Want to go with me? Ever been to Maine? It's very pretty."

He smiled broadly. "I go with you."

"I need to get the car washed."

"How long we go away?"

"I dunno, two or three days."

"I go home, get clothes." He stood up. "I know we go to Ted. Is okay."

Packing for me is a very quick task. I usually take only a black duffel bag when I travel, one that fits easily into the carry-on sizer they have at the airport. I can easily get enough clothes into it for at least four days. Four each of undershorts, t-shirts, button-up shirts, socks, two pairs of pants, swimsuit. No shoes other than the ones on my feet when I leave the apartment, and I wear a blazer or some kind of jacket if it's going to be cold. Couple of books, dopp kit with hygiene stuff, phone charger and my blood pressure and blood thinner pills (not getting any younger). I have traveled enough with Gabriele to know he only takes one bag, but he's very careful about what he packs. I'm usually a t-shirt and jeans guy unless I need to dress up for something, but Gabriele always looks like he stepped out of a magazine. How he does it, I do not know.

I gave Gabriele a key and told him to let himself in if I didn't answer the door, because I was going to get the car washed while he was getting his clothes packed. It was a beautiful late summer day, some fluffy white clouds in a blue sky. Hot and a little muggy, but a wonderful day to be outdoors.

"Do you mind if I drive over to Ricky Coniston's house before we take off for Boston?" I asked him when we left.

He shrugged and hugged me. It was okay.

When I pulled up in front of the Coniston estate and looked down the driveway, there was a silver Mercedes outside the garage. I couldn't see the license plate, but figured it was the one that was registered to Ricky or Ann. I turned around to say something to Gabriele but he was gone. I looked across the street and saw something moving in the woods, then he popped out of the undergrowth.

"*More!*" he yelled. "*Guarda!*" He was telling me there were blackberries in the woods. Not a surprise, and they ripen in August usually, too. As it happens, I love blackberries – something that Gabriele knows well, because they keep them for me at Ora di Pranzo year-round. I had no idea that he did as well. I put the top up on the car and locked it, found a plastic shopping bag in the trunk and we walked into the woods to pick some berries. There seemed to be no end to the blackberry patch, which stretched what looked like acres.

"You make pie," he said happily, filling the plastic bag quickly.

"I can't make a pie in a Boston hotel."

"Then we go home instead and you make pie. Then we go to Boston to meet Ted after we eat pie."

I like to make pies, especially blackberry pies and pecan pies. When I was a small kid living with my grandparents in a small town in Texas, my grandmother made pies from wild blackberries called dewberries. And jam, which I have never tried to do. My mom taught me how to make pie crust, which I don't make any more – I buy pre-made pie crusts rolled up and sold in a refrigerated box. I do like to cook, but making pie crusts is more than I want to get involved in. Italians don't have pies the way Americans do. I like to make peach pies, too, and I know Gabriele always wants two or three servings of any kind of pie.

When we walked back out to the car, Ted Coniston was standing there looking at my car.

"Hi, what are you doing here?" he said with a smile.

"Picking blackberries," I said, and gestured to the bag Gabriele was holding. "But I might ask the same of you. I thought you were heading to Boston."

"This is where Uncle Ricky and Auntie Ann live. I just wanted to pop in and see how she was doing, and how Ricky was coping with everything."

"Looks like quite a spread," I said, and pulled out my keys. "But I know Mr Coniston is pretty well off, so I guess it's not surprising."

"Why here?"

"I have relatives all over Westchester, just happen to know where some of the good blackberry patches are." I pressed on the unlock button on the key, and the lights blinked and there was an unlocking sound. "Looks like quite a spread. I hope things are better than they were when you brought the boys over here. You know, Mrs Coniston's situation."

He said something noncommittal, like they were taking it day by day.

I asked him whether the gatehouse dated from when the house was built.

"No, and it's not really a gatehouse. I think it was added before the First World War. The house is early nineteenth century, I think. If you go inside what you called the gatehouse, it looks like it was built to be a playhouse for kids, what we call the Kids' House."

"Did you play in there when you were little?"

He smiled, but backed up a little. "No. Uncle Ricky wasn't living here when I was a kid. They moved in here about when Ricky took over Coniston Companies after Uncle Eddie died. We were living in

Manhattan, not with Uncle Eddie. We were on the west side, eighties."

"Look, I should get going," he said. "I already said goodbye to them, and I want to get home before it gets dark."

I opened the door to the Jag and got in, put the key in the ignition and put the top down.

"Nice car."

"Thanks, I guess it's my middle-aged crazy car. I always drove sedans before I got this. And it's old enough now to tell you how long it's been since I was middle-aged."

"I think it's still one of the most beautiful cars on the road. Looks like you've kept it in good shape."

Gabriele got into passenger seat and said, looking straight ahead, "Is too hot, maybe raise *capote* and turn on AC?"

As soon as the top was up, he said to me, "Ted not lie, but he not tell you everything."

I hung a U-turn and headed back toward the City. "I'll make the pie and we can drive up toward Maine tomorrow, if that works for you?"

He smiled broadly, made me feel warm. He turned on the radio and set it on the classical station. It was an orchestral piece, sounded like "Till Eulenspigel," what they call a "tone poem" by Richard Strauss. Upbeat but beautiful. He was nibbling on the blackberries.

"Stop that. Leave enough berries for the pie." He reached over then patted me on the shoulder, but he closed the bag and gently put it on the back seat, a joke of a passenger area that could accommodate a small child, but nobody over about ten years.

"Ted afraid from something, *forse* from Ricky Coniston."

"Didn't seem that way to me."

"He scared."

The sky had clouded over, so I switched to an all-news station to see if I could get a weather report. Sure enough, the forecast was for a thunderstorm or two, lasting into the evening, which seems like an almost daily event in late summer around New York City. I felt relieved, because I would not have wanted to be driving to New England during a downpour.

Gabriele reclined his seat as far as it would go, and drifted off to sleep.

My phone automatically syncs with the car's communication system when I turn on the ignition. One of the safety features is that if I get a text message, the car will read it to me so I don't have to try to read it on the phone. While I was driving back to Long Island City, a notice appeared on the little screen on the dashboard, saying there was a message from Ted Coniston. I started to motion to Gabriele to look at it, but he was asleep. So I pressed the "Accept" button. An automated woman's voice read out Ted's telephone number and then said "Mister Miller, I wasn't truthful in what I told you, and would like to stop by your apartment to explain." Gabriele didn't wake up.

I pulled off the parkway at the next exit, and pulled into a gasoline service station. Before I filled the tank, I replied to Ted, saying that I was in Yonkers on my way home, and I would be happy to see him any time.

Gabriele woke up when I stopped the car, and watched me texting, which I do with one finger, not with both thumbs like younger people do.

"*Quello che è successo?*" (What happened?)

I showed him my phone with Ted's message and my response to him. "*Ti ho detto che non stava dicendo la verità.*" He was rubbing it in that he'd told me Ted wasn't telling me everything. Then he settled back and closed his eyes while I was gassing up the car.

In fact, as I drove down the street my building is on, I saw a silver Mercedes idling in front of the building in a no-parking zone. I pulled into the garage entrance and drove up a ramp to the second floor where my parking place is, then took the elevator one floor down to the lobby, then walked out the front door. When I got up to the door of Ted's car, I jerked my head back to tell him to come with me. Gabriele was in the lobby looking out the window. He smiled slightly and turned to go to the elevators.

"Where can I park?" Ted asked.

I told him to drive around the block a couple of times and take whatever spot he could find.

"There's no place for visitor parking here?"

"Sorry, no. But there are usually places on the street. I'll go upstairs and wait there. Gabriele is here, too, by the way."

It apparently didn't take him long to find a spot, because within a few minutes, he was ringing my doorbell. I turned around and realized that Gabriele had disappeared, but I ushered Ted into the living room and saw the bag of blackberries sitting on the kitchen counter. Then I heard the shower in my bathroom – the one off my bedroom – turn on. Seemed odd, but if Gabriele wanted to take a shower, that was his business. Maybe he just didn't want to be part of a conversation with Ted.

"So, you wanted to tell me something?" I asked, and offered him a glass of wine, which he declined.

I poured one for myself – a well-aged *aglianico del vulture* from Basilicata, the instep of the Italian boot.

Ted was obviously uncomfortable, paced around the living room while I sat on the couch and sipped my wine.

"I didn't tell you the truth when I told you about picking up my cousins and taking them to Uncle Ricky's house."

"Where did you take them then?"

"I took them to Uncle Ricky's, but I didn't take them to the Botanical Garden after that."

"Where did you take them?"

"Nowhere. They stayed at Uncle Ricky's. They wanted to go to that building you thought was a gatehouse. There are some video games there, and ping-pong and stuff like that, and they wanted to stay to say hello to Uncle Ricky when he got there."

"That sounds innocent enough. Why did you tell me you dropped them at the Botanical Garden?"

"Because I know they were killed and I didn't want anyone to think I did it. It was stupid."

"Why would anyone think you killed your cousins?"

"Because maybe their father had my father killed, which I don't think happened. But I didn't do anything. They were my family. I loved them."

As he finished saying that, Gabriele appeared at the door to the living room with a towel around his middle and drying his hair with another towel. "Hi, Ted," he said, and the towel around his waist fell to the floor. Gabriele grabbed it and put it back on. "See you in a minute," he said, and disappeared back into the bedroom.

Ted looked what I would call astonished, and his face was red from blushing. "He's amazing looking," he said.

I smiled. "Yeah, it's funny what happens when he walks into a room. Everybody stares. Probably happens to you, too. You're a hunk."

He blushed again. "Nahhh." He looked puzzled, but then said, "Are you two –?"

"Not. I'm the age of his father, if his father was still alive. And I have children who are around his age."

"Hugo belongs to me," Gabriele yelled from the bedroom. No accent.

It was my turn to blush. I shook my head and said, "Just good friends. And good company. No hokey-pokey." Then I frowned to emphasize what I said. "Well, it's the truth."

"It wouldn't be true if I was in your place," he said.

So that's it.

Gabriele appeared looking like a commercial for a big designer, somebody like Hugo Boss. He was wearing one of my dress shirts and one of my ties, but his own jeans. No shoes. Big smile.

Chapter Nineteen

"Well, that was awkward," I said to him after Ted left.

Then I told him what Ted had told me about leaving the boys at Ricky Coniston's house instead of taking them to the Botanical Garden, like he said before. "He said they wanted to go to that tallish building that looks like a gatehouse. It's for young people, has a lot of video games and so forth."

"You can't fool a fooler," he said, again with no accent.

"I wasn't trying to fool anyone."

"I know. Ted was not saying true things. I can see if man is gay as soon as I look at him."

"Why does your accent go away sometimes?"

"Because I learn American when I come to New York, not want to be a foreigner."

"Why don't you talk that way all the time?"

"It's difficult, I have to think about everything I say. Besides now I like being a foreigner and work with Dante."

"Do you think Ted was involved with one of the boys?"

He shook his head. "*Non vuole che la famiglia sappia*. He afraid."

The accent had returned as he said, in Italian, that Ted didn't want the family to know (that he was gay).

"What other languages do you speak?"

"*Napoletano, Siciliano*. Spanish. Impossible run *ristorante* in New York if you not speak Spanish. I can talk dirty in some other languages." Broad smile.

"What language did you speak at home in Capri?"

"Napoletan. *Qualche volta* Italian."

"How different are they?"

"*Un romano non può capire un napoletano*." He was saying that a Roman cannot understand what somebody from Naples says.

"*Italiano* is language I learn from school. If I born Roma or Firenze or Milano, mamma speak *italiano* all time. In Venezia, mamma speak *venetano*, different language. Some places people still talk Greek."

"Guess I'll make a blackberry pie," I said, looking at the bag of berries on the counter.

Since I use pre-made pie crusts, pies are super easy to make. When you cook berries, they give off a lot of liquid, and if you make a berry pie the way you make an apple pie, it will taste fine, but it will be soupy and difficult to cut and serve. I use tapioca flour and cornstarch to keep berry pies from being sloppy and messy. Neither one adds anything to the flavor, but they soak up the extra liquid so you can cut a clean piece of pie without getting it all over the table. Also, berry pies have to cool on a rack for a couple of hours after they come out of the oven to 'set'.

Gabriele watched me make the pie, which took all of about fifteen minutes; just long enough for the oven to pre-heat. So about an hour after I started mixing the berries with sugar, flour and lemon juice, I was taking it out of the oven and putting it on a wire rack to cool.

He wanted to have a piece of pie right away, but it would be a mistake if we cut it before we cooled it; it still needed to firm up. More to the point, if you put something in your mouth that just came out of a three hundred and seventy-five degree oven, you'll burn your palate and tongue. Blowing on the first bite won't help. That pie would be hotter than boiling water.

"I'm surprised that in today's world, Ted would be so worried that people might find out he's gay," I said, thinking about my gay brother in California.

"Family throw him out of house?"

"That doesn't explain why he lied about taking the boys to the Botanical Garden, though."

"Afraid of family after he leave boys there."

That one I could understand readily. A lot could be riding on it if he left the boys there when their mother was frantic, and stayed frantic until their bodies were found in the woods – dead from a fall, but with gashes scratched into their backs that made it look like they were attacked by a bear or maybe Bigfoot (neither of which is in Westchester County and Bigfoot probably completely imaginary).

"Interesting that the boys wanted to go to the kid's playhouse that we saw by the front gate. Tall skinny tower-like building with a flat roof."

"You think maybe boys fall from roof?"

"Maybe. Or maybe they were pushed. It's too early to say that's what happened. But it's a possibility, and we don't have many of those."

"What we do now?"

"I'll tell Mike what Ted said, and he will do whatever he thinks needs to be done."

"We not investigate Ricky Coniston?"

"Not you and me. Not Ruth. Remember, Ricky Coniston had surgery that same morning. I have no idea if Ann Coniston could even find her way to the gatehouse. Maybe the NYPD will focus on Ricky if they think he might be involved. No way to tell now."

"We go Maine? And Ted?"

"Speaking of Ted, that was quite a stunt you pulled, dropping the towel and what-not."

"I know he's gay, but I want you know same thing."

"It worked. Now I know it. What good does that do?"

"Is not what he worries about."

"What is his problem?"

"*Non lo so.*" (I *don't know*)

"How do you know there is something wrong with him?"

"He look bad, like in trouble. Not bad man, but not good man, something wrong."

"How can you tell that?"

"*Non lo so.*"

"Do you think he was after the boys for sex?"

"No."

"What could it be?"

"*Non lo so.*"

"Maybe he feels guilty because he left the boys in danger?"

Shrug. "We try find what is problem."

"You mean now you want to go to Ted's home?"

"Si."

"Do you still want to go to Maine?"

"Si."

"Maybe we can go to a game at Fenway Park."

"Baseball?"

I nodded.

"Whatever you want." No sour look, but I could tell it was at the bottom of his list.

"We don't have to go. I was just making a suggestion."

"Baseball very complicated. Very hard understand what happen."

"It is complicated, and there are too many rules, but it's a game I love, even in Boston."

He smiled at the last part. "New York no like Boston."

"Boston is beautiful. We like Boston, we just don't like their sports teams. And if you wear a Yankee cap, they'll pour beer on you. Hey, do you have to get to Ora di Pranzo?"

He said he told Dante he wanted to take a couple of days off, and Dante agreed. "So I sleep here tonight and we go Boston tomorrow."

The sunsets were still late, around eight o'clock, but my stomach has its own clock and I asked Gabriele what he felt like eating. "Wherever we go, we can have some pie for dessert."

"Maybe I have pie before dinner," he said. "When I at Ora di Pranzo, I eat cannoli before dinner. I not American."

The pie was completely cooled and easy to cut. I cut a large piece and put it on a salad plate, handed it to him with a salad fork. "Vodka?"

Yes.

I poured chilled vodka into two martini glasses, and poured a splash of olive juice in them. We sat at the dining table and clinked glasses. He made growling or maybe purring noises while he ate the pie, which disappeared in a surprisingly short amount of time.

"Maybe I eat more pie after dinner," he said with a huge smile.

"If you do, I have some vanilla ice cream I can put on it."

We decided to leave early the next day. That way we would get to Boston early, so we ordered some Thai food to be delivered and went to bed early as well. Gabriele did indeed eat another piece of berry pie – with a scoop of ice cream on it. I drank a couple of fingers of scotch instead of the pie, probably a similar number of calories.

There was a spectacular lightning storm during the night. I recalled waking up with a crack of thunder, but fell back asleep. Gabriele slept in the second bedroom, which also functions as my office. He says I snore sometimes. My two wives never complained about it, but I'm a good deal older than I was when I lived with them.

I woke up to the smell of coffee brewing. Light was streaming into my bedroom. Gabriele was clattering around in the kitchen and I realized there was the smell of cinnamon, too. As it turned out, he was making French toast and had mixed cinnamon and sugar with the butter. He handed me a mug of black coffee. He pointed at the French toast sizzling in the skillet, "Is pay you back for pie."

After breakfast, we hit the road for Boston, but I felt a magnet drawing me back to Ricky Coniston's home, so we drove there first. As before, we did not go into their property, but I wanted to have a look at the gatehouse, or kids' playhouse, or whatever. It was clearly three stories tall, looked like its floor plan was a square or nearly a square. I walked across the road to the other side, and I could see what looked like an umbrella like one that would be over a table. I pointed to it, Gabriele nodded that he could see it. *"Ombrellone,"* he said softly, meaning a beach umbrella or at least a very big umbrella. *"Se i ragazzi cadessero da lì, li ucciderebbero,"* he said, meaning "If the boys fell from there, it would kill them."

I took a couple of photos with my smartphone, and sent them via text message to Mike, with a note that it was by the front gate of Ricky Coniston's home in Chappaqua, and suggesting that it might be good to get a warrant to search it.

Almost immediately my phone rang. Mike wanted to know more. "What makes this gatehouse thing so important?"

I explained that it was not a gatehouse, but had been outfitted for children and had video games. "Ted Coniston told us that the boys wanted to stay when Ted left, so that they could see their uncle and play video games. He originally told us he dropped them at the Botanical Garden, but he retracted that and said he left them at the Chappaqua house, where they had spent summers several times."

"So why should I get a search warrant?"

"If Ted is right, that the boys stayed there to see Ricky and play video games, they would have been there in that gatehouse-looking building," I said. "As far as I know, that would be the last place they were before they were found in Pocantico Hills. Fingerprints? DNA? I dunno. There seems to be a terrace-like place on the roof. We could see part of a beach umbrella up there. It's high enough up that if they fell, it might kill them. I'd say thirty-five or forty feet tall."

He said he would get the search warrant, and told me to get away from there fast. "They probably have cameras everywhere."

"If they do, that might go a long way toward proving the boys were there."

We took his advice and hauled ass out of there. Next stop Boston.

Gabriele wanted to drive with the top down, so when we were a safe distance away, I stopped and put it down. I also opened a hotel booking app on the phone and got a reservation for two at the Langham Hotel, a landmark building that had formerly been the Federal Reserve of Boston, and had been turned into a hotel some years before.

"Have you ever been to Paul Revere's house?" I asked him somewhere around Hartford.

"Who Paul Revere? Why we go his house?"

I did my best to explain to him how Paul Revere was a hero of the American Revolution, and his house, now a museum, was only a short walk from the hotel. He was game. I wanted to go to the Union Oyster House for dinner; he agreed.

I turned on the radio and flipped the dial around until I found a classical music station. Prokofiev's "Romeo and Juliet" ballet music, one of my all-time favorites.

"We ask Ted for dinner, too?"

"Sounds good. Can you text him while I drive?" I handed him my phone and showed him Ted's text string, which had his phone number. "Send it from your phone. He was very impressed with you, especially when you dropped the towel."

He grinned and nodded. "I not want Ted for my man," he said, "but he try be good man."

I knew that.

Ted answered Gabriele's text right away, wanted to know where and when to meet.

"Tell him to come to The Langham Hotel at seven o'clock. We can meet in the lobby and find a place to have a drink, then walk over to the restaurant for dinner." I pulled over to the shoulder and put the top up on the car. "I want to put on the air conditioning," I told him, and he nodded.

When we got to the hotel, it was about five-thirty. I wanted to take a shower; I felt like I was covered with dust, as though I had been outdoors in a high wind all day. I drank about four glasses of water because I felt dehydrated. Driving with the top down on a sunny day is fun while you're doing it, but it can leave you feeling like you were dragged behind a horse later.

We went down to the lobby just before seven o'clock, and Ted was standing in the middle of the room, looking around, obviously waiting for us. When he saw us, he waved. Gabriele was wearing a tight black t-shirt and a pair of jeans that looked like they were molded onto him. Ted's jaw dropped a bit as we shook hands. The bar at the hotel was closed for renovation, so we walked over to Faneuil Hall and had a drink there.

"Did you have a smooth ride home?" I asked Ted, who was drinking a Heineken and staring at the bar.

"Yeah, some traffic after I passed Hartford. But not bad. I was home in time for dinner with Mom."

"Do you stay home most of the time?" Gabriele asked.

Ted looked up and looked Gabriele in the eye. "A lot of the time, but I go out sometimes. Sometimes a club, sometimes a ball game, sometimes just hang with friends. I bet you're a man about town, aren't you?"

Gabriele looked puzzled. "Man about town?"

"Oh sorry, that's just a phrase we use for someone who goes out a lot."

"In that case, no. I mostly work at night. I have restaurant in SoHo."

"You cook?"

"I good cook, but in *ristorante, il mio nipote* Dante cook. He is cousin. I am *maggiordomo,* stand at front door, welcome people, make feel good. But is still work. I help waiter if more than four people at one table. Also sommelier, *adetto al vino.*"

"Gabriele is an excellent cook, even though maybe Dante is a better chef for a restaurant. Gabriele is a magician with food. He is also a magician with people. At his restaurant, he makes everyone feel at home. Some time when you're in New York, maybe we can get a table at Ora di Pranzo. That's the name of Gabriele's restaurant. Your Uncle Ricky is there often, too. Maybe he can join us."

I thought I could see Gabriele frowning, but decided it was just the lighting.

"Talking about food, let's finish up here and go over to the Oyster House. One of my favorite restaurants in the world."

I finished off my dirty vodka. Gabriele tilted his head back and swallowed the rest of his red wine, probably chianti or Nero d'Avola. Ted was standing, looking out the front window, and had already paid the tab.

We both thanked him, and as we walked, I asked him to tell us something about his mother. "You said something about Eddie Coniston being responsible for you father's death. Did your mom think that?"

"She still thinks that, but we don't talk about it. She knows how I felt about Ed and Dick, and she knows I think Dad drowned by accident. She knows I love being with Uncle Ricky and Auntie Ann. So we don't talk about it. I just don't believe it, but she's my mom and we have agreed not to bring it up. My dad fell into the water while he was on his yacht. Nobody else there. No way anybody was responsible for it happening. It was just an accident, that's all."

"Why would anybody think Eddie was involved in your father's death?"

"They didn't get along. My dad sued to try to throw Eddie out of the Coniston Companies. He wanted to be the big guy himself, I guess. I was just a kid, and I never heard my dad talk about it, frankly. But Eddie didn't like that old rumor about him not being his father's son."

"I thought that came from Eddie's mother when her brains were scrambled from dementia," I said. "And it must have been a long time back."

"I think it was when Eddie said he was going to marry Aunt Lizzie. Grandma wanted him to marry some other girl. A rich one, I think, but I don't remember who she was. So she told anyone who would listen that his real father was some guy she had an affair with, so he wasn't really a Coniston. Hard to imagine, really. But in the long run, the bad blood in the family was why we moved to Boston."

The Oyster House is only about a football field from Faneuil Hall, so it didn't take long to get there. I had reserved a table. The place is pretty old, early nineteenth century, although the building itself is much older, like 1704. The seafood is some of the best I've ever eaten, and served in a kind of 'family' style. They serve hot fresh cornbread and fresh sweet butter with every meal, and even though they put sugar in the cornbread – something my southern-born mother couldn't abide – it's perfect with seafood.

"Do you think the boys were alive when they left the house in Chappaqua," I asked Ted, deciding to dive directly into the water, instead of wading in.

I could see Gabriele's eyes narrowing slightly, but he didn't stare at Ted. He looked down at his wine.

Ted looked like someone who had just been slapped across the face. He nodded.

"Yes, you think they were alive?"

Another nod.

"Where could they have gone from there? Was Ricky Coniston

home by the time you left?"

Negative shaking of his head.

"So, you didn't see him?"

"I didn't see him."

Gabriele turned to look at Ted. He nodded to me.

"But boys alive?"

Ted nodded, and Gabriele nodded again at me.

"You were frightened when he asked you that."

"Of course I asked myself the same questions, over and over. There's no way Uncle Ricky hurt them."

"Why did you tell us that you took them to the Botanical Garden?"

He shrugged. "I don't know. I was panicked."

"Why? Did you hurt the boys?"

His eyes opened wide. "No, of course not."

"If you didn't hurt them, and Ricky didn't hurt them, who does that leave?"

He didn't answer.

"An accident? Maybe they fell off the roof terrace of the building by the gate?"

Gabriele put his arm over Ted's shoulder. "Is okay. We know you not hurt boys, and you not know what happen. We know you trying to help." Ted leaned into Gabriele and shook like he was crying.

Chapter Twenty

We ordered food. For me, eighteen oysters on the half shell, which came with fresh crushed horseradish and some of that red sauce that seems always to be on the side of any platter of shellfish. Same for Gabriele, who dived into his cornbread as soon as the waiter put it on the table. Ted ordered scrod, which is usually described as small cod, but actually can be anything – "Catch of the Day." It's always good.

I suggested to Ted that he should have a whiskey while I squeezed lemon on the oysters. He nodded. "How 'bout dem Yanks?" I quoted a funny line from a play called "The Boys in the Band." Ted looked puzzled. "Never mind, it was a joke," I said, and smiled in as fatherly and friendly a way as I could muster. I signaled to the waiter, who came over to the table.

"Give this young man a smooth blended scotch, neat, please."

He nodded and walked off, came back quickly with a lowball glass that had about two fingers of scotch in the bottom. Tobacco-colored, or maybe a little lighter. I looked at the waiter, and said, "I'll take one of those too, please."

Gabriele raised his hand to make it three. I had never seen him drink scotch, but he had a wicked smile that acknowledged that he was doing something new.

"Did you drive to get here?" I asked Ted, realizing that all three of us had finished eating.

"Nah, I took the MTA. Will I ever return? No, I'll never return, and my fate is still unlearned," he said with a real smile, quoting an old campaign song from a mayoral election after World War II.

"Thanks, Charlie," I said, acknowledging the name of the singer, who was a candidate for mayor. "Since you don't have to drive home, how about another drink?"

He shook his head slightly, stood up and held out his hand to me. I took it, and shook it with both hands. Gabriele hugged him and we said good night. Gabriele and I sat back down to finish our drinks. The waiter came over and asked if we wanted dessert or coffee. I asked Gabriele if he'd ever had Boston Cream Pie. He looked puzzled, so I told the waiter we'd both like to have Boston Cream Pie, which I knew was a specialty of the house.

Gabriele loves sweets, which makes it even more frustrating that he is in such good shape. The only fat on him is his rear end. He beamed like a child when the two million-calorie desserts arrived. I took one bite and knew I was finished. Eating oysters is not filling, but I had downed two pieces of cornbread with the oysters. Of course, a yellow butter sponge cake with about an inch of *creme patissière* between the layers and milk chocolate fondant slathered all over the top is, well, very sweet – "sweet enough to make your teeth hurt" as my mother used to say.

And of course, when he finished his portion, he asked if I was going to eat all of mine. Needless to say, he virtually licked the plate and I thought *well damnation!* Because I knew he wouldn't put on an ounce of weight from that sugar splurge.

I threw back the rest of my scotch and said to Gabriele, "I never saw you drink scotch before."

"I never have scotch before this time."

"What did you think of it?"

"Is burn in throat, like cognac."

"Well, it has the same amount of alcohol as cognac, and it's the alcohol that burns, but it doesn't taste like cognac. Cognac is made from grapes. Scotch is made from barley, a grain."

"I like Boston Cream Pie best."

"I could tell."

"What did you think of Ted?" I asked. "Was he telling the truth about the boys being alive when he left Ricky's home?"

"*Sì, era la verità*," he said.

As a walking lie detector, Gabriele is amazing. So when he said Ted was telling the truth, it was good enough for me.

"Does that mean Ricky probably killed the boys?"

He turned scrunched his shoulder closer to his neck and turned his palms up in a classic "How would I know?" Easy to understand.

I knew from seeing more than one side of Ricky that he was probably an expert at telling people what they wanted to hear. But that didn't mean he killed his nephews. We took a detour as we walked back to the hotel, and I showed him the old State House, and told him that the Revolution started there, when British soldiers shot some civilians. "The history books call it the Boston Massacre, but I believe only five or six people were shot. But it sure pissed some colonists off."

"Is very nice city, no?" he said, glancing around and then back at the lights in Faneuil Hall, which is like a small shopping mall, but with all local merchants. No fast food chain stores.

"It's a good city, except the Red Sox, Celtics and Patriots," I said. Then I added, "The baseball, basketball and football teams."

"If you say football, you mean NFL. If I say football, I mean real football." He was grinning ear to ear.

"*Va bene.* Then add BCFC to the list. And remember that NYCFC plays at Yankee Stadium. So they have to win."

The grin dropped off his face.

"When NYCFC plays Napoli, we bet."

"They not play together. Napoli is Serie A Italia."

"World Cup?"

"NYCFC? *Pazzo.*"

"Napoli hasn't won a World Cup either."

"How you know that?"

"I make it my business to know what my best friend cares about. I admit I was guessing about Napoli."

Standing in Post Office Square, Gabriele hugged me, and whispered in my ear, "Ti amo."

"Me too, Ri-Ri."

He stepped back when I used his baby nickname. It always makes him almost – but not quite – angry. I think it was something his grandmother called him, and he hated it, but he knows that I know he

137

hates it.

"*Lo so che mi ami*." It wasn't news to him.

"Tomorrow we drive to Kennebunkport, and you can have real Maine lobster fresh out of the ocean. Then we stop at the New Hampshire Liquor Store on the way back, and buy some wine."

We walked back to the hotel as light-hearted as Dorothy and her friends following the Yellow Brick Road to Oz.

Chapter Twenty-one

Anyone who's been to Kennebunkport already knows how beautiful it is. Rugged seacoast, lots of picturesque places and houses. A late season for lilacs, because it stays cold there longer than it does in the Mid-Atlantic or the South. There were a few laggard lilacs when we walked around, smelling sweet and fresh, even though the flowers were looking wilty and near the end of their beauty. A lot of lilacs were planted where there had been outhouses before indoor plumbing – they thrived on the fertilizer in the ground.

The presidential Bush family has a home on the water in Kennebunkport, and of course it is one of the sights we wanted to see. We didn't stop, just drove by. Big modern-looking home with lots of glass looking out on the beautiful seacoast and white-capped ocean. The town has no shortage of restaurants, almost all of them hawking Maine lobster dinners. We picked one, and, I suppose predictably, Gabriele ate a three-pound lobster with more drawn butter than a person should eat in a week. Fresh bread and cole slaw that was actually pretty tasty, with an odd combination in the dressing of mayonnaise, vinegar and pepper. Fries, lots of fries.

I don't happen to be a fan of whole lobsters, or even of lobster tails. So I had lobster thermidor, which seemed appropriate, given that when we were there, it would have been toward the end of the French Revolutionary month of Thermidor (the second month of summer). It was delicious, but I couldn't eat much of it, because it was swimming in heavy cream and butter, and I knew I would have nightmares if I had all that in my stomach when I went to bed.

The highlight for me was stopping at the New Hampshire liquor store. New Hampshire is one of those states where all liquor is sold in state-owned and state-run stores. There is a narrow band of New

Hampshire that is on the highway from Boston to Maine, and on the way back there is a huge, neon-lighted liquor store the size of a Home Depot, stocked with every kind of liquor and wine you could imagine. All at cut-rate prices! I bought a case of blended Scotch and a case of assorted Italian red wines, all of which Gabriele picked out. Heavy on the southern reds, the not-so-refined ones that taste of tobacco and what wine critics call 'dirt'. Not polite wines at all. My faves. Nice to have a car with a trunk that can accommodate a couple of big boxes, along with our traveling stuff.

Even with a fair amount of sightseeing, we were able to be back at the Langham Hotel by what would normally be dinnertime, though neither of us wanted to even talk about eating. I felt like if I shook my hips like a hula dancer, there would be a sloshing sound that would be easily audible ten feet away. I drank a lot of water, even though I knew I would be up several times in the night to get rid of it. But lots of water seems to prevent a lot of morning-after woes, at least for me. I opened a bottle of scotch, we had three fingers each in those plastic cups that are in plastic bags on top of the mini-bar. When I drink from cups like those, I always feel like I am going to cut my lip, but it doesn't actually happen.

I noticed that the phone was blinking in the hotel room, so I pressed the 'message' light. There was a plaintive message from Ted, asking if we might have time for breakfast in the morning. I sent him a text message saying yes, we could meet in the lobby of my hotel at nine o'clock. I don't like texting, but I didn't feel much like talking while I waited for the almost-bloat from the lobster and dairy products to calm down. My belt felt tight, ugh.

We were sharing a room with two double beds. I like having a bed to myself because I'm too tall for most beds, and with a double bed I can sleep at an angle without bumping into someone. Gabriele is a guy who showers at night instead of in the morning. That makes us compatible bathroom-wise, because I am a morning showerer. I sleep in shorts and a t-shirt. He sleeps in just a t-shirt, and tends to walk around naked a good deal of the time. I've always been a bit of a gym rat, and try to stay in shape. But Gabriele looks like something that Michelangelo would have sculpted in marble – and annoyingly, I've never seen him work out or run or do any type of structured exercise. I think he likes being ogled, and I suspect that he would parade around in his sleeping t-shirt (or less) if Ted were visiting. He is a bit of an exhibitionist at times, like the strategic drop of the towel that had been fastened around his waist when Ted was in my apartment. It was no happenstance that we were meeting for breakfast downstairs in the lobby.

I was pouring a cup of coffee from the little in-unit coffee maker when Gabriele appeared in the door with a bath towel fastened around his waist and a hand towel mopping his face that had a speck here and there of shaving cream.

"You gonna drop the towel?"

He grinned. "If you want me to drop it, I will drop it."

En garde. Point for Gabriele.

"Coffee?"

"*Si, ho bisogno di caffè.*" I poured a couple of packets of creamer into a mug and threw a spoonful of sugar in after it. Then the coffee. I offered to clink mugs, which he ignored because he was already sipping his. "He gonna tell you he lie again."

"Why do you say that?"

"Because I know is why he ask for meet. He understand I know when he say something not truth. Is why he want to tell all truth now."

"What is he going to tell me?"

"*Non lo so. Vuole parlare dell'omicidio.*"

I knew that, don't know why I asked. He is a human lie detector, not a mind reader. Of course, if Ted wanted to talk about something, it would be about the murders of the boys. I shouldn't ever belittle Gabriele. He has everybody's best interest in his heart, especially mine. I have always figured I am a stand-in for the father who died when he was a kid. Certainly, in my mind he is a stand-in for my son who basically pretended I was dead when his mother and I divorced. They're about the same age.

I have wondered ever since same-sex marriage was legalized why more same-sex couples don't get married, even if they're not in love. Marriage allows spousal privileges in times of hospitalization or death, and sharing of property and assets. There's nothing worse than being old and completely alone. Honestly, when I start to get really old, I know that I will ask Gabriele to move in fulltime and help make sure I take my pills and have a cane with me when I go out. Marriage would make sense in that situation. Think Henry Higgins and Colonel Pickering, or Holmes and Watson.

He was a sex worker earlier in his life (when I first met him he still was an escort – he happened to be tangentially involved in a case I was working on with Mike di Saronno – and I think he tends to see a lot of close relationships through a sex prism), even though I don't think he craves sex, as I don't. In my case, I think it's age and two failed marriages; in his case, it is something else. From my point of view, I am two strikes and no balls, two outs in the bottom of the ninth. Three strikes and you're out. Besides, we would be ludicrous as a couple, and one of the last things I want is to be a laughing-stock. They say pride goeth before destruction, but I hope if the proverb is true, destruction waits in my case until I have time to work something out with Gabriele.

As the clock got closer to nine, I shaved and got dressed in jeans, a t-shirt and a blue blazer, with penny loafers. Gabriele transformed himself from a male Maggie the Cat wrapped in a big towel to a GQ model with my Hawaiian-style rayon shirt and jeans. Gucci loafers, woo-hoo. We hit the lobby a couple of minutes before nine, and Ted was standing in the middle of the room waiting for us.

We went to Cafe Fleuri, where we were met by a majordomo who was standing in front of a sign that announced that Cafe Fleuri would be redesigned and renovated in a few months, along with the renovation of the hotel itself. Breakfast was a buffet that had a variety of foods hot and cold: Irish oatmeal, breads, rolls, sweet rolls, fresh fruit and three kinds of berries, several recognizable types of cold cereal and granolas, Greek yogurt with fruit at the bottom. There was a chef at a hot station with bacon and breakfast meat, including sausages, home-style potatoes and eggs cooked as you wanted, or omelets made to order with your choice of spinach, cheese, mushrooms, crumbled bacon, diced ham, chopped tomatoes and a bunch of other possibilities. There was a thermal coffee pitcher on the table when we got back to the table. The waiter offered us fresh juice and put a rasher of wheat toast on the table with a small bowl of individual servings of Irish butter.

Ted sat down and almost immediately said, "I think I may have misled you when you asked me if the boys were alive when I left."

Uh-oh.

Gabriele pursed his lips a bit and looked at me knowingly.

"As I remember, you said the boys were still alive when you left."

"I walked them out to the Kids' House, where they wanted to play video games until Uncle Ricky got home. What I didn't tell you was that after I left them at the Kids' House, I walked back to my car and left, without checking on them again. They were certainly alive and all over the PlayStations when I left them. But I didn't stop to check on them when I drove away. I didn't know they would turn up dead a few days later."

"Had your uncle come home when you left?"

"No."

"Where was your aunt?"

"She was with the nurse, going for a stroll, apparently toward the horse barn, or at least in that direction."

The waiter came over and took our orders. I'm boring, always want scrambled eggs, hash browns or whatever kind of potatoes they have, and rye toast with butter and marmalade. Gabriele is adventurous, and decided he would take the buffet, as did Ted.

"Where is the horse barn?"

"More or less behind the house, a little more to the north than the house, about a hundred yards or so, a bit higher because the elevation gradually increases by a few feet. You can feel it in your calves as you walk. It can be noisy and smelly, so you wouldn't want it to be real close to the house."

"Are there barn workers in the barn usually?"

"Yes, cleaning stalls, for instance. The grooms are grooming and currying, walking or running the horses, feeding, shoeing them when they need it. Keeping an eye on the horses' health and alertness. Generally, the stable boys are the ones cleaning and maintaining the stalls and the building. Sometimes they take the horses out to pasture for some exercise. Not painting, the barn gets painted by professional painters from one of the towns around there. Same with plumbing and sprinklers to put out fires. There are guys inside the barn twenty-four/seven. Horses are valuable, and the guys who work there are horse-lovers. They don't make a lot of money, but they like what they do."

The waiter brought my breakfast and filled my coffee cup. Gabriele and Ted wandered over to the buffet and came back with some fruit and several types of bread things – 'everything' bagels, Danish pastries, croissants, and some cold meats like pepperoni or salami, ham, bacon, all kinds of things with nitrates or nitrites in them. No eggs. Go figure. Looked like heartburn on a plate to me.

"Would your aunt and the nurse have visited the boys in the Kids' House?" I asked Ted.

"I don't think they knew the boys were there, now that you say that. I think when the boys and I left to go to the Kids' House, I said we were leaving."

"Why didn't you tell us that to begin with?"

Gabriele rolled his eyes in a signal that I was being ridiculous.

"I forgot to tell you that I didn't stop when I drove by the Kids' House. I wasn't trying to mislead you. I just forgot."

"Not really a problem," I said. "I wish I had seen the horse barn. When I was a young kid I lived on a ranch. A cattle ranch, but there were a bunch of cow ponies that knew everything about herding cattle. Your Arabian horses would be much taller and bigger than a cow pony. What I think you might call a quarter horse. Kinda shrimpy compared to a thoroughbred, but smart as all heck."

"You'd feel at home in the horse barn. I know a lot of the guys used to spend summers there with Ed and Dick. Horses are great animals. I understand how people get really attached to them.

He changed the subject. "Big swimming pool with a diving board, too, right near the house. I offered the boys to go for a swim, but they only wanted video games. It gets muggy out there, especially in the middle of the summer and the Kids' House is air conditioned. I would have taken the pool over the video games."

"Do you know if there was an adult with the boys when they went to play video games?"

"I don't know for sure, but I think they were alone. I didn't see anyone there when I took them inside."

"It looks like there's a patio on the roof. You can see what looks like umbrellas from out in the street."

"The roof is flat, and there are some tables with umbrellas – three, I think – good place to have lunch if the weather is good. But there's a pony wall that kinda looks like a castle all the way around, to keep anyone from falling off. That includes animals, like dogs. Now that I think about it, I think there might have been a dog there when the boys went in. Probably one of Ricky's German shepherds. The boys loved those dogs."

"Did the kids in your generation have a hard time getting along with each other?"

"There weren't all that many of us. Now I'm the only one left."

"But when all of you were still alive, did your parents' problems make you and your cousins distant or unfriendly?"

He shook his head. "We loved each other. Our fathers maybe not so much with their brothers, but they grew up in a different time. When Eddie and my dad were kids, that house on 5th Avenue had a couple of dozen live-in servants. If my mom is right, there was a lot of backstabbing in the family. "

"You and Edward Coniston, Ricky's son, were fairly close to the same age."

Gabriele was plowing through his breakfast treats, but stopped to watch Ted. Ted was feeling peculiar; even I could see that. He was flushing and his lips were trembling.

"We called him Ned. He was a great kid. I'm a couple of years older than he would be if he was still here. The Ed Coniston who disappeared was ten years younger than me, and Dick was fifteen years younger than me. But we took care of each other." He was tearing up.

Gabriele stood up and walked around the table to Ted and squatted down next to him so that their heads were at about the same level. "Is okay to cry," he said, and patted Ted on the shoulder. "I not learn to cry until I was man and live in New York."

Gabriele has a natural-born, built-in psychology degree. Or maybe he's a warlock. That would actually be very cool, if he was a warlock.

Chapter Twenty-two

I reported everything I could remember from our conversation with Ted to Mike di Saronno. I gathered that much of it seemed to jive with what Mike already knew, from his lack of questions and seemingly accepting attitude.

I asked him if he knew the boys had been in the gatehouse that Ted calls the Kids' House. "What I thought was a gatehouse was apparently outfitted as a play area for children. Ted took them there because they wanted to play video games."

"If they were there, they may have had quite a wait if they wanted to see their uncle," Mike said. "Ricky Coniston was stuck on a MetroNorth train between Hartsdale and White Plains. It was held for well over an hour because of signal problems in North White Plains. At least they had electricity, so the air conditioning was on."

"But then he could have found the boys dead when he got home."

"If he did, he should have called 9-1-1 or the police to report what happened. No such report. And remember he had some surgery that morning; apparently had several pressure bandages on his face."

"Have any CSIs checked out that building? I know it might be Westchester CSI's, but it would help to know if there was evidence of blood, for instance."

"It has been searched and tested with luminol; no evidence of anything."

"How about the ground outside the building. Maybe they could have fallen off the roof?"

"If they fell thirty feet and hit the ground, there would for sure have been blood. No evidence in the building or in the area around it."

"How valid is luminol on the ground outside? What if it rained, for instance?"

"Nothing lasts forever, but blood lasts fairly long on the ground. If there were any trace of blood on the ground, the luminol tests should have picked that up. I don't know what would happen with a rainstorm. Blood is organic, maybe it could soak into the ground in a heavy rain. Certainly, a heavy rain could ruin luminol results on the grass itself, because the rain could basically wash the blades of grass."

"Did they find any traces of blood?"

"On some gardening instruments, like a hand cultivator, but not enough blood to be able to tell whose blood it was."

"A hand cultivator could have made the bear-claw marks on the boys."

"Yeah, I thought about that, but there would have been more blood someplace if they were ripping bodies up."

"The boys were still in their school uniforms when they were found, right?"

"Pieces of school uniforms, yeah."

"Had they been stripped?"

"Not exactly, but animals had made short work of their clothing. No sexual abuse was found if that's what you're asking."

"Not what I was thinking about, but I guess that's good."

"What were you thinking?"

"Just didn't recall whether they were wearing different clothes than when they went missing, that's all. That would have meant they either changed clothes or somebody changed their clothes after they were dead."

"We didn't find their backpacks," Mike said. "That's troublesome."

"Could they have left the backpacks in Ted's car?"

"Could have. Call Ted and ask if he found the backpacks, or if the boys were still wearing the backpacks when he took them to the gatehouse. Okay?"

I told him I would do that and get back to him right away. Then I called Ruth.

"Well, if it isn't the famous Hugo Miller!" she hooted into the phone when she picked up.

"You busy? I can call back later."

"Just pulling your leg, that's all, sweetie. Not busy. What's up?"

"I've had a couple of revealing talks with Ted Coniston. Gabriele and I drove up to Boston on our way to Kennebunkport. He'd never been to Maine, and he'd never been to a baseball game, so we were going to try to get into Fenway if we could get decent tickets. Anyway, I told you, I think, that Ted had told us he picked up the boys the day they disappeared."

"Yes, I was surprised."

"I was too, especially when he said he drove down from Boston because the boys wanted to visit their Uncle Ricky and his wife."

"Must have had time on his hands. That's four or five hours each way."

"He's just graduated from college and living with his mother. Probably antsy just to get away, I'd say. But he was also close with Eddie's sons, even though he's a good ten years older than Ed."

"Happy to talk about Ted any time. In case you haven't noticed, by the way, I think Ted is kinda sweet on your Italian dude friend."

"I know. Gabriele pulled a stunt that made it painfully obvious."

"Changing the subject, another Coniston cousin has shown up. His name is Hank. He's younger than Ricky by a good bit, but he's clearly on track to get rid of Ricky."

"Get rid of him? As in kill him?"

"Sorry, I didn't mean that at all. He wants to throw Ricky out of the Coniston Companies. Probably wants to take over himself."

"Did he just parachute in from the sky? Why didn't we know about him before?"

"He grew up in England, and more recently has been living in France. I don't think he's ever been in America. By the way, he has a title and is what they call an Oxford man."

"Title?"

"Baron Huntington, from his maternal great-grandfather. The families are related way, way back, but his father was American, so I guess he probably has dual citizenship."

"The title came through his mother?"

"Yes, but she never called herself Countess of Huntington, maybe because she was married to an American, or maybe because women sometimes can't inherit titles. Don't know. Her grandfather was Earl of Huntington. The title moved through her because her father didn't outlive his own father. She died a few years ago and a reduced version of the title landed on Hank."

"So, he's a Lord?"

"Not if you mean the House of Lords. Most of the hereditary members were thrown out a few years back, except for some dukes and a few others who are appointed by the monarch when the Prime Minister requests it. If Hank is a dual citizen, he might not want to be in the government, because he's only got one foot in the UK, so to speak. From what I can find, he's been a fund manager for a big French bank, most of his clients being British, which makes sense.

"I looked up Huntington online," she said. "The title was created during the Wars of the Roses. It more or less replaced another earldom called Pembroke. Pembroke is part of Wales, so maybe there is a Welsh bloodline that Hank carries, too."

"Does Ricky know about this?"

"I can't imagine he's in the dark. He's gotta know he's a target for any malcontents in the family."

"So where is Hank Coniston now?"

"He goes by Huntington, not Coniston."

"Okay, so where is Hank Huntington?"

"Paris, from what I can tell. If I look him up online, there's not a lot of information. I suspect he's well-off, and probably not anxious to publish his personal information. Like movie stars don't want their addresses published."

"Where's the connection to Coniston?"

"I think his mother was a cousin of Ricky's mother. The free genealogical sites online aren't very helpful when it comes to nobility."

I asked if she had time to meet me at Mike's office so we could go over this with him. She was proud of herself for finding this new guy and said yes immediately. So, I sent Mike a text telling him we had some news on the Coniston case and asking if he had time for Ruth and me to stop by to brief him. He texted back right away, that sooner was better. I told him we'd be there in a half-hour or so, and sent a text to Ruth.

Did you speak w Ted?

Not yet. You'll see why.

Ruth was already there when I got to Mike's precinct. True to form, she was wearing a coarse-woven, wheat-colored linen Chanel jacket over a white pullover shirt, and tight jeans. Red-bottomed Louboutin heels. The editor of Vogue would have approved. I'm what people might call a 'shlump', not slovenly, but not remarkable for anything except being taller than average. T-shirt and Levis with penny loafers. Both of my best friends look like magazine covers. Go figure.

The three of us sat in an interrogation room so Mike could have the conversation recorded. Ruth explained what she had found out about Hank Huntington, and that it seemed he might be trying to displace Ricky Coniston at the Coniston Companies.

"He's related through his mother? Is that what you said?" Mike asked.

"Ricky's mother's maiden name was Neval. Hank's mother the same. That's also Ricky's wife's maiden name, although she was a distant cousin, like a third cousin. I believe Hank's mom and Ricky's mom may have been closer cousins."

"Would it have benefitted Hank if Eddie's two boys were dead?"

"No way to tell unless we can get the shareholder lists of the Coniston Companies," she said. "If he is not on the list, he could be trying to get whatever he thinks is his fair share. If he is on the list, he could be planning to agitate from the inside."

"Hugo, we need to see what Ted has to say about Mr Huntington."

I texted Ted there and then. *Hi Ted, hope everything's good in Boston except the Red Sox. Do you know someone named Hank Huntington? Hugo*

No immediate response. Maybe he was driving or taking a nap or a swim.

"I'll see about getting a subpoena for shareholders and dividends or pay-outs from the Coniston Companies."

I asked Mike if he had lunch, or if he'd like to grab something with us. He said he needed to get cracking on some things, so he stayed in his office. Ruth and I walked the few blocks to Thalia, where the air conditioning was going on high and Brian had two dirty vodkas on the bar as soon as we sat down. I took a sip of the vodka and my phone buzzed. It was a text from Ted.

Sorry, I don't know anybody by that name. Mom says Huntington is a cousin that lives in France. She's never met him. Go Red Sox. Ted

I forwarded it to Mike and showed it to Ruth.

"Do you believe him?" she asked.

"I'm not very good at knowing who's telling the truth. That's Gabriele's super-hero weapon. Ted changed his story about what happened to the boys two or three times. I just don't know whether he's telling the truth, but I'm inclined to believe this text message. Maybe because he ends it with a Red Sox crack."

"But his mother knows Huntington, or at least knows who he is."

"I got the impression that Ted and his mother may not be receiving dividends or payouts from the Coniston Companies. He told me that his father left the two of them well off when he died, and from the way he said it, I thought they weren't on the list of people who got regular paychecks."

"If they're not getting dividends or whatever, that might make them sympathetic to Huntington if he is trying to oust Ricky Coniston," she said with her head cocked, like she was asking herself a question.

"I hear what you're saying, but that's quite a leap. We haven't even met Ted's mother. And remember, Ted spent summers at Ricky's home. I doubt he would have any part of trying to booby-trap Ricky."

"But he's a kid, right? A kid who lives with his mommy. Not normal. I wonder if he has a girlfriend."

"As if there was something wrong with Ted for living with his widowed mother. He just graduated from Boston College in finance. I wouldn't be surprised if he wanted to work toward a master's degree. Ricky did that, by the way. He and Ann lived on the West Side before they moved to Chappaqua, but Ricky lived in the Coniston Mansion until he and Ann married. Not with his mom, although she was still around at that point, but bunking in with his big brother and Lizzie."

She shrugged and threw back the rest of her vodka. "Just thinking, that's all." She waved at Brian and made a little circle in the air with her index finger that every bartender recognizes as "another round." I drank the rest of my vodka before the new ones arrived, and asked Brian if we could have an order of fries with some mayonnaise on the side. I know it sounds almost un-American to eat fries with mayo instead of ketchup, but that's the way I like them. I first encountered mayo with fries in Belgium, and I never looked back. I don't eat ketchup on anything. It's not food. It's like eating refabricated chips made from powdered potatoes and packed into cardboard cylinders. Not food.

I felt a hand on my shoulder. It was Mike. "Hey, buddy, looks like we are fated to have lunch together. We have the warrant to search the gatehouse-type building. I think it'll be served on them tomorrow. A few of our CSI's will do the search alongside the Westchester team." He and Ruth did the kiss-kiss thing (Mike's Italian, after all). He asked Brian for a sparkling water with lime.

"Two martini lunch?" he asked in a friendly tone.

"I guess so," I said. "I'm planning to have some spaghetti with red sauce. Not exactly what you'd expect to be a first choice at Thalia, but I like it."

There weren't any seats at the bar where the three of us could sit, so I asked the majordomo for a table in the back of the restaurant that isn't usually full at lunch. He took us to what they call the 'balcony', which is not a balcony, but it is a couple of steps up and has a guardrail kinda like what a balcony might have. The same place we'd been seated the last time we'd all eaten there together.

"Do you guys have any kind of work-up on Huntington?" Ruth asked Mike.

"Not chapter and verse, but we have his bio. We know he is not married but apparently has been in touch with the Westbrooks. Interpol thinks he may be negotiating to marry one of the Westbrook girls. That would make him Lizzie Coniston's brother-in-law."

He showed us a photo on his cellphone. A strapping young guy who looked like Eddie Coniston might have looked when he was young and still slim. Tall, fair-haired, broad-shouldered, looked like he might be a soccer player. Not at all like Ricky Coniston, who appeared shorter than average, with dark, messy-looking curly hair, and looked more like he might be a swimmer than a competitive athlete, either that or maybe he's just skinny. Nice-looking, but wouldn't turn heads. If the photo was accurate, Huntington seemed to radiate charisma, youth and good looks.

"I wouldn't want to run against anybody who looked that good," I said under my breath.

I turned to Mike. "Is it possible to find out if he enters the United States? Like can Immigration notify the NYPD?"

"Practically speaking, the answer to that is negative. How could the federal government notify all the airports and border crossings in the country to call Mike di Saronno if somebody named Hank Huntington tries to enter the country? And if they could, why would they? Has somebody accused him of a crime? No."

"Well, as to the question of how, all the Immigration officers have computers at their stations that they use to make sure you are who you say you are. I know those computers have notes in them about people who might be bad guys. I've seen people escorted away from Immigration at JFK to be interviewed. That's all."

"And who is going to decide that this rich man from France is a bad guy?"

"I don't know. You said Interpol sent you a bio of the man. Doesn't that mean they're keeping an eye on him?"

"I doubt that. What it meant regarding Mr Huntington is that the man is prominent and well-known in France, and Interpol sent us his bio when we asked. Immigration officials are not part of the police, just like the police are not part of Immigration. I don't know what they're looking for when people cross the border or go through Immigration at an airport.

I know that in New York, police do not help Immigration find undocumented people."

"Scuse me, gents," Ruth said. "If you're interested, I have been tap-tap-tapping on my phone and I know where Mr Huntington lives."

"Paris," Mike said definitively.

"No. Any other guesses?"

"Cap Ferrat?"

"Getting warm, but no cigar. He lives in Monaco, in an area called La Condamine. It's a part of Monaco that tourists seldom see because it is sandwiched between the 'Old City' where the Pink Palace is, and Monte Carlo, which is the part of Monaco where the James Bond flick 'Casino Royale' takes place. Never been there myself, so anything I tell you is something I found on the Internet."

"As it happens, I've been there," I offered. "No idea where La Condamine is, but most of Monaco except the Old City is high rise. Everybody wants a view of the Mediterranean."

"Well, what I found is an article in a very upper-crustish beautiful homes magazine with a French name. Apparently, he bought a stand-alone house. Something that I gather is very rare."

"Must have cost a pretty penny. I'm fairly sure I didn't see a house like that anywhere when I have been there."

"The article said it was purchased for more than a hundred million euros," Ruth said, and added an off-tune but heartfelt rendition of the first couple of lines of "If I were a rich man" from "Fiddler on the Roof."

"That's a pretty piece of change," Mike said. "I doubt he flies economy when he travels."

"I walked all around the Old City, which is very small and on a peninsula that curves around to create the yacht harbor and the cruise ship terminal. I stayed in Monte Carlo for a few days while I was at a conference on climate change. All of Monaco is fanatically clean, and it seems like they plant new flowers every night to replace old flowers that have the audacity to not be blooming. Kinda like a Disneyland version of an old European city. And wouldn't you know the seaside road in Monte Carlo is called Boulevard Princesse Grace, after Grace Kelly."

"I feel a field trip coming on," Ruth sang in a comic soprano-ish voice.

"Not something to undertake lightly," I said. "It's more than expensive, and you have to fly to Nice and then take a taxi to Monte Carlo. As I recall, the taxi fare is about a hundred euros each way."

"I see myself in a wide-brim white picture hat and classic Chanel."

"Up to you. Gabriele would never forgive us if we went without him."

"I hate to interrupt," Mike said. "What do you think you'd be doing in Monaco?"

"Shopping for a home," Ruth said in her best imitation of a *grande dame*. "What did you think? Maybe we'd just walk up to Mr Huntington's front door and ask to interview him?"

"And your goal with regard to the case of the two Coniston boys?"

"I think we'll be able to find a way to meet Mr Huntington. It seems like we'd be better off if we knew something about him."

"You won't be acting as a representative of the NYPD."

"Heaven forfend."

"Mike, I agree with Ruth. I'm worried about the cost, but we can look into it. I promise we'll behave if we go."

Mike put two twenty-dollar bills on the table. "I gotta get back to the office. You both and Gabriele are valuable assets for yours truly. Take care of yourselves."

As he walked out, Ruth was sending a text to Gabriele.

Chapter Twenty-three

As it turned out, Ruth was not flying blind. She had indeed thought seriously about a few days in Monte Carlo and took it far enough that she had already looked into flights and hotel rooms. As far as she was concerned, we were going, period, end of statement. She has been more hermit-like since Murray died, and I think she saw an opportunity to kick up her heels.

I know better than to walk into a buzz-saw, so I just smiled and waited for a speed bump that would prevent us from going. It seemed unlikely to gain for us any knowledge that would help with the Coniston Case. Even if Mr Huntington was out to oust Ricky from his job, that would be in the future, and the boys died in the past.

Gabriele was beyond excited and insisted on moving in with me while we got ready for the trip. He is well-fixed financially, due mostly to the huge success of Ora di Pranzo. He had been to Monte Carlo as a teenager when he worked as a steward on a cruise ship that docked there. But I gathered from what he said that he hadn't had time to see much of the city, even though it is postage-stamp small: one square mile, but strung out in a narrow strip along the water, culminating in the rocky stronghold of the Old City that curves back around to form the harbor.

"You know it's going to be seriously hot in Monte Carlo at this time of year?" I lobbed at Ruth.

"Give up," she snarled. "Like it's not hot in New York at this time of year? Besides, I looked it up and the average high this time of year is eighty – with almost no humidity. Perfect."

She is a volunteer at Carnegie Hall, and has been a contributor to their various charitable funds that help maintain the beautiful old hall that on its own would be bankrupt. She called some friends there and at the Metropolitan Opera, and asked if they knew – or knew of – Henry

Huntington, who stays in Monaco most of the time.

Bingo. It worked. Two trustees of an arts program I had never heard of, that funded small dance companies and museums that do not have heavy foot traffic but have unique collections, like the NY Historical Society on Central Park West, which is frequently so uncrowded that it seems almost empty, but has *all* of John James Audubon's original artwork, knew Huntington.

"A little finagling and we're going to have drinks with Mr Huntington," she punctuated that with a loud exhalation, hands on her hips, like she had been working up a sweat laboring in the full sun.

"You're the best, you know I love you." No speed bump. "What about flights and hotel?"

"Done. I may not be executive platinum on American Airlines for much longer, but I still have all of Murray's gazillion miles, enough for all of us business class. We have to fly to Heathrow or Frankfurt or Zurich and take a plane from there to Nice."

Murray was her husband who passed away a couple of years back; he was a 'garmento' and traveled all over the world fairly constantly to buy new lines of clothes for his business. He spent a lot of time in China, needless to say, and India, I guess, Viet Nam, places like that. Also, Mexico.

I don't know how she managed to keep his miles after he died, not something I've ever tried to do. But she usually gets what she wants. We've been buddies for ages.

"By the way, they have Uber in Nice, so we won't have to wander around with our luggage looking for a taxi."

Like I said, she usually gets what she wants. Not unexpectedly, so does Gabriele. I think one of the reasons I am so attracted to the two of them is that they are so self-sufficient, so determined, and they hang on to what they want like a bulldog.

Gabriele arrived with a duffel bag that looked fairly stuffed with whatever was in it. "What's in that?" I asked, pointing at the bag.

"Is clothes. *I miei vestiti sono nella borsa.*"

"Clothes? I thought maybe you packed a pillow in there." I took the bag from his hand and said, "It's heavy enough to be bricks."

He turned to Ruth. "When we go Monaco?"

She smiled and said, "How about tomorrow? It's Saturday, usually a good day to travel, and better prices, too."

Gabriele beamed and looked at me. I nodded, and said, "If we want to go to the casino or the opera, remember they want people to dress properly."

"I bring *abito nero* from Ora di Pranzo."

He meant he brought his tuxedo. I have a tuxedo, too, but it's tighter than it used to be, and yes, I'm perfectly aware that suits do not shrink, but bodies get larger. I can still wear it, but I don't like the idea of taking a monkey suit on a fact-finding trip. By the way, Ruth has ridiculed me in the past for not wearing 'correct' (patent leather) shoes with a tuxedo. Not gonna pack those either.

I nodded to Gabriele, "Maybe a tuxedo would be a little too much. You don't need to look like James Bond. No need for Ruth to take an evening gown, either. I usually pack a navy-blue suit or wear a blue blazer and pack some grey or tan slacks. Maybe I should take the suit this time. And dark, solid-color ties. In Monte Carlo, you'll have less need for casual clothing – other than swimming gear."

We did indeed go the next day. I sent Mike a text telling him we'd be back from Monaco in a few days and would let him know anything that turned up.

Gabriele is a very eager flyer, and no matter how many times he has flown across the ocean, he never gets over the privileges of flying in business class, on chairs that recline to flat beds, of palatable food and endless wine, not to mention a television screen that has pretty much whatever you want. He has got to the place where he doesn't start pushing buttons the minute he sits down, but he is a very 'active' passenger once the plane is in the air.

Airplanes are the only location where I will drink whisky before five o'clock. This time around, Gabriele joined me in a scotch on the rocks after we took off on the midnight flight from JFK to Heathrow. I sometimes have a drink at lunch if I am at a restaurant, but very seldom drink anything outside the hours of five o'clock to midnight. Here we were drinking whisky at about one-thirty in the morning New York time – when I would normally be asleep. Gabriele is more of a night-owl, due to his work at Ora di Pranzo, which doesn't close the doors until about one o'clock.

All three of us only take carry-on luggage. The long-haul planes have more overhead storage space, and the business cabin has fewer people per overhead bin. But if we had checked anything, it could have been checked through to Nice, via a British Airways flight about four hours after we were scheduled to land. American and British are partners in a worldwide group of airlines that honor each other's frequent-flyer programs. So, if you have enough miles, you can fly from JFK to Nice without paying any folding green other than a small fee for using the service. Since Ruth still had all of what was left of Murray's miles, that is exactly what we were doing. Everything's better when it's free (or when it seems free). Of course, once we're on the ground, we were back in the not-free normal world. But even in Monte Carlo, three nights in a beachfront hotel is a lot less than a business-class ticket back to New York.

When I was still traveling on business, I used to go to a conference every March in Monte Carlo (deductible and partially covered because it was for clients who partially reimbursed me). At that time, I usually stayed in the Monte-Carlo Beach Hotel, which is at the far eastern end of Boulevard Princesse Grace. I had told Ruth what I knew, but Ruth found a Fairmont Hotel where we could get two rooms with two double beds for about half what it cost at Monte-Carlo Beach. Fair enough. Between Gabriele and me, neither one is a snorer, so two double beds is perfect.

As it turned out, the Monte Carlo Fairmont is largely built on pylons in the water of the Mediterranean, although the front of the hotel is on dry land. It has a good spa, a sparkling big swimming pool, and several places to eat. The rate included – as it does in most hotels on that side of the Atlantic – breakfast. I couldn't recall whether it was there the last time I was in Monte Carlo, even though I walked to the conference near the casino and back every day I was there, and would have been walking right by it. I was always captivated by the Lamborghini showroom on the other side of the Boulevard, which may be the reason why I had a blind spot for a fairly large building. There is also a small botanical garden that showcases cactus and succulents.

There was in fact an Uber car waiting at the airport for us, and the driver whisked us away with a minimum of fuss and bother. Even so, it took the better part of an hour to get where we were going, even though the Nice International Airport is virtually on the beach – there are serious mountains not far inland that rise up to the Alps pretty quickly. That would make it unwise to build an airport there. I had booked the car on my cellphone, so the bill was automatically charged to my credit card. I was also paying for a piece of Ruth's room, since I was only paying half of the room Gabriele and I would be staying in. Ruth and I both figured we owed Gabriele for the many lunches and dinners and drinks that had been comped over the years, so Ruth and I planned to split meals half-and-half, so that Gabriele would be 'comped'.

I'm not wealthy. I have enough income to live well. But I couldn't go on this kind of jaunt often.

When I checked in, there was a message waiting for me from somebody named Clint Caine, with a phone number. I put it in my pants pocket and forgot about it, since I had no recollection of that name. I figured it was a scam artist, or somebody looking for someone else, not me, maybe whoever was in that room the day before. Alliterative names like that have an odd smell to me, like they were made-up, like a *nom de guerre.*

As Gabriele and I were unpacking and hanging things in the surprisingly spacious closet that needed to let wrinkles hang out, the phone rang. I figured it was Ruth, but it was Clint Caine.

"Mr Miller? My name is Clint Caine. I left a message for you at registration. Sorry to be a bother, do you have a minute?"

He sounded like a real person, slight French accent behind what sounded more like an American voice, which would not be unusual in Monaco, since it is surrounded on three sides by France. "I'm in the middle of unpacking, but I can take a minute out. What can I do for you?

Have we met?"

"I do not believe we have met. I live here in Monaco, but I have family relations in the United States. I was hoping to be able to buy you a drink while you are here."

"If you're selling time-shares, I'm not interested."

"Not selling anything. I work with Mr Huntington."

"Henry Huntington?"

Gabriele looked up when he heard that name, and stopped hanging up shirts.

"Yes. His name is familiar to you?"

"Yes. I have made the acquaintance of some of his relations in the Coniston family around New York and New England."

"My research tells me that you have been in the field of public relations for quite some time," the man on the phone said.

"I was, still am in some ways, but the company I built is entirely concentrated on sports teams or athletes. I did not travel here on company business."

"Are you on holiday?"

"Sorry to be uncivil, but I really don't know who you are, and I don't see that question as appropriate."

"My apologies. I didn't mean to be impolite. Might it be possible to have a drink?"

"I'm not here alone. Two friends are with me."

"Please feel free to bring them along. I can meet you in the Saphir24 bar in your hotel."

"Tell you what. I'll talk to them and see if they are interested in meeting, and I'll let you know. I have your telephone number, the one you left on your message."

"I appreciate your time, and look forward to meeting you."

Click.

"I help?" Gabriele asked.

"Maybe you could see if Ruth is settled in, and whether she might have some time to talk."

He left. As it turned out, Ruth's room was on a different floor, but

Gabriele was back very shortly after that, with Ruth in tow.

They were both ready to meet Clint Caine whenever he wanted to have that drink.

"When you were contacting real estate agencies a house in Monaco, did you come across Mr Caine?"

"Sorry, no."

"I told him I'd let him know if we wanted to have a drink with him."

I sent a text message to Mr Caine saying we would be happy to meet him for a drink at his convenience.

My phone buzzed shortly after I sent the text message.

I can be there in half-hour.

There are three of us. I'm tall and a senior citizen, grey hair, and I usually wear a baseball cap because I'm partly bald and a cap keeps me from getting a sunburn on my scalp. My friends are happy to meet.

I'm tall too. Originally English, fair skin and hair. I'll be in a blue linen jacket.

See you in the lobby. I'll probably be wearing a navy-blue jacket and jeans.

C U soon

The bar was in an outdoor terrace with glass pony walls to keep people from falling into the water. Quite beautiful, and by the time we got there, it was getting on for twilight. Clint Caine was waiting for us next to the door, and spotted us when we got off the elevator.

He introduced himself to the three of us, and thanked us for joining him.

Ruth held her hand out to him and said, "Nice to meet you, Mr Huntington."

"I'm Clint Caine," he said, taking her hand and starting to bend over to kiss it.

"No, you're not, you're Hank Huntington. I've seen your photos."

He dropped her hand and looked like he might turn and leave. He was taller than me, looked like a surfer dude in his late thirties. Sun-bleached hair, blue eyes, could easily have been a runway model.

Gabriele shook his hand and offered his name, Gabriele Cortese.

"As the lady said, I am Hank Huntington. *Piacere di conoscerti, Signor Cortese.*"

"*È un piacere conoscerti anche tu,*" Gabriele said, with a slight bow from the waist.

"As I am told, you work with the New York Police Department."

I spoke up. "I do, and my friends are good enough to help with what I do for the NYPD."

"Are you here on New York police business?"

"No. We are working on the case of the Coniston boys in New York City, but we are not here on behalf of the NYPD."

"Why are you here?"

"To enjoy this beautiful city and country, and to meet you," Ruth answered.

"To meet me? Why?"

"I'm interested in a *pied a terre* here in Monaco, and I read an article that said you have one of the most beautiful homes in the country. I wanted to see if you have any hints for me on where to look, although I'm only looking for an apartment."

Gabriele was sizing Huntington up, his arms crossed.

"I don't have any hints. I have a house, not an apartment, and it was luck that I found it."

"Why did you want to see us?"

"Because I thought you were working with the police, and I believe my cousin, Richard Coniston, had his nephews killed."

"Hmm, I think we should have that drink," I said.

Huntington had a table reserved on the terrace, one with a big umbrella over it. We sat down and he signaled to the waiter, who appeared to know Huntington.

"Margarita with salt?" the waiter asked.

Huntington nodded.

"What may I bring your guests?" he said, looking at the three of us.

I ordered a dirty vodka straight up with olives. Ruth and Gabriele wanted the same. The waiter left.

"Why would Mr Coniston have the boys murdered?" I asked.

"They were preventing him from taking over the Coniston family fortune," he said matter-of-factly. "It's a lot of money. Better men than Richard Coniston have committed crimes for money."

"Your relationship with the Conistons is what?"

"My mother and Eddie Coniston's wife, Elizabeth, are cousins. I've never met Elizabeth, and never met Eddie. I met Richard because my hedge fund co-invested in a leveraged buyout with the Coniston Companies."

"He goes by Ricky, not Richard," Ruth said. "And apparently the dividends being paid by the Coniston Companies are significantly higher than they were under Eddie Coniston."

"I have no way of knowing that. I own no shares in the Coniston Companies, so I do not receive dividends."

The waiter brought the drinks, and put a small bowl of roasted, salted nuts in front of each of us. Gabriele raised his martini glass, smiled and said "*Cin Can,*" an Italian toast more or less like the American toast of "Cheers." We all took a sip of our drinks.

"It is a pleasure to meet you," Huntington said, gazing at each of us in turn. He took another sip of his margarita with a salted rim.

"I've known the Conistons for decades," Ruth said. "I knew Eddie and Lizzie Coniston from the Opera Club at the Metropolitan Opera, and met Ricky and his wife, Ann, when they used Eddie's tickets from time to time. Your statement about Ricky being involved in the murder of Eddie's sons is the direct opposite of what I know of Ricky, a decent man who has had to cope with tragedy in his family. His wife has a rare form of dementia and doesn't recognize anyone, including Ricky. His only son died as a teenager a couple of years ago. He is very much alone, and apparently has grown the Coniston Companies significantly since he took over when Eddie stopped working because he was sick. That was just a few months before Eddie died."

"Signor Huntington, I also know Ricky Coniston for long time. He come *frequentemente a la mia ristorante*, Ora di Pranzo, many time.

All *famiglia* like him. I like him. Not believe Ricky kill boys."

I refrained from gilding the lily, since Ruth and Gabriele had said it so well.

"I understand you are friendly with Mr Coniston. I have never met the man, but from what I have learned from people in my family, there may be a darker side of Richard Coniston, unlike the man you know."

"And if you are correct, what do you think should happen?" I asked.

"The family should replace him at the Coniston Companies, and the police should investigate Mr Coniston regarding the deaths of the boys."

"Replace him with whom?"

"Someone honest and competent, with a great track record."

"Like yourself?"

"I enjoy living here in Monaco, never even thought about visiting New York City."

He sat back in his chair and smiled. He had a very impressive and charismatic way about him, but I found myself thinking he wanted Ricky Coniston's job and control of the family fortune.

"But you are a portfolio manager, and even Ricky Coniston has said that managing the Coniston Companies is more like managing a family office than operating a company," Ruth chimed in.

"We're not trying to make you out to be a bad guy," I said. "As you can imagine, I probably know more than you do about this sad turn of events that ended with two young boys losing their lives. I know that many people have theories about what happened. I've been up close and personal with this crime, and I guarantee you that the solution – when we find it – is not going to be as simple as arresting one person for doing it."

"You should come New York. Great city, good food, good people," Gabriele said. "I make you best dinner you ever have in you life."

"Look around you. It's nearly impossible to find anyplace better than Monaco."

"Any chance we could see your house?" Ruth asked.

"Unfortunately, I'm leaving town this evening for two or three weeks. I'll be in Paris working with our financial department on an audit of the hedge fund. I'm having some work done in the house while I'm gone. So it is not a good time to tour the house. If you haven't been here before, go to the casino, Cafe de Paris, and The Grill. Then walk around the Old City. Be sure to see Monaco Cathedral. It's not ancient and breathtaking like Nôtre Dame de Paris, but it is beautiful. The Old City is very small. You won't be tired after you walk around it. If you have a chance, go to Eze, a village just west of Monaco, in France, Provence. You can get there in a taxi, very short ride, or I can send my car and driver if you would let me; since I will be away, he will have plenty of time. Beautiful place, lots of architectural interest, too. Don't forget to have a late dinner at The Grill. Quite a treat. It will surprise you."

I had finished my dirty vodka. Ruth had sipped at hers, but seemed to be ignoring it. Gabriele had finished his and eaten all the roasted nuts at his place, as well as mine. Of course, he never gains any weight.

Huntington looked at his watch, and said, "I am afraid I have to leave. I need to get my luggage and be at the airport within the next two hours. My apologies. I have told the waiter to put the charges on my account, so don't hurry. My thanks to you for agreeing to meet."

He pushed his chair back and stood up, so all three of us did the same. He shook my hand and Gabriele's, and bowed to Ruth. She smiled at him and held her hand out. He shook it carefully.

When he turned and walked out, we sat back down. "I think I'll have another drink," I said. "What do you think?"

"About Huntington?" Ruth asked.

I nodded and signaled to the waiter, who scurried over to the table. "We'd appreciate another round." He bowed and hurried away.

"He's a hunk," she said. "I bet he never gets turned down for a date. One of the biggest homes in Monaco and looks like a movie star."

"Listen to you," I said, cocking my head a bit.

Gabriele laughed.

"You noticed, too," she said to Gabriele, and blew him a kiss.

He nodded and gestured to the waiter, who arrived with the drinks, and three small bowls of potato chips mixed with salted pretzel sticks.

The waiter was ogling Gabriele, who pretended not to notice.

"Looks like you have a fan club, too," Ruth said to Gabriele. Big smiles.

Ruth's phone buzzed. She looked at it and said, "It's a text message from Mr Huntington, saying he hopes we will let his driver take us to Eze tomorrow morning. I think we should accept. Is ten o'clock good with you two?"

I nodded, and Gabriele seconded me. She tapped a bit on her phone, and hit 'Send', then said to both us, "Odd when he blurted out that Ricky had the boys killed, don't you think?"

"That made no sense to me," I said. "But he didn't blink when I stared at him."

"He want take Coniston money," Gabriele said.

"I think you're right, as usual." I pushed my bowl of salty goodies toward him. "I can't eat that kind of thing and not gain weight." I picked up my martini glass and took a healthy slurp of the salty, olive-flavored vodka.

"Not only are you right, you're better looking than Huntington," Ruth said with a wink. "But I think he's on thin ice accusing Ricky Coniston."

"Mike will be interested to hear our post-mortem on this."

She held her glass up and said, "Here's to Mike di Saronno. A good cop."

Chapter Twenty-four

"Actually, I doubt he has anything a court would call evidence. I think if he did, he would have said so," I said to Mike, after telling him about our conversation with Hank Huntington. "Even if he didn't want to share any of the specifics." I was responding to Mike's simple question about whether Huntington backed up his accusation with anything tangible.

Mike drank his coffee and stared at the mirror in the interrogation room where we were sitting. "So," Mike said slowly, "what do you think we should do?"

I told him that I didn't think Huntington was interested in visiting the United States. "When I said something to him about replacing Ricky Coniston, he was very clear that he was not going to live either in or near New York City. If he is interested, maybe he thinks he could run the Coniston Companies from Monaco, or that he could meld it with his existing business in Paris, and close down the headquarters office in New York. But the impression he was trying to convey was that he had no interest in running the Coniston Companies. Is that true? I doubt it."

"You think he is going to try to get Ricky Coniston thrown out?"

"He's a hedge fund guy. I think he was sending up a trial balloon, not firing a shot across the bow. He pretty clearly knew that it would get back to Mr Coniston, but he may have no intention of following through."

"Hugo, do you have plans for today? I mean, are you jammed for time?"

"Nah. I seldom go to the office any more, and I'm jet-lagged after two planes and a five-hour layover at Heathrow coming back from Monte Carlo."

He said he had to take a phone call in his office, and asked if I would wait. I said okay.

Ruth, Gabriele and I did in fact go to Eze the next morning after meeting with Mr Huntington, but we didn't use Mr Huntington's chauffeur to get there. It is very medieval-looking, built entirely from stone and perched on the top of a hill, with a real wall around it. I took a bunch of photos on my phone. Gabriele was less impressed than Ruth and I were, but maybe it looks like a lot of places on Capri, where he spent his formative years. We also spent most of the afternoon and evening after Eze seeing the sights of Monaco. It is very pretty, and as clean as a Disney theme park.

I had never been in Le Grill, thought it would just be a run-of-the-mill high-end eatery and watering hole with super-expensive prices. I was wrong. The food was better than just good, and just before midnight, there was a slight rumble, like a machine turning on, and the painted ceiling parted in the middle and retracted to open the room to a full view of the stars and the moon. Apparently, they do that every night unless it's raining. The retracting roof was installed decades back when the building was remodeled and Le Grill ended up on the top floor. It was dismantled and reinstalled after a major renovation in the early 2000s. It really is a surprise when they do it. Maybe not enough of a surprise to justify the prices, but what the heck, right? They did send over three snifters of Louis XIII cognac after dinner, which was apparently in response to Gabriele handing his Ora di Pranzo business card to the majordomo. We flew home the next day, which was the day before my meeting with Mike. Ruth didn't look at any apartments – no surprise since it would take a miracle to transplant her from her Park Avenue classic eight to anywhere else. Well, maybe Cobble Hill in Brooklyn, where she grew up.

Mike sauntered back into the room with a broad smile. "Ricky Coniston is on his way over here. I told him what you told me about Mr Huntington. I couldn't tell what his reaction was, but clearly it has some priority if he's dropping everything to find out more."

I said nothing, but it was probably easy to tell that I would have preferred not to be at a meeting with Ricky Coniston to talk about his distant cousin's accusation.

"How about a coffee?" Mike asked.

I have come to realize over the years that he uses coffee as a cure-all, the way some people use a glass of wine or a dirty vodka. "Sure, just black for me, thanks."

I had only taken one sip when Ricky Coniston appeared at the top of the stairs. Mike walked to the doorway, waved and offered Coniston some coffee. He declined.

He looked at me, and said, "Detective di Saronno told me you met with Hank Huntington in Monaco."

"Yes, we did. Two friends and me. We had a couple of drinks in the hotel bar. He asked if I worked with the NYPD, and I said yes, but that I was not in Monaco on NYPD business. My friend, Ruth Jensen, was interested in finding a small apartment somewhere in Monaco so she could escape from New York winters if she wanted to."

"How did you happen to meet Mr Huntington, if I may ask?"

"We didn't happen to meet him. He called me at the hotel and invited us for drinks. We hadn't even unpacked. But I knew that he was probably a distant cousin of yours, and accepted, since I have been assisting Mike concerning your nephews."

"How do you suppose he knew you were there?"

"No idea. Maybe he has connections at the airport, or maybe he has someone here in New York who keeps an eye on things for him."

"What did he have to say?"

"He said almost right away he thought you were behind what happened to the boys."

"You're right. We are probably cousins, but very far removed. He has been in touch with my sister-in-law, Elizabeth, and apparently he said something similar to her. He also brought up the subject of possibly marrying one of Eddie's daughters, who are, of course, my nieces. That would bring him very close to me. I've never met him, as far as I can recall."

"He's very well put together, makes a strong impression, seems very friendly and accommodating. I'd say good looking, too."

"And he thinks I'm a criminal, or at least that's what he said."

I nodded.

Mike leaned forward looking at Ricky Coniston and said, "But he didn't offer any evidence for why he said what he said. Right, Hugo?"

"He basically just accused Mr Coniston of being behind the boys' deaths. No backup that I heard. I thought it was odd that he would make an accusation like that and not back it up with anything. Like I told Mike, I think it could be a trial balloon of some kind, maybe something that he was not sure would work. He's a hedge fund manager, so he probably understands the politics of making an accusation like that."

"If he thinks he's going to marry one of Eddie's daughters, he probably would try to throw mud at me so he could take over the Coniston Companies."

"He said he had no interest in visiting New York, much less living here."

"His business is in some ways quite similar to what we do at the Coniston Companies. He probably thinks he could do it remotely, from Monaco or Paris."

"I take it you don't think that would work."

"If I could manage our investments from home, I'd be doing it already. It's true we don't have an active hand in managing any of the companies we've invested in, even the ones we own all the shares of. But we have Board seats on each and every one of the portfolio companies. That means I have to spend all day every day keeping up with what's going on."

"But you can't sell your shares, can you?" Mike asked. "I mean, your companies aren't public, right?"

"That's correct, our companies are all privately held. Many of our investments are what you might call Private Equity. There are significant cash flows associated with those investments. But if a company goes sour, we've been able so far to unload investments successfully. I suspect his hedge fund's investments are all traded publicly someplace. That way he can hedge them, protect them from downdrafts in valuation."

"Have you had any communication with Mr Huntington?" Mike asked.

"Not so far, but I have a feeling I will hear from him soon." He didn't look worried; no wrinkling on his forehead. He looked healthy and relaxed. "Detective, I want you to know that Huntington's idea about me is hogwash. Pure crap."

Mike looked at the ceiling and said, "We believe the boys were killed, whether on purpose or by accident, at your home."

He looked like he'd been startled. He stood up and looked directly into Mike's eyes. "Why haven't you told me this before?" Now he was angry. He stopped blinking his eyes and glared at Mike.

"The last place they were, was in the gatehouse-like building near the fence."

The anger disappeared. "How did you find that out?"

"Ted dropped them off there, because they wanted to play some video games, and they wanted to wait until you got home because they wanted to see you."

"Ted?"

"Your nephew from Boston."

"How did they find out I wasn't home?"

"The boys apparently told Ted they wanted to visit you and their aunt. He didn't know you had a surgical procedure scheduled for that day. He had just graduated from college and had some time on his hands, so he drove from Boston and picked them up on Columbus Avenue near their school. They drove to your place, found that you were not home, and visited your wife briefly, but of course she didn't know who they were or anything about you. The nurse or caregiver took Mrs Coniston for a walk in the direction of the barn. Ted offered to take the boys home, but they asked him to let them stay to see you. That seems to be the last time they were seen alive, at least by anyone we've talked to."

"Why didn't you tell me that Ted picked them up? I could at least have tried to track them down. They were in the Kids' House? Nobody ever told me." Now he was losing his composure, tears rolling down his cheeks, trying to stay under control, but he had a frantic look in his eyes. "Ted used to stay with us in the summers, back when my son was still healthy and the boys were hero-worshipping the older boys." He put his face in his hands and sobbed.

"Probably nobody knew where they were," Mike said. "Mrs Coniston and the nurse walked in the opposite direction. The boys got into Ted's car and he drove off. But if the nurse saw them, she didn't know he dropped them off at that building as he was exiting the property."

"You've had a hard time, Mr Coniston," I said. "I wish I could help."

He shook his head and choked out the words that meant he had to leave. Then he left.

Chapter Twenty-five

As I was getting ready to text Gabriele and Ruth to see if they could come over to my place, my phone buzzed that I had received a text, which turned out to be from Ted Coniston.

You told Ricky that I dropped the boys off at his place the day they went missing?

I didn't, NYPD did, also told him that Henry Huntington accused Ricky of being behind the deaths of the boys

On my way to New York. Can U C me?

Not right now, later ok.

I'm not even to Hartford yet. Maybe 2 hours or so?

LMK timing. No worries. Keep calm and carry on

Fortunately, Ruth and Gabriele both said they'd be right over. I took a shower and put on a fresh t-shirt and clean jeans. Also made a smallish screwdriver and swallowed it fast in a couple of quick gulps. I have an 'essential tremor' in my hands from time to time, usually when I'm being stressed. It's a genetic thing, lots of my relatives have it, too. If I drink something with alcohol in it, the tremor is repressed for a while. Oddly enough, although I sometimes have a hard time using a fork, the tremor doesn't seem to affect my ability to use a keyboard. Go figure.

Gabriele got to my place first. He lives in Brooklyn Heights and he can take the G train, not a long ride to a subway station near my apartment. Ruth rang the bell a few minutes later.

"I need a drink," she said.

"Your wish is my command, madame."

I heard the toilet flush and Gabriele walked into the living room buckling his belt.

"We're going to have a drink," I said. "You want one?"

"Whisky," he said. "Neat."

"Bowmore okay? Or Lagavullin?" He looked a little puzzled so I said, "The Bowmore is smoother, easier to drink. Lagavullin is what bartenders call 'medicinal-tasting,' a little bitter."

"Bowmore," he nodded, "three fingers." I handed him a whisky glass that once belonged to my grandfather. Irish crystal (he had a lot of relatives in Ireland). I found the bottle of Bowmore and handed it to him. Then I retrieved two martini glasses from the cabinet, filled them about halfway, and poured in a bit of the liquid from an olive jar, threw a couple of olives in each glass and handed one to Ruth.

"Cheers," she said.

Gabriele lifted his juice-glass-sized drink and sipped the light-colored whisky. Ruth and I clinked lightly, so as not to slosh the vodka over the edge. Gabriele winced a bit, clearly not much of a whisky-drinker. I smiled at him. He made an "I don't like this" face.

"How about one of these instead?" I said in his direction, lifting my glass. "Here, just take mine and give me your glass." I took his glass into the kitchen and put it in the sink, made another dirty vodka for myself. When I walked back into the living room, I raised my glass and said "*Salud.*" We all took a sip.

I ran over what happened at the meeting with Mike and Ricky Coniston, and the brief text exchange with Ted, who said he was on his way and would arrive in a couple of hours. "He was somewhere north of Hartford when we had the text chat, which was shortly before you got here."

"What was Ricky like when you and Mike met with him?" Ruth asked. "Nervous? Mad?"

"He seemed intent on finding out what Huntington said to us. He was upset that nobody told him that Ted dropped the boys off at his home, and the last time Ted saw them was when he let them out of the car at that Kids' House. He was curious about how we came to meet Huntington. I told him that Huntington contacted us, not the other way around.

"He wanted to know how Huntington knew we were going to be there. I told him I had no idea. Do you, Ruth?"

"I probably mentioned his name to some of the real estate agents

I spoke to, because I had read that article about the house he bought. Other than that, I don't have a clue. Nobody at the NYPD but Mike knew we were going, as far as I know. You didn't tell Ted, did you?"

"I don't think so, no. Of course, if he has been talking to Lizzie Coniston, he could be aware of my name, and it *was* my room he called. He could have a mole at the airport or in Immigration. It would probably be easy to find out what hotel we'd be staying at. I bet hotel reservations are shared with the Société des Bains de Mer."

"What's that?"

"It's theoretically a publicly traded company, but the state owns control of it, so it is basically an arm of the government. Dates back to the 1890s, I think. Aristotle Onassis bought control of it when it was freely trading because he wanted to build some hotels in Monaco, but Prince Rainier approved the issuance of a lot of new stock for the Société and dropped Onassis's ownership to less than a third. The state bought all the stock. It runs the casino, Le Grill, the Opera, Café de Paris, Hôtel de Paris, and One Monaco, which is where a lot of business conventions are held. I suspect they know everything worth knowing in Monaco."

"Anyway, I guess it doesn't matter," Ruth said. "However he found you – and us – we got what we went to Monaco for. We got to meet him."

"Remember, he used a stage name when he called my room. Clint something. So he wasn't planning to reveal himself."

"He *mascalzone,* not good man," Gabriele said. "*Maloik.*" (Naples slang for "evil eye".) "He want hurt Ricky Coniston."

"I figured that out when he accused Ricky of killing the boys. What is *mascalzone?*" My Italian vocabulary is mostly okay, but this was one I had never heard before.

"*Mascalzone* is bad person, not tell truth, stab in you back."

I found an Italian-English dictionary on my cellphone. It said the translation was 'scoundrel'. My guess is it would be a much less polite word than 'scoundrel' though. Not something you would say if your mother was in the room.

We decided to have another drink. Gabriele went into the kitchen and had a gaze at the contents of the fridge. There was an avocado on the counter. He whipped up some guacamole and I told him there was a bag of chips in the pantry.

He put a basket of chips on the table with the fluffy green dip. "*Eccola!*" he said, standing back and looking at his creation. "Is very pepper. *Stai attento.*" He warned us to be careful.

My cellphone buzzed. It was Ted. He was circling around the block looking for a parking place. I told Gabriele and Ruth that he would be up shortly. Gabriele scooped up some of the avocado dip with a tortilla chip and put the whole thing in his mouth. Big smile. He took a bow.

"*Ted vuole fare sesso con te,*" I said it lickety-split in the hope that Ruth wouldn't understand. I was reminding him that Ted was gay and attracted to him.

"*Grazie,*" he said to me and winked. "*Lo so.*" He already knew that, he was saying, and he handed me a chip with a splotch of guacamole on it. He was right, it was spicy, but I like it that way.

The doorbell rang. I opened the door and welcomed him with a polite hug. When I turned to take Ted into the living room, Gabriele was standing there looking at me. Then he looked at Ted and held out his hand to shake. Ruth was standing in the kitchen doorway and waved to Ted.

I asked him if he wanted a drink and pointed to the three martini glasses on the coffee table. "A couple of fingers of scotch?" he asked me. "I get anxious driving fast on the New England Thruway. A drink would hit the spot."

I got another of the small whisky glasses down from the cupboard. "Neat or with ice?" I asked him.

"Some ice please. It's hot out and I try not to run the AC in the car," he said. "Because it makes the gas mileage lower. I know it sounds silly. My mom tells me all the time that saving a quarter or fifty cents is not a good reason to turn the AC off."

"I thought you said your father left you and your mother comfortable."

"You're right. He did. I don't have to pinch pennies. I turn off the AC so it will decrease the greenhouse gas coming out of the tailpipe."

"So, you're a tree-hugger," Ruth said with a smile when I handed the scotch to him. She offered her martini glass for a clink, which he accepted. "The guacamole has a lot of spice to it. Gabriele just made it, so it's fresh. Give it a try, but take a small bite first."

"Pepper sauce in guacamole," Gabriele said to Ted as he shook his hand up and down like he was trying to get water off.

"My Uncle Ricky was all over me for dropping off the boys and not letting him know. I understand why, but I had no idea anything would happen to them. You have to believe me," Ted said, looking straight at me.

Frankly, it had never occurred to me to think Ted could have been involved in the deaths of the boys. I nodded to him and patted him on the shoulder. "I think you're a good guy, Ted. We'd like for you to go over what happened as you were leaving and dropping off the boys. Did you take them into the building? What did it look like inside? Was there anybody inside when they got there?"

He looked like he was having a hard time keeping his composure. He plopped down on the couch and stared out the balcony window across the room from him. I ate a couple of chips with the fiery avocado dip. I loved it, and gave Gabriele an enthusiastic thumbs-up, as I reached for another one with the other hand.

Ted sipped at the scotch and ate several chips with guacamole in a row. "I didn't realize I was so hungry," he said. "Anyway, yes I did stop and walked with them into the downstairs playroom. If there was somebody else there, I didn't see them; it seemed to me that nobody was there. The lights were turned on, which I thought was odd, but I didn't think that meant somebody was lurking someplace in the shadows. The boys headed straight to the video games and started shooting down bad guys. I walked up the three flights of stairs to the roof. Nobody there either. I made sure the boys had their cellphones, and that they plugged them in to charge them. I wrote down Uncle Ricky's number. Then I left."

"I was under the impression that the boys didn't have cellphones, because we tried to ping the numbers and there was no response," I said.

"They had them. Maybe they were powered down. I didn't

check."

He looked up at the ceiling, like he was trying to remember something. "You know, I should have stayed there until Uncle Ricky got home. I wanted to get home. It was a long day and I was tired. I always thought of Uncle Ricky's house as a place where I was safe all the time. It never occurred to me that something might happen to the boys."

"You said you walked up three flights of stairs to the roof," Ruth said. "What's on the second and third floors?"

"Oh, bedrooms on the second and a kitchen on the third. It's usually stocked with healthy food and fresh fruit, but there's a stove and oven, so you could cook there if you wanted."

"But you didn't look in there?"

"No, I wanted to see what kind of shape the outdoor roof furniture was in, since I hadn't been there in ages. You know, I wanted to see if there were bird droppings all over, but there weren't any. The roof is flat, with a kind of pony wall all the way around it, probably five feet tall, so you couldn't accidentally fall off the edge. When I was a kid, I used to walk on the top of the wall and pretend I was a tightrope walker. But it's almost two feet wide, easy to walk on."

"If you did fall, what's the ground like below?" she asked.

"Grass I think, but I never paid any attention." He thought for a minute. "Yeah, grass. But I can tell you from experience that the ground around there is pretty solid. Hard to get a shovel to make a dent in it, even if you put your whole weight on the top of the shovel blade. I think if somebody fell from the roof, they'd have to break some bones, depending on how they fell. Ribs for sure. It's probably thirty feet down."

Gabriele leaned forward. "Boys walk on wall, too?"

"No idea. I don't think I've been on the roof other than when I dropped them off for maybe ten years. No, maybe six or seven years. Before I went to college. When I was a kid, my cousin, Ricky's Edward, would walk on the wall. I think he saw me doing it. When he was alive people called him Eddie Ricky, and they called me Eddie George." He started to smile, and thought better of it. "But I like Ted better."

"If boys walk on wall, fall happen easy. Even strong wind make fall."

"The Medical Examiner in Westchester determined that the cause of death was blunt force trauma, probably from a fall," I said.

"Oh my God. It's my fault, isn't it?"

Poor Ted. He can't be responsible for any of what happened after he left.

"Hold on, man. We don't know what happened. And it's certainly not your fault, given what you've told us. But I think it would be best if we went over to Mike di Saronno's office, and you can tell him what you've told us."

"I need a lawyer?"

"No idea. Anyone's entitled to one if they're arrested. Not sure if that goes for just a conversation that doesn't end in an arrest." I paused before asking, "Do you have a lawyer?"

"Probably. I mean I'm sure my mom has one. But probably for business stuff. Not for being arrested. My dad was arrested a couple of times. I think it was when he was drunk. But I haven't ever even had a traffic ticket, and for sure my mom hasn't."

"Maybe you want to call your mother and talk to her about it."

He nodded, then stood up and said, "No lawyer. I know what I know and that's all I know and I will tell the truth. I shouldn't need a lawyer. This is America." He looked shaky, though.

Gabriele stood up and walked over to Ted and stood close in front of him. He smiled and said, "I go with you, is okay." Then he kissed Ted briefly, full on the mouth.

Chapter Twenty-six

Mike reacted about the way I expected. I sent him a text asking if we could meet someplace so that he could hear what Ted Coniston had to say. Ted had been at my place with Ruth and Gabriele and me, and had filled us in on a number of things having to do with his last interaction with the Coniston boys – and some physical details about the recreational building where the boys wanted to wait for their uncle,

"You want to come over here?"

"Well, it's late enough that maybe we could meet someplace where we could eat something. That okay with you?"

"Sure, name the place and I'll meet you there."

"The Oyster Bar at Grand Central in a half-hour?"

"See you there."

Ruth and Gabriele were all in for the meeting with Mike. I brushed my teeth and put on a clean shirt. I offered Ted a change of clothes if he wanted, but he was okay.

Ted and I got to Grand Central before Mike did, so I got a table in the back corner. Gabriele walked in right behind us and glad-handed the head-waiter, so I thought maybe we'd be comped. Ruth walked in wearing classic Chanel and very high heels, maybe four-inch.

Mike walked in and spotted us. He was looking very put-together. Tie in a proper Windsor knot, suit looked like he just put it on, and there was a glint of cufflinks on his sleeves. He had also gotten a haircut and had a fashionable scruff that looked like an incipient beard.

He and I shook hands and I said, "You're looking like a man about town. It becomes you."

"*Signor detettivo*," Gabriele said, and they exchanged the traditional cheek kisses.

Mike and Ted knew each other from the time in the interrogation room at Mike's precinct. Ted stood up and shook Mike's hand. I liked him. His posture was straight-up like a marine, and he knew how to interact with much older adults. He looked like a man, not a boy, but he accorded people of thirty and up with a degree of submission that was very old-fashioned and admirable.

For me, it's usually fish and chips when I go to the Oyster Bar. Yes, they have a big selection of oysters, but I don't know anyplace that has better fish and chips, so that's what I stay with. In spite of the fact that I love oysters on the half-shell with fresh horseradish. I ordered a Tito's vodka straight up (no olive juice), which means chilled in a shaker with ice and served in a martini glass. For some reason, cold vodka seems right with fried fish. Wine doesn't work for me with seafood, probably because I don't drink white wine. It's for cooking, not drinking.

"Our crime scene investigators found some indications of blood in the soil under the grass at the back of the building," Mike told Ted. "That could mean they did fall off the roof and land on the ground. Unfortunately, there had been a couple of heavy downpours in the intervening time that degraded the blood that might have been there, so there was no way we could determine whose blood it was – or even if it was human."

Ted's forehead wrinkled and his eyes look watery.

"So, you can imagine that your information about the boys being in that building playing video games when you left is of interest," Mike said. "One thing we do know from the Medical Examiner is that the boys most likely died from a fall, which she said could have been from a tree or a roof or a cliff of some kind, like a rock formation. They both died almost immediately from broken necks wherever it happened."

Mike ordered an assortment of oysters and a plate of fries. Gabriele was having shrimp scampi and mixed vegetables. He joined me in a Tito straight up, and seemed to approve when he took a sip with one of the shrimp. Ruth had some kind of broiled fish, maybe branzino, which is served in a lot of restaurants in New York City because it is farmed in the Mediterranean off Italy, where branzino is a favorite. It's a small variety of sea bass; the name is northern Italian. In the area where

Gabriele grew up, it is called *spigola*. Not even similar. Go figure.

Ted went back over what happened when he parked next to the Kids' House and walked the boys inside. He checked out the ground floor and the roof, to make sure the furniture was clean, since it was not protected from rain or birds, which sometimes deposit droppings as they fly. He hadn't checked the second or third floors, which was where the bedrooms and the kitchen area were, respectively. He also was sure to go over the fact that there was a five-foot parapet around the roof that was two feet thick to prevent any kid from falling.

"The only way to make sure a child doesn't fall is to watch carefully like a lifeguard does at a pool or the beach," Mike said.

That did it. Ted choked and started to cry. "I didn't know what was going to happen to them. I had a four-hour drive ahead of me and I was tired. But it was my fault if they fell."

"No, it wasn't your fault," Mike said. "Even so, I imagine your uncle might be upset with you for not staying with the boys until he got home."

Ted nodded and looked down at his shoes.

"Is there any possibility that your aunt went to the Kids' House and found the boys on the roof?"

He shook his head. "First of all, I doubt she could get to the Kids' House without a nurse to show her the way. Her memory is almost completely gone, not to mention she's very overweight and very frail. She can walk, but she'd get lost before she got there. She has no idea who anyone is, not even Uncle Ricky, much less Uncle Eddie's sons. She doesn't even know herself in the mirror. That nurse is with her twenty-four/seven. She can still talk and even carry on a conversation – but she's delusional, so talking to her can be very disturbing sometimes. Basically, the Auntie Ann I know isn't there any more. It's somebody else in Auntie Ann's body. It's a terrible disease she has, called Pick's Disease, or Frontal Lobe Dementia. Not Alzheimer's. It's worse than Alzheimer's. Nobody knows what causes it, and there are no medicines that help, except with symptoms." He teared up and said, "Uncle Ricky is a saint to go through all of this. Ned dying, Auntie Ann losing her mind, and the boys being killed and dumped in the forest. And he is the CEO of the company that basically provides an income for most of the people in the family. A good man."

I asked Ted if he was going to order anything, because he had been studying the menu when the waiter took orders. He shook his head negatively.

"That's not a good idea, Ted," I said, trying to sound parental.

"Okay, then I'll have what you're having."

"Fish and chips, with a chilled vodka straight up? That's what I'm having."

"Fish and chips great. I'll pass on the vodka. Water is fine."

I waved at the waiter, who came over right away.

Ted said he'd like to have fish and chips. "What kind of fish is it?"

The waiter said, "It's cod. That's every day. Here fish and chips means cod."

"What can I do to help?" Ted asked Mike directly after the waiter walked away.

"Would you consider going with us to Chappaqua to your uncle's place?"

Nod. "What would you want me to do?"

"Give us a tour of the house, the barn and what you call the Kids' House. Show us where the boys were when you last saw them. I'm hoping that Hugo will be able to go with us."

I nodded and smiled, looking from Ted to Mike and back.

"Is tomorrow okay?" Mike asked.

"Yeah," Ted answered, "but I have to figure out where to stay. Maybe there's a hotel near your office, Detective di Saronno?"

"If you want, you can stay at my place, Ted. I have a second bedroom with its own bathroom," I said. "Then we could take the subway over to Mike's office tomorrow."

He blushed slightly. "I wasn't asking you to put me up, Hugo."

"I know that. I was just offering. I won't be offended if you decide a hotel is better. I used to live very near Mike's office, and I know how cool that area is. Up to you."

Gabriele had been watching Ted. "Hugo apartment good place to stay. Maybe I stay there tonight."

"Well, then the second bedroom would already be occupied," Ted said.

"Maybe, maybe no. Maybe I sleep with Ugo." He paused then continued, "Maybe I sleep with you."

Scarlet blushes on Ted and Ruth. Mike was looking at the ceiling. Gabriele was grinning. *Gotcha.*

"You have no shame," I said to Gabriele across the table, but with a smile.

"If you took him at face value, you'd be making a mistake," I said directly to Ted. He was looking like a deer caught in headlights.

"You were teasing me?" he said to Gabriele.

Gabriele looked down at the table. No response.

"I'll take that as a yes," Ted said.

I waved at the waiter after we had finished our meals and asked for dessert menus. "Desserts are on me," I said. "I'm gonna have a hot fudge sundae."

Ruth opted for a pistachio praline and chocolate torte. Mike passed. Gabriele wanted lemon ice cream.

"And for you?" the waiter asked Ted.

"Hot fudge sundae always sounds good."

"Well, if you can be at my office by about eleven o'clock tomorrow morning, that would be good," Mike said to Ted. "Maybe half-hour earlier for you, Hugo?"

I nodded, and Mike stood up. "I tried to get the waiter to bring a check, but it seems that somebody, Mr Cortese, has arranged to have the meal comped. Thank you, Gabriele. Even so, I have to work," he said genially. "I've already been gone long enough that the desk sergeant is probably getting ready to send out a search party." He shook hands around the table and left.

Ruth kissed Gabriele and me on the cheek and held out her hand for Ted to shake.

"I can do as I please," I said, "but I need to call my stockbroker and see what the market's doing, so I'm heading home, too."

I am in awe of women walking in high heels, especially very high, high heels. Ruth pulls it off every time. She never wobbles. I'd be in an ambulance with a broken ankle. She doesn't even make a sour face when she stands up. I'll never understand it.

After Ruth left, I said to Ted and Gabriele, "Who's staying at my place tonight?"

Gabriele raised his hand. Ted did likewise.

"Cool. You guys decide who's going to sleep on the couch in the living room."

They looked at each other and smiled. Gabriele raised his hand again.

Chapter Twenty-seven

When I woke up the next morning, I realized there was a garlicky fragrance in the air. Gabriele and Ted were already sitting at the dining table drinking coffee and eating toast with fig jam. Gabriele was reading the Arts section of the paper. Ted had Sports. They were a magazine picture of healthy youth, at least from my point of view. Ted was taller and blond, the proverbial barefoot boy with cheeks of tan. Gabriele was almost twice Ted's age, had black hair and tanned skin, features like a Michelangelo sculpture, and the body of a swimsuit model. They were both wearing the kind of white tank-top shirts that are sometimes called 'wife-beaters' and boxer shorts. They didn't realize I was standing there, and I was tempted to take a picture of them, but didn't.

"I thought I smelled coffee," I said, and they looked up.

"Coffee in kitchen," Gabriele said. "*E focaccia.*"

"When did you have time to make focaccia? Doesn't it have to rise before you bake it?"

"*L'ho fatto impasto ieri sera,* bake in morning. *La focaccia è ancora caldo dal forno.*" (He made the dough last night, and it was still hot from the oven.)

Focaccia is a type of yeast bread that is very popular in Italy. It's more or less similar to pizza crust, but sometimes flavored with garlic and oil or fresh rosemary. It's a flat bread, perfect for breakfast. I could smell the garlic, and it started the salivary glands in my mouth. What a luxury to have a friend who is a real Italian chef. I should have guessed he would make something, because he doesn't like to eat American bread. At his restaurant, they bake fresh bread every day.

"It smells wonderful. Was there yeast in the pantry?"

"*Ho portato il lievito in tasca.*" (He brought yeast in his pocket.)

"What?" Ted looked puzzled.

"We were talking about the bread. He doesn't eat American bread, so I guess it wasn't a surprise. Nothing important."

Gabriele stood up and hugged me. I felt awkward. He giggled.

It was about eight o'clock. "We should leave in an hour or so. Gabriele, there's a fresh towel in my bathroom. I'll eat some focaccia while you take a shower."

Ted washed down the rest of his focaccia with coffee. After he swallowed, he said he would take his shower. I told him I had put a fresh towel in his bathroom on the counter by the sink.

"Are you and Gabriele a thing?" Ted asked nervously.

"What do you mean, a thing?"

"Are you partners?"

"We're friends. He's about the same age as my son in California. His father died when he was a child."

"Does he have a girlfriend?"

"You'd have to ask him about that. Go take your shower."

"Do I have to wear a tie?"

"If you want to wear a tie it's okay, but you don't have to."

"Are you going to wear a tie?"

"No."

He quick-walked down the hall to his bathroom and disappeared. Fortunately, there is ample hot water for two showers at the same time, with plenty left over for me.

We were walking to the subway station by nine fifteen. "This is a nice area," Ted said. "Beautiful views of the city."

"You should see where Gabriele lives in Brooklyn Heights. It's a breathtaking neighborhood, maybe the most beautiful in New York City."

Ted was looking nervous. Gabriele threw his arm over Ted's shoulder and said something to him that I couldn't hear.

"Mike isn't going to put you in a compromising position. Don't worry," I said.

"That's what Gabriele just said to me," he said with a smile. "It's just that I don't want to be on the wrong side of Uncle Ricky."

"I don't know him well, but he's not somebody to fly off the handle. That's just my impression, but I seriously doubt you have anything to worry about with your uncle." He looked doubtful. "Try taking deep breaths and get yourself better oxygenated. It's natural to have some anxiety when you're doing something you've never done before."

When we got to the precinct, Mike had an ugly surprise for us. Apparently, there was a tweet-storm in process, kicked off by a tweet from Hank Huntington or somebody with the handle of @MonacoHank.

Relatives are telling me that Richard Coniston is behind the deaths of his two nephews. Anybody have evidence? I'm thinking of going to New York to nose around.

There had been several hundred thousand responses, many of them clearly by bots repeating and retweeting, but some purporting to be from the Coniston and Westbrook families.

"Very few of the tweets are in favor of Ricky Coniston," Mike told us. "One of the tweets that was clearly on Ricky's side was from *@LizzieC123,* clearly meant at least to appear to be Lizzie Coniston. No way for us to tell, but it looks like the platform managers have been deleting bot tweets. They're vanishing, sometimes while you are looking at the screen, but the overall number of tweets keeps climbing."

Gabriele pulled out his phone and showed me how fast the tweets were moving by – much too fast to be able to read any of them. And then while I was looking at the screen, one vanished. "I saw one vanish, must be a bot tweet."

"It seems that the man you met in Monaco has decided to attack and get Ricky Coniston thrown out of the Coniston Companies," Mike said.

"Well, Huntington's been the head of a big private hedge fund company," I said, "so not a lot different from what Ricky Coniston does. Ricky characterizes his work as managing a family office, which means it is very similar to a hedge fund, but entirely devoted to one extended family – the Conistons."

"It's a disingenuous tweet," Ted said. "The one from Huntington, I mean. He's trying to look innocent, which makes me think he may not be innocent."

"Have you ever spoken with Mr Huntington?" Mike wanted to know.

"No, I have not," Ted said. "But I know some people in the family have been talking to him. Like most of the Westbrooks."

"How about your Aunt Elizabeth?"

"I don't know. I haven't seen or talked to Aunt Lizzie for a long time. But she was a Westbrook before she married Uncle Eddie. She may be trying to fix him up with one of her sisters or Westbrook daughters. That would tell us why there is a fierce tweet in favor of Ricky from somebody who looks like Lizzie."

"How do you know that other people in the family have been in touch with Mr Huntington?"

"My mom told me."

Mike said that the CSI hackers were working on the tweet-storm. "They'll keep us up to date on whatever they find out, so we should get going up to Chappaqua."

I was worried that we would be going in NYPD-marked cars, but as it turned out, it was an unmarked Ford Expedition.

"This must get about the same kind of mileage as an old Hummer," I said aloud, and then thought it would have been better if I just thought it.

Mike laughed. "Single digits, but it has a big gas tank, so we don't have to worry about running low."

One of Mike's colleagues was the driver, in civvies.

"And you have a search warrant?" I asked.

He pulled it out and handed it to me. "Looks like we're going to be able to look wherever we want. I think I recall that when Ted left with the boys to take them to the Kids' House, Mrs Coniston and the nurse were walking toward the barn. I bet there are more than a couple of employees working there. The Conistons are well-known horse people. I'd guess they have a lot of horses."

"They do," Ted said. "Always have, as long as I can remember. I learned to ride there. I wish I could have a horse and someplace to keep it."

"I bet that wouldn't be a problem," I said. "Horses aren't as expensive as you might think. It's the tack that costs a lot. Well, if you're buying a thoroughbred, it could be expensive, but feeding them and so forth isn't going to wreck you. If you expect the grooms at wherever you keep the horse to do all the work, that would cost more."

"I need to get my master's and a job before I even think about a horse."

"I bet your mom would be happy to get you set up."

"You don't know my mom. She's like someone that grew up in the Depression; always worried about money. She clips coupons every day."

Veddy interesting. Why haven't they talked to Ricky about budgets or dividends?

We were turning from the New York State Thruway to the Saw Mill Parkway, so I knew we were close to Chappaqua. I looked at Ted, who also clearly knew how close we were. He was staring out the window, and acting fidgety. He was sweating enough for it to be running down the side of his neck.

He's really nervous. I wonder if it's just worry about seeing Ricky, or whether he hasn't told us everything. It wouldn't be the first time.

Mike turned around in his seat and looked back at Ted. He was seeing what I was seeing. I looked back at Gabriele, who was staring at Ted from behind.

"Ricky's place is just up there," he said, and gulped down another shot of air.

He's afraid of Ricky.

I leaned over to him and whispered, "Are you afraid of Ricky?"

He nodded almost imperceptibly and looked at me with a weak smile. He grabbed my hand and squeezed it hard.

"I'm here with you," I said very softly. "So are Gabriele and Ruth. We won't have to get out of the car while they serve the search warrant. You can probably stay in the car until we stop at the Kids' House on the way out. Nobody would be able to see you through the tinted glass."

He shook his head. "Better to be hung for a sheep than a lamb."

"Stay oxygenated, and it'll be over before you know it."

As we drove into the driveway, I could see the tendons in Ted's neck tighten, but he didn't say anything. When we pulled up in front of the house, the front door opened, and Ricky Coniston stepped out in a gray business suit, white shirt, striped tie. He smiled and waved. Mike got out of the car with the police driver, and presented the search warrant to him. Ricky nodded as he read the warrant. He pointed to the Kids' House and nodded again. He beckoned to Mike and they walked down the side of the house. When they got to the corner, Ricky pointed at something we couldn't see.

"Is he pointing at the barn?" I asked.

Ted nodded.

"When was the last time you were in the barn?" Ruth asked.

"Last summer."

"Lotsa people working there?"

"Maybe ten or twelve, mostly guys."

"Some women work there, too?" Ruth was surprised, but interested.

He nodded. "One of the grooms is a girl, or was last summer anyway. She was just graduating from high school, so maybe she went off to college. Kinda pretty, but strong as an ox."

"Did you ask her out?"

Nod.

"She said yes, but then I thought maybe it was because I was part of the family. That kinda turned me off. I'm not super-interested in girls either." He looked away.

I looked at Gabriele, who was clearly listening to everything.

"It's hard to have children in a same-sex marriage," I said.

"I had been thinking of asking Uncle Ricky for a job in the barn. That was before all of this happened, though. I've been looking for a job, but there aren't many openings I'm qualified for."

"You don't have to have any special education to work in a mail room. Or to wait tables."

"A waiter?"

"Is good job, waiter," Gabriele offered. "Waiter learn many things about people. The way they act."

I added, "But, Ted, you said you really like horses. Maybe you should swallow your pride, go ahead and ask your uncle if you can work in the barn. You'd learn things about horses you could never learn anywhere else."

"I can't ask him if he's mad at me."

"Why he be mad with you?" Gabriele asked.

"If he thinks I had something to do with Ed and Dick getting killed."

"I doubt he thinks that," I said. "Even the little I know of you, you're not the sort of person to get involved in something like that. And you don't have a motive."

"What kind of motive would make somebody want to kill kids?"

"Most commonly, money or jealousy."

"Like Mr Huntington, you mean?" Ted's question came out of nowhere.

"I hadn't thought about it, but yes. He pretty clearly wants to throw Ricky out and take over himself."

Mike was walking back to the car with the driver-cop, and Ricky was walking with them. I could hear Ted suck in air. Ruth reached over the seat from behind to pat him on the back.

Ricky stuck his head in the open car window.

"Who've we got here? Hey, kiddo," he said to Ted. "Good to see you. What are you doing with the cops?"

Mike answered. "Ted has been very helpful about telling us what happened the day he picked up the boys after school. I asked him if he would be willing to show us around the Kids' House, and he said he would."

"I was going to show them the barn, too," Ted said.

"You didn't need a search warrant, you know," he said to Mike. "Next time just ask." He looked at Ted. "How's your mom?"

"Okay, stingy as ever." Ted smiled a real smile, not a pasted-on one.

Ricky started to laugh, then didn't.

"Inside joke," he said to Mike and the rest of us. "I tried to get Ted and his mom to move out here with us. Ann was still okay then and our son was still alive. The house is big enough for a lot more people, and Ted is like a son to me. But his mom was set on moving to Boston. We couldn't persuade her to change her mind. She was still mourning George, who was my brother and her husband. George drowned in Avalon Harbor in California, maybe ten or eleven years ago."

"Twelve," Ted said.

Ricky nodded as he was looking down at Ted's feet or mine.

"Mr Coniston, have you been in communication with Henry Huntington?" Mike asked, standing behind Ricky just outside the car.

Ricky backed out of the car and stood up, leaning on the car roof. "No," he said. "I've never met him. Our mothers were related to each other several generations back up the line. He lives in France, I think. I know he's been talking trash about me, but I don't know why."

"He lives in Monaco," Ruth said.

"Monaco is almost part of France. I thought he lived in Paris, but no matter."

"His business is in Paris," Ruth said. "I think he spends a good deal of time there, but home is definitely in Monaco. He presents himself well, good speaker, good eye contact."

"Sounds like you're on his side," Ricky said.

"I'm not on a side. I just want to find out what happened, and let the dominos fall where they may." She did her best haughty look, and Ricky blinked, looked down at his feet.

"To give the devil his due," I said, "I wouldn't want to run against him in an election. Very self-possessed, strong dose of charisma. I found it difficult to trust him. He never explained how he knew we were there, and that we had some connection to the NYPD. And he used a fake name when he called."

"Fake name?"

"Clint Caine, but Ruth recognized him from a picture she had found online."

"Mr Coniston," Mike said, "I presume you know that Mr Huntington may have been proposing marriage to one of your sister-in-law's relatives."

He nodded and said nothing.

"Now, it would be good to have a look-see at the barn and the Kids' House," Mike said.

"Ted," Coniston said, "why don't you show my guests around? You know them better than I do anyway."

Ricky walked back toward the house and didn't look back. Ted motioned to us to follow him. When we got to the corner of the house, he pointed toward a group of buildings up a slight grade.

"Doesn't look like a barn," I said.

"You mean it isn't red with a pointed roof," he said, smiling. "But this is what a real, working horse-barn looks like."

The barn was considerably larger than I had envisioned. I grew up as a small kid on a ranch in Texas. We had a barn and we had eight quarterhorses, which were called 'cow ponies', due to their smaller size compared to thoroughbreds or the taller, stronger kinds of horses that pull wagons or various kinds of old-fashioned vehicles that you still might see in a parade, or around Central Park. Point being, we were a small ranch, even though to my eyes it was perfect. Our barn smelled of straw and manure, and the horses were in stalls, with a couple of stalls left empty. When we had a mare that was going to foal (have a baby horse), that mare was put in one of the empty stalls, and the cowboys would tend to her if she needed help.

The Coniston barn was five or six times the size of the one I grew up with. The thing that first caught my eye was the tack room – something we didn't have. When I was a kid, our saddles – 'western' saddles with a saddlehorn and much bigger than English saddles –were thrown over something that basically looked like a sawhorse, but wider. The Coniston tack room looked like a showroom at a fancy saddler. Of course, all the saddles were English, which required a totally different type of riding than the saddles we had. A racing jockey basically rides standing up and leaning forward. In a western saddle, you basically sit like you would on a stool, but lean forward to avoid bouncing up and down if the horse had to run. That bouncing can leave the rider very, very sore – something called 'saddle-sore'.

I think the best way to describe the Coniston barn is to say it looked more like the facilities at a big fancy race-track. The stalls were much larger, closed with a gate, and the horses were fed with grain, fruit and vegetables – not hay. Basically, there was about one groom to every two horses. Horses are usually not house-broken like dogs or cats, so there was still the smell of manure and straw, but the stalls were clean, compared to a barn on a working truck farm or livestock ranch. The grooms were well-dressed compared to our cowboys, and they spent a lot of time currying the horses and spoiling them with carrots and turnips. I couldn't count the number of horses or grooms because we didn't tour the entire facility. It was just too big.

Shortly after we got to the barn, a suntanned fellow probably in his mid-twenties, walked over to us and suddenly he and Ted were hugging like brothers.

"Teddy, where the heck have you been?"

"I just graduated from college, so I have some time on my hands. Maybe I'll be here more often, Jack."

Ted introduced Mike, Ruth, Gabriele and me to Jack, who looked Latino to me, but with no discernable accent. "I'm just showing my friends around. They're with the NYPD, and they're trying to figure out what happened to Ed and Dick."

Jack looked down at his feet and shook his head. Then he wiped his eyes and looked at Ted without saying anything.

"Jack and I grew up together, at least in the summers. Right here, where we're standing."

They hugged again, then Jack turned away and walked farther into the barn.

"He's gotta take care of his horses," Ted said. "And he was having a hard time keeping from crying."

"Where's he from?" Ruth asked.

The Coniston Curse

"Around here someplace, maybe Katonah. I don't really know. His dad is from Puerto Rico, I do know that. But Jack's a natural-born American citizen; he went to high school somewhere close around here."

"He very sad about boys," Gabriele said. "Maybe he know something happen."

"I had the same feeling," Mike said. "I'd like to talk with him."

"He does some gardening here, too. I think he was the one that found some hand tools with blood on them."

"We knew about a hand cultivator with four prongs, but not any other hand tools," Mike said. "We have that cultivator in the evidence room. The lab couldn't tell much about the blood, but there were some bits of skin. It was one of the boys, or maybe both of them. We figure it was used to make the fake 'bear claw' gashes on the boys' backs. No fingerprints. Probably whoever was holding it was wearing gloves."

"Maybe it was just one tool then."

"We need to find out for sure," Mike said.

"I didn't mean to stir things up."

Mike smiled at Ted. "That's how you find out what happened – you stir things up. Otherwise, you'd never learn anything." He patted Ted on the back. "Maybe we should go and have a look at the Kids' House."

Ted trotted down the same way that Jack had left. "Gimme a couple of minutes," he twisted around and shouted, then broke into a run.

Very shortly after that, Ted and Jack were back with us. "There was a trowel that might have had blood on it, but it disappeared, or got washed and put away with the other trowels," Jack said.

"What do you mean when you say it 'might have had blood on it'?" Mike asked.

"We couldn't tell. It had dirt all over it. I had been planting zinnias with it."

"Zinnias? Where?"

"At the Kids' House," Jack said. "There's a flower garden that goes almost all the way around it. Just more of a border, I guess, so the foundation of the building was hidden."

"Why don't you come with us – we were just on our way over

there to the Kids' House."

"I'll have to ask my boss if it's okay. There he is over there," he said, gesturing toward a man leading a horse into the barn.

Mike went over and had a brief talk with the man, who nodded his head, and Mike came back. "He said you have a hall pass, Jack."

"That horse is one of the ones I take care of. His name is Vesuvius." He went over to the horse and snuggled his head against the horse's and said something into his ear, then patted him on the side of his neck below his mane. The horse shook his head and whinnied. Friends.

"What did you say to the horse?" Ruth asked.

"Nothing. I said 'That's my boy'. He's my good buddy, and I give him carrots." The tears were coming back.

We walked back toward the house and up the driveway to the tall slim structure that I originally thought was probably a gatehouse, but we know now is called the Kids' House, and is basically an indoor playground.

There was indeed a narrow flower garden that looked like a skirt where the walls met the ground. And there were zinnias in full bloom. Zinnias always meant that summer was coming to an end when I was a child. Such beautiful, vivid colors, and they last well if you cut them and put them in water. My grandmother was an avid gardener – well, garden planner, since she had two men who came six days a week and did all the work. She had a particular soft spot for zinnias.

The door to the Kids' House wasn't locked, so we walked right in. Ted and Jack showed us the video games that were hooked up to flat-screen, wall-mounted, high-def LED televisions. The ceiling of the first floor was probably about ten feet up – higher, anyway, than the usual eight feet. We would find that the second and third floors were more normal, closer to eight feet. There were some classic touches like crown moldings in all the rooms except the bathrooms. Most of the ground floor was devoted to a single rec room, with several bright-colored overstuffed chairs which held three old-fashioned pinball machines as well as several PlayStation-type consoles where several people could play "Grand Theft Auto" or other well-known multi-player games, or virtually antique

"Dungeons and Dragons" types of games. There was even a screen where you could play "Hitchhiker's Guide to the Galaxy" from pre-historic times.

There was a library of DVDs with games on them. Just behind the wall that held the big TV screens were a small nap-room for kids who played themselves to sleep, and a bathroom with a shower stall.

"So, this is the last place I saw Ed and Dick when I dropped them off to wait for Uncle Ricky to get home. They both knew the ropes, because they stayed out here for several weeks in the summer each year – that's how we got to know each other like friends, not just cousins."

He walked over to the staircase leading up to the second and third floors. The second was entirely about five small bedrooms and three more bathrooms with stall showers. The third floor was almost completely devoted to a combination kitchen and eating area with stools arranged around a counter-top that covered one entire end of the room, and curved around and up the side. There were eight stools at the counter, and two more at the end of the counter. He showed us a pantry with healthy snacks and hot meals that could be easily microwaved. Also, popcorn, a fridge full of bottles of flavored water, an OJ machine with fresh oranges in a dispenser, and the normal kitchen equipment – double stove, six-burner stove top, cabinets with dishes and various sizes and types of glasses (most of them plastic and unbreakable).

Then Ted took us up to the roof, which was set up like the area around a swimming pool, with round tables that had umbrellas that stood up through a hole in the center of the tables, and stackable white plastic chairs. He pointed out the half-wall that went around all four sides of the roof. The walls were about chest-high on me and they looked to be about two feet thick.

"It'd be kinda difficult to get up and stand on the wall, it looks like to me," I said.

"Not if you stand on a chair," Ted said. He hopped up on the wall and showed us how easy it was to walk around. Then he hopped down onto the roof again. He pointed to the signs on the walls that read "It's Dangerous to Walk on the Walls."

"That's like daring a kid to do it," Ruth said to Mike.

"Yup," he said with a smile.

He leaned over the top of the wall and hoisted himself far enough up to look over the side. "It's all grass down there, except the narrow flower garden. But it would be a long enough fall to do a lot of damage, especially if you landed head-first."

"What do you think, Mike?" the driver-cop asked.

"I think this is where the boys met their maker." He rubbed his chin. "But a lot happened before the boys were found in Pocantico Hills."

He turned to Jack. "How would you transport two dead boys if you had to move them, Jack?"

"C-mon, that's not fair," Ted said. "You can't ask him to pretend he's a criminal."

"It's okay, Ted," Jack said. "Probably the safest way would be to put them in one side of a two-horse trailer, and put a horse in the other side. Hook it up to a truck or an SUV, and drive until you get someplace where nobody can see you, then do whatever you do."

"That's kinda what I was thinking, too," Mike said. "I'm guessing you have enough horse trailers to be able to spare one for an emergency like that."

"We got three double trailers, and they don't get a lot of use."

"They out by the barn?"

Jack nodded.

"Hey, Danny," he said to the driver cop. "We have some luminol spray in the car?"

Danny nodded. "Two bottles, I think."

"Jack, we need to spray a chemical on the floors of the double trailers that tells us whether there has been any blood there. It glows blue if it touches blood, because it reacts with the iron in the blood. It's safe, won't harm people or animals."

He turned to Gabriele. "We need to take photos of the whole procedure. Can you hold steady and take the photos?"

"*Si, signor detettivo,*" he replied, "*posso farlo.*" (*Yes, signor detective, I can do that.*)

201

Chapter Twenty-eight

Long story short, the luminol showed what looked like small puddles of blood on one side of one of the double horse trailers. Gabriele's photos passed muster with Mike, and we stopped by the house to thank Mr Coniston for his help. Mike told him about the luminol and asked him if it would be okay if Mike arranged somebody to pick up that trailer so the Westchester CSIs could go over it.

"Of course," he said. "Does that mean this is for sure where my nephews died?"

"Not necessarily," Mike said. "All it shows for sure is that there was some blood on the floor of one of the trailers. If the boys were transported in that trailer, it could explain that blood. But if somebody's German shepherd was hit by a car and transported to the vet hospital in that trailer, that would also explain it. So would a fresh-killed chicken or a deer or quail or duck or a fisherman's striped bass. That's why I want the CSIs to go over it. Maybe they can salvage some DNA to help us. That would tell us if the blood is human and male, at least. With luck, it could also tell us approximately how old the bloodstain is, how long it's been there. Even if it's human and male, if it's been there a year, it's not the blood we're looking for."

Mike's phone buzzed, indicating a text had arrived. He looked at it and showed it to Ricky Coniston, who acknowledged it with a slight nod. Then Mike turned to us and said, "Mr Huntington called the office, and asked if I will call him back."

I started to ask a question and thought better of it.

"It's a problem for later, maybe tomorrow," Mike said loudly enough for all to hear, including Ricky Coniston. "I told Mr Coniston that you three met Mr Huntington in Monaco recently."

I put my hand up, followed by Ruth and Gabriele doing the same.

Mr Coniston waved back. He looked up and flashed what looked like a grimace briefly. "The mysterious and aggressive Hank Huntington, *en garde,*" he said, loud enough for everyone to hear.

We got back in the car and Danny turned the car around and we turned left when we got to the road. Nobody said anything until we were a mile away. Mike signaled Danny, who pulled the car over to the shoulder and put on hazard lights.

"Everybody out," Mike said. "We're going to sweep the car for bugs, listening devices."

Danny produced a wand with a loop of metal like a tennis racket without the strings, from the trunk and carefully went over the entire interior of the car. "Didn't find anything, Detective," he said.

"I didn't think you would, but it's protocol to check."

"Did your email tell you what Huntington wanted?" Ruth asked.

Negative.

Mike told us that he had all the conversations we had on his phone, and he would have it transcribed overnight. "I think it'd be a good idea if Hugo, Gabriele and Ruth could join me as listeners for the call with Mr Huntington tomorrow."

"What kind of take-aways did you get from the tours today?" I asked.

"Well, for one thing, it scared the pants off me to see Ted cavorting around on that wall around the roof. If the boys were on that wall and were startled or pushed, that would have been the end of them. I'll wait for the CSIs to look at the bloodstains in the horse trailer, but it is looking very likely that the boys died at the Coniston estate. They knew their way around because they had spent time there many times, so they may have gone up to the barn on their own hook, to see the horses, or to say hi to anybody they knew in the barn. They could have been bludgeoned inside the horse trailer, but I don't think so because there would have been more splatter, so I'm guessing that, like the Medical Examiner said, they died from a fall. The M.E. said it might have been from a tree, but I'll put my money on that wall around the roof. Both their necks were broken, so they were dead as soon as they hit the ground. The

M.E. thought some of the abrasions might have been from hitting tree limbs as they fell."

"If there were a lot of abrasions, what could have caused them in falling off the roof?" Ruth asked.

"Frankly, animals had been eating at them, so the M.E. was just guessing about some of it. He found saliva from coyotes, racoons, a variety of rodents, a fox, and a lot of birds, maybe vultures. If it wasn't for DNA, we could never have identified them."

"Too much information," she said, and turned away.

"Sorry," Mike said. "I rattle on about things like that without thinking sometimes. That happens when you're in homicide. It's not that you get used to it, but you get used to talking about it. It makes me sick sometimes, too."

Gabriele said, "Mister Ricky seem calm, not worry. Not look guilty."

Mike smiled. "I try to keep an open mind, but I have a hard time imagining him knowing anything about what happened to the boys. Not that he's a softy, because we know he's not. Not if he can build up a one-family hedge fund to the place where it supports a good piece of the entire extended family. If the inside detectives at NYPD are right, the Coniston Companies has close to one hundred employees with entirely company-paid health insurance. That can't be cheap. He seems upset by anything in his family that goes wrong. He has a heart, but he also has a temper that shows in flashes of anger, like what he muttered about Huntington. But I'd bet whatever we find out will be as much a surprise to him as it might be to us."

When we got back in the car, Danny put on the radio to WQXR, the classical music radio station from NPR (used to be owned by the New York Times, but they sold it to NPR). It was a blessing, because they were playing ètudes by Chopin; very soothing, and devilishly difficult (or impossible) to play. I used to play Baroque and Rococco music on my harpsichord, but Chopin has to be on the piano, and because the keyboards are different sizes and the style of music is so different, I was never able to play even 'simple' Chopin (there's really no such thing). My fingers didn't seem to extend far enough, and I couldn't get accustomed to playing one chord with seven notes, so I had to use both hands crossed over each other. I just got my fingers tangled up every time I tried. But I had been trying to learn out of a book, not with a teacher, and that was probably the root of the problem.

I could hear Gabriele's breathing get slower and louder. He was falling asleep. Ruth kept tapping on her phone, obviously sending text messages to her followers or friends.

By the time we got back to the precinct, it was after four o'clock, and Mike suggested we wander over to Thalia for a drink. He whispered to me when the others were in the washroom that he kept seeing those boys in his mind cavorting around on the wall around the roof, and he could use a drink. It was good to know he had feet of clay sometimes, like a normal human being. Mike sent an email to the email address that Huntington had left, saying the best time for him would be around eleven o'clock New York time, which would be around five o'clock in Paris or Monte Carlo. He got a confirmation quickly for that time, and sent Mike the number to call.

I felt like I had been ridden hard and put away wet, to use horse-barn language. You never leave a horse wet from a ride; you towel him off all over and curry him if you don't want him to get sick, and if it's the least bit chilly, you put a blanket on him, maybe give him an apple. I felt dog-tired and used up. Dirty vodka was the answer, as it so often is for me. Actually, I used to drink scotch on the rocks with a splash, but I got to liking the taste so much I was afraid I would overdo, so I switched to dirty vodka, because I knew I would sip that, not gulp it down. Vodka is more or less lacking in taste of any kind, which is why people seldom drink it straight. It does help me relax, but it doesn't make me want to overdo.

Chapter Twenty-nine

I could feel that we were coming to a point where we would know what happened, but there were still parts of the solution that were blanks.

Ted and Gabriele went back to my place with me – a short walk through Times Square to the shuttle entrance at 43rd Street, then a quick change at Grand Central to the 7 line, and one stop to Long Island City's Vernon-Jackson subway station. We stopped at a market and picked up some chicken breasts, shredded mozzarella and fresh-picked basil so that Gabriele could make some chicken parmigiana. I told them I had the rest of the ingredients already in the fridge and the pantry.

Ted was worried about his friend Jack, who might have been working on the flower border when the boys arrived to play games while they waited for Uncle Ricky to get home. Little did they know that Ricky Coniston was stuck on a motionless MetroNorth train that was unable to start up again after some sudden signal problems on the Harlem line that could take him eventually to North White Plains or Pleasantville.

I texted Ruth, asking what she thought about Hank Huntington threatening to travel to New York.

He said he was gonna be in Paris. He can fly direct to JFK, could be here tonight

I thought about that. And he probably doesn't care about cost

Wonder what Mike is going to do

He told me a day or two ago he might be able to post a notice on the immigration computers at all ports of entry about Huntington

Wonder which one of Eddie C's daughters Hank is after

Probably the elder one. I think her name is Elizabeth too, but I haven't met her.

I asked her if she could meet Gabriel, Ted and me for lunch the next day at the Tarallucci e Vino restaurant that was part of the Cooper-

Hewitt Museum on 5th Avenue. She agreed and said that would be just a short stone's throw from the Coniston Mansion a couple of blocks uptown on 5th. We would meet in front of the museum, where I was a member, and then we could make our way to the outdoors seating, where we could find some shade and get away from the crowds indoors where there was air conditioning.

Wouldn't want to talk about all this where other people could hear us.

I didn't want Ted and Gabriele to be put in a compromising position, and encouraged Gabriele to head home after the chicken parm, and then to meet us at Tarallucci e Vino at noon. He agreed and looked a little relieved.

"I am yours, not his," Gabriele said emphatically.

"Like I have said all along, I hope you realize I'm nearly twice your age, and not inclined to form a same-sex relationship after two failed marriages," I said softly. "I'm not trying to get rid of you. I love you in some odd way, and can't imagine ever being happy without you. I think I feel about you the way I always wanted to feel about my two sons – neither of whom ever wanted anything to do with me. But if you find someone you want to be with, I'm not gonna be in your way."

About then Ted wandered into the living room, looking a little lost. I asked if he wanted a drink or a snack or whatever.

Negative. I told him I was going to make a dirty vodka and turn on the news, or CNN or MSNBC if I couldn't find any network news.

"I've always been a news junky," I announced to whoever was listening. "It was heart-breaking for me when I cancelled my subscription to the Times, but the old newspapers were stacking up in the recycle room across the hall, and truthfully, I can read everything I need online for a lot less money and fewer trees cut down – trees extract oxygen from carbon dioxide and make it easier for animals and people to breathe."

"Tree-hugger?"

I nodded.

"Good thing my mom isn't here. She thinks climate change is a hoax, like certain politicians keep saying."

"Poor you, to have to cope with that kind of attitude."

"Listen, my mom is my mom, and she's weird in more ways than just that. I told you she clips coupons from the newspaper every day, even though by almost any measure we're pretty well-off. Some day you'll meet her, I hope."

"Bring her with you the next time you come to New York. I'm sure Lizzie Coniston would be happy to see her. She seems pretty much stranded high and dry, like a beached whale or a ship on a sand bar. Loneliness is one of the worst things to have to cope with."

I realized Gabriele was not in the apartment, just as I heard the doorbell ring. It was Gabriele, brandishing a shiny purple eggplant. "Best parm is with *melanzana*," he said, and headed into the kitchen. "I call Dante and tell him I be at Ora di Pranzo for dinner time tonight. Then I go home. Then I meet you at Tarallucci e Vino tomorrow at twelve. Dante make parm better than me anyway." He leaned into me and I hugged him.

"Is good place, Tarallucci e Vino. Maybe we make Ora di Pranzo like that, have new place on Upper East Side. Just need to find chef like Dante and *maggiordomo* like me."

He was certainly at home in the kitchen, singing tenor arias while he breaded and fried the eggplant and chicken breasts. He made the parm with both eggplant and chicken, and layered them into a glass Pyrex casserole dish with the other simple ingredients: basil, oregano, shredded mozzarella cheese and lots of red sauce (he used a brand from Rao's, a famous Italian restaurant in East Harlem, well over one hundred years old, and impossible to get a reservation), and of course parmesan cheese in prodigal amounts. He gave me instructions for cooking, which came down to baking it at about three hundred and fifty for half hour and then when the cheese is melted, it will be ready to eat.

Then he either high-tailed it to Ora di Pranzo, or probably home to slip into his tuxedo, then to the restaurant. Ted was a little downcast, but I think he understood the situation. He certainly chowed into the dinner when it came out of the oven. I opened a bottle of ciliegiolo, an Italian red wine from the area just south of the Maremma, partly in Umbria (around Orvieto) and partly in the northern part of Lazio, the area that Rome is in. A *ciliegia* is a cherry, so I guess the wine is supposed to have a taste that reminds one of cherries. I've never found that, but I like the wine. So did Ted.

I stayed up to watch one of my favorite cop shows and then got the headlines from the eleven o'clock news before gulping down the rest of my dirty vodka and heading to the corral. Fortunately, I seldom have trouble sleeping, although I have a heart-sinking feeling when I wake up in the mornings, and, given the option, would always roll over and steal some extra zzzs.

Then it was morning, and I heard some noise in the kitchen, which is just outside my bedroom door. Ted was making coffee in his underwear. I wear a t-shirt and boxer briefs to sleep in the summer – it's too warm and humid for pyjama pants, which I save for the colder months. I know my hair, such as it is, stands up all kinds of odd ways when I wake up, because I turn from one side to the other all night. I drink a lot of water, and usually my one surviving kidney (I lost one to cancer some years back) works overtime while I am asleep, so morning urination wakes me up with a start around seven o'clock. Once that's over with, I have my head back on the pillow for another hour or so.

We had a lazy morning dominated by coffee and rye toast with fig jam, something I have loved ever since my Texas grandmother made wild-fig jam every year and filled a shelf in her pantry with the bottles. Then we set out for the Cooper-Hewitt Museum, which is part of the Smithsonian – I think the only museum in New York that is a Smithsonian institution. It's an easy trek, but takes a while, because once you're at Grand Central, you still have to go fifty blocks uptown, and then walk over from Lexington to 5th Avenue.

Of course, Ruth was already there, waiting in the Cooper-Hewitt entrance lobby. She was like a painting or an illustration in *Vogue*: in a linen blouse that was the color of raspberry sorbet, with zero wrinkles in it (how do people do that?), and white linen slacks with white sandals.

"You look like the Goddess of Summer," Ted said to her with a broad smile. She blew him an air kiss. It was about then that Gabriele arrived, having had the longest distance to travel, from Brooklyn. We found an empty table across a sizable lawn from the entrance to the restaurant and made ourselves comfortable. A waiter brought menus and poured ice water into our glasses.

"Oh my God," Ruth said. "Don't look, keep your heads down, but Hank Huntington just walked from the museum exit and is making his way into the restaurant."

I looked up and saw him, wearing a linen blazer and white pants, and peering into the windows of the restaurant, like he was looking for someone. Then he disappeared into Tarallucci e Vino.

"We're so close to the Coniston Mansion," Ruth said. "I wonder if he's been over there courting one of the girls. Who could he be meeting here? He was acting like he was expecting someone important, straightening his tie and so forth. Imagine wearing a tie and jacket in this heat!"

"I think that's something we will have to find out another day," I said. "I suggest we head out now, before he comes back out and spots us." We left one by one, skulking quickly to the back exit, and meeting on the 5th Avenue sidewalk. "Let's reconnoiter at the bar in the Peninsula Hotel, 55th Street and 5th Avenue."

We needed two taxis, but didn't have to wait long, and soon were in the bar where Ruth and I had met up with Ricky Coniston. My favorite bartender, Juan, wasn't there, but we got regal treatment anyway. Soon we were eating salted nuts and drinking either a Tom Collins or a salted margarita, appropriate to the weather. I was tempted to ask for a mint julep, but didn't want to be tipsy, so stuck to the Tom Collins. I hadn't reckoned with the fact that Collins mix is carbonated, and I don't do well with alcohol and carbonation. I started to feel a bit nauseated, what with the taste of the gin (which I seldom drink) and the carbonation. I signaled the waiter and asked him to take the drink away and bring me a Coca-Cola instead, and a lunch menu.

Bars in hotels usually serve food if you want it, because they use the same kitchen as the restaurants. I wanted scrambled eggs, toast and jam, which was not a problem. Ruth joined me in that, and Ted wanted a club sandwich and some chips. Gabriele was happy with his salted margarita.

"We know, or we were told, that Huntington is interested in one of Lizzie's daughters," Ruth said. "Good grief, he must be twice the girl's age."

"That museum that we didn't go into is a cool place, lots of design-oriented exhibits that change fairly often," I offered, trying to change the subject. "I remember seeing an exhibition of hand-painted wallpapers from the early nineteenth century. Landscapes and country homes mostly. Fabulous."

"So, what do you think about almost running into Huntington there?" she asked impatiently.

"Like I said, I have no idea why he was there. And like you said, he appeared to be looking for someone in particular. Could it be a Coniston? Could be. Do we know? No."

Ruth was convinced he was either meeting Lizzie or one of her daughters. "Lizzie has five daughters, two of them Conistons, and the others Harrisons, although I believe they consider themselves Westbrooks, which was Lizzie's maiden name; she married Mr Harrison first, then after they divorced, he died and she married Eddie Coniston. There are apparently a few Westbrooks who have taken up residence in the house. Eddie Coniston was partial to that family, so they may have been there for a while."

"I wonder why the Coniston girls aren't in line to inherit the business," Ted said. "Women have been able to vote since 1920. With the boys dead, why wouldn't the estate go to the girls? Wouldn't you think, in this time when companies are all looking for diversity, that the girls would at least be advising the Board, and probably would be valuable additions to the management?"

"Woo hoo!" Ruth said softly. "Look at you, all modern and stuff. Congrats, Ted, I like your style."

"When I was a kid, and my dad was still alive," Ted said, "my cousin Betty – that's the Elizabeth Coniston who's about my age – and I were very close. When the family got together, we played board games together in the second-floor library. Monopoly, Parcheesi, things like that.

My family lived on the Upper West Side, but Betty lived in the 5th Avenue house with her parents and her brothers and sister. She was a pretty girl, probably still is, haven't seen her in years, but we're close to the same age. She's a year or two older than me, maybe twenty-four. I think she went to Cornell, graduated when I was still at BC. No idea what she majored in, but she's sharp as a tack. She could run the Coniston Companies. It seems to me that, by rights, she should have inherited what the boys owned."

Gabriele was watching Ted, almost without blinking.

Ah hah! What have we here?

Gabriele looked at me and I saw he was grinning ear to ear. He shrugged and sipped on his margarita, looked away from Ted. He stood up and walked over to the bar, asked something of the bartender, then took off in the direction of the rest rooms.

"Sulking, is he?" Ruth asked, looking at me.

"Not that I know of. Looks like he's looking for the men's room."

"Did you say men's room?" Ted asked.

Nod. "I think that's where Gabriele is going."

"Great bladders think alike," he said, and stood up. "Where is the men's room?"

"Other side of the check-in desk and to the left," I told him. I spent many visits to New York at this hotel before my second divorce, which was when I moved from California to Manhattan, and I know the lay of the land at the Peninsula. I lived in the Theater District for ten years, then moved to Long Island City – but I'm still very fond of the Peninsula Hotel and the people I still know there.

Ted walked off toward where Gabriele had gone.

"Trouble in paradise?" Ruth asked. Since she and I were the only ones left at the table, I answered that I thought they both had to pee. "You still drinking Coke?" she asked. "I'd be surprised if you didn't have to pee, too."

"I'm not going to leave you alone at the table, if you're suggesting that I follow the boys where they are, but when they get back, yes, I will avail myself of the facilities just as they're doing now."

My phone vibrated in my back pants pocket. It was a text from Mike.

You in town?

Yup, can I help you? At the Peninsula Hotel lobby bar with Ruth, Ted and Signor Cortese

Just give me a call when you're free. Any idea when that will be?

Want me to come over there?

Sure, whenever you can

I told Ruth that I had a text from Mike asking me to meet him at his office, and waved at the waiter with that air-pencil sign language that means "check, please."

"You don't have to pay for everything," she said.

The waiter came over and told us there was no check because Mr Cortese and his friends were being comped. I put two twenties on the table and headed to the men's room, passing Gabriele and Ted on the way, so I told them I was heading to Mike's office. Then I thanked Gabriele for the lunch and drinks that were comped.

The Peninsula Hotel is at 55th and 5th Avenue. Mike's office is at 54th Street between 8th and 9th Avenues, so it was not a long walk, even on a swelteringly hot summer day.

Chapter Thirty

"Hank Huntington is in town," Mike said when I got to his office door.

"I know. I almost ran into him today."

"How? Why?"

"Ted, Gabriele and Ruth met me for lunch, and Huntington walked in while we were sitting outside. He didn't see us, and we didn't wave or make ourselves obvious, and we got away without being seen, I think."

"What did he look like?"

"About the same as he looked in Monte Carlo when we met him there. As tall as I am, good looking, and could be a runway model."

"That's not what I meant. Was he angry? Was he with someone?"

"Not angry; he was alone, but seemed to be looking for someone, maybe someone he was planning to meet. Kept looking in the windows like he was looking for someone in particular. That's probably why he didn't see us, because we were sitting a way away on the other side of a lawn, behind him. Ruth spotted him, and we all ducked out."

"What kind of a restaurant has a lawn?"

"It was Tarallucci e Vino at the Cooper-Hewitt Museum, which is what used to be Andrew Carnegie's home on 5th Avenue and 91st, I think. Entrance to the restaurant is on 90th, and there's plenty of room for a lawn in what was probably a back yard when the Carnegies lived there. Quite a place. Food is good, but we didn't stay to eat after Hank stalked in."

"Wonder why he was in a museum."

"It's right near the Coniston Mansion, could be why he was there. He is said to be courting one of the Coniston girls. According to Ted, that would probably be Elizabeth Coniston, named after her mother, but called Betty by the family. She's a couple of years older than Ted, so think mid-twenties-ish. Hank is probably about double that in years, although he looks younger than he is. Ted says Betty is very pretty and smart."

"This city has millions of people wandering around, and you almost bump into a person of interest in what may be a homicide that we're working on."

"I don't think he knew we were there."

"If something like that happens, let me know immediately. It could make a big difference."

"Anything else, boss?"

"Yes, the M.E. was able to determine that the blood in the horse trailer was from the Coniston boys. Couldn't do the same for the blood on the ground by the gatehouse tower-building. Could have been animal blood – washed away to a large extent by heavy rainstorms."

"Maybe we should talk to Jack. If we do, it might be good to take Ted along, so Jack won't freak out."

Mike pulled out his cellphone and tapped on the keys a bit. "I'm sending a text to Ricky Coniston asking if we can meet with some of the people in the barn."

"What if Ted picked Jack up and brought him to your precinct?" I asked. "Do you think he would be more willing to open up than if he was at his workplace, surrounded by friends and colleagues?"

"Could be. What do you think?"

"I think the interrogation rooms in the precinct are good environments for telling the truth."

"I don't know Jack's last name. Do you?"

"No, but I'm sure Ted does. They've been friends for years. I do know one of the horses he grooms is named Vesuvius. But maybe I should text Ted and ask him?"

"If you can, that'd be best."

I texted Ted, who came back to me quickly.

I told Mike, "Ramos is his last name. His full name is Diego Ramos, but he goes by Jack. Ted's here in Manhattan; do you want me to get him to come over here?"

Mike nodded, so I texted Ted again and gave him the address. He texted back that he could be here in ten or twenty minutes.

When Ted appeared at the top of the staircase leading up from the ground level, I was waiting for him, and took him into Interrogation Room 2, per Mike's instructions. Mike walked in right behind us.

"Thanks for coming over, Ted," Mike said. "We're thinking that it's likely that your friend Jack might know more about what happened than he let on when we were out at your Uncle Ricky's place."

Ted nodded. It was clear he had been thinking the same thing.

"It's not easy to tell everything you know if you're afraid you might get into trouble," Mike said. "And it's embarrassing to be involved in something nasty like the kids getting killed, even if you didn't have anything to do with it."

I asked Mike when he thought he could get Jack into town for a meeting. He said he thought he could arrange it for the next day, so I suggested that Ted might want to stay over for another day or two. Ted agreed. I imagine that he was thinking he might get to see Gabriele again.

"Maybe we can have dinner at Ora di Pranzo, if you'd like to see the place."

He brightened up right away when I said that. So, I texted Gabriele and asked if he'd mind if Ted and I showed up around seven o'clock.

Maybe I go to you and we eat at Tournesol or someplace there. Then I stay with you tonight in your bed, so Ted understand.

Seven o'clock was okay with Gabriele. He said he would call Tournesol and get a table, and I wondered what he was planning to do. I told Ted that Gabriele would join us for dinner near where I live.

"*Tournesol* is the French word for a sunflower, which 'turns' during the day to face 'sol'," I told Ted, who nodded in an off-handed way that conveyed he already knew what *tournesol* meant. Ted was unusually quiet, and I wondered if he was thinking about whether Jack would be bushwhacked the next day at the NYPD precinct. It seemed like there were several undercurrents in motion.

When Gabriele showed up, he was not looking his best in an oversized, navy blue, loose-knit linen crew-neck pullover and a pair of tan khaki pants that looked like they had been wadded up and

purposefully wrinkled. He made a show of yawning as I handed him a
dirty vodka when he flopped down on the couch. I looked at him and
realized he was putting on a show that was the opposite of what he usually
did.

We walked over to Tournesol, a distance we covered in less than
ten minutes. It is a very popular eatery, even drawing people from
Manhattan, which is very unusual – most Manhattan residents wouldn't
be caught dead in Queens, except when they're going to one of the
airports, or maybe a Mets game (maybe not). Not expensive, but
excellent, mostly traditional French food. I rank their duck confit nearly
as good as that same dish at Chez Napoleon in Hell's Kitchen, which, on
a scale of one to ten (ten being best) was about a twenty-five. Served with
haricots verts (green beans) and *pommes frites* ("French" fries, which
actually originated in Belgium). Gabriele had steak frites and a side of
epinards a la crème (creamed spinach). We ordered a bottle of Cahors, a
wine from the southwest of France that is made from seventy percent or
more Malbec grapes blended with a bit of merlot. In the ancient town of
Cahors, it's called *Auxerrois*. Most Americans associate malbec grapes
with Argentina, but it is a French grape, also used in some Bordeaux and
Loire Valley reds.

Ted tried to start conversations, but Gabriele wasn't having any,
just wolfing down his steak and tearing up some bread rolls to drag
through the green pepper sauce. He seldom wants to go to an Italian
restaurant, which is easy to understand, since his own place serves the
pinnacle of Italian food on Manhattan Island. I happen to know, though,
that he favors the pizzas at Grimaldi's, which is very close to his
apartment in Brooklyn Heights. I was finding myself amused at his 'new
self', more slovenly than I had ever seen. And quiet, not conversational
at all.

Ted ordered a Toulouse-style cassoulet, which is a casserole made
with white beans, ham, special Toulouse-style garlic-pork sausages, and
duck confit like I had ordered. Even I thought it smelled wonderful, and I
was tempted to taste it, even though I haven't eaten red meat – including
pork – in more than thirty years.

As we walked back to my apartment, there were clouds that looked like rain. I hadn't watched the local news, so didn't know that there was a prediction of thunder and lightning. But then there was a bolt of lightning that lit up the whole sky, followed in less than a second by a very loud crack of thunder. It must have been very nearby, and all the lights went out as far as we could see, including Manhattan. The three of us started to run, just made it to the lobby when the rain started. It was pouring and there was a strong wind that made it rain sideways, so it was pounding on the windows. My apartment is on the tenth floor, so we took the stairs, which had emergency lighting. There was also emergency lighting in the hallway, but no juice at all inside the apartment.

Fortunately, I grew up in Texas at a time when we lost electricity fairly often with big thunderstorms, so I have always put lots of candles on the tabletops, and had a box of wooden matches on the pass-through from the kitchen to the living room. I lit several of the candles, and then realized that the Chrysler Building was lighted up, so there was a likelihood that the blackout was only local. Gabriele found a bottle of California red wine with a screw top and opened it. I got out some water glasses, and warned Ted not to open the fridge, because if the electricity stayed off, the food might spoil.

A short few minutes later, there was a brief mechanical noise and the lights came back on outside. I quickly blew out all the candles and turned on a couple of lamps and the television.

"I hope it stays on," I said out loud.

Gabriele hugged me for an uncomfortably long time. Ted concentrated on the television, using the remote to click through the stations, probably looking for news bulletins or weather alerts.

"Try New York One if you're looking for news. I think you'll find it on channel twelve," I said to Ted, removing Gabriele's arms from my back. Gabriele walked off in the direction of the bathroom. I heard the door close.

"What's with him?" Ted asked me. "He's acting like there's something wrong."

"Everybody's entitled to be moody sometimes. Even Gabriele,

who's usually smiling and looking like a movie star," I said. "Sometimes the world is harder to tolerate. Give him some space. He'll be better tomorrow."

Ted said he was going to take a shower and go to bed, and walked down the hallway to the second bedroom. I heard the shower running in the master bathroom, Gabriele trying to wash off the dust and whatever.

The next morning, I was the first one up, so I made the coffee, and used dark roast coffee that I had in the freezer. It smelled wonderful as it was dripping into the glass coffee pot. I heard the second bathroom's shower turn on, so I knew Ted was up and about. Sure enough, about ten minutes later, he appeared at the kitchen door, smiling, and wearing nothing but boxer shorts. He was built like a runner, strong legs and slim torso, but with an unboyish thatch of hair on his chest. I poured a mug of coffee for him, and told him that there was milk in the fridge, and sugar in the canister on the counter, patting the top of it.

"Just black for me," he said.

I took a mug into the bedroom for Gabriele, who was still asleep. I had put milk and sugar into his coffee, so I put it down on the bedside table and sat down on the edge of the bed. He woke up.

"Smells wonderful," he said. I pointed at the mug and he sat up, swung his legs off the edge of the bed. "How's Ted?"

"About like you, but he's in the living room drinking his coffee in his boxers." He looked up at the ceiling. "I think you're safe to go back to normal," I said.

He smiled and nodded.

"I think I'll text Mike and see what time he wants us to be there for the meeting with Jack," I said. "Mike is big on morning meetings. My money's on eleven o'clock."

I was wrong. The meeting was set for one o'clock. The three of us headed for the subway about half an hour before noon, intending to stop someplace in Times Square for a quick lunch, or at least a quick drink, since the forecast was for a hot humid day. I decided to wear a short-sleeved linen shirt and suggested to the boys that they should dress for the weather, and not try to look like investment bankers. When we got off the train at Times Square, I wasn't feeling like eating much, or at least only eating something light.

We ended up walking over to 9th Avenue where there are several Thai places that are reasonably priced. I learned years back that if you want to eat light, make a meal off the appetizers at a Thai restaurant. When we looked at the menu, I ordered Golden Purses, which are like fried wontons stuffed with crabmeat and spicey sweet chili sauce, and a green papaya salad. Also, a Thai beer and a glass of water, since I try to stay well hydrated in hot weather. Gabriele and Ted both ordered noodle bowls and Thai beer. I told them I was paying for all three of us, because I can get reimbursed by the NYPD, and it was not likely that we would get comped anyway.

We were a few minutes later getting to Mike's office than I had planned, and Jack was already in Interrogation Room 1. Mike was waiting for us in his office, and told us we would be sitting in the interrogation room with him, and not in the observation room behind the mirror. There were several bottles of water on the table, and Jack was clearly happy that Ted was in the room. They hugged each other like Europeans.

Mike started the meeting by thanking Jack for coming into town for this meeting, and explained that the reason for holding the meeting in this room is that the room is equipped with recording devices that would allow us to get a transcript on paper within twenty-four hours of the meeting. Then he asked Jack a personal question: "If your given name is Diego, why do people call you Jack?"

"Most people say that the English version of Diego is James, and Jack is a nickname for either John or James. The kids in school called me Jack, and I liked it. My parents still call me Diego; some of the relatives call me Jack, others call me Diego."

"Is it okay for me to call you Jack, in that case?"

"Sure."

"So, Jack. Were you working on the flower border behind the Kids' House the day that Ted brought his young cousins to visit Ricky and his wife?"

"Earlier that day, I was working on the flowers, but not in the hot part of the afternoon, when I worked in the barn. So, I wasn't working there when they arrived to visit Mr and Mrs Coniston. I heard later that they had been there, and eventually went back over to the Kids' House to say hello to them."

"And were they there?"

He looked at the table. "They were, but when I opened the front door, I didn't see them."

"Isn't there a doorbell? Or is the door just left unlatched so you could just walk in?"

"It's usually unlocked, although there is a deadbolt on the door so that once you're inside you can lock the door. It can be opened from the outside with a key, I think. At least there's a keyhole there. I don't know who has the key, probably Mr Coniston."

Mike asked him if he then left, or if he went upstairs to look for the boys, and then added, "And what were your intentions? Just to find them and say hello?"

"I guess so. I've known them for a long time. They usually stayed with the Conistons for a few weeks each summer, and I've been working with the horses for ten years. It turned out they were on the top level of the House. I guessed that, because that's where the food is. Most kids are hungry all the time."

"So, you went upstairs?"

He nodded and ran his hand through his hair, looking worried. "Yes."

"What happened?"

"They weren't in the kitchen, so I looked out on the terrace. They were standing on the wall. I walked outside and when I let go of the door, it slammed shut. There was a breeze, and it must have blown the door. It made a loud noise, and Dick turned and clearly looked like he was losing his balance. I told him to stay where he was and I would help him, but he grabbed Eddie's shoulder and both of them fell off the wall. I ran over to the wall and looked over, and neither of them was moving, so I ran downstairs, but I couldn't find a pulse on either one. I didn't have my cellphone with me, so I ran back to the barn to call 911, but I saw

Vesuvius – he's one of the horses I groom – and he could tell I was upset and started to paw the ground in front of him with his hoofs. Horses are very observant and very smart, and Vesuvius more than a lot of other horses, at least around me. He was trying to break out of his stall. So, I started talking to him and calmed him down, petted him on his neck and forehead."

"But you didn't call 911. Nobody did."

"I couldn't find my cellphone, so I ran back over to the Kids' House. Of course, they were exactly where they were when I ran off. I rolled them over, and Eddie had fallen on my hand cultivator. It was sticking in his back. I left it on the ground there that morning. I thought maybe that killed him, but it hadn't been bleeding much, so maybe not. I thought it was probably just the fall. I was really scared, and I don't know why, but I ran back to the barn, hooked up one of the horse trailers to one of the pickup trucks, and put Vesuvius in the trailer. Then I drove back over to the Kids' House and picked up the boys and put them in the other side of the trailer, and drove off down the road. Ended up driving over near Tarrytown, not really very far, but it would have been a very long hike if you were on foot."

"And what did you do when you stopped?"

Ted's mouth was hanging open like his jaw was broken or something. Tears were pouring down his face. Gabriele put his arm around Ted's shoulder, and Ted started to sob.

Jack stared at Ted, and said rather loudly, and with a lot of emotion, "I took the boys out of the trailer, and put them under a tree, leaning on the trunk. They looked like they were okay. And then I was really, really scared, because I knew what I had done was probably illegal, even though I didn't hurt the boys." He kept looking at Ted and said, "You know I couldn't ever hurt them?"

Ted nodded and stood up, walked around the table and hugged Jack. "I know you wouldn't hurt them, no matter what. "

"I didn't tell anybody what happened because I was scared. I couldn't sleep, I couldn't eat." He burst into tears and collapsed against Ted, falling to his knees. "Please don't hate me."

Joseph Allen

"I couldn't hate you, Jack. You've always been my friend," Ted choked out. He grabbed Jack's arm and pulled him up to standing. "You're a good person, Jack, and I'm glad you were there when the boys fell off the roof."

Mike told Jack that the things we discussed would be passed along to the local police in Tarrytown or Hawthorne. "We'll try to help you, but they may decide to press charges for leaving the scene or disturbing the scene of a crime or something like that. The Medical Examiner's cause of death was the same for both boys: broken necks, severed spines. They wouldn't have been in any pain. Very fast death, and you had nothing to do with it."

"You'll have to tell Mr Coniston," Jack said to Mike, making it sound like a question.

Mike nodded and Ted jumped in and said, "I'll tell Uncle Ricky. Better me than a policeman. Who's going to tell Aunt Lizzie?"

Mike said he would go over to the Coniston home on 5th Avenue and break the news to Mrs Coniston, and he would also tell the mayor, who would probably tell the media.

Chapter Thirty-one

The mayor didn't hold a press conference and apparently didn't leak the news out to the media either. I watched the television, with Ted, pretty much from four o'clock until about midnight – nothing about the Coniston boys. Ted was morose, and spent a good deal of time on the telephone with his mother, who was clearly distraught to hear what Jack had told us at Mike's precinct.

Gabriele showed up shortly after six with two bags full of food that either he or Dante had cooked. I was humming very softly an old Woody Guthrie song called "Hard Times in the Mill" when the doorbell rang. Gabriele put the bags on the counter in the kitchen, and produced a plastic container of dried *orecchiette* pasta. He looked in the cabinet where I keep pots and pans and produced a pasta boiler, which is a deep pot with a strainer that fits inside it so that you can boil the pasta and lift it out without pouring the water into the sink. That's because Italian chefs use that water that the pasta has cooked in to thicken the sauces they make to put on the pasta. In this case, the orecchiette (so named because they looked to somebody like 'little ears') would be accompanied by turkey sausages and broccoli rabe (called *rapini* in Italian) sauteed in olive oil with lots of garlic.

I asked him what he was doing, and he said it was important to eat when you're upset or having a bad day. I hauled two bottles of Italian red wine out of the wine rack and pulled the cork on one of them so that Ted and Gabriele and I could whet our whistles.

"Nothing on the news about the boys yet," I told him. "Maybe the tabloids will run it in the morning. Hard to imagine that it won't leak out, but so far nothing on the TV."

Ted, who had been sitting in the living room watching the television, stuck his head into the pass-through to the kitchen to tell us that his mother, Isabelle "Izzy" Coniston, was taking Amtrak to New York City so that she could visit Lizzie Coniston and hold her hand. In spite of the ill will that Eddie and George Coniston held for each other, their wives had always been close. Now all the male children of the Coniston brothers were dead, except Ted. Ted would meet her at Penn Station and go with her to the Coniston Mansion on 5th Avenue.

"Does that mean that Eddie's daughters are likely to inherit control of the Coniston Companies?" I asked Ted. "Or will you inherit?"

He shrugged and said if there was any justice, Betty would take over her brothers' positions, but it was probably up to the Board. He said he was going to take a shower and put on some nicer clothes, since he would be going to visit Aunt Lizzie. I couldn't resist saying that it would be the Lizzie and Izzy show.

My cellphone vibrated in my pocket, meaning I had a text message. It was from Ruth, who wanted me to call her. I did. She told me that there was something going on in Twitter that had to do with Ricky Coniston. I knocked on the bedroom door where Ted had been sleeping. He opened it and I asked if he minded if I used the computer, because the room doubles as an office as well as a guest bedroom. He was just ready to leave to meet his mom at Penn Station, so I sat down at the desk and logged into Twitter. Of course, it signed me into my own account, so I searched "Coniston," and had no trouble finding Ricky's account.

There was a lot of activity on Ricky's account with several new bot-generated tweets appearing over the course of about a minute. They all seemed to be related to a tweet from @Hmonaco123, which looked to me like it had to be Hank Huntington. It was asking for info on Ricky Coniston, and especially anyone who knew where the Coniston boys were before they disappeared. I scanned over several dozen of the most recent tweets, and there were several that said the boys were dead, but none that attributed their deaths to Ricky.

I called Mike di Saronno and told him what was going on at Twitter. While we were talking, I looked at LinkedIn, and found the situation was very similar to Twitter. Lots of activity, and much of it looked like the work of bots – same words over and over again.

"Doesn't look like the mayor has leaked anything about what Jack Ramos told us," he said.

"Nor Lizzie Coniston or anyone else, who by now would know what Jack said."

Mike said he would inform the CSIs about this and see if they could come up with any intel on it. He also told me he had found out that Mr Huntington was staying at the Pierre Hotel, certainly the snootiest and fanciest hostelry in a city that has no shortage of snobs and mega-rich billionaires. Like the song says, "there's nothing more sure, the rich get rich and the poor get children. In the meantime, in between times, ain't we got fun." I felt totally certain that Hank Huntington was enjoying his life in the brilliant luxury of New York's most best-est, the Pierre.

Another text, this time from Ted: *Mom here on our way to Aunt Lizzie*

I found myself hoping that Mike had already made his visit to Lizzie Coniston, so that Ted and his mother wouldn't have to break the tragic news to her themselves.

I texted to Ruth that Huntington was staying at the Pierre. Of course, she knew the hotel's manager, who was a member of the Opera League – which means that Lizzie Coniston probably knew him, too. Maybe even Ricky Coniston, since he had used Opera League tickets several times. Ricky Coniston would be someone to befriend if you were the manager of the Pierre, being by reputation one of the patricians of New York – an old rich family, whose home was on the same avenue as the Pierre, and across from the same park.

She called and asked me if she should get in touch with her friend at the Pierre. Just because I was curious, I suggested that if she did call him, she might find out what kind of accommodations Huntington had booked. As it turned out, Hank was bedding down in the least expensive room available, no view of Central Park, on a lower floor. Interesting. I had figured he would have taken a large suite with a grand piano in it. Was he being thrifty? Interesting.

It occurred to me that it might be advisable for someone from Mike's office to brief Ricky Coniston on what was going on – with Ted and Isabelle Coniston calling on Lizzie, who might well want to have some explanation from Ricky of what was going on at his home in Chappaqua. Mike disagreed, saying that it was not NYPD policy to get involved in family issues, especially in families of the ilk of the Conistons. I told him I still thought it would be good if Ricky Coniston knew what was in the wind, and especially if he knew what Jack Ramos had told us – I pointed out that Ted, who said he would bring Ricky up to date, was escorting his mother to the Coniston Mansion, and might not have had time to call Ricky since his mother arrived without much notice.

Mike told me he had indeed made his visit to Lizzie Coniston, who took the news without showing much emotion. "She said it was something of a relief to know it had been an accident, and not intentional on anybody's part." She had called Betty into the parlor-type room where Mike and Lizzie had been talking, and told Betty in front of Mike a summary of what Mike had told her. Betty, unlike her mother, burst into tears and said that Mr Huntington had told her that many people suspected Uncle Ricky had something to do with what happened to her brothers.

"Son of a bitch," Lizzie said, as though it were a normal everyday phrase. Then she told Betty that Mr Huntington would not be welcome in her house any longer, even though he was a distant relative. "And he's twice your age, young lady." Mike said that Betty wheeled around with her back to her mother and marched out of the room, pausing at the doorway to say with a sneer to her mother that Mr Huntington had been a perfect gentleman. *"Get out of my face, Mom!"*

A few minutes after the talk with Mike, my cellphone vibrated. It was a text from the concierge downstairs in the building lobby that Mr Cortese was on the way up. I had no idea that he was coming over; it was odd, because, although we spent a lot of time together, he almost never showed up unexpectedly.

Sure enough, the doorbell rang. When I opened the door, he was looking down at his feet, and didn't look up right away. When he did, he had an almost funereal look on his face, like he was carrying the burdens of the world on his back. I asked him if he would like to have a drink. He opted for a bottle of Nero d'Avola, a Sicilian red wine that is sometimes called 'Calabrese', but not in Sicily. Theoretically, it was originally grown in or near a town called Avola, which is just west of Siracusa, that spectacular ancient Greek city at the southernmost tip of the island that had been the home of Archimedes – who, it is said, used concave mirrors to set enemy ships in the harbor on fire by redirecting and concentrating the sun's rays on their sails. But in reality, Nero d'Avola grapes are grown all over Sicily, not to mention California and Australia – even Turkey.

Gabriele is normally talkative and outgoing. After all, he is the majordomo of one of the most popular restaurants in Manhattan, but on this day, he was morose and quiet.

"What's wrong?" I asked.

He shrugged. "Nothing, I guess."

"There's obviously something amiss," I said, and put my hand on his shoulder. "Tell me."

He said he had decided to leave Ora di Pranzo and move to Boston, where he could find an apartment that he and Ted could share.

"What does Dante think of that?"

"He not have trouble, but he want me stay."

"Why did you decide to do this? It doesn't sound to me like it is something you want to do."

"Because I love Dante. I love Ora di Pranzo. And I love you," he said, finally making eye contact with me. It was looking like a "Dear John" episode, but that didn't make sense because there was not that type of relationship between us.

"Why Ted?"

"Because he love me and he is good person. I need to be with somebody that love me."

"You know I love you. You are like my son."

"But I not want you be my father."

"I know. I understand. But you know that I'm not the type of person you need to be with all the time."

He smiled and shook his head. "I not know that. I know what I know. Ted and me, we can be happy together."

"But leaving Ora di Pranzo? That's too much. You have made it such a wonderful place. Everybody loves you there."

"You not mind I be with Ted?"

"Why would I mind? I agree with you that he is a good person. But why not stay at Ora di Pranzo and invite Ted to move in with you in Brooklyn Heights?"

"Because in New York I want be with you instead of him."

"If that is true, it would be true in Boston just as much as Brooklyn." He turned his back to me and drank most of the wine in his glass. "What does Ted think of all this?"

He said he hadn't spoken with Ted about it. They had talked about moving in together once, and Ted liked the idea, but that was some time back.

"Do you think you and Ted would get married?"

He shook his head and shrugged, probably meaning he didn't know.

"Let's go for a walk," I said. "Fresh air is good."

We walked along the waterfront along the East River, which isn't a river at all, just a connection between Long Island Sound and New York Harbor. It's all ocean water, and people catch striped bass off the piers in front of the building I live in. He didn't say anything, just put his arm around my back. I'm several inches taller than Gabriele, so he was reaching up, and was pulling down on my shoulder.

Clearly, I didn't want him to leave. But I myself had been telling Gabriele for years that he should find a partner to be with, that there was no way he and I would be partners in that way. I am attracted to Ruth, but I would never be able to live with her either. The love of her life was her husband, Murray, who had died a couple of years earlier. I have known Ruth since before she met Murray, but I am a two-time loser in the marriage world, and I don't see the point of trying it a third time.

We walked up to Vernon Avenue, and wandered over to Dominie's Hoek, a favorite watering-hole for the area where I live, named after the Dutch moniker for the area that became this part of Long Island

City. I had a dirty vodka, my usual poison of choice, and Gabriele joined me in that.

"I would miss you terribly if you left," I said, looking directly into his eyes.

He teared up, and so did I.

Chapter Thirty-two

Ted and his mother, Isabelle (or "Izzy"), showed up at my apartment shortly after Gabriele and I got there, having spent most of the afternoon with Lizzie Coniston. Isabelle was about the age of my eldest daughter, I judged from her looks – mid-40s or thereabouts. Pretty. A *zaftig* brunette with a nice figure, must have been almost still a teenager when Ted was born. And then to lose her husband and have to raise Ted as a single mom. *She must be strong as an ox,* I thought.

She was wearing a navy-blue shirtwaist dress with a thickish white leather belt and a strand of pearls that was shorter than opera-length, but not a choker. The dress looked snug on her, and I wondered how she would dress when she wasn't visiting her sister-in-law's mansion.

She accepted a glass of red wine and sat down in a caned armchair that had been in my grandmother's house when I was a child. Probably an antique, but comfy, especially in hot humid weather such as we were having, because it kept you from sweating. I had the AC on too, but that wouldn't necessarily help if you had been outside walking. I offered her a lumbar cushion, which she took with a smile.

"How was your visit with the New York Conistons?" I asked.

Ted answered, "Nice. I was worried that Aunt Lizzie would be grief-stricken, crying a lot. But she wasn't. She was acting like herself. She said it was a great relief to find out that what happened was accidental, but then we just talked about summers at Uncle Ricky's place, and how nice it was to be out in the country."

I poured myself a couple of fingers of scotch and then threw in two ice cubes and a splash of tap water. I put a bowl of roasted salted nuts on the coffee table, and scooped a few into a small container for Isabelle. Ted and I were both sitting on the sofa, and could reach the coffee table easily.

"Terrible time for Elizabeth," Isabelle said. "She doesn't show her feelings, puts on a brave face, but to have both of her boys gone – it must be torture for her. My Ted is the only Coniston boy left now. Ricky's son is gone too, and with Ann in the condition she's in, it doesn't seem possible that they will have another child. Very sad." She looked around the room. "You have a lot of paintings. Are you an artist?" she asked me.

"Not at all. Just have very little willpower when I see a picture that I like."

She smiled and said, "Where do you find the pictures?"

"Most of them were purchased in galleries. Several of them from galleries in Santa Fe, but some from New York too, and some from places in California, where I used to live." I motioned to a pencil sketch of an elderly woman, nude. "That one was my first purchase, when I was about nineteen, long time back, *molti anni fa*, as the Italians say. Cost me all of about twenty-five dollars at a charity silent auction in one of the United Nations' embassy buildings. I felt like a bigshot then, but I still like it all these years later."

"Do you speak Italian?"

I nodded and said, "Not very well, though. Just enough to ask street directions, or order basic food in a restaurant." I paused, then added, "I can figure out what newspaper articles are about, but sometimes get lost even with that. And I can't follow Italian television. They talk too fast. But I try."

"I visited Italy once, loved it. My husband was a traveler, loved exploring new places, places he'd never been to. Have you been to Italy?"

I nodded. "Mostly the west coast of Italy, and the islands. Sicily, Sardinia, Capri, places like that. Lampedusa. Never have made it to the east coast. Never been to Venice or Ravenna, for instance."

"Venice is wonderful, but we were there in the summer, and it smelled bad a lot of the time," she said.

I noticed that she had no wine left in her glass and offered to pour some more. She smiled and said she would appreciate a glass of water, which I got from the kitchen; a chilled bottle of Perrier from the fridge, and a glass with ice in it.

I turned to Ted. "Are you heading back to Boston? My guest bedroom is still yours if you want it."

"Mom and I will be driving to Boston when we leave. She came on the train, because I have her car."

"I know Gabriele will be sad that he missed you this afternoon."

"Gabriele?" Isabelle asked.

"Italian guy, owns a very fancy restaurant in Manhattan," Ted said quickly. "Kind of a celebrity, I think."

"I think of Gabriele as my adopted son," I explained. "He's frequently here, and I am frequently at his restaurant, which is in the SoHo area, on the downtown side of Greenwich Village."

"Mr Miller has met Hank Huntington," Ted said.

Isabelle perked up and smiled. "I hear he is very handsome," she said.

"He is good looking, and seems very athletic, too. No idea how old he is, but he looks to me like he might be mid- or late thirties. I met him in the Fairmont Hotel in Monte Carlo. He has a house in Monaco, which is pretty unusual because there are only a very few houses in the whole country – people live in high rises, not houses. I remember thinking I wouldn't want to run against him for a political position, because all the women would vote for him."

"Not nearly as good looking as Gabriele Cortese, I bet," Ted said. "That's the restaurant owner, looks like a movie star or someone who just stepped off a magazine cover."

There was an awkward pause in the conversation as Isabelle looked questioningly at her son. Then she looked at me and said she understood I worked with the police.

"I am what they call a civilian criminalist in the NYPD, but yes, I do work with one of their lead detectives on some cases," I said. "One of the cases I have been on is the case of the Coniston boys when they disappeared. I have met Mr Richard Coniston, and have been to his home in Westchester County. Quite a place. Also, Mrs Edward Coniston, Ted's aunt."

I realized that Isabelle knew her son was gay, and I decided to change the subject to Mike di Saronno. "I value my relationship with the detective I work with. His name is Mike di Saronno, and he's one of my best friends as well as being my boss at the police department. I was in Monaco specifically to find out what I could about Mr Huntington."

"How did you get to meet him? Did the police help you make an appointment?"

"No, they didn't. As it happened, Mr Huntington got in touch with me almost as soon as I checked into my hotel. I never found out exactly why or how he knew who I was, or that I was even there. But money makes a lot of things possible, and Monaco is such a small place that a billionaire who wants to know who's coming and going is probably a snap. He initially introduced himself under another name, though – not Huntington. But my friend Ruth had seen a picture of him in a real estate magazine and knew who he was right away, so trying to be incognito was pointless."

"Is your girlfriend an NYPD person, too?" she asked.

"She's not a girlfriend, first of all. We've just known each other for decades. I'm divorced and Ruth's husband, Murray, died a couple of years back, so we're both home alone a good deal of the time; we are comfortable with each other, so we spend time together, but it is not a romantic relationship – never has been, never will be.

"Ruth helps out with my NYPD assignments though; she calls herself 'Ruth the Sleuth' because of that. Mr Cortese is a loner, too – no real romantic emotions as far as I know, although I know he admires your son a lot. He has more social contacts than a bear has fleas – he was on friendly terms with Ricky Coniston, for instance, because Mr Coniston likes to dine at Ora di Pranzo. But Gabriele spends a surprising amount of time on police cases, and he seems to be able to tell with uncanny accuracy when people are not telling the truth.

"Both Ruth and Gabriele are super-connected with the great and the good in the Tri-State area. Ruth is a big opera fan – goes to the opera every Monday during the seasons with the Opera League, and a volunteer at Carnegie Hall, too. Gabriele knows everyone who is anyone because of his fancy restaurant, where even celebrities and rich people have to wait in line to get in."

Ted stood up and said he needed to use the restroom, would be back shortly, and flashed a smile at his mom.

"I should have asked you if you wanted to use the facilities," I said to Mrs Coniston. "There are two full bathrooms in this apartment, so there's no standing in line necessary. There is a bathroom right behind that door over there (I gestured to the door to my bedroom, which is just across from the kitchen). It's attached to my bedroom."

She smiled, shook her head slightly, and said she was fine.

While Ted was down the hall, I told Isabelle quickly that I thought Ted and Gabriele might be developing a relationship with each other. "Gabriele even told me he was thinking of moving to Boston, which would mean he would have to leave his restaurant and his cousin, Dante, who is the restaurant's chef, and a half-owner with Gabriele."

My cellphone vibrated. It was Ruth. I texted to her that Isabelle Coniston and Ted were here, and that I would call her back if it wasn't an emergency.

Okay talk later. Anything new on Huntington?

Why?

Wondering if he's still in NY. Seeing tweets about Ricky. Maybe H stirring the pot

Will call you soon as I can

I told Isabelle I needed to make a couple of calls and went into the bedroom and closed the door. First, I called Mike.

"Hey, bud," he said. "What's up?"

I told him that Ruth had just called to say she was seeing tweets about Ricky Coniston. He said he had seen some, too. "Not a storm yet, but I'm seeing more every time I look."

"Ruth was wondering if Hank Huntington was still in New York," I said.

"As far as I know, he's still staying at the Pierre."

"Might be a good idea to check."

"Will do."

"Let me know what you find out. I'm thinking it might be a good idea to meet with Ricky Coniston to find out what light he might be able to shed on what Huntington could be up to."

"Good thinking. I'll try to get something set up," he said. "Maybe it would be best to do this in Chappaqua, instead of asking Ricky to meet in Manhattan someplace. I want to see inside the Kids' House again at any rate. The CSIs from Westchester took some pictures, but didn't write much about what they saw there."

"Text me if you get something set up," I suggested, remembering that I had told Ruth I would call her. I peeked out of the bedroom. Both Ted and Isabelle were there, so I waved and told them I had one more call to make that wouldn't take long.

"Mike's going to try to arrange for us to meet with Ricky Coniston at his place in Westchester," I told Ruth. "You up for that?"

I told her we hoped to get another tour of the Kids' House where it seems, according to Jack Ramos, that the Coniston boys died by falling from the roof terrace when the wind slammed a door and startled them.

Ruth was enthusiastic about that, especially to see the place where the boys may have fallen with fresh eyes.

I went back to the living room after a short talk with Ruth and told Ted and Isabelle that I was hoping to have a meeting with Ricky Coniston and another tour of the Kids' House there.

I asked him if he wanted to go along with us, because we were hoping to see Jack again, and try to fill in some of the blank places in what we knew.

"Do you know that horse that Jack was grooming? Vesuvius?" I asked him. "I'd kinda like to actually meet him. I grew up with horses. Well, actually quarterhorses, much smaller than thoroughbreds like the Arabians that Ricky Coniston is probably raising. But so smart you wonder if they're smarter than people."

Ted nodded and said that he had even ridden Vesuvius, although Ted admitted that he was a good bit heavier than the small-frame riders who trained horses that were still racing. "You have no idea how smart those horses are until you spend time with them. And Vesuvius can be completely, one hundred percent your friend if you give him a turnip or a carrot, or especially an apple. Most horses are happy to be around people. They're like dogs: friendly, playful, loyal and completely domesticated. Not like cows, who are dumb as dirt."

I told him that when I was a kid, I found out how dumb cows are, because my grandparents owned a cattle ranch. If a cow walks into a pond and get its front feet stuck in the mud, it can't even figure out how to back up. It'll just stay there until it dies. You have to pull them out by tugging on their tails. Same if they walk into a fork in a tree looking to eat the leaves, they can't figure out to back up unless you pull on them. They just eat, that's all they do. And make 'cow pies' that can be turned into fertilizer.

Isabelle volunteered to take Amtrak back to Boston, so that Ted could stay in New York with the Mercedes. "I like the train ride. It's very pretty at this time of year, before the leaves turn color and fall. Of course, it's pretty when the leaves turn, too. It'll be pretty until around Thanksgiving. Just make sure you come home when you're finished here, so I won't have to worry about where you are."

Chapter Thirty-three

Mike was able to arrange a drive to Chappaqua the next day. Ricky Coniston would meet and tell us whatever he knew about what happened that fateful day, all subjects okay. Ted took his mom to Penn Station to catch the Amtrak train to Boston, and insisted on carrying her suitcase, even though it was small and didn't weigh much.

I texted Gabriele and asked him to come over for dinner with Ted and me. It would be a surprise for Ted when he got back from taking his mom to the Amtrak platform at Penn Station in Manhattan. He texted back that he'd talked to Dante and would be happy to join us.

As it happened, Gabriele got to my place before Ted got back. He had a bag of groceries, and I knew he was planning to cook.

"I was thinking we could go out, maybe the crab shack," I told him.

"Maybe I just make some pasta and we stay here," he said, without making eye contact. "Why is Ted mama go home so soon?"

I explained that Mike had arranged a meeting in Chappaqua with Ricky Coniston, and we thought Ted should go to the meeting, especially since we would probably be spending some time with his friend, Jack Ramos. "So, instead of driving back to Boston, Isabelle decided to take Amtrak, which she said she enjoyed more anyway," I said. "And I thought it would be an opportunity for you, Ted and me to spend some time together."

He looked at me and there were tears in his eyes. "Is you I love, Ugo, not Ted. But I sometimes need be with a man who love me. Maybe can be Ted." He looked away. "I make pasta. We have good dinner when Ted come." Turned out he had also brought two bottles of Barbaresco, a northern Italian red with a slightly fruity taste combined with a slight similarity to the famous 'Sunday wine', Barolo.

"How about a dirty vodka while you cook? I'm going to have one."

He nodded. So, I pulled two martini glasses out of the freezer and poured a bit of the liquid from the olive jar into them and then filled most of the rest of the glasses with vodka, also stored in the freezer. We clinked our glasses together and my eyes teared up. "Of course, I love you, but not the way Ted might love you," I said, and took a big slurp from the vodka, which burned as I swallowed it, but it was a good burn, not a bad one.

I turned the television on, and set it to CNN, which is news and opinion twenty-four/seven. Maybe too much opinion, but I don't pay much attention to that part. Vodka is my friend when I'm feeling shaky. And I always feel better when the news is on the TV.

Soon there was the wonderful smell of olive oil and garlic, and I heard the sizzle of hot Italian turkey sausage being sauteed, one of the best kitchen smells in the world. I peeked into the kitchen and saw Gabriele chopping *rapini*, which in English is broccoli rabe. One of my most favorite dishes, something Gabriele has known for years (and he'd made it for me often).

I poured another couple of fingers of vodka into my martini glass as I heard the doorbell, which I figured was announcing that Ted was back from taking his mom to the train station.

"Hey, Ted, did Isabelle get on a train okay? What a nice person she is," I said, shaking his hand. "I'm very impressed, and understand how you got to be the fine young guy you are. Good genes. Nice mom. Pretty, too."

He hugged me, not like somebody would hug their uncle or dad, more like someone would hug their only friend. I backed up and told him that the smell was Gabriele cooking dinner for the three of us. He ran his fingers through his hair to see if it was mussed, and walked into the kitchen. When I got there, the two of them were kissing each other in a not-on-the-cheek way. Gabriele looked up at me and then looked down at his feet. I followed Ted into the living room and found my vodka, which was no longer cold. I refilled it in the kitchen and offered to refill

Gabriele's, but he covered it with his hand and shook his head.

"Don't worry about things," I whispered to him. "I'd be happy to dance at your wedding, as Ruth always says about me and you. You and Ted look right together. And we both know he'd say yes in a heartbeat if you patted him on the butt."

I put the plastic table cover on the dining table, and then put an old calico tablecloth and cloth napkins out for the three of us. Cloth napkins look festive, but they're cheaper than paper napkins because they last forever, and I never iron them, just smooth them out when I take them out of the dryer and fold them carefully. They always look fine. I like to put silver flatware on the table, so I did, and put some nice old Lenox dishes that I inherited when my mom died (I think they were a wedding gift). Nice tulip-shaped, tall-stem wine glasses. The table looked like it should have flowers on it – the calico tablecloth had little flowers that would have to stand in for real flowers. Then I realized that one of the orchids was blooming, so I grabbed it out of the windowsill and put it on an old, pre-Civil War silverplate tray that I keep in the middle of the table. I inherited it from my oldest aunt who died a widow a decade or so ago.

The smells from the kitchen were heavenly. I still had a bit of vodka in my martini glass, so I grabbed it and plopped down on the sofa to watch some CNN news. I find the Beltway stories from Washington, DC boring, and that's mostly what it was that evening. Ted was watching the TV intently, though. I flipped the remote to channel 7 – ABC – to catch the Evening News. At least there would be some sports coverage to break any political monotony, and maybe something other than White-House-type intrigues.

Ted was looking like he wanted to talk. He stood up and walked to the balcony, slid the glass door open and went outside, then came back and sat down again. I turned the sound down on the television, and said, "Ted, if you don't want to watch the news, I can turn the TV off. I know pretty much what's going on, don't need to watch this half-hour of news. I know I'm a news junkie but not everybody is."

He smiled at me and said he'd like to ask me a personal question. "Would that be okay?"

I nodded, and he asked me if Gabriele and I were lovers.

"No, we're not. Never have been, and I doubt that would ever change. I love him like a son, I think. Certainly, he is very important in my life, and he and I have talked about this. If you want to date him or whatever, just ask him. I'm too old for that kind of thing, and anyway, I'm attracted to girls. Have you talked to your mom about this? Does she know you're gay?"

He nodded and said his mom was cool with it.

Gabriele appeared from the kitchen with a large platter with the pasta dish he had made with the sausages, garlic and rapini. He had used the ear-shaped pasta. That sort of pasta holds the olive oil and garlic well – much better than spaghetti, which is my default favorite. I like twirling it, too.

"That looks splendid," I said to him. "You certainly know what I like. Thanks. That's my favorite dish," I said, and took the platter from his hands and put it on the table.

He ducked back into the kitchen and emerged a minute later with the two bottles of Barbaresco, and put those on the silver tray in the middle of the table top, one on either side of the orchid, which had a tall spike of magenta flowers. Wine-colored flowers and good Italian red wine.

"Dinnertime, I guess," I said. "Ted, why don't you pick where you want to sit. There are three places set."

When we were all seated, I suggested that Ted and I pass our plates to Gabriele, who could serve them. "Everybody help yourselves to the wine."

Gabriele had made a large quantity of the pasta and doused it with a lot of grated Romano or Parmesan cheese. He served it onto the plates with a large fork and spoon. I could tell that there was probably more food there than the three of us could eat. The rapini was shiny and forest green, slightly wilted from the cooking, but perfect in every way. One thing that Gabriele and I always agree on is that there is no such thing as too much garlic – and it's a super-food anyway, keeps the doctor away better than the proverbial apple a day.

I said a quick grace and Gabriele proposed a toast *"Ai miei buon' amici,"* meaning "to my good friends," then adding the usual *"Cin Cin,"* and we all took a sip of the wine.

I proposed another toast, "To the Coniston family, long may they prosper."

Ted grinned, and added, "Especially the women."

Gabriele left his chair and walked around the table, put his arm around Ted's shoulders and squeezed him a bit. "To Ted," he said, and ran his hand through Ted's hair, before he walked back to his chair and sat down.

Ted was staring at Gabriele. Gabriele blew him a kiss.

I thought *this is looking more and more like a soap opera,* so I excused myself and went to the bathroom, brushed my teeth and gargled with some mouthwash, then went back to the table. The episode was apparently over, and they were both eating some of the mouth-wateringly wonderful pasta with oil and garlic, sausage and rapini. There was a big bowl of freshly grated Romano cheese on the pass-through from the kitchen, so I picked it up and put it on the table.

The television was still on, tuned to CNN. "Do you mind if I turn the sound up a bit on the TV?" I asked. "I just want to find out what's on the top of the news, is all." Pause. "The pasta is fabulous, as usual. You are a great chef, and I hope you and Ted will find a way to spend more time together."

Ted looked up from his food and flashed a big question mark at me by opening his eyes wide and slightly wrinkling his forehead as he cocked his head.

"I love cook food for you," Gabriele said. "You always say nice thing when you eat my food." Pause. "Ted and I will go for a walk after food."

Ted nodded, stood up and reached for the platter, then served himself a big second helping. You can always tell with a young man that the way to his heart is through his stomach. Maybe an old man, too.

They both cleared the table after the food was largely gone, and hand-washed the silver, the old Lenox plates and bread-plates, and the wine glasses, which were in fact Waterford that had belonged to my grandparents. I had been careful some time back to tell Gabriele that all the 'good' stuff had to be hand-washed so that the dishwasher detergent wouldn't scratch them up.

I could just imagine my grandmother looking grim while she was watching someone put one of her dishes in the dishwasher – not something I would ever let happen. All the family stuff is going to be in as close to perfect condition as possible when I pass on. I have considered leaving the tableware and so forth to Gabriele, because I know he would take good care of it. But I suppose my kids and grandkids would feel deprived if they didn't get the lion's share of my stuff – especially the paintings and *tchotchkes* and knick-knacks that are scattered around the living room and dining room. To be truthful, every usable bit of wall space is taken. I can't buy more paintings because I would have to take something down in order to put anything else up. Just as well, I suppose; I've been a spendthrift most of my life, and lucky to be able to support myself living where I do.

The next thing I knew, Ted and Gabriele were gone. I walked out on the balcony and could see them walking along the water's edge of the East River. Ted stopped to pick up something off the ground – must have been a rock – and he skipped it across the surface of the water. *Well done, Ted my man.* Then I ducked back into the apartment so they wouldn't see me watching them. I felt relieved. Of course, I knew Gabriele was thinking seriously about decamping to the Boston area. Maybe he would open a new Ora di Pranzo in one of the vacation spots in New England. P-town maybe, or Hyannis.

Good thing Isabelle is fine with Ted's life choices. These days a gay couple can adopt a child, or maybe even find a surrogate who could carry a baby for the two handsome men. How cool would that be?

I could feel my eyes getting watery, and realized I had never felt that way about my own children, probably because I seldom saw them. That's what nasty divorces do to people. I have to find out what my children and grandkids would want when I am gone. But I will leave some of the things – even family heirlooms – to Gabriele, and probably some to Ruth, too.

Truthfully, I felt good about Ted and Gabriele potentially being a couple, and maybe even having a family. I was never good at any of that. My two wives got the mucky end of the stick when they married me. Running the business was my life for a long, long time. That didn't leave a lot for either of them to love. Interesting how melancholy I tend to be when I look back on my life. I wouldn't want to be young again – youth is too difficult, too stressful. But there are nuggets from those years that I love to remember. Being in the delivery room when my kids were born, cutting the cords. Taking them swimming at the beach. Watching them watch dogs or cats deliver litters. Graduations. I guess we make our own families if we need to. I loved taking my wives and kids on vacations, too. Hawaii. England and Wales. Cabo San Lucas. Puerto Vallarta. Acapulco. Good times that I seldom think about except when I'm feeling sorry for myself.

The doorbell rang. I looked at the clock, and an hour had passed. It was Gabriele and Ted.

"How was your walk?"

"Nice," Ted said. "There was a little breeze off the water. Maybe the dog days of summer are past, and we're moving toward fall."

Gabriele smiled and kissed Ted on the mouth, which Ted didn't resist in the slightest. It was a chaste kiss, but a kiss anyway.

Young love.

Chapter Thirty-four

As I found out the next morning, Gabriele slept in the living room, and Ted retired to the guest bedroom. I woke up when I smelled the coffee that was already made in the kitchen. *Gabriele knows exactly what to do. Ted's going to be a lucky guy if they become a couple.*

I checked my phone and indeed there was a text from Mike di Saronno, saying that we should get to Mike's office as early as we could, so that we could drive up to Chappaqua for the meeting with Ricky and another tour of the Kids' House. The door to the guest bedroom was closed when I looked down the hall. Gabriele took a mug of coffee to the bathroom in my bedroom and chugged it down while he waited for the shower water to get warm enough. I decided to wake Ted up so that we could get to Mike's office as soon as possible. Turned out he wasn't still asleep, just reading a book. He followed me to the kitchen and eagerly poured a mug of coffee and put two spoons of sugar into it. *I thought you wanted it black.*

We hit everything just right. When we got to the subway station at Vernon-Jackson, a train was just pulling in, and when we got to Times Square, we got an uptown number 1 train right away. We were at Mike's office a good bit before eleven o'clock. Mike had arranged for a fleet car, which turned out to be a very large Ford Expedition that could have carried nine people, where we were only four. Plenty of room.

Traffic was lighter than usual, and we were on the West Side Highway heading north quickly. I took the shotgun seat, with Ted and Gabriele in the second row of seats, leaving the third-row empty. It was an almost-cool day that made it look like summer was winding down, although the trees were all still green, no seasonal color changes yet. I asked Mike, who was driving, if he minded having the radio on. He was okay with it, so I found 1010 WINS, which is an all-news station ("You give us twenty-two minutes; we'll give you the world"). It was quickly obvious that there were no big headlines, so I switched it to WQXR, which is the classical music station that used to be owned by the NY Times, but had been given to NPR some years back. No commercials. Most of the music was of the "chestnut" variety, so almost everything was familiar.

When we got to Westchester, Mike took the Saw Mill River Parkway, which more or less parallels the Hudson going north, and then angled a bit inland as we passed the 287 ("Cross-Westchester Expressway"). Pretty soon we were pulling off the highway and onto the road that would take us to Ricky Coniston's horse ranch. As I looked out the window, I saw a lot of smoke ahead. I pointed to it, and Mike said it looked like a house fire, because the smoke was so black.

The closer we got to the Coniston estate, the more it looked like the fire was likely to be there. When we got to the white-washed plank fence, we could see that the fire was roaring out of all the windows of the Kids' House.

"No tour of that today," Mike said. "I wonder what happened." There were several fire trucks, including two hook-and-ladder trucks that had hooked into a fireplug that was next to the road near the cattle-gate. They were trying to douse the fire, and the color of the smoke seemed to be getting lighter, probably as the water created steam as it hit the hot spots. There was a lot of noise, and firefighters were high enough on the trucks that they could aim the water stream down onto the top floor of the building.

"Looks like a total loss," Ted said. "So many memories there."

As we pulled up, Mike showed his credentials to the captain who was in charge of fighting the fire. Then we drove off the driveway and around the fire trucks to get closer to the Coniston home. There was a clump of people watching the fire; one of them was Ricky Coniston, who was standing next to Lizzie Coniston, who was easily taller than Ricky, and she wasn't even wearing high heels.

We walked over to the group of spectators. Ricky welcomed us and told us that his two German Shepherds were in the building, and he was worried. Shortly after he said that, someone ran out of the building carrying one of the dogs. It was Jack. He put the dog down on the ground and ran back into the building, re-appearing shortly thereafter with the second dog. Then, astonishingly, he ran back into the building, which was still looking like a three-story bonfire.

"No, Jack, don't go back in there!" Ricky yelled. He ran over to where the dogs were shaking themselves. They were soaking wet, and didn't look to be hurt – at least not badly hurt. They were all over Ricky when he got close to them. "Jack!" Ricky yelled. "Come back out here!"

Two firefighters with gas masks and huge yellow helmets came running out of the building. They ran over to where the chief firefighter was standing, and reported something to him. Ricky ran over to where the three of them were standing, then walked slowly back to us. He hugged Ted and told him that Jack was trapped on a staircase, and the firefighters had not been able to get to him.

Ted looked devastated. "Is he still alive? Is he hurt?"

Ricky said he didn't know, but there was probably a chance that he wouldn't be okay. "I'm so sorry, Ted. I know you've been friends for years." He hugged his last surviving nephew.

"How did the fire start?" I asked Ricky.

He shook his head and shrugged. "No idea. I just looked out the window from the house and saw the fire."

Lizzie started to cry.

Another car pulled up on the road, and stopped outside the fence. It was a light-colored sedan, and a man got out of the driver's door and walked over to the fence.

"That's Hank Huntington," I said quietly to Ricky and Lizzie. "I met him in Monaco."

"Yes, I know," Lizzie said, and shifted her shoulder-bag from one shoulder to the other. "What the hell is he doing here? I wonder if he had something to do with this god-damn fire." Mr Huntington spotted us and waved, probably to Lizzie Coniston. She gave him 'the finger', then shooed him away with the back of her hand. "Get out of here, you bastard," she hissed.

Mike said, "Be careful, Mrs Coniston. He has a gun. He's got it holstered under his jacket. I can see it."

"Of course, he does, but so do I, and I know how to use it."

Ricky took a step back and said to Lizzie, "Don't say that. There's no reason to think he had anything to do with the fire."

Lizzie made a hand gesture that looked like she was flicking an insect in the air, but it was meant for Huntington. He reached under his jacket. Lizzie unshouldered her bag and produced a handgun.

"He's going for his gun," Mike said. "Be careful. Don't let him know you have one, too. Remember there are other people here, too. You don't want all of us to be collateral damage. And you don't want to shoot your gun at a human being." He held his hand out to Lizzie. "Give it to me. I have a gun myself, but I know what to do with it if it needs to be done."

Huntington held his gun in his right hand, and pointed it in our direction like a wild-west cowboy. Clearly, he had taken no instructions on how to use it. Mike said, "Don't let him make you do something you would regret for the rest of your life."

"That bastard wants to steal my daughter, and find some way to get Ricky thrown out of the family business. Sometimes it seems like this family is cursed. He's the curse if there is one. He's like a rat in the subway." She spread her legs out and leaned forward, holding her pistol with both hands. Then she fired it, and Huntington jerked backward with blood spurting from his shoulder or his upper right arm.

"Damn," she said. "I aimed for his forehead." Then she handed the gun to Mike.

Huntington scrambled into his car, managed to get it started and drove off.

I realized that the fire was either out, or about to be out. Two firefighters came out of the building with their face shields flipped up, carrying a body bag.

"Oh my God, no!" yelled Ted. He ran toward the men carrying the body bag. "Jack! What the hell? Jack!"

The chief firefighter walked over toward us, and pointed to Mike.

Mike nodded. The chief told us that they were opening an investigation into the fire. "We saw what could be marks of an accelerator in the kitchen area on the third floor. Could be arson, but at this moment, we don't have enough evidence to know for sure."

Mike said to the chief, "Was that the young man who got the dogs out of the house?"

He nodded and said, "Probably smoke inhalation. They tell me no obvious burns."

Ricky said to Mike that he would have to call Jack's father to tell him what had happened. "You want to stay here, Ted?"

"No thanks, Uncle Ricky. I've got the car at Hugo's place, and I sent Mom home on Amtrak yesterday afternoon, so I think I'll just dead-head back home. Mom worries about me. I sent her a text about Jack. Jack and I were BFF's." No slowdown in the tears.

Mike grabbed Ricky's hand and shook it, saying, "I think I'll take my guys and head back for Manhattan. I hope the building is salvageable."

Ted couldn't stop crying, or maybe I should just say tears kept coming, because he wasn't continually sobbing. I watched him in the mirror once we were back in the car. He took out his smartphone and sent a text to someone. I turned around and asked him who he was texting.

"Mom." More tears.

Gabriele was a little weepy, too, probably sympathetic tears. *Good man.*

When we got back to Mike's office, he told us to take off. It was mid-afternoon, and no point trying to get started on anything new. "I doubt there's anything left in that building," he said. "Looked like a total loss to me." He looked up at the ceiling, and said, to all of us at once, "Mrs Coniston really lost it. I hope, for her sake, that man, Huntington, isn't badly hurt. Otherwise, she may be up the creek without a paddle. And unfortunately for her, a jury might hold her wealth against her. Although I suspect she has access to really good lawyers."

"I think she was trying to protect Betty," Ted said. "They're super-close, but Betty may have been interested in being courted by somebody like Huntington. That wouldn't go over well with Aunt Lizzie. She and Uncle Eddie were always holding hands – really in love – but a lot of people in the family thought she was a gold-digger – you know the type of thing. A woman who marries for money, earns it."

When we got to the subway, Gabriele said he would head downtown to Ora di Pranzo and surprise Dante. Ted and I headed for Long Island City and he said it was early enough that he might just head home. He said he was parked on the street and might have a parking ticket for leaving the car in the same place for too long.

"Maybe Mike can help with that if you have a parking ticket. In New York City, parking tickets can be really expensive, like hundreds of dollars. He seems to be really connected down at One Police Plaza."

Chapter Thirty-five

When we got to my place, Ted packed up his duffel bag with the clothes and books he had brought, and trundled off to the elevator for his drive to Boston.

No sooner had he left than my cellphone rang. It was Mike, telling me that Ricky Coniston was on his way over to Mike's precinct office for a talk, and told Mike that it would be just as well if Ted could be at the meeting. I tried to explain that Ted was on his way to Boston, but Mike was in a hurry and said, "Try to get him on his cellphone and turn him around. I think he will want to be at this meeting. Actually, I'm fairly sure of it."

I was able to get Ted and get him turned around, and shortly thereafter we were on our way to the subway at Vernon-Jackson. When we got to Mike's office on 54th Street between 8th and 9th Avenues, Ricky Coniston was already sitting in Interrogation Room number two. Mike was standing in his doorway as we came up the stairs, and walked us over to the room where Ricky was waiting. Ricky stood up and greeted Ted with a bear hug, and me with a handshake.

"Sorry to interrupt your plans, Ted. Detective di Saronno told me you were on your way to Boston. I took the liberty of calling Isabelle to tell her what I'm going to tell you. This was a very sad day, because we lost Jack Ramos. As you might guess, his parents were very upset and sad when I called them to tell them that Jack was caught in a fire and died. Of course, I'll pay for the funeral and so forth.

"All the things that happened yesterday and today made me look carefully at everything that was going on. I've made some decisions, and one of them involves you, Ted." He told Ted to sit down, and I could see that Ted was very anxious about what his uncle was going to say next.

"First of all, we believe that Mr Huntington was not badly hurt by the bullet that hit him. He was seen by Mt Sinai's ER, and was sent home to his hotel room to rest. So, I hope that will let your Aunt Lizzie off the hook. Anyway, she was firing at him because he was pointing a gun at all of us. Self defense."

Mike added that he was impressed with how Lizzie had handled her weapon. "She must have taken lessons, because no novice could hit a target at that distance. She knew exactly how to hold the weapon. She looked like a pro. She made me want to go to the shooting range and put in some time."

"But more to the point," Ricky said, "I've decided to retire from the Coniston Companies, and I intend to nominate you as my replacement, Ted, and to nominate Betty as the Chairperson of the Board. We need diversity; this isn't a man's world any more, hasn't been for decades, since the Eisenhower days."

"Oh, Uncle Ricky, thank you so much for that, but I can't do what you do," Ted said in a rush of words. "I'm really just a slightly grown-up kid, you know." He had tears running down both cheeks. Ricky grabbed him and threw both of his arms around the young man.

"I've been watching you pretty closely, Teddy Boy, and I think you inherited good genes from your parents – my brother, Georgie, and Isabelle," he said. "I'll stay on for long enough for you to get the hang of things, and then I'll stay on the Board – Betty's Board – so I'll be there if things get in a pickle. But you're going to have to put your shoulder to the wheel, because there are a heck of a lot of people who will be depending on you."

"You're scaring me, Uncle Ricky."

"Don't worry. I wouldn't be doing this if I had any doubts about how you will handle the job," Mr Coniston said, still hugging Ted. "You have an excellent education; you're a good person and you're sharp as a tack. And we all love you, you know."

Ricky said he had asked Isabelle to come for a visit in Chappaqua, and she had said she would like that. "So maybe when you see your mother, you and she can decide about when to have that visit. Meantime, I'm planning to take your Auntie Ann to Central America soon. There are some good doctors in Mexico, and I'm hoping they can help her. As far as we know, there is no cure for Pick's dementia, but there is some research being done on ways to slow it down."

"I guess I should get an apartment in the City," Ted said.

"As it happens," Ricky said, "we – I mean the Coniston Companies – maintain several apartments that we use to house people in training, and regional managers from around the world who come to visit." He patted Ted on the back. "No worries, and you can move in as soon as you want. You'll be in training, so TCC will pick up all your expenses. There's a really nice apartment with nice views in a historic building on 47th Street. They have a gym in the building, too. It's completely furnished, two bedrooms and two baths, but you can change it however you want. Beautiful tree-lined street with some views of the river, and it's right close to the Theater District. Always something happening. Nice place for a young guy like you to be. You'd be able to walk to work, weather permitting."

Ted was staring at his uncle, and his jaw dropped while Ricky was talking.

"If you don't like that place, we can find a different place," Ricky said.

Mike was smiling, and looked like he might chuckle. "I live in Hell's Kitchen, right near the Theater District, and you couldn't drag me away from there with a team of Clydesdale horses. I love where I live – the theaters, the food, the people, and I love being able to walk to work," he said, then, with a nod and a grin to Ricky, "weather permitting, of course."

Ted was listening to all this with a somber look on his face. He stood up and said, "I have something I need to tell you, Uncle Ricky. I'm a gay man, always have been gay, and always will be, as far as I can guess. You may not want an openly gay CEO for the Coniston Companies."

"I know, Ted. Isabelle knows, and it doesn't make any difference in what we think of you as a capable and honest person. You know, we're all Episcopalians, and Episcopalians welcome gay people to church and to the clergy. A predictable percentage of people in any culture are gay –

some male and some female. Even the Pope says gay people should be able to have families, just like anybody else. We are all God's children, and we are all family, especially in our family. What happened to your father was not fair, and we have all been living under the shadow of what happened for far too long. I will myself try to rectify the differences between how you and Isabelle have been treated by the Coniston Companies, and how others in the family are treated – maybe even including some of the Westbrook relatives. We owe you and your mother, and we will make you whole."

"Can I ask you a blunt question, Uncle Ricky?"

"Of course, Nephew Ted."

"Why wouldn't you consider talking to Henry Huntington about being the CEO? He's obviously more experienced than I am, and way more mature."

"I'd disagree with you about the 'mature' part, because I think he has been acting like a child. But I take your point about his experience as a fund manager. There are those who think I am a fund manager, but I'm not a fund manager. I run what the government calls a 'family office', but the Coniston Companies are not a family fund. The Coniston Companies are a family way of helping people – the people in all the companies we invest in, including the companies we own completely or nearly completely. And we give a really significant amount to many charities – healthcare charities, clean-air charities, the arts, children's charities and scholarships, groups who are helping women and minorities break through the ceilings that have been holding them down for centuries.

"As CEO, you'll be spending as much time giving away money as you will be running the company. Why do you think Uncle Eddie and Aunt Lizzie were such loyal members of the Opera League? One of the categories we help on an annual basis are the many opera companies in the United States – each one losing money each and every year and would go out of business without donations from companies like ours.

"Your job won't be easy, but it won't in any way be a nightmare. You'll know that you'll be helping the poor and downtrodden raise themselves and their children up. You'll be saving lives. And to answer your question, my judgment is that Mr Huntington is, in fact, a fund manager, and would see charitable giving as a waste of profits. That's not who we are, and I don't think it's who you are, either."

Ted looked at his feet. "What if Betty wants to be with Mr Huntington?"

"She's an adult. Don't ask me questions like that. Ask her if you want to ask someone. But remember that we love her unreservedly and forever. You're my only surviving nephew, and Betty is one of only two nieces." He held out his arms, "What do you say, Nephew Ted? Wanna join us?"

Then Ricky walked around the table and, once again, bear-hugged Ted, who smiled and wept at the same time.

I couldn't wait to tell Gabriele about all of this.

Chapter Thirty-six

After Ricky Coniston left, Mike took Ted and me to his office. He wanted to tell us that shortly before all of this happened, he had received notice from JFK Airport that Hank Huntington had left in a private jet to go back to Paris, landing at Orly Airport, not Charles de Gaulle. Orly handles more general aviation flights and very short hops, so since he was in a private plane, it made sense that he would be heading for Orly.

"He was apparently recovering, although his right arm was in a sling, as you might expect," Mike said, "and apparently he knows there wouldn't be any point in trying to bring charges against Lizzie, since he was brandishing a gun before he was shot. No question that she shot him in self-defense."

It occurred to me that one of the things a fund manager had to know was how to get out of a bad investment. *This isn't likely to follow Huntington back to France, much less Monaco.*

My phone vibrated, telling me I had a text message. It was from Gabriele, wondering if Ted made it back to Boston. I told him Ted was with me at Mike's office, and I handed the phone to Ted.

The conversation was short. I didn't hear the first part, because Ted was facing in another direction and was speaking very softly. Then he turned around and looked at me.

"And I told Uncle Ricky that I'm gay."

Pause, I assumed while Gabriele said something.

"He already knew, because my mom told him."

Another pause while Gabriele responded.

"Anyway, I may be living in Manhattan myself, if I take the offer that Uncle Ricky made me – to work at the Coniston Companies."

Pause.

"I'd love to, but I need to see if Hugo has plans."

Pause.

"Are you sure?" Then he looked at me and covered the phone with his hand. "He wants me to have dinner at his restaurant, which I don't even know where it is. He said you would be welcome to join us." He looked questioningly at me and said very slowly, "Yes, we have kissed, but we haven't done anything else. No worries. No problem."

"I'd love to have dinner with you and Gabriele at Ora di Pranzo, and I could get there blindfolded."

Ted uncovered the phone, and told Gabriele that both of us would be there at seven o'clock.

"In the meantime, Ted," I said to him, "I think you should talk to your Aunt Lizzie and your cousin Betty, to make sure they are up to date, and that they know that Huntington is going to be okay, and will be back in France later today, travelling in a private jet heading for Orly Airport, the older airport near Paris, kinda like LaGuardia Airport in New York, which is old-timey and small compared to JFK Airport, the huge modern airport where the trans-Atlantic and transcontinental flights land. Be sure to tell them that Detective di Saronno said that since Huntington was waving a gun around, there won't be any problem for Aunt Lizzie, because she was acting in self-defense, and there are lots of witnesses, probably including the firefighters."

Mike said he had to go to a meeting, so Ted and I left and walked to the downtown subway at 50th Street and 8th Avenue, beneath a tall office building called Worldwide Plaza. Once there, it was only ten minutes or so before we were in Long Island City and walking to my place. The subways are the fastest way to travel in New York City, especially in Manhattan.

While we were walking, Ted said, "I think Gabriele is maybe planning to move to Boston, just when I'll be maybe planning to move to Manhattan, so I can work with Uncle Ricky."

"The way I understood it," I responded, "Uncle Ricky feels like going out to pasture, like Vesuvius, the horse Jack was grooming. He's handing things over to you and Betty."

When we got to my apartment, Ted said he was going to call his mother and then Betty, to tell them what had happened, and he disappeared down the hallway to the bathroom.

I called Gabriele, who picked up on the first ring.

"I thought I should call and go over what happened at Mike's office today," I said. "I know Ted told you some of this, but long story short, Ricky Coniston is retiring, and he wants Ted to step up to be the CEO. Also, Ricky plans to install Betty Coniston as Chairperson. Ted will have to move to Manhattan, where the Coniston Companies will provide him with an apartment fitting to the CEO of the family office. Ted's kinda worried that you might be planning to move to Boston, just when he'll be moving to Manhattan." I felt a little out of breath when I finished.

"That's a lot," he said. "I can't be with Ted here. I told you I can only be with him in Boston, where I am far from you. Because I love you. I love you every way I know to love."

"I wonder if you might be more comfortable if I have dinner at home tonight, instead of going to Ora di Pranzo with Ted." I felt like my voice was going to crack, and my eyes went bleary with tears that were filling my eyes.

"No," he said. "You must be here, to make me strong." His accent disappeared, as it is prone to do from time to time. "I can't do this without you."

"Do what? The dinner tonight?"

"No. The rest of my life. I am happy when I am with you, even though I know that we are not going to be *amanti* and that doesn't make me *triste*." The accent came back slightly, in a way that told me he was regaining his composure – he sounds like an American when he feels super-stressed. When he's just being himself, he sounds like the Italian majordomo of a fancy Italian restaurant in Manhattan.

"Okay, see you at seven then, with Ted."

"*Forse* we have good Aglianico with food." That's my favorite red wine.

Chapter Thirty-seven

Gabriele looked every bit the upscale maître d': starched, high-collar formal shirt with black bow tie, black dinner suit trimmed with satin, and patent leather slip-on shoes. In spite of his extraordinary good looks, he emanated a lack of self-confidence that made him look like someone I had not met before. He had a smile pasted on his face, and he showed us to a roomy corner table in the back of the room, where we could see that the room was filled with designer-dressed people, and many of the women wore jewelry that absolutely looked like real precious metals and real gemstones.

Ted was fascinated with the interior of Ora di Pranzo, staring at the brilliantly colored velvet and silk window curtains in loud greens, reds and yellow-golds, with gold rope sashes holding them to the sides of the windows. Or maybe he just didn't want to meet Gabriele's gaze.

"Do restaurants in Italy look like this?" he asked me when we sat down.

I nodded and said, "Yes, this place reminds me of a hotel I stayed in at the beginning of Via Vittorio Veneto, named after a battle of World War I, and built by the Kingdom of Italy after Rome joined the country in the late nineteenth century. It originates at Piazza Barberini and is more or less associated with the area around Venice, although I don't think the road goes all the way up the boot. It's not far from the Trevi Fountain and the Villa Borghese."

"I've always wanted to go to Italy," Ted said. "I bet it would be fun to go there with Gabriele."

"I bet he knows every foot of the places you'd want to see. He was born in Naples and grew up on the Isle of Capri. The chef here is his cousin, Dante, who is originally Neapolitan. Fabulous food."

About the time I said that, a waiter brought three dirty vodkas, put one each in front of Ted and me, and one at the third chair, obviously where Gabriele would be. Sure enough, as we stared at the martini glasses frosted over, Gabriele appeared, sat down and raised his glass.

"*Cin Cin*," he said, the traditional Italian toast, pronounced chin-chin. We tapped our glasses together and each took a sip. "So, tell me about this job Ricky Coniston is offering you," Gabriele said, making eye contact with Ted.

"Umm," Ted made an uncertain noise. "He wants to retire, I guess, and he thinks I should learn to run the Companies. I'd be CEO, and part of my compensation would be what sounds like a palatial apartment in Hell's Kitchen."

"Well, that sounds like the chance of a lifetime, doesn't it?" I said, directing it to Gabriele.

"Sounds to me like driving a car into a wall," Ted said. "Recipe for failure."

"Stop it," Gabriele said to him, covering Ted's hand with his own. "You're one of the smartest people I know, and one thing I've learned is that when you get a chance like this, you take it. It's like when Dante and I started this place. Neither one of us had ever had a *ristorante*. Dante is great chef. I got lucky, but I was afraid I would fuck everything up. You're going to be a great CEO for a great business, following a great builder named Ricky."

Ted didn't know what to say. His jaw dropped.

"I think your uncle is a smart man. He didn't offer you his whole company just to be nice. He thinks you're going to do a good job. I bet he's right. Maybe you can come here for dinner sometimes, like Ricky does now."

"I bet this is a really expensive place," Ted said.

Gabriele nodded. So, did I.

"The CEO of Ricky's company is going to be able to afford anything he wants."

"And you and I are going to be best friends forever."

Ted looked like he had vertigo, like his head was spinning and he might black out. He reached for his vodka, spilled it on his shirt, and dropped it on the floor, where it broke into a bunch of pieces. He started to pick up one of the pieces.

"No touch!" Gabriele said with a laugh. "Not cut hand, not sue Dante and me for lotta money." No accent.

"Fat chance!" I said with a friendly smile.

Gabriele was on his feet and waving at one of the waiters. He said something to the waiter in Italian, and the fellow fast-walked toward the swinging doors to the kitchen. About ten seconds later, a younger man with a bucket and a mop appeared at the kitchen door and walked carefully over to our table. He picked up my napkin with thick kitchen rubber gloves and carefully picked up the broken glass and put all the pieces in the napkin, then folded the napkin over itself and handed it to the waiter, who had returned to the table. The waiter headed to the kitchen with the napkin, and came back shortly with a platter of *contorni*, mostly herb-roasted or fried vegetables that are commonly eaten as appetizers in Italy. In Rome many restaurants have buffet-like tables at the entrance to the dining room. There are stacks of small plates, and guests help themselves once they have been seated. I particularly love the deep-fried crispy zucchini strips, but also a fan of roasted bell peppers and turnips or yams. The younger man quickly mopped the floor and then disappeared back into the kitchen.

The waiter also came back with a small glass pitcher that looked to be full of water – but he had a new martini glass, and refilled all the martini glasses with it, so it had to be chilled vodka. I watched Gabriele slurp into his refilled glass and figured he was feeling stressed.

"Everything's going to be okay," I said to Gabriele.

He winked at me and nodded.

Ted apparently thought I was talking to him, and he responded, "I'm not worried, no problem."

Liar, liar, pants on fire.

Gabriele waved to the waiter, who brought over and opened a bottle of 2009 Cantine del Notaio Il Sigillo Aglianico del Vulture, which is from the instep of the boot of Italy. There are fierce local dialects where this wine originates, and some people still speak a mash-up of Corinthian

Greek, dating back to the time when Corinth was colonizing what's now Sicily and southern Italy. The wine is really special, probably because the grapes have been grown there for nearly three thousand years. I hadn't ever tried that label or that year, but I figured Gabriele knew it well. He's a real wine expert – as long as the subject is Italian wines. Not much interested in Bordeaux or California Cabernet Sauvignons (and almost no white wines, thank you very much).

He tasted the wine and made a thumbs-up sign. Then he handed me the bottle. I poured some into my wine glass and some into Ted's.

"This looks special," I said, and then tasted it. "Oh my God! It's more than special! *Mille grazie!*" I burbled. "It's fabulous."

He smiled and nodded. "Dante bring a case when he come back from Napoli last year," he said. "Is for special times. We having *penne arrabiata* with this *vino*."

"Wow," Ted said. "That's a muscle-bound wine. What the fuck?" He grabbed the bottle and read the label. "Gabriele, when the bottle is finished, can somebody in the kitchen soak the label off, so I can get some of this for my Mom?"

"We soak it off, fine, but this wine not in America. Not anyplace. If you want, I will send a bottle to *Mamma*. She like strong Italian wine?"

Ted nodded. "She always keeps a bottle of Nero d'Avola ready to drink. This bottle reminds me of her wines, but this is much better."

"You know, when I met Gabriele, I thought he might be from Brazil," I said. "That was actually when I was helping Mike di Saronno for the first time. Almost twenty years ago."

"Why Brazil?" he asked, and looked at Gabriele, who was smiling.

"Because he was so good looking, and Brazilian men are famous for being handsome and sexy."

"What are Italians? Chopped liver?" Gabriele said with no accent. Suddenly he looked like himself again.

"Tell me about it," I said.

The wine was a perfect match for the fiery red-pepper and tomato sauce, and the sauce was more pepper than tomato. I love it that way, but it made me think about heartburn. Fortunately, no problems that night.

Gabriele told Ted that he had been thinking about moving to Boston, and maybe starting a new Ora di Pranzo either in Boston or maybe Cape Cod, or even Hyannis Port. "But I have to stay in New York. Dante need me here, and I not just move away," he said. "If you move to Manhattan, maybe one day you come to Brooklyn Heights and I make you best dinner of your life. Ugo and me, we are very lucky to know you. You know Ora di Pranzo is where that stuffed bear was sent, addressed to Ugo. If that bear not here, maybe we never get to meet you." He reached over and patted Ted on the shoulder."

"I'm the lucky one, thanks to a teddy bear with long fingernails," Ted said. "A bear named after me, and I bet Jack sent it, to tell me that he knew what happened to my cousins."

I could tell from looking at Ted that he was feeling emotional.

"Poor Jack," he said, "what a terrible way to die – in a burning building. But the more I think about it, the more sure I am that Uncle Ricky will be a great teacher for me. It'll be fun to work with him and Betty, and I will get to travel all over the place. And it's time for me to move away from my mother's house anyway, I think. Who knows? Maybe I'll meet Mr Right."

He winked at Gabriele and flashed a toothy grin, with his hands folded together like he was saying a prayer and said, "Maybe it was fate, and you helped me grow up. I feel like I'm grown up now, and I felt like a kid before all this happened." He held his wine up and said, "To my friends, Gabriele and Hugo."

Of course, I teared up. I do that more than I did years back. I felt like the two of them were like my sons at that table.

Chapter Thirty-eight

A few weeks later, I drove upstate with Ruth to 'visit' Murray, her husband who had died several years before. She had scattered his ashes in a lake in the Catskill Mountains, and once a year or so, she wanted to go up there to that lake, and talk to him.

While we were driving in my old Jaguar XK8 with the top down, she told me that she had just renewed her membership in the Opera League, and asked me if I would go with her to one of the operas the first week in October.

"Which opera?"

"Well," she said, "it could be a new production – they're introducing a new 'Traviata' for instance – or it could be an oldie-but-goodie like the Zeffirelli production of 'Turandot.'"

"I love 'Turandot'," I said. "That production is so fantastic, the audience gasps every time the curtain goes up. That would be my pick. Especially if they have a good soprano and a good tenor."

"I think we're going to grow old together," she said with a grin. "You ought to join the Opera League."

"I'm already old," I riposted. "I'm on Medicare and get a Social Security check every month, but I doubt I can afford to join the Opera League, and go to the opera every Monday like faithful Opera Leaguers do."

She was looking out on the landscape. I wasn't driving fast, but the top was down, and she had a fancy Hermes scarf tied tightly around her hair. I kept thinking it might blow off, but it didn't. Ruth doesn't like her hair flying around, even though it's relatively short. She's very pretty, and always looks like she just got dressed.

"You know, when we first met, old John thought we should be a couple."

"Old John was a natural-born yenta. He was always trying to fix me up, and I'd guess he was trying the same with you." She turned on the radio, which was set to WQXR, the classical music station that the New York Times had sold or given to National Public Radio. It was all just static – too far from the signal. I told her that there were some CDs in the glove box in front of her. She opened it and seemed delighted when she found Handel's "Water Music" and "Music for the Royal Fireworks."

She chose the Royal Fireworks first, but set the volume fairly low. I reached over and turned it up a lot. "It's fireworks, needs to be loud. I was in this car playing that same CD on September 11, 2001 on my way down 5th Avenue to work when I saw what looked like green fire way up high on the World Trade Center twin towers. I didn't see the plane hit the tower, probably because I was driving, not looking up. I turned off the CD and switched to 1010 WINS, which was just running a bulletin that a 'small plane' had crashed into the North Tower. I remember thinking what kind of a stupid lummox would run into the World Trade Center. Who knew it was Osama bin Laden's terrorist gang?"

Ruth said she was still at home that fateful morning. She and Murray were watching "Good Morning America," so they virtually saw it all unfold in real time. "But I didn't know you actually saw it happening in front of you."

"Being a Californian by nature, I wanted to drive to work, even though I was living in Manhattan and working at 5th Avenue and 20th Street. I drove to work every day, from 48th Street about fifty or sixty feet from Broadway. What I should have done was take the subway, but I was too stupid. That morning there wasn't a cloud in the sky, and I blared the Royal Fireworks music as loud as I could stand it, but not loud enough to get a traffic ticket, or a fine for disturbing the peace. I turned the volume way down when I switched to the news station.

"When I got to the office, everybody was watching television in the conference room, probably CNN, although I don't remember for sure, because all of the networks would have been all-news that day. I told them all to go home, and actually was standing on the sidewalk on 5th Avenue by myself when the second tower collapsed. Even when I saw it happen with my own eyes, I couldn't believe it. I guess everybody knows where they were when the Twin Towers collapsed, and all the stations kept running footage over and over of that one plane hitting one of the towers."

"I couldn't bring myself to go to work that day. I never left the apartment," Ruth said. "Murray the same. We both just sat in front of the TV like we were hypnotized."

"I think everybody stared at their TV screens most of that day. Of course, we didn't know how many planes were crashing into buildings. Then there was the Pentagon, and the plane that crashed in Pennsylvania. I remember feeling like I was tied up and couldn't move all day long."

"Stunned, I guess. Must be just how Lizzie Coniston must have felt when her boys disappeared," she said. "Paralyzed, unable to move. Half-dead. Hopeless."

We got to the lake where Murray's ashes were scattered. I parked the car on the side of the road, and we got out. There was definitely an autumnal feeling in the air.

"September," I said. "The warm days are probably gone until next year." *I grew up in Texas and southern California, so I have no love for cold weather. A lot of my relatives are exactly the opposite, but my blood runs cold when I smell fall in the air. About the same time as I get my flu shot. At least it doesn't usually get super-cold until around Christmas. And snow, brrrrr.*

Ruth is a Brooklyn girl, and the change of seasons doesn't get her down, so she wandered off along the lakeshore and apparently communed with Murray. She's a very stable person, and she doesn't chat with the dead. She just wants to go to this particular place where she can remember scattering her husband's ashes, and also walk back in her mind to whatever time she needs to re-live, in order to feel close to Murray as he was when he was still alive.

I stood by the car and waited. Pretty soon she was back, and ready to go back to Manhattan.

"How you feeling?" I asked her.

She smiled. "Better, closer to Murray." She held her hand out to me, and I took it and squeezed it. "You're a good man and a good friend," she said. "I know you understand that I miss Murray every day. I apparently don't fall in love easily, and I don't expect it to happen to me again. So, the time I had with Murray will probably be the only time of my life when I really loved someone. I don't have any children to love either. I have brothers and sisters, but most of them are fairly distant physically, and all of them are distant psychologically. Yes, there is familial love, but it's different, isn't it?"

"Don't you feel close to Murray when you're at home?"

I was thinking that it was very much Murray's apartment that she lived in. Before she married him, she lived on Riverside Drive on the West Side. I suddenly realized that she was wearing her wedding ring, a lovely emerald-cut diamond that she took off when Murray died, and that she hadn't worn – at least not that I had seen – ever since.

"You're wearing your ring," I said to her. "I figured you wouldn't put that on again."

She smiled. "I put it on because we were coming here today."

"Does the ring make you feel closer to him?"

She nodded and stared off into the distance.

Epilogue

Ted hot-footed it back to Boston, to get his mother's car back to her. He was back in town a day later, and Ricky Coniston had him installed in a Hell's Kitchen apartment the day after he arrived. I've been there, in that apartment, which was on 47th Street. It was in an old building that had once been a brothel in the nineteenth century. It was big, with two very large bedrooms, a dining room, lots of windows and details like crown moldings throughout. Fully furnished with a combination of sleek modern furniture and interesting antiques. Several nice paintings that looked to be nineteenth century Hudson River School, all of them landscapes. Very homey. Isabelle showed up and kept Ted company for a few days. While she was there, she also bought several oriental carpets to cushion the golden oak floors when people with shoes walked on them, as well as some lamps to replace the old-fashioned and lacy, slightly feminine ones that had been in the apartment when Ted moved in.

Sure enough, Ted could walk to the Coniston Companies (TCC) office, which was on 7th Avenue at 49th Street, on a floor that was higher than most of the surrounding buildings. Betty Coniston accepted the appointment to the TCC Board, and was clearly delighted to be working alongside her cousin, Ted. Ricky Coniston had a second desk moved into his spacious office, and installed himself there, with Ted sitting at the big mahogany desk that had been Ricky's before Ted got there. Then the three of them – Ricky, Betty and Ted – left to visit some of the larger companies that were in the TCC portfolio, which took them to northern California, Japan, Korea, Germany, England, France, and a variety of towns and cities across the USA, and in Mexico, Brazil and South Africa.

Gabriele stayed in New York, and continued to be the maître d' of Ora di Pranzo. He and I stayed close, but I cut way back on eating at his restaurant, not wanting to be a parasite and, maybe more importantly, not wanting to find myself coming between Gabriele and Ted, although I thought that any chance of the two of them becoming an item was highly unlikely. That was partly because Gabriele continued to insist that he wouldn't spend time with Ted in New York, although he might have in Boston. But I also realized that Gabriele was about the same age as Hank Huntington and Ted was about the same age as Betty, so there would have been a fairly large gap between them.

Hank Huntington's investment business became more and more successful, with assets under management growing to a size that made Huntington Investments one of the largest private fund managers in Europe. Then he merged his company in Paris with an even larger fund manager that was headquartered in New York City and was traded on the New York Stock Exchange. That would have enabled him to cash out over some period of time, but when the stock started to drop, it seemed like he had drawn to an inside straight and lost (never try to time the market, they say). As far as I know, he has never yet come back to New York, even though he sold his home in Monaco and moved back to Neuilly, which is near Paris.

Ricky Coniston took his wife to Mexico to consult with a medical scientist who was working on patients with a variety of types of dementia that were not Alzheimer's. Unfortunately, Ann Coniston's health did not improve, and she died in Chappaqua, in home hospice administered by a well-known hospital in the Bronx. She was buried in Kensico Cemetery in Valhalla, New York, in a plot where several Conistons had been laid to rest, including Eddie Coniston. Then Ricky gave his estate – lock, stock and barrel – to Betty Coniston, and moved himself and almost all of his horses to a horse farm in Kentucky. Vesuvius and a couple of other horses stayed in Chappaqua. He must have sighed in relief when he got settled in. Lizzie and the rest of her children moved to Chappaqua so that Betty wouldn't be alone, and she gave the Coniston Mansion on 5th Avenue to the Opera League, which used it for fund raisers, and to house guest artists. Bronze statues of Eddie and Ricky Coniston were placed at the entrance to the Opera League Mansion.

The Westbrooks moved back to the Hamptons, which is where

most of them grew up.

Betty Coniston was admitted to the Stern School of Business at NYU and completed an MBA in less than two years. She married an investment banker whom she had met in grad school at NYU; they had a daughter, whom they named Cecily.

The Coniston Companies prospered under Ted Coniston's administration. Dividends rose and the number of shareholders grew, among them Isabelle Coniston and all of Lizzie's Westbrook/Harrison children. Ted and Betty were approached by a SPAC and considered going public at a multi-billion-dollar valuation that would have also invested an additional seven hundred million dollars. But it would have changed the character of the operation, and it would have changed the shareholder base to be largely, though not majority, non-family. They decided not to do it, but they did raise salaries and hourly pay rates at all the companies they owned, and the Board decided to institute year-end bonuses for one hundred percent of the employees, giving each worker the equivalent of a month's pay in one lump sum.

Betty and Ted concentrated their philanthropic grants on climate change projects – principally offshore wind-power projects off the east coast of North America and wave-power projects off the west coast and Hawaii.

About the Author

Joe Allen's first success in "trade" books (books for retail buyers) was *Sandcastles: The Splendors of Enchantment* (1981). His first mystery novel, *Rocky Point Road*, was published in 2015, followed by *The Monteverdi Manuscript: A Hugo Miller Mystery* in 2016. *The Hanging Man*, published December 1, 2018, is a second Hugo Miller Mystery, set largely in Manhattan. With characters including a murderous "gypsy" dwarf, a papal legate with an overactive Twitter account, a woman promoting canonization for a nineteenth century New Yorker, a long-dead gangster who may have left buried gold in the basement of a condemned building, the wife of a murdered man on the lam with her infant son, and a tribe of possibly mutant males who live in tunnels underground on the west side of NYC.

His other novel about a sprawling New York family from the Eisenhower years to 2015, *Where All Past Years Are*, published September 1, 2018, is set largely on the west shore of Lake Champlain in New York near the Canadian border. *A More Perfect Union*, published early in 2019, is the third Hugo Miller mystery, following the fortunes of Eddie Hall, an African-American lawyer and politician whose intended same-sex marriage is cancelled by the murder of his intended on a sidewalk in SoHo. He is currently working on a sixth Hugo Miller mystery and a mystery, *Boom!* that starts with a deadly explosion at a fireworks factory in Arizona.

Joe is also the author of five nonfiction books, including *Effective Business Communications: A Practical Guide*. His *Systems in Actions: A Social and Managerial Approach* was used as a text in advanced problem-solving in several MBA programs, including the UCLA Anderson School of Management. He contributed chapters to two Aspatore (Thomson Reuters) books on investor relations.

Most of Joe's business career was with Bozell & Jacobs and then at Allen & Caron Inc., a consulting and investor relations firm he founded in 1981 in Irvine, California. Under his leadership, the company worked with clients in the UK, Ireland, France, Belgium, Sweden, Denmark, Italy, Greece, Germany, Poland, Switzerland, South Africa, Singapore, Australia, New Zealand, Brazil and Argentina, among other countries.

Joe served on the boards of several small companies, was vice chairman of the United Way in Orange County, California, has written on a variety of topics for numerous leading magazines and newspapers, and has published interviews with financial luminaries on SeekingAlpha.com.

Joe studied Classical Languages and English Literature at UCLA in the 1960s, prior to becoming an editor of scholarly journals at Sage Publications, and was then a marketing manager at Benziger Bruce & Glencoe, a college publishing subsidiary of Macmillan. He was married for forty-seven years. Now widowed, he has two children and two granddaughters.

Fools Playing Fools

No sooner has handsome, partially disabled Ned Savage moved into the apartment next door to Hugo Miller than he is apparently murdered with a heavy candlestick to his head while he is collapsing into anaphylactic shock in his living room, due to a fungus that is commonly found on marijuana plants. The action happens in and around several productions of "Twelfth Night" in NYC and at a nearby Shakespeare festival. Hugo, Gabriele and Ruth travel to California to see a high-tech cannabis operation, to London to visit Ned's pregnant wife (a secret marriage), and to Istanbul to meet a famous author who has invested in Ned's career. Ned's sexuality and his pregnant wife's preferences aren't clear, and Gabriele Cortese is part of a love triangle involving both of them. But the keys to the solution are found on a stormy night filled with lightning and fools in New York City.

Chapter One

When I heard the commotion in the hallway outside my door, I opened the door a crack and looked out. Cops, white-coated CSI workers. They were talking to each other, but it was so muffled that I couldn't understand what they were saying. I guessed someone had died.

We were in the middle of a thunderstorm, an almost every-afternoon phenomenon anywhere near the Hudson River or New York harbor in the sweltering summer humidity. Zeus was slinging thunderbolts right, left and center, and the giants were bowling in the sky, creating rolling peals of ear-splitting, bomb-like explosions. It was the kind of storm that throws boats onto dry land and smashes sailing vessels against rocks and piers. Fortunately, these summer storms usually come and go fairly quickly, and then the sun comes out to dry the streets and sidewalks.

The apartment the CSIs were filing into was occupied by a young man whom I had not met, mostly because he had just moved in. Because it was still summer, I was trying to keep windows open when it wasn't raining and frequently propped the front door to the apartment open with a small but heavy fake-marble lion statue I bought at the Metropolitan Museum some years back. A cross-draft is a blessing in a New York heat wave. So, I had seen the young man going back and forth when he moved in. Never said hello.

He was boyishly handsome with almost shocking rock-star hair of a chestnut-auburn color, a fashionably scruffy almost-beard, enormous dark eyes and the regulation Levis and black t-shirt but with black leather lace-up shoes. He had a problem with his right side, holding his right hand in a cupped position that was at odds with the angle of his arm, and he almost dragged his right leg when he walked but didn't use a cane and walked in a straight line. Looked like a long-term problem, not the consequence of a recent fall off a motorcycle.

He wore a headset and was clearly listening to music or a radio show, was smiling and occasionally laughing quietly. Not talking on the phone. He looked happy. I paid attention because for some reason I was surprised that someone who looked to be crippled was in such a good mood on moving day, which I surmised must have been difficult at best for him. I considered introducing myself, but he seemed to be busy, so I thought I'd wait.

Well, it turned out I missed my chance to say hello because when the CSIs arrived a couple of days later, he was dead. Couldn't possibly have been over thirty, maybe as young as twenty-five.

My name is Hugo Miller, and I'm mostly retired from a business I started that specializes in public relations for sports teams and players. But I am also a civilian criminalist with the NYPD—mostly an honorary designation that lets me work on cases assisting a detective I know in the Midtown North precinct of Manhattan, Mike di Saronno. I kinda fell into this because of a homicide case in Manhattan where I was potentially a witness of something relevant. That was several years back, and since then I've worked with Mike on four or five cases.

That's all well and good, but I live in an area of Queens called Long Island City that's on the East River directly across from the east end of 42nd Street and the United Nations. My Manhattan credentials don't carry much weight with the local cops. To be fair, I used to live in the Theater District on 48th Street—until I got priced out of Manhattan by skyrocketing rents. And although I continue to work with Mike when he calls me, I hadn't introduced myself to anyone at the 108th precinct that was a couple of long blocks up my street.

I called Mike, who poked around and told me what he found out. The victim was Ned Savage, twenty-seven, an Equity actor who had worked on Broadway and in smaller theaters in the area. Went to acting school in Los Angeles where he grew up but had lived in the Theater District for several years. He rented the studio apartment on my floor and told the leasing agent he would be living there alone. Apparently, someone had conked him over the head with a brass candlestick.

"Must have happened quickly," I said. "My apartment is directly next door, and I think we share a wall in my guest bedroom. I never heard anything, so there must not have been much of a scuffle."

He said he thought the detectives would be knocking on my door to ask me some questions since my apartment shares a wall with Mr Savage's place. As it happens, though, my apartment is a large two-bedroom, and I sleep on the opposite side of my floorplan from the hall or that apartment.

"Still, I think if there had been people throwing things or yelling, I would have heard some noise," I told the detective who was now asking me questions. "And since it's been hot, I've been keeping the sliding glass door open to the balcony to catch some breeze." I showed him and his partner the living room, with the sliding door open, a screen door keeping bugs out, and balcony directly upstairs forming a ceiling that kept it mostly dry during rainstorms. "If the balcony in that apartment was open like mine, I would for sure have known what was going on."

They were there to get information, not to give it to me, so I didn't bother to ask them anything, because I knew they'd clam up if I did. Figured Mike could find out and let me know.

I don't trust coincidences, but Mike told me Ned had moved into the apartment next to me from a high-rise across the street from where I used to live on 48th Street. I'd been living in Long Island City for almost five years and when I heard that, I tried to remember if that building was even ready for occupancy when I moved away. Anyway, he had to be well-off to live in a new luxury building in that area, because rents were sky-high; through-the-roof ridiculous. When I moved out of the Theater District my rent was almost five times what it had been when I moved in ten years earlier.

"For sure I don't remember seeing him when I lived on 48th Street," I said. "I would have remembered. Very striking fellow. Combination of rock-star and person with disabilities. Like somebody who had fallen off a trapeze with no net, or been thrown from a horse jumping over a hedge."

Mike suggested it might be good if he and I could get together. It was almost mid-day so I suggested we meet for a quick lunch at Ariana, a hole-in-the-wall Afghan restaurant on 9th Avenue at about 49th Street that combined good food and cheap prices. He agreed.

To get from my place to Times Square is easy. Take the 7 train from my subway station, three stops—maybe eight minutes—and you're at Times Square, exiting onto 43rd Street. It was a warm day, no rain, so I could walk to Ariana in ten minutes. I took a quick shower, decided I didn't need to shave, and was on my way, tapping on my cellphone to retrieve text messages from relatives in California.

These days there is free WiFi on the subway platforms, so I stood and texted until the train pulled up, about three minutes after I got there. I was at Ariana before Mike, who only had to walk five blocks from his office. Go figure.

I'm fond of Mike, though we are not friends in a social sense. He lives right near where I used to live and before I met him professionally, I would see him in this and that restaurant or bar from time to time and never knew he was a cop. But I have a good memory for faces and after a couple of sightings, I recognized him, but we never were introduced or shook hands. So, when I did meet him, it was a shock that he was a police detective. Very normal-looking, Italian features, slightly bronze, even in the winter, good symmetrical features, hazel eyes, taller than normal but not as tall as me.

I grabbed the table in the front bay window so I could watch for Mike and stare at people who walked by. I am a born voyeur; there's nothing more fascinating than watching people, even if they're just walking by. It's a little like watching a fire in a fireplace, very calming and I can't take my eyes off the parade of people meandering or scurrying by.

Mike was all apologies for being late.

"You're not late. I was early. No prob."

He told me before he looked at the menu that he was going to be working on the Savage case. The guy had been directing a production of *Twelfth Night* at an off-Broadway theater just off 8th Avenue in the 40s. Talk was that he was a *wunderkind*, a young prodigy. The kind of charismatic genius that everybody loves, especially in show biz.

"He looked really young, almost like a kid."

"Maybe you're getting old, Hugo. I never met him, but his photos don't look like a kid to me." He told me some of the things the CSIs had found. First of all, Savage didn't seem to have any immediate family, or at least there were no entries on his computer or in an old address book. They packaged up a drawerful of manila envelopes with papers in them and took them to the lab to make copies. At that point there was no next of kin to notify.

Second, the apartment had not been ransacked. Savage's body was found on the floor between the coffee table and the front door. The cushions on the couch that was also a pullout bed were rumpled, so it appeared that he might have been sitting there before whatever transpired that left him on the floor. The candlestick that appeared to be the cause of his death was on the floor but closer to the door than the body. It had blood and bits of hair on the base, indicating it had been grabbed by the top. The wound was on the right side of Savage's head, indicating that if the person holding the candlestick was facing Savage, he or she was left-handed. If he or she was behind Savage, then the indication would be right-handed. The M.E. would have to make the determination as to where the assailant was standing or sitting.

Mike went on to say it seemed logical that I help him on this case if I had time. Since I had an official tie to the department, there would a modest paycheck attached to the assignment. Enough to cover expenses and maybe go out to eat—once.

"Got nothing but time, Mike," I said. "Okay if I talk to Ruth and Gabriele?"

He smiled a friendly grin and nodded vigorously.

I texted Ruth and Gabriele on my way to the subway to see if we could meet up that evening for a drink. "The game is afoot," is how I ended the texts. It's a quote from Sherlock Holmes, and it actually comes from what the Brits call "shooting." The "game" are the birds—grouse, whatever—the shooters are after. And they can be heard running around in the brush, so "the game is afoot." I always thought it had something to do with a game, like a game you play. Nope. Brits are different from Americans.

Yes and yes. We agreed to meet at Dominie's Hoek, a watering-hole on Vernon Boulevard about a block and a half from the subway station on the 7 line. It's an old Dutch name for the area from before the Brits took over in 1664. Kind of a silly operetta of a take-over. The Brits arrived in the harbor and signaled to the Dutch that they were going to lay siege to the city, which was then just a cluster around what we call Battery Park. The Dutch figured they were joking, said no, go away. Then the Brits signaled that if the Dutch resisted they would "sack" the city – in other words, burn it, steal everything they could find, and rape the women. Seemed like an over-reaction, so the citizens of New Amsterdam refused to defend the city from the English ships. They gave up, much to the chagrin of Peter Stuyvesant, who had been the director-general and autocrat of the colony of New Netherlands for eighteen years. He was known to history as Peg Leg Pete, because he lost a leg in a naval battle somewhere in the Caribbean. Even though he was no longer in charge, he hung around on his big estate on the East River and died in Manhattan in 1672, so it couldn't have been a terribly hostile time between the two Protestant powers. He was buried in St Mark's in the Bowery, which was built on the site of the Stuyvesant family chapel.

Anyway, Dominie's Hoek is a place where you can get a good drink and sit outside in warm weather in a garden-ish patio in the back. They make burgers and such. Mostly it's a noisy neighborhood bar where you can wave at people you recognize, even if you don't know their names. Just about everybody is in a good mood.

Gabriele was early and arrived downstairs at my building at about six. The concierge called up, and yes, of course, send him up. He rang the bell, and when I answered, he was gesturing at the yellow crime-scene tape that was all over the end of the hallway just feet from my door. I nodded and he came in.

"Kid just moved in a day or two ago. Young guy, apparently in the theater business, directing a Shakespeare play near Times Square."

"What happen?"

"Well, I guess that's what we'll be trying to find out. Mike is heading the investigation because the kid was working near Mike's precinct and used to live in that zombie Irish building on 8th Avenue, the tall, super-skinny one. You remember it?"

He nodded and hugged me. He's a hugger. He's from Capri, with a lot of relatives in Naples; not sure, it seems different from time to time. He and his cousin, Dante, have a popular white-tablecloth restaurant in downtown Manhattan called Ora di Pranzo ("dinnertime"). Heavenly food. Gabriele is one of those confident Italian guys who attracts every eye in every room he walks into. I always look at his hair, since I am thinning/balding myself, but remember how nice it was to have hair when mine was still brown. I met him because he was a person of interest in a fairly sordid homicide several years back. He didn't do it, and we found out who did do it. Gabriele and I have been fast friends ever since. He says he's in love with me, which I try to smile through, but secretly it pleases me. Myself, I'm a two-time loser, two ex-wives with assorted kids, all on the West Coast. Limited contact. Not interested in hooking up again, but if I were, I would be aiming at Ruth, not Gabriele.

I live on the tenth floor; nice view of the Chrysler Building and the UN. Also, that crazy tall Trump building that's across from the UN. Since he was early, we had a very short snort of whisky at my apartment to get loosened up and then walked over to the bar to meet Ruth.

Ruth is a fashion plate for the modish set who are into "classic" looks. In Ruth's case, that means older Chanel clothing, nubby fabrics that approach Turkish toweling at times, kinda Joan Crawford shoulders sometimes, usually worn over fairly tight tailored jeans that made it clear she had Betty Grable legs. Ruth is comfortably well-off, a widow with some family issues – her husband's ex-wife and her own brothers. Her father was a rabbi, and Ruth was observant, at least at the important times of the year. "Acerbic" would describe her personality, but smiley and sweet on top of the film-noir attitudes. She was a picture in Chanel pink that evening, with pink and white Vans. Gotta love a woman in comfortable shoes. I read somewhere that an average woman in spiked heels exerted the same amount of pressure on the floor under the spike as a full-grown hippopotamus. Impressive.

She does good entrances and paused in the doorway at Dominie's Hoek to be silhouetted by the sun.

"You did that on purpose, didn't you?" I asked as I bussed her on both cheeks like a European.

"Did what?"

"Stood in the doorway with the sun behind you."

"Pish-tush," she said, pulled out a chair at one of the tables and sat down. She made me smile every time I saw her. I re-appreciated that she didn't carry three handbags, which is what a lot of New York women do. Men use pockets more, and women use pocketbooks, purses, or backpacks, sometimes all three.

So I briefed them on what Mike had told me about Ned Savage. "I guess there was no real evidence of any kind of tussle, so the assumption is that either he was surprised or he knew whoever it was that hit him and didn't feel in danger. Nothing yet on next of kin, or whether he had any close relatives."

"Did you say he was an actor?" Ruth asked.

"What I was told was that he was directing a production of a Shakespeare play," I said. "I think it was *Twelfth Night,* in some off-Broadway theater."

"WSR," she said. "West Side Rep. I'm on their mailing list. I've met him. He was Bottom in their *Midsummer Night's Dream* a year or so ago. Good looking, has a limp." She pulled out her cellphone and tapped on it. "Here," she said, flashing a picture of Savage. "Brings out the mother instinct in me," she smiled.

"Yeah, that's him," I said. "Small world?"

Gabriele grabbed the phone from Ruth and looked at it. "He come Ora di Pranzo maybe two times, *con amici. Parl' Italiano, ma bruto. È una brava persona.*" (*He brought his friends and spoke Italian, but not well. Good man.*)

I wouldn't say that's why I love both of them, because it's not. I've loved them for years on their own merits. But the fact that Ruth is involved in what seems like every arts charity in Manhattan and Gabriele owns a restaurant that you have to reserve a month in advance to hope to get in – it don't hoit, as they say. There I was, living next door to an apartment where a man was murdered a couple of days before, and both of my best friends knew him. Go figure. What? Eight million people living in the five boroughs? I live in Queens. Ruth lives in Manhattan. Gabriele lives in Brooklyn. All three of us turn out to know this one guy, and I had only seen him, never met him even though he lived next door.

I made a mental note to look up West Side Rep and see what I could find out. A waiter took our orders. Glass of red for me, glass of white for Ruth, dirty vodka for Gabriele. It felt good to be sitting with them on a warm summer day and to be working together on a puzzle. When I was a kid, my favorite thing was to work on jigsaw puzzles – big ones, lots of little pieces, lots of areas of color that look the same on the boxtop. You find all the edges you can find, and work your way in toward the middle. There's a lot more in the way of blind alleys and dead ends when you're dealing with a homicide—don't get me wrong—and it's a good deal more somber than trying to fit the pieces together in a picture of bright seas and sailboats.

Gabriele said that Savage had been to Ora di Pranzo at least twice, both times with a group of young people, probably actors or people he was working with. I asked if they were well-behaved. He said something noncommittal, like he didn't remember.

Other Books by the Author
at
Rogue Phoenix Press

Rocky Point Road

When his ex-wife drowns in a hot tub in California, Denis Rosa sets out to bury her and sell the house. He confronts her philandering history and her fixation on young Chicano boys and is the victim of a vicious attempted murder without ever knowing why. The house on the cliffside on Rocky Point Road holds a ghost, a hidden treasure of some kind, and decades of memories for the Rosa family. When Detective Sue Mason is assigned to the case, her son and his soon-to-be husband and two dogs move into the house with Denis to protect him from further attacks. Is it drug-related? The wife was alcoholic and smoked grass, but nothing hard. Denis confronts his ghosts as he finds himself attracted to Sue. The key to the plot is found when Denis slides off the edge of the cliff.

The Monteverdi Manuscript

The action revolves around the death of a famous musician, who hits the pavement outside Carnegie Hall from the window of his apartment seven stories up. He has recorded keyboard versions of a lost opera by Claudio Monteverdi, the man who "invented" opera. Set in New York, London and Venice, action includes a kidnapping, drug use, prostitution, LGBT characters, one character who comes back from the dead, and three classic New York detective characters led by Hugo Miller.

Where All Past Years Are

Starting on Thanksgiving Day 1954, the Chadwick family encounters wars, financial crashes, 9-11, and the Great Recession. As a family with a WASP history they discover the wider world that is America, marry across religious, racial and ethnic lines, live, love, laugh and celebrate Thanksgiving and Independence Day at the Old Home on the shore of Lake Champlain near the Canadian border in New York.

The love of husbands and wives, the closeness of relatives who are an increasingly rainbow-like group, the touching beauty of the Old Home on the Lake as some family members move back to the property into new cottages—all are major themes. Children running a three-legged race watch the young man, Gray Chadwick, drop to his knees to beg his pregnant girlfriend, Melissa, to marry him. Births, deaths, burials, 4th of July fireworks, boating and bass fishing, and the strengthening power of love lead to a final surprising and unexpected reunion of two branches of the family for the first time in over three hundred years.

A More Perfect Union

Former ADA Eddie Hill, divorced African-American father of two, plans to marry Jimmy van Gelsen, wealthy gay man who, like Eddie, has been unlucky in love. Eddie is injured in a car accident on the NY Thruway, and Jimmy is shot in the forehead, killing him instantly. Was it Eddie's gun? If so, with Eddie in the hospital upstate, who pulled the trigger? Hugo, Ruth and Gabriele sort through a thicket of clues—a stolen Bentley, a shabby vacation home on Antigua, a multimillion-dollar co-op in Greenwich Village with fabulous art. Major political demonstrations with thugs and tiki torches, reminiscent of the Charlottesville riots with protesters battling in the streets—one at a prayer vigil, one a "Million Woman March" down 5th Avenue, another outside the Copley Plaza in Boston. Eddie runs for Congress from a mixed-race district in Brooklyn. Jimmy's will left a fortune to Eddie, who doesn't want any of it. Is it a right vs left murder? A gay-bashing murder? A robbery gone wrong? The answers are close to home.

The Hanging Man

When wealthy investment banker Luigi's body is found hanging from the crossbars of the George Washington Bridge, it is immediately thought to be a Mafia hit. Is it? Not according to a Catholic bishop with a diplomatic errand from the Vatican and an out-of-control Twitter account. As the truth unfolds, the reader meets a mad dwarf who eats insects and small rodents, a long-dead candidate for canonization, a deceased gangster who owned The Cotton Club in Harlem, and a tribe of mis-shapen males whose lives have been spent in tunnels under Hell's Kitchen.

Explosions, whispers coming from walls, mysterious billionaires from Grand Cayman, Luigi's terrified young wife with a suckling baby at her breast, treasure-hunters looking for buried gold in the basement— provide a frightening backdrop to a mystery that literally goes deeper and deeper into Manhattan as the story develops.

Hugo Miller, Ruth the Sleuth, handsome Gabriele Cortese and stalwart NYPD detective Mike di Saronno pool their considerable resources to solve a series of crimes that may hark back as far as seventy-five or one hundred years.

www.ingramcontent.com/pod-product-compliance
Lightning Source LLC
Chambersburg PA
CBHW071450170626
46811CB00007B/2529